Marriage, Friends & Lovers

Marriage, Friends & Lovers
ISBN: 978-1-7391726-8-8

First published in Great Britain
in 2023 through Amazon self-publishing
service Kindle Direct Publishing

Produced in the UK by The Book Writers'
Resource
www.tbwr.co.uk

Dedication

To all the lovers.

Photo taken and permissions granted by courtesy
of Matt Glover Brand Photographer

Acknowledgements

This project has been an odyssey of discovery for me. Not just in the fact I have learnt about processes such as editing and typesetting, to compositing images for the cover of this book, I have also discovered I have many friends who are ardent supporters and cheerleaders.

Firstly, I must recognise and show thanks to my long-term boyfriend, Steve Burrows, as without him, I would not have seen this project through to it's conclusion. Steve's support has been unfaltering and has given me the courage and strength to believe in myself.

Similarly, my dad, Roger Hood, has been my main supporter for the last 43 years. When I first mentioned I was writing a steamy romance, on our way to watch Leicester Tigers, my dad showed interest and said, 'if it's what you want to do, then do it,' and again when I had made the decision to publish my work, my dad encouraged my decision and has shown enthusiasm for every achievement along the way, be it large or small.

I would like to thank my mum, Jane Hood, and my sister, Christine Hood, for showing support regarding my published book.

I must show gratitude to David Hambling who has patiently worked with me, yes patience is required, sorry David... David has taken my first draft, just on a Word document, and has worked to bring it to life, to make it the book you hold in your hands now. David has edited the book, made suggestions to add to the drama of certain scenes, and typeset the book. We have worked together to design the book cover, David listened to my ideas and designed the finished cover you see now. However, above all of this, David has supported me and encouraged me, especially when I may have felt this project was not worth pursuing. Thank you David, your expertise is invaluable.

I am eternally grateful to Karen Hall for designing the map of Upper Loughton for me. After seeing my freehand attempt, Karen, who is a graphic designer, took inspiration and asked if I would like her to design a map of Upper Loughton. At first I was amazed, however after Karen convinced me she was serious, I agreed. I asked her to keep it simple, I didn't want to take up too much of her time. I must say, I am most awestruck with her final design and immensely grateful.

I would also love to thank Paul Evanson for working with me to design a fabulous website. I'm not very tech savvy, lol... and Paul was on hand to assist with any queries I had and after just one initial conversation, he designed a website which is exactly what I would have chosen. Thank you so much Paul for all your hard work and dedication to helping me.

I would love to thank all my early readers, who without I would not have known what the public consensus of the story was. You have all been amazing, I have loved the excitement you have all shared for this book and the infectious enthusiasm. Thank you so much, it means a tremendous amount to me.

I would very much like to show my appreciation to my very good friends, Stephen Goddard and Philip Brooks-Stephenson, who have shown me their unwavering support throughout this project and continue to do so. Thank you so much, both of you.

And last but by no means ever least, I would love to thank my best friend in the whole world, Anaida Doran. Anaida has supported me every step of the way, she is the most honest friend anyone could wish for and I am grateful to have her in my life. Thank you so much Anaida, love ya!

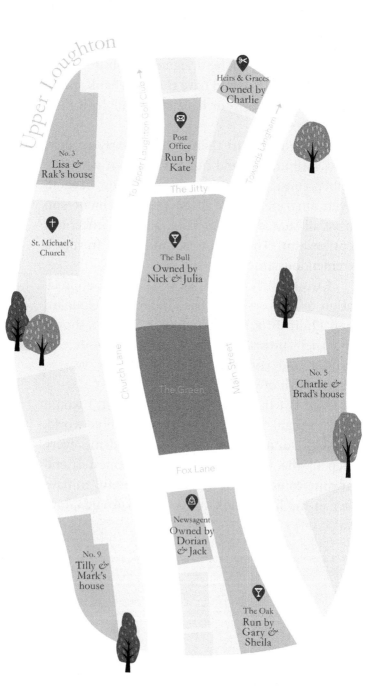

Marriage, Friends & Lovers

Caroline Hood

1

Friday Night
The Bull

"You have got to be kidding? There's no way you can compare 'The Stones' to any of today's shit." Rak was insistent that most, if not all, modern music was manufactured crap.

"No, you see mate, that's where you're wrong, there really are some fantastic bands around now. Take this cover band we've got on in here tonight, they do all sorts, modern and the older stuff." Nick was insistent the band him and his wife, Julia, had booked would spice up the Friday night at *The Bull*. Nick had owned *The Bull* for fifteen years, however, it had been in his family, the Carr family, for forty years. Nick wanted the pub to be a 'place to be' on Friday nights so had started putting on live music. Rak Banerjee, Nick's best friend for the past thirty years, wished him well. Even if he did enjoy winding him up. "What do you think Lisa? Do you think your disillusioned husband is right?" asked Nick, with a smile on his face.

"My husband stopped being right a long time ago but of course, as his best mate, you wouldn't agree." Lisa was not laughing. Rak looked dejected, he wasn't expecting Lisa to start another argument tonight, especially as they were in company.

The rest of the table looked at each other with resignation as they were aware of what was to follow. Lisa and Rak had been married five years. To see them together you could imagine it more to be twenty-five years, they were not a happy pair. Tilly and Mark French were good friends of Rak and Lisa but even they wondered how they stayed together. Tilly gave Mark a look exclaiming she knew a row was brewing.

"Right, who wants another drink? It's my round," asked Mark, trying to get the evening back on track. Everyone around the table responded by getting their order in.

"I'll give you a hand, you'll never manage all that," offered Charlie Worthing, quickly getting to her feet to help Mark and possibly avoid the potential atmosphere which she sensed was about to fall over the table.

Charlie owned the local hair salon and was married to Brad. They always had a few drinks in *The Bull* on a Friday night, however tonight it was just Charlie as Brad was away on business. She did not want to be caught in the crossfire of a famous Rak versus Lisa, Friday night special.

"Lucky escape, eh?" quipped Mark "That's not going to end well, I don't know how he copes with her."

"It does seem to be a tricky balance with Lisa," agreed Charlie. "I certainly don't envy him".

As Charlie and Mark returned to the table with the drinks and various flavours of crisps and nuts, the band started up. Their first track was a cover of 'Satisfaction' by The Rolling Stones. "This is really quite good," Rak announced to anyone who was listening around the table. He caught Charlie's eye and she gave him a full smile which reached her eyes. Charlie felt sorry for Rak, she knew Lisa had a great life with him if only she would see it. Charlie was Lisa's go to stylist and the amount of money she spent in her salon in a month, most women wouldn't spend in a year. Rak was always trying to keep Lisa happy, *much to the detriment of his own happiness,* Charlie thought.

"Are you getting satisfaction mate?" asked Mark with a lightness to his voice and a smile.

"Me? Satisfaction? Not in years mate, believe me." Replied Rak, laughing.

"How dare you discuss our personal life in the middle of the pub, you fucking prick! I've had enough, Rak, enough of having you put me down in public, enough of your demands. Enough is enough." With that Lisa grabbed her designer handbag and stormed out of the pub.

"Are you going after her?" Tilly asked Rak.

"No, fuck her." Rak responded just as the band stopped. The entire pub looked in the direction of the table, shocked to hear Rak, a usually mild-mannered man, raising his voice in anger.

Both Kate McGuire and Dorian Smyth, the postmistress and the village newsagent respectively, shot a look at Rak. They both lived for gossip, and this was just too juicy to miss. "She's a complete bitch to that man you know, Kate," whispered Dorian. "He's such a gentleman, and she treats him like something on the sole of her shoe."

"I know. She's totally intolerable." Agreed Kate, "I never liked her, she's too obsessed by what people have, not who they are."

"I heard his first wife was very different, compassionate and kind. They have two children together you know. I wonder what happened there?" mused Dorian. "Well, I say children, I believe they're grown up now. Still, can't have been easy for them, the divorce." Both women sat there considering the plight of Rak's first wife, Amira, and their two children, neither having met them previously.

Despite Lisa's best efforts to disrupt the evening, it had been good fun. The band had been a success, the drinks had kept flowing and Rak actually enjoyed himself. "Who's for one more for the road?" he asked.

"Not us, Rak, thanks anyway, we've got to take Russ to a football try-out in the morning. Best be getting off, cheers, great night." Mark said before he and Tilly were on their feet and ready to leave. Russ, their 19-year-old son, was a budding footballer and was hoping to secure a scholarship.

"Charlie, are you up for another? Don't leave a sad old man by himself, please, honey." Rak mimicked begging at Charlie's knees.

"Oh, go on then, there's only an empty house waiting for me," replied Charlie, smiling and laughing at the same time.

"There's only an empty hearted bitch waiting for me." Rak quipped back with a smile. Charlie found she could not stop laughing, although she knew it was true.

Nick was just arranging another booking with the band when Rak approached the bar. "Yeah, sounds great, once a month will do to start with, cheers." Nick waved the band mates off.

"Are you ok darlin'?" Julia asked Rak.

"Yeah, I'm ok thanks, I have to be. May I have

two large whiskeys please, Julia?" asked Rak.

"Yeah, course you can, your usual?" Julia knew Rak had expensive tastes and always kept a bottle of Chivas Regal behind the bar for him.

Rak reached for his wallet, however, Julia waved her hand. "On the house, you deserve it darlin'" she gave him a smile as she said it.

Rak smiled back and mouthed 'thanks.'

When Rak returned to the table Charlie was quite surprised to see two whiskeys, especially since she had been on red wine all night. Rak sensed her surprise. "Just a treat. Anyway, thank Julia, on the house y'know."

They sat talking while finishing their drinks, Charlie was sipping hers, not wanting to wake up with a hangover. In the morning she would have her Saturday regulars to contend with; the one that was always late and would throw her timings out for the morning; the one who wanted a perm every other week and who Charlie would persuade that it would not be of any benefit, and then in the afternoon she would pull in her money clients—the colours and highlights.

As they got up to leave the pub Rak offered to walk Charlie home, after all it was late and very dark outside, and she was a bit tipsy. "Night you two, make sure he behaves, Charlie!" shouted Nick from the other side of the bar, laughing as he said it "I've known him a long time, you have to watch him."

Charlie was laughing now too, however Rak mocked injury to his reputation, miming being stabbed through the heart by his best friend. "Don't forget golf tomorrow, Nick, tee time is booked for midday." Rak was aware his friend would not have remembered.

"Oh, yeah. Cheers mate, I'd completely forgot about that, hopefully so has Julia." Nick smiled, knowing he would be in the doghouse for leaving Julia on her own on a Saturday lunchtime. Oh well, she might have to ask Adam to help out for an hour, her son and Nick's stepson, was always grateful for the extra cash.

Once outside, the air was cold and fresh. The temperature was not that high for late June and Rak saw Charlie shiver. "Here, put this on, honey." Said Rak, taking off his jacket.

"Awww, thanks. Knew I should've brought a cardi with me, didn't think I would be out 'til closing, not on a school night." Joked Charlie. She took his jacket from him and placed it around her shoulders, she could smell his aftershave, musky and manly. He put his arm around her, and she looked at him, questions in her eyes.

"Well, you've got my jacket, hun, this shirt's thin. Help a guy out." As they made their way to Charlie's house, which in all honesty, was not a million miles from *The Bull*, she had to admit, he made her feel safe.

When they arrived at the front door, a pink composite front door no less, which incidentally, her husband, Brad detested, she looked at him. "Would you like to come in?" she asked. "I've a decent bottle of red and I'm not tired enough to go to sleep."

Rak nodded his head and followed her inside. He had been inside Charlie and Brad's house many times, he knew the drill, shoes off. This time however, it felt somewhat different. Like he was going beyond boundaries, possibly because Brad was not home. They headed for the kitchen, Charlie had a massive kitchen, her favourite part of the house and the reason she had begged Brad to buy it, even though it had stretched their budget.

She took two wine glasses out of the cabinet and poured two large glasses of Rioja. She passed one to Rak and slowly took a sip from her own glass. They both sat at the island, sipping their wine when Charlie decided to put on some music. "Have you heard of her?" she asked, holding up a Norah Jones CD.

"No, you know me and new music, I'm not very up on popular culture." Rak was laughing now.

"It's not pop music. I hear enough of that in the salon. It's what I suppose you would call easy listening. Shall I put it on?"

Rak was intrigued now so nodded his head. "Yeah, why not?"

As they sat there, the first track playing, Charlie asked, "why do you stay with her, Rak?" He looked shocked and for a brief moment she thought she had upset him.

"Good question. I suppose the truth is I can't afford, or actually want to pay her off." He paused and looked at Charlie's face. "You see, when Amira and I divorced that cost me a lot of money. But I didn't mind as much, she had given me two beautiful kids and I'd been a twat. She was owed. Lisa on the other hand gives me nothing but grief and I will not give her the satisfaction of clearing me out to boot".

Charlie had an overwhelming desire to hold him. She didn't know if it was the drink, after all, she had drank quite a bit, or that she wanted to feel what he would feel like in her arms. She leant over to touch his hand and then found herself standing in front of him. He took her into him and held her close for what felt like an eternity. He smelled delicious, musky, manly and hot. She raised her head and looked into his eyes, deep brown eyes. Eyes she could get lost in if she dared herself to look for long enough. He was looking into her eyes, she could feel the pull towards him. He made a move to kiss her, and she let him, slowly at first, lingering. Then his tongue was in her mouth, she responded, wanting more of him. He was using his tongue to lick and flick her own. She could feel herself becoming wet between the top her thighs, her nipples were hard, she was becoming breathless. She had never been kissed like this before, with so much passion. He moved closer still, and she could feel he was hard. She couldn't take any more, she took his hand and led him upstairs to her bedroom, the bedroom she shared with Brad.

They continued to kiss passionately, she was unbuttoning his shirt, she wanted to touch his chest. Her hands wandered along his chest, down towards his stomach. As he removed her dress, his hands caressed her body. She was wet now and she could see his jeans tightening around the front. She loosened his belt and undid his top button and fly. She was tugging at his jeans, trying to get them off as quickly as she could. His Ralph Lauren boxers were tight, tight around his cock. She put her hands between the boxers and his hips to pull them off.

"Are you sure you want this, Charlie? There will be no going back, you know that don't you." Rak needed to be sure, he needed to hear her say it.

"Yes," she whispered, "I want you, I want you right now. No regrets, I promise." She was staring into his gorgeous brown eyes and willing him to touch her.

He took her bra off and fondled her breasts in his hands, then he was kissing her neck, little kisses all the way down her neck to her chest. He took her nipples in his hands and placed one in his mouth, she let out a gasp and placed her hand in his boxers.

His cock was massive, she could feel it throbbing in her hand. She pulled his boxers off and pushed him onto the bed. She was dripping wet now, she needed him, now.

She took his cock in her mouth, he whispered her name, "Charlie, baby, yes, yes. Oh my God. That's so good." He gently pushed her blonde hair further down, her mouth taking more of his throbbing cock, the head filling her mouth.

She placed her hand over his balls and could feel them tighten almost immediately. "Stop now hun, stop" he whispered. She was startled but did as he had asked

"Why, what's wrong baby?" she asked, concerned he may be having second thoughts, she need not have worried.

"I don't want to come in your mouth sweet, I want to fuck you".

He rolled her onto the bed and kissed her breasts, gently and softly. He moved down to her stomach and slowly caressed her whilst kissing her. His hands were in between her thighs now, she was waiting with anticipation for him to touch her pussy. She wanted him so badly she was aching for him. He moved further down her body, caressing every inch of her. He slowly and gently parted her legs. He was kissing the inside of her thighs now. She was already feeling breathless when he lightly touched her wet pussy. "Ahhhh, yes, yes, Rak."

He responded by inserting a finger inside her, she thought she might come there and then. Then his head was in between her legs, his tongue licking her lips, lightly, slowly.

She placed her hands on his grey hair and held his head there. "Rak, Rak, don't stop, please, don't stop." She wasn't aware, but she was screaming now. Next his tongue was on her clit, flicking and licking. He was more intent now, she wanted to come so badly but she didn't want this pleasure to end. "Rak, baby yes, yes, yes. Oh my God, yes!" he responded by licking her softly, he slowed down. She felt herself regain some composure, then he sucked her clit and licked her so strongly she could not stop herself. "Rak, I'm coming! I'm coming, baby! Ahh, God! Yes, yes, yes..." It was the best she had ever had. She took his cock in her hands and guided him inside her.

He looked into her eyes. "Baby, you feel so good. Your pussy feels so good." He began thrusting into her, she was getting wetter and he was getting harder. "How do you want me to fuck you hun?" he whispered.

"Hard, hard and deep. I want to feel all of you," she shouted back. He lifted her legs and took her even deeper, she felt so good he wanted to come but slowed himself down, he didn't want this to end. She met his thrusts and he lifted her onto him, they looked into each other's eyes as she came again. Stronger this time, more intense. She saw a kaleidoscope of colours, she felt weak yet strong at the same time. She felt his body tense, she looked into his eyes "I'm coming, honey. Oh fuck. Yes! I'm coming!"

2

Saturday Morning
Rak

Rak had not wanted to leave Charlie's arms. They lay in her bed, holding each other, neither daring to move. The alarm clock on the cream, art deco effect, bedside table read 1:28am. "I should go, baby. We don't want prying eyes in the morning," his voice was tinged with sadness.

"Stay a while longer with me, just a while." Charlie wanted him to stay all night but knew he was right.

He looked into her eyes and kissed her so passionately she never wanted to let him go. Rak felt his cock becoming hard, he placed his hand between her thighs and was amazed by how wet she was. "Charlie, honey, one more time?"

She wasn't sure if he was asking or telling her, the only thing she was sure of was that she wanted him all over again. He pulled her on top of him and slowly fingered her wet pussy until she nearly came. She grabbed his throbbing cock and sat on him, an immediate feeling of pleasure radiating through her body. He felt her begin to move, him inside of her, slowly this time, slow and long. As she quickened her pace, hips moving in a circular motion, he knew he needed to come. He slowly and deliberately massaged her clit, he knew she was coming, her pussy had tensed around his throbbing, hard cock. He let himself go and together they collapsed into each other, a feeling of warmth and breathlessness between them.

Rak left at 2:05am. As he made his way from Charlie's house towards *The Bull*, he briefly wondered if Nick would still be awake. This thought was quickly replaced by a need to be alone. As he walked through 'The Jitty' towards his own house, he took out his mobile to use the torch, he wasn't feeling very stable on his feet. Two missed calls from Lisa, great. The last one registered at 1:15am. No voicemail. He prayed to God she would be in bed now and not spoiling for round two.

As Rak got towards the front door he noticed

all the lights were turned off downstairs, he sighed with relief that Lisa would have given up waiting for him and gone to bed. He let himself in and tried to be as quiet as possible. He headed straight for the kitchen, opened the drinks cupboard, took a cut crystal tumbler from the cabinet and poured himself a large Chivas. Rak sat at the kitchen table, cradling the glass. He needed to make sense of what had happened. Questions were going through his mind at a million miles an hour. How did that happen? What just happened? How did he feel about Charlie? Was it a one off? Did he want it to be? Or did he want more? He couldn't answer any of them. The only certainty he did have was that he had just had the best sex he'd had in years.

Lisa and Rak had been having problems for more than half their married life. When they first met, they would be laughing and joking all the time. He fell for her quickly and within a year of meeting they were married. Rak liked being married, it suited him. They had moved to Upper Loughton four years ago. Rak was always over visiting Nick and playing golf and it made sense when 3 Church Lane came onto the market, to buy it. Lisa loved the house; however, she loved the postcode more, the area being very desirable.

After a year of moving to the village their problems had started. Lisa was extremely jealous of Rak's friendship with Nick. She could not comprehend how two people could be best friends for nearly thirty years, having not experienced long-term friendships herself. She began to make excuses not to socialise with Julia and Nick or Tilly and Mark come to that. Lisa wanted Rak all to herself, however, when he would do as she had asked and cancel plans with friends, she would not talk to him all evening. Rak believed she was punishing him for being likeable, something Lisa struggled with. Then the biggest problem that Rak could imagine materialised, Lisa stopped giving him any affection. Rak would openly admit he loved kissing, he loved sex and being passionate with a woman. During his first marriage to Amira, he had never experienced any kind of rejection. She was as passionate as him and loved making love with him. Rak was not a selfish lover either, he enjoyed giving pleasure to a woman, watching her come.

Rak drained his glass of the whiskey and decided he should get some sleep. He couldn't make any sense of anything right now. He took the spare room, the better option he concluded.

The sun was coming through the curtains. Rak awoke suddenly. He looked at the time on his mobile, 10:22am. He couldn't believe how late it was, he rarely slept in these days, hadn't for years. He got up and made his way to the adjoining en-suite and straight into the shower. It suddenly occurred to him he was washing her off, washing Charlie off his body. Just the thought of her made his cock twitch, he felt himself with his right hand. This had been the only way he had been pleasured in the last three years, by himself. He closed his eyes, the warm water from the shower washing over him. He could picture Charlie, her breasts, her stomach, her thighs, her pussy. He recalled how good it had felt to come inside her, to actually feel something. "Ahhh, God, ahhh, ahhh." He had come in his left hand. He felt shaky and his cock was too tender to touch.

3

Saturday Morning
Charlie

Charlie had not wanted Rak to leave her. She wanted to wake up with him next to her and make love to him all over again. As she lay in bed, the alarm reading 2:37am she knew she should try to get some sleep. The salon was almost fully booked and she didn't want to feel exhausted. However, she could not rest her mind. The same thoughts were running through her head on a loop. Would she see Rak again? How good it had felt coming with him at the same time, this had never happened with Brad, she was lucky if Brad ever managed to make her come at all nowadays. Brad, what was she going to do about Brad? He couldn't find out, it would destroy him. But she couldn't be without Rak, she knew that too. He had ignited something in her, something she knew she needed to feel again and again. She wondered if he felt the same. Or was it just a one-night stand to Rak? He was married, admittedly not happily, but could she ask him to risk his marriage?

Charlie had met Brad through a mutual friend twelve years earlier. She had been twenty-three when she met him. She was the manager of a successful hair salon and was doing well for herself. Charlie had never had a problem attracting men, just the wrong sort. Before Brad, she mainly had flings that would fizzle out after a month or two, or one night stands that meant little to her. Charlie enjoyed the single life however, making her own decisions, suiting herself. But then she wanted a family.

Charlie had always dreamed of having four children, preferably two girls and two boys, although that really didn't bother her. She knew she needed to meet someone solid if this was to happen for her. Someone she could depend upon. Her oldest girlfriend had already met her dream man and suggested his best friend could suit Charlie. They went out on a double date and she met Brad. She found him attractive, not up to her usual standard but then again, he wasn't a player either, unlike her usual type.

They married two years later and Charlie was extremely keen to start a family. She didn't want to be in her forties running around after toddlers, she wanted to have the energy to enjoy her children. She had also planned to buy her own salon once the kids were older and she didn't want to leave that too late either. She and Brad started trying almost straight away, Charlie naively thinking she would conceive first time, she had been so petrified of becoming pregnant by a one-night stand for all those years it was a relief not to take precautions and enjoy a spontaneous sex life.

In the beginning Charlie loved it. Brad would grab her in the kitchen and fuck her over the kitchen table, or finger her in the middle of the night until she came then make love to her until she came again. They were enjoying early married life and the prospect of a baby. However, month after month, regular as clockwork, Charlie would start her period. It was beginning to destroy her. She was approaching thirty now and knew the time was running out. She had begged Brad to seek medical help with her, 'there must be reason!' she would yell at him. Brad was too embarrassed to speak to anyone, let alone admit that there was a fifty percent chance he was the problem.

When she reached the age of thirty, having been married five years, they decided to move house. A fresh start. Charlie saw 5 Main Street, Upper

Loughton, online and booked herself a viewing. She knew Brad would rage about the price but she loved it and wanted to see it with her own eyes. As soon as she pulled up onto the driveway, she knew she had to have it. The owners were welcoming and allowed her to walk around by herself. The whole house was beautiful, everything was to her taste. Then she walked into the kitchen. It was huge, running the length of the back of the house, bi-fold doors opening onto an expanse of manicured gardens. The kitchen also offered an island unit in the middle, something she had always wanted. She had to have it.

Then to her amazement during a conversation with the owners they mentioned they were retiring abroad and also selling their business. The village hair salon. Charlie knew this was right, with no prospect of a baby now she recognised she needed to move on and start her next adventure. All she had to do was persuade Brad.

That was no easy feat. "How do you imagine we can afford a house in Upper Loughton and buy you a salon?" he guffawed after she had shown him the house and the salon online. She was shocked, he was just laughing at her. "I'm a sales manager Char, not a fucking CEO!"

Charlie had been saving money since they had gotten married, she guessed they would need it once the kids started coming and she wasn't able to work as much. "I have savings Brad, for the baby. But as that's not likely to happen we should put the money towards this." She watched his face go from one of mockery to anger.

"Not likely to happen? Is that what you've decided, is it? Why? Because you want a fucking salon now and to be the big business owner? Are you seriously giving up? You fucking bitch!"

She was close to tears but didn't know what of, sadness or anger. She explained how she cannot put her life on hold for another five years with month after month of disappointment. Their sex life had become a chore, checking temperatures, the right time of the month for ovulation and then a quick, meaningless fuck. Brad would come quickly, thinking his job was complete. He hadn't paid any attention to Charlie's needs for a while.

After much more rowing and shouting, Brad relented. He put an offer in for both the salon and the house. They got a good deal as they wanted to buy both, giving the agents less stress. Unfortunately, their problems were much more deep rooted now.

It was 8:45am. Charlie was just letting herself into the salon when her mobile rang. Her first thought was Rak. She grabbed her mobile out of her bag the name displayed read Brad. Her disappointment was tangible. "Hiya, how's it going?" she asked, attempting to sound light and breezy.

"Hi babe, yeah good thanks. I've got a quite a few orders in the bag. Should be home around 4:00. Can you book a table at *The Bull* tonight? Fancy taking you out."

Charlie panicked, *The Bull*, Rak would be in on a Saturday night, guaranteed. She couldn't risk it. "Can we go to *The Rose & Crown* in Langham instead? Really fancy the chicken and ribs combo they do." She hoped that would work.

"I don't wanna drive to Langham babe, I've got the three hour drive back as it is."

Shit, shit! "All right, I'll drive then, give you a rest, is that okay?" she detested driving at night, especially that dimly lit lane from Upper Loughton to Langham.

"Yeah, if it means that much to ya. See you later, have a good day. I love you, y'know."

She didn't know what to say. "Look, my first client has just arrived, see you later." And with that she hung up.

The day dragged slowly, every time Charlie saw someone pass the salon window, she looked up from what she was doing to see if it was Rak. It never was. She hadn't seen him all day. Now she didn't know what to think.

4

Saturday Afternoon

Upper Loughton
Golf Club

Upper Loughton Golf Club was the main attraction for the men of the village, after *The Bull*, of course. The old saying, 'most deals are done on the golf course', really did apply here. Only the previous week, Mark French had secured enough building work to take him into the middle of the next year. The payoff for husbands playing too much golf, meant their wives were granted their long-awaited extensions or loft conversions. This was the main reason

Mark joined the club, he struggled with golf to be fair, much preferring watching sport to actually playing it. Nick and Rak had persuaded Mark that joining the club would be the most lucrative way of growing his business, and they weren't wrong.

Mark ordinarily would have joined his friends for a round of golf on a Saturday afternoon, it was also proving a good escape from Tilly. However, after ferrying Russ to his football trial and back, he was now pricing up a rather substantial extension. Their usual tee time was 2:00pm, after the lunchtime rush in *The Bull*, however, the club was hosting an annual tournament between the two local secondary schools this afternoon so Rak had agreed midday with Ted, the course manager.

To be fair, both Rak and Nick were slightly relieved, Mark did hold up their game and it could be frustrating, but what could they say, he was a mate. "Should get round pretty quickly today mate, then I'm buying you a few back at my place, looks like you need shaking up."

Nick was trying to be funny but Rak really wasn't in the mood. "What? What do you mean?" he asked, a little tetchily.

"I'm just saying mate, you look like you've got out of bed the wrong side, are you okay?" Rak knew Nick knew him better than he knew himself sometimes.

"Yeah, sorry mate. Bit of a hangover y'know,

getting too old for live bands and drinking 'til kick-out time." It was left there.

Rak was having a terrible game, Nick was beginning to feel embarrassed for him. A thought crossed his mind that even Mark could've thrashed Rak this afternoon, he was missing easy shots. Rak had been friends with Nick for thirty years, he was his oldest and most trusted friend. Nick knew of all the women Rak had thought about over the years and the ones he had done more than think about.

Rak knew how Nick really wanted *The Bull* to be a success with him at the helm. Nick's relationship with his father had not been the greatest and he wanted to be better than him. Similarly, Rak had a poor relationship with his own father, they had not spoken in almost twenty-five years.

Nick decided it was time to play his favourite golf course game, 'Hypothetically.' Nick would always come up with a scenario and ask Rak, 'hypothetically,' what he would choose or what he would do. They would discuss everything; nothing was off limits when it was just them two. "Right then mate, hypothetically, if you were proper loaded, I know you are loaded, but even more loaded." Rak did have to smile at this, he would only be loaded, as Nick put it, if he sold everything, as Nick already knew. "Would you have a Lamborghini or a Ferrari?"

Rak laughed out loud this time. "Not this again, I've told you many times, a Ferrari. You only keep asking this one hoping I'll change my mind to the Lambo because that's what you want, and you'd want to borrow it." They both started laughing and then Rak finally started sinking some putts.

★ ★ ★

Charlie finished her final client of the day at 4:45pm. She was absolutely knackered and really just wanted a long, hot soak and very large glass of red. As she locked up for the evening and the weekend, she saw Rak outside *The Bull*. He was speaking on his mobile. She raised her hand to wave. He didn't look at her. Perhaps he hadn't seen her. Charlie really couldn't be bothered driving to Langham, then she remembered, she had completely forgot to book the table. *'Oh, for fuck's sake!'* They would have next to zero chance of getting a table at *The Rose & Crown* on a Saturday night without a reservation. Brad, she knew, would not be happy.

As she walked through the front door Brad greeted her with, "Hello." Just 'hello'? She really wasn't in the mood for an altercation so chose to ignore his unaffectionate welcome.

"Hi, look I've had a mental day. I forgot to book *The Rose & Crown*, shall we just get a takeaway?" she was hopeful he would be tired from his journey and agree.

"No babe, don't worry about it. Mark rang, he and Tilly are eating at *The Bull* tonight, asked if we wanted to join them. We're booked in at 6:30. There, all sorted."

Charlie could not believe what she had just heard. She knew Rak was at *The Bull* already, having just seen him. She knew he had been avoiding her line of sight and now she would have to see him again. The thing that she really could not fathom was his coldness towards her after the night they had shared only hours before. She reasoned there was no point in raising suspicion with Brad so decided to go along with the plan. She opted for a shower over a bath, that would only send her to sleep, a shower would wake her up. She blow-dried her choppy blonde bob perfectly and applied her make-up with precision. She decided to wear a figure hugging red dress, being a size fourteen, Charlie could carry it off, having all the right curves in the right places. She also wore hold-ups instead of tights, she wanted to feel sexy. When she walked into the living room to grab her watch even Brad looked twice at her.

"Wow! Looking good, babe."

And they were out the door.

5

Saturday Evening
The Bull

Rak had been propping up the bar since around 3:00pm and was well on his way to being a little worse for wear. Mark had joined him and Nick was relaying Rak's attempt at a round of golf that afternoon. "Honestly Mark, I'm not being funny but I reckon you could have had him today. Totally off his game, only got one birdie. He was totally shameful." Both Mark and Nick laughed at their friend's expense, even though Mark was actually laughing at himself too.

"Now hang on Nick, the accused is allowed a

defence. Rak, what are you claiming as your defence?"

Rak knew exactly what his defence was but could not possibly admit to it here, or anywhere come to that. "It's been a long week mate, I'm fatigued, what more can I say?" Rak was smiling and trying to look happy. "Do you want another?" as he gestured to both Nick and Mark. They both took him up on the offer and the conversation moved to a new car that Nick was interested in looking at. "Is Tilly joining you tonight, Mark?" Rak asked, usually they would be out together on a Saturday evening.

"Yeah, she's just sorting that bloody dog out, honestly mate, she cares more about that than me and the kids." Tilly had recently acquired a Labrador from her boss as he was really getting too old to look after him and was thinking of putting him in a dog shelter. Tilly being kind-hearted could not bear to think of the dog in a shelter every night so begged Mark to let her take him.

"We're meeting Charlie and Brad in here for dinner, actually, do you wanna join us? Bring Lisa too if you want." The last offer was an afterthought, Rak and Nick were aware, but at least the offer had been made. Rak was more concerned about seeing Charlie again. He still hadn't been able to decide what he wanted or think what she might want.

"Errr… no you're all right mate. I don't really fancy playing gooseberry tonight and I still need to sort things out with Lisa. Thanks anyway." Rak had no intention of trying to make amends with Lisa as he well knew but he also could not stomach seeing Charlie with Brad.

The bar at *The Bull* was large and curved round. From where Rak was sitting he could see the bar entrance. The door opened and there she was. A figure of beauty. Their eyes met for what felt like an eternity. He felt his cheeks flush and quickly took a large gulp of his pint. Then Brad followed, into the bar. Rak could take no more. He jumped off his bar stool and went to make his way to the gents, mumbling to Nick and Mark, "what goes in must come out." Once in the sanctuary of the gents he took a few deep breaths. He splashed his face with water and then looked at the reflection of the man staring back him in the mirror. This grey haired, fifty-year-old man. Lines around his eyes, from years of stress and happiness, although not in equal measure. His shoulders were still broad and he wasn't fat, at 6ft he carried himself well. He heard himself say aloud, "what would she want with you? She could have anyone." He felt deep inside that he was too old for Charlie and he really didn't want to ruin her life.

It felt as if he had been in the gents for an eternity. He knew he would have to face the bar soon. Rak found the courage to return to the bar to see Charlie sitting with Brad. He had his hand on her knee and she was laughing. Mark and Tilly were with them, he quickly picked up they were laughing at a story Mark was telling about Tilly's dog. Charlie's laugh was infectious and the whole table were happily enjoying each other's company. Tilly saw Rak first. "All right, Rak? Would you like to join us? You can help me defend Rollo, my dog. I need some allies." Tilly was smiling and lightly smacking Mark in jest, who was just shaking his head. Charlie turned round to see Rak, her eyes saying more than words ever could.

"No thanks, Tilly, I'm really not feeling it tonight. Thanks for the offer though." And with that Rak left.

He took himself to sit on the bench on 'The Green'. The cool air was refreshing, and he needed to collect his thoughts. He had not heard from Lisa since a text message earlier that day, informing him she was going shopping. To be honest, he could not have cared less. A figure appeared in front of him, he raised his head to find it was Charlie.

"Are you going to keep avoiding me then?" Her voice was fragile and he sensed it

"Hun, we can't do this. You have too much to lose. Don't you see, I'm no good for you." He sounded defeated and like his world was about to end.

Charlie did not have the words to respond, just tears that were falling so hard now she could not stop them. Rak could not bear to see her so upset, he knew what he wanted to do. He got to his feet and took her in his arms, comforting her, protecting her and most of all, wanting her.

Charlie felt his body close to hers. She wanted him. She wanted to kiss him, right now, right here. She looked up into his brown eyes, they were glistening with moisture. She knew he felt the same, but she sensed he was scared of the consequences of the actions they may take next. "Brad is in the pub, I told him I had a headache and was going home for a lie down. Why don't you join me?"

His hand tapped her bottom and he nodded "Come around the back, into the kitchen. I'll unlock the side gate." She wasn't asking, she was telling.

As soon as Charlie had let herself into the house through the front door, she rushed to the side door in the kitchen and unlocked the side gate. Rak was there already, waiting to be let in. Once in the kitchen they could not wait to kiss each other, passionately, wanting nothing more than to feel and taste each other. Her hands touched his bottom, his hands touched her breasts. He lifted her onto the island and started to lift up the bottom of her dress. When he saw she was wearing hold-ups he smiled. He used his finger to push her knickers to one side and then fingered her with two fingers "Rak! oh, Rak! Yes, yes!" she wanted him right there. She undid his belt and his jeans, they fell to the floor. His boxers were tight around his hard, pulsating cock. He ripped her knickers off her and began licking her clit. She was coming and she couldn't stop "Rak! Yes, yes, yes. Don't stop. Don't you dare stop..." She pushed his head further onto her. She used her hands to pull his cock from his boxers, hard and massive. He pulled her to the edge of the worktop and then he was inside her. He still had his shirt on, she still had her dress on. It was frantic and hot. He was thrusting into her, harder and harder. Rak knew he was going to come quickly but he did not want to slow down, he had a profound need for Charlie. He let out a scream of pleasure.

6

Upper Loughton

Six Weeks Later

Tilly French and Julia Carr had been friends for over twenty years. They both had a common dislike of Lisa Banerjee which also bonded them. Tilly had invited Julia to join her on her morning walk with Rollo, the Labrador. Tilly knew Julia would have liked to have had animals herself, but the commitment of *The Bull* was already enough.

"He really is adorable, Tilly, you must be over the moon to have him." Remarked Julia as Rollo ran after the ball she had just thrown for him.

"Yeah, he is. I'm so happy I decided to take him on. He's given me a new lease of life too."

Julia knew Tilly had previously suffered slightly with depression and she could see Rollo was helping her to see the lighter side of life. Tilly and Mark had encountered money worries a few years ago. Mark's building company was not doing so well and unbeknown to Tilly he had incurred quite a substantial amount of debt. She only became aware after she ordered a new sofa for the living room without consulting Mark, they had never really discussed interiors and Mark had always given her free reign. Julia recalled how Tilly had appeared at the bar of *The Bull* in floods of tears, desperate for her friend to help her. Mark had seen the order for the sofa on an email and he had let rip at Tilly. That was when the truth of how much trouble they were in became apparent to Tilly.

After Mark had been open with Tilly, they began to work together to resolve the situation. Tilly took a part-time job at the bus station, initially as office manager, she had trained in clerical work and previously worked as a P.A. to the managing director of an engineering company—Rak's company. Rak had offered Tilly her job back when he heard she was looking, however, she didn't want to feel she was moving backwards, although she was grateful. Tilly had been a kept woman and it was hard enough contemplating returning to work, if she was going to do it, she needed something new. Tilly found she actually enjoyed working at the bus station. The banter suited her and she began to feel she had a purpose. She realised that being at home all day, by herself had actually been getting her down. Once Mark's business began to pick up again and they had cleared some of their debts, he offered Tilly the chance to finish at the bus station, he wasn't comfortable with the idea of sending his wife out to work. However, at the same time an opening for a job share arose within the bus station, as part-time station manager. Tilly applied and was successful. She had never looked back since.

The two women and Rollo were approaching the newsagents and saw Dorian outside cleaning the windows. "Hiya Dorian, you can do mine after if you want." Shouted Tilly with a smile on her face. Tilly was a petite woman but what she lost in stature she made up for vocally.

"Oh, don't Tilly, I've been on at Jack for the past two days to clean these bloody windows. The lazy bastard won't move unless he's going over the road." Jack and Dorian had been married twenty-five years, although they had been together nearer forty, and to say familiarity breeds contempt would be a fair description. Julia was laughing now too, as 'over the road' referred to *The Oak*. The other pub in the village, leased by Sheila and Gary Tyler, not natural publicans by any stretch of the imagination.

"Blimey, he must have to be telepathic to know what time they're going to open up" laughed Julia, as *The Oak* had a reputation for random opening hours, dependent on how much Gary had drunk of his own supply the previous night.

Dorian was happy to stay and chat longer with the two women, always with the hope of gleaning some new, juicy gossip. "I must say Julia, Kate and I had a wonderful evening last night. You and Nick are doing a fantastic job with the place."

Julia took the compliment but could also sense Dorian was after something else "We were very surprised to see Rak looking so happy, I mean y'know, with how his wife is and all."

'Here we go,' Julia was thinking and gave Dorian a smile. "Yes, it is good to see him looking happy, Dorian, he deserves to be happy but then again doesn't everyone?"

Dorian was desperately trying to scramble her mind for something else to pick at. She and Kate had been discussing the Banerjee's the previous evening and she desperately wanted to impress Kate with more information. However, before Dorian could say anything further.

"Right, I need to get back to help Nick get ready for opening, are you coming Tilly?" Tilly realised the correct answer was yes and walked on with Julia, Rollo in tow. Dorian was left cleaning her windows and feeling very disappointed.

The two women continued walking towards *The Bull* when Julia suddenly came out with, "you know what though, Tilly, the old cow's right, Rak does seem very happy and has done for a few weeks now. Do you reckon he's got a new woman on the go?"

Tilly looked surprised but not shocked. She had been working part-time for Rak when he and Amira had divorced. She knew from some personal papers he had asked her to look over that the reason cited was adultery on his part. Tilly did not know if Julia was aware of this and still felt loyalty towards her old boss and friend so decided not to disclose it. "Hmmm, I don't know, I mean who with? He's always on his own." Tilly really did not want to be having this conversation.

"Is Mark playing golf this afternoon, Tilly?" Julia was plotting, Tilly could feel it.

"No, he's got a big job on, working Saturdays now. Still, gives me chance to enjoy a bit of peace."

Julia's eyes lit up. "Right, Nick can get to the bottom of this, I'll get him to find out what's going on".

As soon as Julia arrived back at *The Bull*, she was on to Nick. "Nick, I need you to do something." She shouted as soon as she came into the bar. Nick was bottling up ready for opening in half an hour.

"Yes, sunshine of my life." he retorted.

Julia knew he was being sarcastic, but she didn't have time for his stupidity at the moment. "I want you to find out if Rak is shagging someone, y'know doing the dirty on Lisa."

Nick nearly dropped the crate of mixers he was carrying in disbelief. "You what? You're bloody mad, you are. Careful, you'll finish up like the two nosey cows that were in here last night." He put the crate on the bar and made to return to the cellar.

"That's exactly why I need to know Nick, Dorian has just insinuated that he might be and if they start gossiping... well, you know."

Nick was more than aware that his wife had a soft spot for his best friend and would not wish any harm to come to him. "I'll see what I can do, no promises though."

She knew not to push it further.

7

Saturday Afternoon

Upper Loughton Golf Club

Nick was not looking forward to asking his best friend if he was having an affair. Apart from the belief that if he was, Nick would already know about it. He knew if he was and Rak hadn't mentioned it, it was for a very good reason. Although Nick did have to agree with his wife, Rak had been extremely buoyant these past few weeks, more of a spring in his step.

The sun was shining and there was no wind, *the perfect weather for a round of golf,* Rak thought as he took his clubs from the boot of his Jaguar F-Type. He saw Nick waiting near the clubhouse and made his way over. "You're keen mate, we don't tee off for another ten minutes. Is Julia doing your head in?" Rak was laughing as his friend was only ever early if he was exasperated by Julia and needed to get out the pub.

"Yeah, something like that." Nick was non-committal. He was not going to divulge what they had been speaking about earlier in the day. "Good day for it, mate, hope it stays like this for the fundraiser next week." Nick was keen to discuss something else. Every year the village held a fundraiser. It was started by Rak and Nick after their friend of many years passed away after battling with Motor Neurone Disease for so long. They would usually raise a few hundred pounds and then between them match it and donate to the MND charity.

They began making their way around the course. Both men were on top of their game and looked as if they may tie "So mate, hypothetically, if you had to shag a woman in the village who would you choose?" This was the only way Nick could raise the subject.

"You what? What sort of question's that?" asked Rak, slightly taken off guard. He started to panic, he wondered if his best friend knew about him and Charlie.

"Well, I was just thinking, we've never done this one before, y'know compared the ladies of the village. I know who you'd choose anyway, Kate" and Nick laughed. Rak could not work out what his friend wanted to hear but knew he could no longer keep the truth from him.

"Actually mate, there is something I need to tell you but you cannot, in any circumstances repeat it. Not even to Julia." Nick was getting concerned now, was his friend ill? Was his immediate thought, but that was quickly quashed when he thought how happy Rak had been recently.

"Whatever it is mate, just tell me for fuck's sake." Rak immediately replied. "No swearing on the golf course," and laughed as he did so as they both knew Ted had enforced this rule but it was not adhered to. Rak stopped and looked Nick straight in the face. He took a deep breath "Do you remember the first week you had that band on at the pub, on the Friday night?" Nick nodded without saying a word. "I walked Charlie home because she was on her own," he did not want to mention Brad. "Well," Rak was hesitating now and he was beginning to feel a little too warm. Nick was waiting with bated breath but he thought he knew what his friend was going to say next. "I don't know how it happened mate, honestly. We were just having a glass of red, chatting, well not chatting, talking is a more accurate description. Then we were kissing, proper kissing. Then we were in her bedroom, undressing each other. I asked her Nick. I didn't take advantage, y'know." Nick was looking at his friend in disbelief. Disbelief that he had actually done this but more so, disbelief he hadn't told him. "She was all over me Nick, she made me feel like a man again. She felt so good I couldn't stop. She enjoyed herself too, I made sure of it." Rak was looking to his friend for support but mostly approval "I stayed with her afterwards, it was so good to hold her and I didn't want to let go."

Nick suddenly had a jolt. "Hang on, we played golf the next day, early tee time because of the school tournament, why didn't you tell me?" Nick looked hurt and Rak knew it.

"Because I didn't know what I was going to do next, she's married too, remember? I didn't want anyone to know." Rak hung his head slightly, knowing his friend was very aware of the age difference.

Nick was still shocked. "And you were dead funny in the pub after, especially when her and Brad walked in. I remember now, you were in the gents for over fifteen minutes, I wondered what you were doing. Then you left, half a pint still on the bar."

Rak really needed to make his friend understand. "I was trying to decide what to do mate. I know she's younger than me."

Nick quickly interjected. "That's a fucking under-statement."

Rak continued, "I went to sit on 'The Green' to try and get my head together, I'd decided that we couldn't carry on, it wouldn't be fair on Charlie. But she came out and found me. I told her we couldn't have an affair, but mate, she got really upset. Crying and vulnerable, I had to hold her, I had to." Nick didn't say a word, just waited for Rak to continue. "She said she wanted me and I wanted her too, more than I've ever wanted any woman. We went to her place and I shagged her on the kitchen island. Fuckin' hell mate, it was fantastic." Rak realised immediately he had given Nick too much detail.

"Is it still going on?" Nick asked, softer tone this time, remembering to be a friend to his friend rather than judge and jury.

"Yeah… yeah, we're still seeing each other. It's not just shagging Nick, it's more than that. We've told each other really personal stuff, stuff not many other people know."

Nick had to process what his friend had just told him. He was very aware that Rak hid his innermost feelings from people as he found it difficult to be vulnerable. Nick realised if he had discussed his personal feelings with Charlie, it must be serious.

"How do you feel about her?"

Rak looked away briefly, then back towards his best friend, his eyes full of emotion "I'm developing strong feelings for her Nick. I think I'm in love with her." Nick could see his friend was getting emotional, not a sight he had seen too often, even in the thirty years they had known each other. "You can't tell Julia, no one else can know. I don't care about Lisa but if Brad finds out, Charlie will get hurt. Do you understand?" Rak had lost his vulnerability now and was on the verge of anger, he could not and would not have Charlie hurt. He knew he loved her and he could not risk losing her

"Ahh, come on mate. You know what it's like. I can't keep secrets from my wife, you're putting me in a difficult position." Nick was acutely aware that Julia would be expecting a full report after closing that evening and he couldn't lie to her face. Rak could feel his body tensing, he did not want to fall out with Nick, that was incomprehensible, however he feared for Charlie being hurt or being made the subject of gossip.

"What happened to mates before dates?" Rak forced through gritted teeth.

"Right back at ya." Nick was getting angry now. "I can't believe you would ask me to lie to my wife to protect your girlfriend."

The two men abandoned their game and went their separate ways.

8

Saturday Afternoon

Heirs & Graces

The salon had been busy all morning, Charlie had skipped lunch and was ready for a break. Earlier that afternoon she had to be pleasant and personable to Lisa. As usual, Lisa had called the salon around an hour before she actually wanted her appointment and demanded Charlie fit her in as she had a very important dinner date. With Rak.

This was not new information to Charlie as Rak had mentioned he would have to indulge Lisa on Saturday night earlier in the week. It was Rak's birthday the following day and Lisa had insisted she wanted to eat out at *San Marios* on the Saturday night. *San Marios* was an exclusive restaurant situated the other side of Langham, it was more well known as a place to see and be seen rather than offering decent food, even if it did arrive with a decent price tag.

Charlie was not the least bit phased by this, she had expected Rak to fulfil his obligations to accommodate Lisa occasionally, even if it was in celebration of his birthday. The other reason Charlie was being reasonable was that her and Rak were going away on Sunday morning and not coming back until Monday afternoon. Charlie had received a trade flyer advertising a trade fair in Stratford-upon Avon to be held on Sunday the 18th of August. The timing could not have been better. She had a ready-made excuse to be away from home for the night. She had already booked the hotel, a boutique-y number, which prided itself on offering super-king size beds. She couldn't wait.

Earlier Lisa had been explaining how awful it was to live with Rak. "You just can't imagine, Charlie. He's quite a nightmare. Temper tantrums at the drop of a hat. I really don't know how I cope with him. If he becomes upset, he's a terrible nightmare, the mood swings are the worst." Lisa was waving her arms around to add to the drama. "I really believe I am the only woman who can tolerate him."

Charlie didn't know how she kept her tongue or a straight face, being privy to more information than Lisa could ever imagine. Charlie was desperate to defend Rak, but did not want to remind Lisa too much of her husband's qualities. "I'm sure every couple has their own issues," was the best she could offer, whilst really trying not to scratch Lisa with her comb.

Charlie was both relieved and drained when Lisa had left. She was not going to let her spoil their weekend. Charlie had not known what to buy Rak, when she had asked him what he would like his response had been, 'You, baby, just you. All night long.' So she treated herself to a matching set of sexy underwear, hoping she would not be wearing it for too long.

9

The Bull

It was around 2:45pm, the bar was thinning out now after the lunchtime crowd and Julia was looking forward to a break. She had not been able to concentrate on anything since her earlier conversation with Nick. She was hoping and praying he would talk with Rak and find out what was going on in his life. She was not, however, prepared for what would happen next.

Nick came slamming through the entrance door to the bar. His face was like thunder. At first Julia thought he was having a heart attack or something.

She left the customer she was serving and rushed to his side. "Nick, what's happened? You look awful. You're back early, are you feeling ill?" Nick still could not speak, he was livid. The next question pushed him over the edge. "Where's Rak?"

Nick saw red, he really could not believe that Julia was enquiring regarding Rak's whereabouts. "There you go again, fucking interfering. Why can't you keep your fucking nose out of other people's business? And why are you so obsessed with Rak?"

The customers in the bar were looking now. Julia tried to calm the situation by dragging Nick into the back "Adam, watch the bar" was all she could say.

Julia was scared, she hadn't seen Nick like this ever before. She wanted to ask what had happened but didn't dare to. She sensed whatever had happened was being blamed on her. On the way back to the pub, Nick had decided in his head that if Julia had not asked him to interfere in Rak's business, then he and his best friend, possibly the person he loved most in the world, would not have had their altercation. Instead, they would have enjoyed an afternoon of great golf and a few beers after. It was his friend's birthday tomorrow and now she had created all this bad feeling between them. He had also considered that his wife had an unhealthy obsession with his best friend and this angered him further. Julia found her courage. "Nick, please sit down and calm down." She was telling him now. "What has happened?"

Nick was now in a sticky situation. He did not want to betray Rak's trust, he knew that. He also knew his friend had been right in reminding him, 'mates before dates', a mantra they had lived by in their younger days. He knew he would have to explain his outburst. But he could not let go of his anger for his wife. "Leave me alone Julia. This is none of your business." With that he stormed out of the pub and took solace on the bench on 'The Green', head in his hands.

10

Saturday Afternoon

Rak

After he left the golf course, Rak threw his golf clubs into the boot of the Jag, slammed the boot as hard as he could, got into the driver's seat, slamming the door behind him and sped off out of the carpark. Rak was so angry he could not comprehend his feelings. He left the village by the main road and drove out into the country. Rak knew he was speeding but he didn't care, he was angry, emotional and confused. The radio was playing 'Layla' by Eric Clapton and the guitar rift just encouraged him to press the accelerator. He was taking sharp bends too quickly, he nearly lost the front end into a hedge. This still didn't slow him down. Then, BANG...!

11

Saturday Afternoon
Charlie

Charlie was just finishing a cut and blow when her mobile rang. She hated leaving clients to answer the phone, however this was different. The ringtone was the one she had selected for Rak. She had wanted to know if he was calling so she could move to another room before answering the call, ensuring Brad would not hear her on their calls.

Charlie looked at the salon clock, it read 3:15pm. Rak should be playing golf. She apologised to her client and went to get the phone before it went to voicemail "Honey, baby, I errr..." she couldn't understand what he was trying to say,

"I can't hear you, you'll have to speak up." Charlie turned the CD player off and went into back. "Baby, what's happened?" She was concerned.

"Hun, I've crashed the car. I'm bleeding. I don't know where from."

Charlie's heart was in her mouth, her stomach hit the floor, she was shaking. "Where are you baby?" Charlie was crying now; her client had heard and came in to see what the commotion was about. "I'm really sorry, can you please go home? I have an emergency." and she closed the door. "Rak! Where are you baby?" she was shouting hysterically now. The line went quiet, then nothing.

Charlie ran outside in panic. She would get her Mini and go and look for him. She had to find him. As she approached her house, she saw Nick sitting on the bench on 'The Green'. "Nick! Nick!" she shouted. He heard her but didn't wish to talk to her. He ignored her. "Nick!, It's Rak. He's had a car crash. Please! Please, help me!"

Nick looked at her in horror, the bottom dropping out of his world. "Where is he?" He was on his feet now.

"I don't know, he said he was bleeding then the line went quiet." She did not want to use the word 'dead'. Charlie was sobbing as she went to unlock her car.

"Hang on, we'll take mine. If anything happens

to you, he'll kill me." At that moment she knew Nick knew.

Nick ran to the pub carpark and got his Porsche, drove out the carpark and waited while Charlie got in. "We had an argument, Charlie, this is all my fault. He was in a vile temper. I should never have got involved."

She knew he was referring to the affair her and Rak were having. "I'm sorry Nick, it just happened. I love him Nick, I want to be with him for the rest of my life." She was sobbing now, heartfelt sobs interspersed with wailing.

"Come on, babe, keep it together for Rak, eh? Help me look for him." Nick's anger for Julia was now unprecedented, *'if she hadn't fucking interfered'*. He thought. They were driving along the main road out towards the countryside. Nick knew Rak had often commented he liked getting his foot down on this road, 'it's all about the bends mate, gorgeous.' He could hear his friend enthusing to him in his head.

"There, Nick there." Charlie was pointing to the back end of Rak's car, the front buried in fencing.

Nick immediately put on his hazard lights and jumped out of the car. Charlie followed. They found Rak. He was slumped back in the driver's seat, the airbag blooming out from the steering wheel, his head was cut and bleeding quite badly. The driver's side door was open. Charlie reached for her mobile and dialled 999 "Ambulance please. My boyfriend has crashed his car, he's bleeding. Please, hurry up."

Nick heard Charlie describe their location through her sobs and felt guilty for giving his friend a hard time. Why could he not be happy for him? Hadn't he had enough shit over the years? Charlie immediately opened the door further to hold Rak. Nick managed to somehow to move her out of the way so he could reach in to unclip Rak's seatbelt, the only thing that may have saved his life, then he pulled his friend out of the car.

At that moment the ambulance arrived. Two paramedics got out, one man, one woman.

"What's his name?" the woman asked.

"Rakesh Banerjee," replied Nick. "But everyone calls him Rak."

She nodded. "And his date of birth?"

Nick couldn't think straight. "He's fifty-one tomorrow, he will be fifty-one tomorrow" his voice was full of intent.

The paramedics were telling Charlie to give Rak space, but she needed to hold him. Nick led her away, he could see she was not helping Rak.

"Tell me he'll be all right, Nick. Tell me!" she was hysterical again.

"Calm down!" Nick did not want Rak to hear his girlfriend in distress. "Charlie, you've gotta calm down, ok? That's how you'll help Rak, do you understand?"

Charlie nodded and Nick took her hand and held it tight, he was scared himself and needed Charlie to support him too.

"Ok, we're going to take him to St. Luke's," it was the female paramedic. "It's not serious love, ok? He'll live. He's just cut his head and passed out from shock. He's conscious now." She was talking to Charlie now. "We're just taking him in to get checked over, would you like to come in the ambulance?"

Charlie immediately replied. "Yes, yes, I would. Is he talking?"

The paramedic replied "Yes, he is, a lot about Charlie, is that you?"

Charlie nodded, dumbstruck. Nick got his car keys out of his pocket. "I'll follow on, he'll be ok Charlie, there's life in the old dog yet." Then he hugged her, more for his sake than hers.

12

St. Luke's Hospital

Charlie and Rak were finally alone. Rak had given a statement to the police, insisting a rabbit had ran into his path and he had no choice but to swerve to avoid killing it. With no witnesses to the contrary, they reluctantly accepted his version of events. Nick had gone to call Julia, his anger now subsided slightly, and because Rak had told him to.

"*The Bull*, how may I help you." Julia sounded worried and annoyed in equal measure.

"It's me, look Rak's had a car accident."

"What? Is he ok?"

Nick knew he had to reassure his wife. "Yeah, bit bruised, cut to the head but he was lucky according to the doctor, I'm at St. Luke's now. It could have been worse, Julia. Look, I erm… I'm sorry I shouted at ya. I can't explain here but I will as soon as I get back." Nick could not go into detail over the phone, he needed to talk with his wife face to face.

"Have you let Lisa know? I mean, I know she probably won't care but she should know, Nick." Nick hadn't bargained for this question.

"No, don't do that, they're letting him go home tonight anyway." Nick didn't want Julia to know about Charlie yet.

"Ok, well you drive carefully home, are you waiting for Rak?"

Nick breathed a sigh of relief that Julia hadn't pushed it. "Yeah, look I might be a while. I love you, Julia."

"I love you too, tell him I'm pleased he's all right." With that Nick ended the call.

"What happened baby?" Charlie was still upset but so relieved. She also had experienced the realisation of her true feelings for Rak.

"I just lost it, hun. I was going too fast and lost it on the bend." Charlie wanted to ask more, to ask what had happened between Rak and Nick but she didn't want to stress him out.

"I'm sorry about the weekend, I was looking forward to it. I wish we didn't have to sneak around,

I might look at renting a flat or something for us, what do you think?" Rak was searching her eyes, he wanted to move their relationship on but knew they needed somewhere to call theirs.

"Yes, that would be fantastic. I need to be with you, Rak"

Just at that moment the doctor walked in "Well, Mr. Banerjee, all your tests have come back clear, you're free to go." the doctor was around Rak's age if not a couple of years older. "I would recommend some bed rest." Charlie could have sworn he was smiling as he said it and couldn't have agreed more.

Nick had overheard Rak and Charlie's conversation and on the way back to Upper Loughton, he took a detour.

"Where are you going mate? I'm the one that's had a bump to the head."

Nick smiled at his friend, his best friend in the entire world. "You'll see." Was all he said. Rak did see, he saw they were approaching Pam's Cottage.

"What are we doing here mate?"

Again, Nick replied, "You'll see".

Pam's Cottage belonged to Nick's mother, Pamela Carr. It was just far enough away from the village to avoid prying eyes but close enough to be convenient. Pamela had been left the cottage by her best friend some years earlier. Nick's parents did not have an easy marriage, and this became Pamela's bolthole. However, a few years ago Pamela had gone on holiday to Spain and hadn't returned, having met the love of her life out there. Nick let the cottage out periodically, however at the moment it was empty.

"Charlie, come and see what you think to this place." Nick said, gesturing towards the front door. Charlie could not believe what she thought was happening.

"Why? I mean I'm not being rude, but Rak needs to rest."

Rak gestured for her to follow Nick as he followed her. Charlie could not believe how secluded the cottage was, spread across one level and tucked away from the main road. Once inside she loved it.

"It's yours if you want it. I'm not saying I agree with what you're doing because I don't." Nick still had a niggling feeling his friend would get hurt but he also wanted to help him be happy. "But he's the happiest he's been in years so you're doing something right. Look after him though, I mean it."

Charlie knew he meant it. "I will, I promise you Nick, I will."

Rak couldn't believe the generosity of his friend. "Are you sure, mate? How much do you want for it?"

Nick laughed. "Nothing, just look after the place and if Mum comes home, you'll have to give it back, she ain't living with me." All three of them were laughing hysterically now.

13

Saturday Night

3 Church Lane

Rak wanted to stay at Pam's Cottage all night with Charlie. He was sure she would kiss him better. However, he also knew Lisa would be waiting to go out to *San Marios*. Now, he was not up to going. "Where the hell have you been? The table's booked for 7:00, it's 6:30 now!" Lisa was livid. She was desperate to mingle with the *San Marios* scene and could not understand Rak's apparent disinterest. She didn't even notice his cuts and bruises.

"I've crashed the car, I've been at the hospital. We're not going out, I'm finished. The doctor advised rest."

Lisa's face was one of horror, not from concern for her husband though. "Where's the car? What do you mean, 'you've crashed it'? How have you managed that? For fuck's sake. Rak!"

Rak was not expecting love, hearts and flowers but he was expecting some concern, for him, not just his Jag. He could not admit to speeding, she would go mental. "A rabbit ran out in front of me, I swerved to avoid it and lost the front end, hit a farmer's fence. I'm sure it's a right off, I mean that's what you're bothered about, ain't it?" Rak was feeling emotional, drained and to be honest, desolate. He needed Charlie.

He went upstairs and took his mobile out of his pocket, he selected the text button and messaged Charlie.

'Hey Charlie, I can't do this, stay here I mean. Pack a bag and meet me in The Bull's carpark. Let's go to Pam's xxxx'

Charlie was in her kitchen, listening to Diana Ross and thinking about Rak. She was concerned for him, especially as he was with Lisa. Brad had just finished watching his fishing programme and joined her in the kitchen. "Would you like a glass of something babe?" He offered.

Charlie was feeling so lonely she would have liked a vat of something. "Errr, yeah. A glass of red please." She tried to impress an air of happiness in her voice. Just as Brad placed a glass of red wine before her, her mobile pinged. She read the text and a wide smiled enveloped her face.

"What's up babe, you won the lottery?" Brad was curious.

Charlie felt as if she had won the lottery, she was on cloud nine. "Oh, it's Anna, my friend in Stratford, she's invited me to stay at hers tonight, y'know, as I'm in Stratford tomorrow anyway." Charlie was acutely aware Brad did not have a great rapport with Anna, who actually did live in Stratford, so was less likely to ask questions.

"Will you be ok driving, Char? It's going to be dark soon." Charlie was already on her feet.

"Yeah, I'll be fine thanks, just going to chuck a few bits in a bag." Charlie almost ran upstairs, she felt suddenly alive again.

'Hi baby, yes. Give me 10 minutes xxxx'

Charlie quickly threw some clothes, make-up and her toothbrush into her overnight bag. She also packed her new underwear, she wanted to give Rak a birthday present he would never forget.

She returned back to the kitchen and grabbed a couple of bottles of red. She was ready to go. Their first night in their first place together.

14

Saturday Night

The Bull

Tilly and Mark were in *The Bull*. Julia had called Tilly after Nick's outburst; she was so upset and angry with him. Tilly had advised Julia to leave him to calm down, she knew Nick was usually placid and easy going. However, around 6:30pm Tilly had suggested to Mark they pop by and check on the situation.

"Yeah, I'm up for a pint or two but I'm not getting dragged into domestic problems. Julia's your mate and Nick's mine, stay impartial, eh? You know Nick, he wouldn't lose his shit if there weren't a reason."

Tilly was inclined to agree, especially knowing how intent Julia was on uncovering the reason for Rak's sudden improved mood.

"Hiya darlin', what will you be having?" Julia seemed more relaxed than she had earlier but still on edge.

"A pint for his lordship and a large glass of rosé for me please. Have you heard from him?"

Julia was now torn between telling her friend about Rak's accident or keeping it to herself, after all, Nick had not said she couldn't tell Tilly, Julia gestured Tilly towards the end of the bar where it was quiet. "Rak's crashed his car, been to St. Luke's. He's ok according to Nick; apparently, he was very lucky."

Tilly couldn't quite take the news in. "How did that happen? Rak's usually such a careful driver. Bloody hell, Julia, that's really shook me up." Tilly had always liked Rak and was beginning to feel hot tears welling up in her eyes.

"Oh, come on, Tills, he's ok. Nick was waiting to take him home." Tilly attempted to recover her composure; she didn't want Mark to see she was upset either.

"What are you two gossiping about? You could give Dorian and Kate a run for their money," quipped Mark.

"Rak's had a car crash, Mark. Julia said he was taken to St. Luke's. Looks like he was lucky, Nick's waiting to bring him home."

Mark sat looking at his pint, in shock. "Bloody hell, Tills, Rak's usually such a good driver, he's so precious about his car. Well, at least he's ok, eh?" Then Mark took a large gulp of his pint to hide his emotion.

The entrance door to the bar opened, it was Nick, thankfully for Julia in a better frame of mind then earlier in the day. "Hey babe, get us one of Rak's whiskeys would you, it's been a fucker of a day." Julia could finally breathe a sigh of relief, it seemed whatever Nick was angry about earlier had dissipated. She would ask him later for details.

15

Saturday Night
Pam's Cottage

She could not believe they were alone together. Alone, without having to watch the time, or listening for the door unexpectedly opening, or a car parking on the drive. Charlie felt so grateful to Nick, he had given Rak and her a priceless gift. They could finally spend some quality time together. She was still concerned for Rak, he was still saying he felt fine, but she could see him wincing every time he tried to move too quickly. "Will you just do as your told?" She was being playful with him as he was insisting on pouring the wine and being the gentleman he so truly was.

"Wow, hun. I can't believe we've got two whole nights together. Did you cancel the hotel? I don't want you worry about that."

Charlie beamed the widest smile she had given in a very long time. "Yeah, can you believe it? Two nights uninterrupted. Yes, I called them, they were really very good and wished my boyfriend a speedy recovery." She moved to kiss him, carefully at first as she didn't want to aggravate his wounds. Then Rak pulled her tighter towards him, he kissed her so strongly, his tongue playing with hers.

He pulled away to say something, "I thought I was a gonner, hun, I didn't know what was happening, I've never passed out before. But before I passed out, all I could think of was you. I love you Charlie Worthing." He was looking so deep into her emerald green eyes now she thought she might melt away.

"I love you too Rak Banerjee, I really, really do."

They decided to explore the bedroom. Charlie undressed herself first, then she undressed Rak. "You need to lie down Mr. Banerjee, I need to check your vitals." She could see his cock was already responding, the shaft was becoming hard. She ran her fingers up and down the length of him, as she did so, he quivered with delight and pleasure. Then she placed his throbbing cock in her mouth, just the head at first, teasing him with her tongue, flicking and licking.

"Ahhh, baby. Charlie, I love you. That feels so good."

She then moved her tongue down the length of his shaft, still licking him, her eyes on his face. Rak pushed her head further and she opened her mouth and took all his cock.

"Oh my god, you are so fucking sexy, yes, yes, yes." He thought he was going to come when she opened her mouth and licked the head of his cock again. "Ahh, you sexy lady, you don't know what you do to me. You make me feel so good." She had all his cock in her mouth now, she was sucking so strongly. "Honey, if you don't stop, I'll come, stop now," he whispered.

Rak tried to roll Charlie over but she could tell he was struggling. She moved herself so as she was lying next to him. She placed her fingers on her pussy and began playing with her clit, she was putting a show on for Rak, his cock was getting harder, he could feel it. She moved further down her pussy, feeling herself.

"Ahh, ahh, Rak."

He pushed her hand away and fingered her with two fingers, slowly at first then gathering pace, quicker, harder. Charlie could feel she was about to come. "God, Rak, please don't stop, please. I'm gonna come!" Rak was feeling the pain but wanted to satisfy Charlie. "Oh my god, yes, yes, yes!" she was breathless.

Rak lay flat on his back again, Charlie straddled him, she was dripping with wetness, she wanted to feel him. She grabbed his hard, throbbing cock and placed him inside her. Slowly and carefully, she began to move, his cock felt so good, she thought she would come again immediately.

Rak was closing his eyes, whispering, "yes, baby, that's it. Yes, you feel so good. The perfect medicine. Ahh, ahh, yeah." she began to quicken her pace, she was careful not to place too much pressure on her lover. Charlie could feel herself becoming weaker, she looked into Rak's eyes, he smiled at her. "I'm gonna come, sexy, come with me, I can't wait, ahh, God yes, yes!"

They both felt a beautiful moment at the same time. They held on together, knowing they had all night.

16

Sunday Morning

The Bull

Julia was still waiting for a full debrief from Nick. She tried to talk with him last night after closing, however Nick was a little tired and emotional. "My best mate could've died today y'know, babe. Fuck, what would I have done then, I don't wanna think about it." Was all she got out of him.

Julia was cooking Nick a Full English with the hope it would help him to open up to her. "Morning gorgeous, how you feeling now?"

Nick looked rough, hangovers never did suit him, which was possibly the reason he usually steered clear of spirits. "That smells great love, thanks. I feel like shit, actually, but I'll survive." Nick knew Julia would still be expecting an explanation of the previous day's events.

"Look, love, I need to tell you something but you must swear you won't tell anybody else, you got that?" Nick had reasoned that he was helping Rak and Charlie, however, why should his marriage have secrets? Julia placed the breakfast on the table in front of him.

"Well yeah, ok. But what is it? Is it about yesterday?"

Nick still didn't know where to start so he ate a sausage first while contemplating how he should begin. "Right, here goes. I will tell you everything I know. So, listen and don't ask any further questions as I won't know the answers."

Julia just nodded.

"Rak is having an affair, you were right. He's seeing Charlie. Has been for around six weeks now. He reckons he loves her and she says she loves him. We had a massive row yesterday at the golf club because he wanted me to keep it from you, which I wasn't comfortable with. Then I blamed you for our falling out, I reasoned if you hadn't asked me to ask him, we wouldn't have fought. I now realise that's not quite the case but it's not totally untrue either, is it?" Nick stopped to continue with his fry-up, bacon and egg this time. Julia said nothing, trying to take all this new information on board. "Rak stormed off in a temper, he was driving too fast, even for him and lost it. Hit a fence. He's lucky to be here. He rang Charlie immediately after but then passed out. She was hysterical when she saw me. We drove round looking for him and when we found him, I realised she does love him. The ambulance woman said she was the first thing he spoke about when he came to." Another pause, this time beans. "At the hospital, after I'd called you, I heard him saying he wanted to rent a place for the pair of them, I would say shag pad but they both reckon it's more than that and I believe them. I wanted to help him, even you said how happy he's been recently. So, I've given Rak the keys to Pam's Cottage. Told him to come and go as they please." More bacon and egg with black pudding now. "I'm gonna get his car sorted today for him, he's with Charlie and they've not had this sort of quality time until now, the last thing he needs to think about is his motor. I've already spoke to Slim Jim about it and he's gonna meet me to extract it from the hedge." Slim Jim was the overly large local garage owner from the next village, Nick and Rak had both been taking their cars to him for years. "There, you know everything. Only you, me, Rak and Charlie know, Julia, if this gets out, I will know where from."

Julia got the distinct impression her husband was threatening her but didn't want to upset the equilibrium further. She was also shocked "Fucking hell, Nick, I can't believe it!" was all she could say. Nick took a swig of tea.

17

Sunday Morning

9 Church Lane

Tilly had been awake since 6:30am. She had quietly made her way downstairs to make a pot of tea and then sat in the kitchen, quietly enjoying her early morning peace. Mark was still snoring away, Russ was staying at his friends and Stella, their youngest at age seventeen, was away at her boyfriend's for the weekend.

Tilly sat at the kitchen table, staring out to the garden, slowly sipping her tea. She was still in shock over Rak's accident. Tilly had been Rak's P.A. before she had even met Mark, in fact it was thanks to Rak she did meet Mark. Rak had wanted some alterations making to his father's engineering business after he took it over and contacted a local building firm.

Mark French had just started his own business, M.F Construct. He came out to quote Rak for the work and immediately fancied Tilly, aged just twenty. Rak briefly showed Mark what he was looking for and then asked if it was ok if he left him in the capable hands of his P.A. Rak was more hands-on in the old days and would spend most of his time in the workshop. Tilly was not instantly attracted to Mark, she secretly had her sights set on her boss.

Rak had been dating Amira for just under a year and Tilly was hopeful it would run its course, most girlfriends would not tolerate the long hours he worked and she had her fingers crossed this would end sooner rather than later.

Tilly was looking at some papers Rak had asked her to check over when Mark tapped her office door. "All right love, I've priced the job up. If I can source the materials locally the job should come in around this figure."

Tilly took the piece of paper from Mark and smiled. "Thanks, I'll make sure he gets it."

Mark made towards the door then turned back to Tilly. "Look, it's Friday, do you fancy a drink when you knock off?" Mark was nervous and Tilly could tell. She didn't really fancy a drink with him but felt a bit sorry for him.

"Yeah, all right, why not? Do you know *the Rose & Crown* at Langham?" Tilly was living in a house share in Langham at the time and knew the pub was good.

"Yeah, I do actually. What time should I meet you?"

Tilly quickly calculated the time it would take to wash and dry her hair and put a face of make-up on "Say, 7:30? Is that all right?"

Mark nodded. "Yeah; yeah, see you then." Mark left her office with a spring in his step. Tilly also had an ulterior motive, she had overheard Rak earlier in the day arranging to meet Amira at *the Rose & Crown* that evening too.

18

The Rose & Crown

Twenty-Nine Years Earlier

Amira Patel was sitting waiting for her boyfriend, Rak, who was yet again late for their date. This had become a regular occurrence since he had taken over his father's business, so desperate was he to prove to the old man he had what it takes. Amira was cradling a glass of Merlot. She didn't want to sit in the pub without a drink but didn't want to get drunk either. Around fifteen minutes later Rak arrived. "Hun, I am so sorry, I completely lost track of time. Then the old man phoned, giving it all that. Old George Potter had been onto him, moaning about the 'service he received,' for fuck's sake, it's about time he retired anyway." Rak finally paused for breath and to order a bottle of Merlot from the bar. Amira loved him and she knew he loved her, she could see how much the business meant to him, if only to prove his father wrong. "Anyway, forget that place until Monday, how was your day?" Amira had a job as a secretary for a house builder, Rak had asked her to be his P.A. before he advertised the position, but Amira was wise enough to decline.

"Oh, y'know, all right. Bloody long day though, invoice after invoice, thought it would never end."

Rak poured himself a glass of red and topped Amira up. "One day you will be a lady of leisure, I promise. I'll keep you in the style you will have become accustomed to, baby."

Amira smiled, "and lots of dirty nappies." They both wanted a family, they had discussed marriage and kids and both wanted to get started. They were right for each other.

Rak was late for another reason too. He had been to the jewellers. He knew Amira was the one, so why wait? He had discussed it with his best friend, Nick Carr, who personally thought he was mad. 'Mate, you're only twenty-two, what's the rush?' Nick was not a fan of commitment, his longest relationship lasting around six months.

'I love her. I want babies with her and I want to be young enough to enjoy it. She's the one Nick, I can feel it.' Rak smiled, and his eyes were bright with excitement of what would be.

It was 7:15pm and Mark sat with a pint at the bar, waiting for Tilly. It suddenly occurred to him that he hadn't asked her name, not being very experienced when it came to dating it had never crossed his mind. 7:25pm, Tilly arrived looking fantastic. She had a new dress on with her high heels and her best handbag, if she was going out, she was going out in style.

"Hello, look sorry, I didn't ask your name earlier." Mark admitted sheepishly.

"I'm Tilly and I know you're Mark because Rak told me."

Mark smiled and gestured towards a table. "Do you wanna grab that table and I'll get you a drink, what would you like?"

Tilly looked towards the table, it was opposite her boss and his girlfriend, 'oh good,' she thought, 'at least I've got a view.' "A G&T please, with ice. Thanks." Tilly made a dash for the table Mark had selected and waved at Rak, and Amira, who she had only met twice.

Rak was not that pleased to see his P.A. and her date sitting at the table opposite. He would now have to think of another plan to propose to Amira, he wanted to do it romantically and did not want gossip around the workshop detailing his softer side. *'Shit.'*

Mark returned to the table and handed Tilly her drink. "Isn't that your guvnor?" he asked in his very strong cockney accent—Mark originally growing up in an east London suburb.

"Oh, yeah, I hadn't noticed," lied Tilly.

"Do you wanna move? You've seen his face all day." Tilly did not really want to move but she was also a good-natured person and could sense Mark felt awkward with Rak being in such close proximity.

"Yeah, ok then, what about that corner table over there?" pointing to a cosy table positioned in the snug.

"Yeah, that looks good," and Mark was up like a shot, picking up their drinks and making his way to the new table of choice.

Rak had witnessed this and was very relieved. Amira was looking at the menu, "I don't fancy anything really; oh, hang on a minute the fish looks good. What are you having darling?"

Rak returned his attention to the menu "Erm... possibly the pie and chips I'm starving, missed lunch again. Are you sure about the fish? Have a pie with me." He was looking right into her eyes, Amira looked at him quizzically.

"Why? What's so great about the pie?"

Rak smiled at her, "because, baby, when you see my dinner you'll want to swap, as usual, and I don't want fish." They both started laughing quite loudly, causing some regulars to stare over, and they couldn't have cared less.

Tilly was trying not to enjoy Mark's company but he was making her laugh, a lot. "So I'm up this ladder right, and I ain't too keen on ladders, prefer scaffold, and this prick comes along and yells at the top his voice, 'free beer, free beer,' nearly fell off the bleedin' ladder, didn't I?" Tilly was enjoying the banter, the previous dates she had been on were with businessmen but they were always too stuffy for Tilly and never made her laugh like Mark was doing now. "So come on then, tell me a bit about you" Mark said when he returned with more drinks.

"Right, well I grew up in this posh area, full of big heads. You see, my dad had a good job in the bank. I couldn't wait to leave and when I saw this house share advertised, I jumped at the chance. I share with two other girls, Patty and Julia. We have a right laugh. Maybe you could come round for dinner one night, if you don't mind tights hanging up everywhere." Tilly was laughing even more now, she could feel tears of laughter in her eyes.

Amira and Rak had enjoyed their food. "That pie was amazing darling, you should learn how to cook like that. Y'know, men are getting involved in the kitchen these days."

Rak knew she was teasing but also thought he would like to play his part too. "Oh, don't worry hun, I will look after you. I'm not like my old man, I know both of us need to work together".

Rak could wait no longer, his nerves were beginning to get the better of him, he had nearly knocked his wine over twice. "Baby, there's something I want to ask you."

Amira looked at him. "What, what do you want to ask me? If it's about pudding, then no way, I'm stuffed."

Rak got up off his chair and went around to stand in front of Amira, she was now looking quite quizzically at him.

"Darling, are you ok?"

Rak looked deep into Amira's eyes. "You know I love you and I want us to spend the rest of our lives together," Amira went to speak but Rak kept going. "Please, please, baby, don't interrupt." He then proceeded to get down on one knee and produce a box from his pocket, containing a diamond ring. "Amira Patel, would you do me the amazing, greatest honour of becoming my wife? I want us to spend forever together."

Amira was shocked and smiling, she had waited so long to hear these words. "Yes. Yes, of course I will. I can't wait!" Amira jumped into his arms and they kissed passionately, for all the pub to see.

Tilly and Mark had heard the commotion from the other side of the bar and wondered what was going on. Tilly was desperate to see what was happening, so went around the bar to see for herself. What she saw knocked her for six, her secret crush, at the bar, smiling the widest smile and ordering a bottle of champagne for himself and his new fiancé.

19

Sunday Morning

Pam's Cottage

Charlie had woken up extra early. She wanted to pop to the convenience store in the next village before Rak awoke. She quietly crept out of the cottage and into her car. She had realised in the middle of the night they had not bought provisions, such as milk or something for breakfast. She wanted Rak's birthday to be special. She drove there quickly, not much traffic being about and picked up some essentials. As she let herself back into the cottage, she heard Rak was awake. "Happy birthday, gorgeous man."

Rak had a huge smile, he had been worried Charlie had changed her mind and gone home to Brad. "Where have you been? I woke up and you weren't here, hun. I missed you."

Charlie loved the fact Rak had missed her. "Just to the shop in Catchford, we needed milk and I wanted to get us some breakfast." Charlie then made her way into the bedroom in just her knickers with a bottle of champagne and two glasses "Happy birthday to you, happy birthday to you, happy birthday you sexy, gorgeous man, happy birthday to you"

Rak laughed sweetly and grabbed his girlfriend, pulling her onto the bed towards him, his aches and pains not feeling as bad this morning, although his head still hurt. "Come here you sexy minx, help me pop this cork."

They both enjoyed sipping the champagne and then looked deeply into each other's eyes. "I love you Charlie, I want this so much, do you know what I mean?"

Charlie felt a warm feeling radiating through her. "Yes. Yes, I do. I love you too. I wish we could be like this all the time." Then she realised what she had said, had she just suggested that they leave their marriages and be together?

"Is that what you want?" Rak was serious now.

"Everything's easier with you, life's fun and we don't battle each other." She looked into his eyes "I wish we could do it, Rak, but I know we can't."

100

Rak sat there for a moment, contemplating what Charlie had just said. "One day, I promise, it will be just us, always. If that's what you want but be sure, Charlie, because once this is out there we won't be able to go back."

She kissed him, softly at first, then with passion.

Rak felt he was becoming hard, so hard he couldn't wait any longer. He placed his hands inside her knickers and pulled them away from her. She let out a gasp as he slowly parted her thighs, running his hands along the inside of them. He was kissing her stomach, slowly, softly, every kiss as sensual as the last. He placed his hands on her breasts as he moved down her body, kissing every inch of her. His mouth was now on her pussy, licking her lips, tasting her. "Ahh, Rak! Rak, you feel so good, please don't stop, please!" he moved his tongue towards her clit, softly, slowly teasing her. His fingers were inside her and she could feel she was going to come but she did not want this heightened pleasure to end. "Oh, Rak. Rak, yes, yes, oh my god, yes." He licked her quicker and flicked her clit with his tongue. "Rak, Rak! Oh, God, Rak!" she had come so strongly, she felt she was floating. His cock was hard and he couldn't wait, he was inside her, thrusting hard, lifting her legs so he could thrust deeper and harder.

"Oh, sexy, you feel so good, so fucking good." He was thrusting faster now, faster and harder, she met every thrust and felt she would come undone again.

He was crying out, "Charlie, oh, God, Charlie, yes, yes!" He looked into her eyes and saw nothing but love, love for him. He wanted to slow down, to last longer for her. He slowed right down; she let out a moan of pleasure. Once he knew he could keep going he thrust into her harder. "I'm gonna bang your brains out baby," he whispered.

"Yes Rak, I want you, I want you now. Fuck me hard!"

His cock getting harder, he moved faster. "Baby, I'm gonna come, I can't wait."

She held onto him as his entire body shook with deep, hot pleasure.

They both lay in bed, holding each other. Charlie's head rested on Rak's chest, listening to his heart beating, her fingers playing with his chest hair. The bedroom opened out onto the secluded garden, they had opened the curtains and were looking out into the garden, watching nature. "You know Pam talked about putting a one-way glass fence in at the bottom of the garden. It's fields the other side you see, imagine that view." Rak looked at Charlie who was admiring the garden and her surroundings.

"It really is an amazing place Rak, how long has Pam owned it?"

Rak shifted round to look at her. "Around ten years. Pam's friend, June, I think, don't quote me on that, passed away. She was aware that Pam's marriage to David, Nick's dad, was not happy. Rumour has it that Dorian had a fling with David before she married Jack. There was suspicion surrounding the parentage of Dorian and Jack's daughter, Sally, but nothing was ever proven."

Charlie was shocked. That Dorian 'whiter than white' Smyth would have an affair and possibly a child with another man. Especially considering how judgemental Dorian is. "So, could this Sally be Nick's half-sister?"

Rak looked away as if in thought. "Yeah, very possibly, if you believe what you hear."

Charlie sat up to pour more champagne. "Does he know?" Charlie was fascinated by this revelation.

"Nick knows, yeah. That's partly why him and his dad fell out, that and the appalling way David treated Pam. When Pam and David ran *The Bull*, it was more like *The Oak*." Charlie was truly shocked by what she was hearing. "Then Pam went on holiday to Spain a few years ago after David had died. She told me she wanted to start living life. Nick was happily running the pub and she felt now she needed those long-awaited holidays. Anyway, she met Paul, he's got a place out there. They fell in love and she's not been home since."

Charlie took a sip of champagne "Well, can you blame her?"

Rak was just about to say something when his mobile pinged with a text.

'Happy birthday darling. Enjoy whatever or whoever you're doing lol. Call me when you can, we need to discuss Geeta. Xx'

Rak sighed with resignation. The text was from Amira, she never did forget his birthday. They had remained civil, for the kids if nothing else. Now he was wondering what his daughter, Geeta, was up to.

"What's wrong baby? Was it Lisa?"

Rak smiled and shook his head "Don't be daft, she doesn't care if I'm dead or alive. She'd prefer dead actually."

Charlie lightly smacked him on the arm "Don't even joke about it, especially after yesterday," then she kissed him where she had just smacked him.

"No. it was Amira, usual sarcastic birthday text. And something about Geeta. Sorry to be awful, but do you mind if I quickly call her?"

Charlie did mind but knew Rak's kids must come first. "No, not all. Would you like me to leave you alone?"

Rak laughed "No, it's Amira for Christ's sake, no secrets for you to worry about."

The phone only rang twice, she knew he would ring straight back. "Happy birthday, darling, sorry to bother you. Are you with the ice maiden?"

Rak smiled and laughed, his eyes laughing too. Charlie could not help but notice. "No, I'm not. What do you want? I am rather busy." Rak winked at Charlie.

"It's Geeta and that fucking boyfriend of hers. He's a total shit, Rak. We need to do something. I know I said it would run its course, but it's not. She was here last night, crying her eyes out"

Rak's face turned to anger. "I'll fucking kill him, what's he done now?"

Charlie could see this could ruin their day.

"He won't get a job, he's using her for money. She hates her job at that snooty salon but can't find anything else. I need you to help me Rak."

Rak thought quickly. "Are you free on Tuesday? I'll come over, we can talk properly."

There was a pause. "Yeah, Tuesday is good, I'll make you some lunch".

20

Sunday Morning

5 Main Street

Brad awoke to silence. The bed he would usually be sharing with Charlie feeling empty. He picked up his mobile to check for messages, nothing. Charlie had texted him the night before to say she had arrived safely at Anna's and he had heard nothing since. He let the phone drop onto the bed and tried to decide how he was going to fill his day.

Brad was not a natural when it came to enjoying his own company, silence tormented him and the thought of spending the entire day alone was unbearable. He got out of bed and straight into the shower, not bothering to have a cup of tea in bed as he usually would with Charlie on a Sunday morning, the only morning of the week they spent together.

Saturdays were different for Brad. Charlie had always worked on Saturday, so he would fill his day by cleaning the house and tackling the supermarket shop before watching sport in the afternoon. But there was something about Sundays, the deadly silence, the feeling of emptiness, the feeling of abandonment.

After his shower and making the bed, he made his way downstairs. Straight to the kitchen, kettle on and also the radio. It was one of those annoying breakfast shows, where the presenters always sound unbelievably happy, like they are on drugs. He changed the station, next he found Love Songs on Sunday. Not exactly what he wanted but the presenter was slightly less annoying. He made his tea and went to sit at the island, looking out to the garden. Brad felt his mind start to wander, what would it be like to wake up with a house full of kids? Would he and Charlie be laughing in the kitchen whilst preparing a breakfast of pancakes and watching the kids play? He felt the hot prick of tears in the corners of his eyes. At the age of thirty-seven he had given up on any chance of becoming a father. They had been married ten years this year and yet nothing.

He also had the distinct impression Charlie was not that bothered anymore. She had excelled in other areas of her life, the salon was doing great, it had proved to be a good investment after all. She had been spending more time with friends recently, friends Brad was not familiar with and wouldn't be introduced to. They seemed to socialise less and less as a couple, especially not with Lisa and Rak, he thought to himself. He was more than aware that Charlie was not a fan of Lisa's but she did always enjoy Rak's company. They hadn't seen Tilly and Mark for a while either. Brad sat and wondered what was happening to his marriage.

The radio was still on but the music finished, the presenter started. "Have you ever wondered if your partner is having an affair? Well, the signs to look out for are, they start wearing a new scent, perfume or aftershave, they make excuses to go out without you, they take more care than usual with their appearance and finally, they seem happier." Brad was only half listening but suddenly it occurred to him that maybe this was happening to him. It was only a fleeting thought. However, it was definitely a thought.

He just sat there, staring out to the garden. *'No, she can't be,'* he thought, *'anyway, who would she be seeing?'* then he concluded, *'stupid fucking radio show,'* and turned it off. His mobile pinged, a text, must be from Charlie

'Hi Brad, just wondering if you wanted to have a pint in The Bull? It's Rak's birthday and we're going over around 12:30. Let me know. Cheers.'

It was Mark. Brad sat looking at the text, trying to decide if he fancied going or not. He was weighing up the odds, he knew Charlie wouldn't be home until tomorrow and how long the day would feel spent alone. He was hesitant, he didn't know if he could face making small talk all afternoon. Charlie was always the more extrovert, always able to hold a conversation. He began to type

'Hi mate, yeah sounds good. It's just me, Charlie's at a trade fair. See you around 12:30. Cheers.'

Brad suddenly felt as if his day had a purpose, he made a fresh cup of tea and a round of toast. He was still acutely aware that Charlie had not been in touch but decided she must be busy. She had mentioned she was interested in some new scissors and brushes so perhaps she was looking at them. He decided she was looking at them.

21

Sunday Morning

3 Church Lane

It was 11:00am. Lisa was watching the shopping channel and had her eye on a new handbag. She was sipping a G&T, perfectly aware that it was not even midday but it was her husband's birthday. She was, however, unaware of her husband's whereabouts.

After that disagreement, as Lisa viewed it, regarding Rak's accident and his abhorrent refusal to take her to *San Marios*, he had just disappeared. He had not uttered a word, just up and left. She supposed he was at *The Bull*, with his little friend, Nick. She could just picture him sitting there, slagging her off and the other two cretins lapping it up and sympathising with Rak's terrible plight.

She still could not comprehend that he had damaged the Jag. *'What's wrong with him?'* she thought to herself, *'he's too old for a mid-life crisis for fuck's sake'.*

Lisa often wondered if she still loved Rak. When they first met it was exciting, he would spoil her with lavish gifts and expensive weekends away. He would indulge her with fabulous meals out at desirable restaurants and give her free reign with his money. However, he had a very hungry appetite for sex, he craved physical attention and wanted to hold her and kiss her all the time. He was a fantastic lover and she was always more than satisfied. However, Lisa had also found his weak spot and used this to her advantage. When she was tired of Rak, she would refuse all physical contact, almost to the point of watching her husband break.

Even she didn't know why she enjoyed watching Rak suffer, after all, she enjoyed making love with him. She always felt special with him and he was always open to trying new things. He wanted her to enjoy it. Truth be told, she had never experienced a sexual relationship like it.

In her younger years, Lisa had struggled with her body image. Always feeling inferior to her sister, Belinda, who was the perfect size ten, all the right curves, in all the right places. Belinda would be fighting off male attention, whilst Lisa found she craved it. Lisa was actually very attractive, at a size sixteen back in her twenties she felt she should have been slimmer, especially in comparison to Belinda. However, still very attractive with long blonde hair, sea blue eyes and rosebud lips. If she would only have believed in her own self-worth, rather than comparing herself to Belinda. Belinda was always confident, extroverted. She lapped up the attention of men and made them feel special, special that she would take the time to acknowledge them. Lisa struggled to communicate with men, scared of rejection or of looking inexperienced. Her lack of self-confidence was actually a turn off. Her incessant need to be reassured and her refusal to believe she was beautiful. Men found her hard work, she was thought of as high maintenance.

Then at the age of thirty-six, she met Rak. He was older than her by nine years, struggling to recover from the break-up of his marriage and he was looking for someone new—he was not a fan of solitude. He was different to the few men she had previously dated, those relationships always ending in heartbreak for Lisa as they would tire of her neediness. He was the oldest man she had ever dated. At first, she was unsure. Unsure if he would find her inexperience a turn off, if he wanted someone with more of a past. She slowly realised he was as lovely as he had first seemed, attentive, quite good looking albeit he was older than her and he could make her laugh.

Their relationship moved quickly and after they had been dating just under a year, Rak proposed. She almost felt he was grateful, grateful to be with someone again, someone younger. She knew he couldn't give her children, however, she reasoned she could live with this, after all, he ticked all her other boxes.

The problem really came around the time they moved to Upper Loughton. Rak would expect Lisa to socialise with his friends, he would urge her to make the effort, saying to her, 'my friends are your friends, please try, baby.' However, she would convince herself they didn't like her, they were judging her. She felt they must imagine she was only with Rak for his money. The truth was, she didn't really want to share him with anybody, not even his children. For the first time in her life, she had found someone who really loved her and she was scared they would turn him against her.

Ironically, she had managed all by herself to cause the distance in her marriage. Rak would still see his children and his friends, he had always been sociable. However, he would see them on his own. They started drifting apart. Rak would endeavour to keep the marriage alive, cooking for Lisa, treating her to presents and giving her whatever she wanted. He also wanted to keep the physical side of their relationship special, he was still in love with her and enjoyed making love to her. Lisa, now feeling wounded that he wouldn't stop seeing his children or his friends, withdrew all intimacy. She was prepared to hurt herself to hurt Rak. If she couldn't have all of him, she wouldn't have any of him.

22

Sunday Lunchtime
The Bull

The bar was extremely busy, even for a Sunday. Julia had texted Adam and asked if he could help out with the lunchtime rush. *The Bull* served a fantastic roast on a Sunday and attracted custom from neighbouring villages. Nick had been out all morning with Slim Jim retrieving Rak's car, which after they had got it loaded onto the transporter, did look as bad as they imagined it would. "He'll need a new bonnet for sure. Is he going through insurance or what? He knows I'll say whatever he wants, after all he's had it around four years now." Slim Jim always put the customer first.

"I dunno mate, I'm not even sure if he'll be in for a drink or not this lunchtime but I'll message him." Nick really did not know if Rak would leave his love nest, and Charlie, to have a drink in *The Bull* on his birthday.

'Sorry to bother you mate, know you're busy… are you planning on dropping in? Slim Jim's here and I think Tilly and Mark were planning on coming over for a drink.'

Nick didn't have to wait long for a reply as Rak and Charlie had already had this discussion and decided it would look odd if Rak didn't nip in for one.

'Hello mate, yeah, I'm going to pop in for one. Officially, I'm still not feeling great, ok?'

Nick understood perfectly.

'No worries, get the picture. Around 1:00pm would be best, you'll see everyone then. Cheers.'

Nick was slightly relieved he wouldn't have to make excuses for Rak being a no show. Tilly and Mark entered the bar with Brad just behind them, *'great, this'll be interesting,'* thought Nick. "Hello you lovely people, what can I get ya?"

Brad immediately offered to buy the first round. "Hiya Nick, erm, two pints please and a large glass of rosé for Tilly, where's the birthday boy?"

Nick was finding this extremely awkward. "On his way I believe, although I must say, I don't think he's really up to it, not after yesterday." Nick was really trying to help his friend to escape early as he had intended to.

"Why, what happened yesterday?"

'Oh, shit, Brad didn't know.' Nick, now feeling further involved in a situation he did not want to be involved in at all. "Oh, haven't you heard? He managed to crash his car up on the main road, lost it on a bend. He's ok, been checked over at the hospital but he's still feeling sore." Nick also thought to himself, *'probably still feeling your wife too,'* whilst trying not to make eye contact with Brad.

"Bloody hell, that's awful. At least it wasn't more serious, eh?" to which Slim Jim chipped in.

"Tell that to the poor car," whilst shaking his head. Brad paid Nick and thankfully Tilly had found a table. Nick breathed a sigh of relief, covering up for his friend was going to be harder work than he had imagined.

Charlie had driven Rak to the edge of the village, paranoid she would be spotted. "I'm going to drop you off here and go back to Pam's. When you've had enough just text me and I'll come and pick you up. Try not to be long, I'll be lonesome without you." She was making a sulky face and mock crying.

"Don't worry hun, an hour tops, ok?" he was smiling, looking deep into her eyes. "I love you baby," he squeezed her thigh.

"I love you too, enjoy yourself." Could they risk a kiss? They both looked round, had a quick peck and he was gone.

As Rak walked over to *The Bull*, he glanced towards his own house. He considered going over, the kids might have sent birthday cards and he didn't want them to think him ungrateful or ignorant, at the same time, he did not want to see Lisa. He decided quickly, he would text the kids later, explain he was away for his birthday weekend and arrange to see them properly at a mutually convenient time. Yes, that would be better.

Rak opened the door to the bar and straight away saw Nick. "Happy birthday mate, another year older, eh?" Nick came around the other side of the bar and hugged his friend so tightly, Rak thought he would have to add broken ribs to his list of injuries.

"Careful mate, bloody hell, you trying to finish me off?" Rak teased.

"After yesterday mate, I never wanna think about that again. What you having? A Chivas? On the house."

Rak smiled at his friend, they had an unbreakable bond. "Yeah, go on then, medicinal, ain't it?" they both continued to the bar together, laughing as they went.

Mark saw Rak first. "Happy birthday mate, how you feeling?"

Without being rude, Rak wished at that moment he could just have a quiet drink with his best friend and not half the village. Then he saw Brad. "Oh, y'know, bit sore still. My head's still aching so a whiskey might help." Rak was really trying to be personable.

"Here you are love, here's your card." Tilly was smiling and this relaxed Rak a little.

"Ah, thanks Tilly, that's really thoughtful of you. Thank you."

Tilly moved a chair towards the table "Will you join us?"

Nick saw this and knew he had to help Rak. "Julia love, I'm just gonna have a drink with Rak and those reprobates, you and Adam can manage, can't ya?"

Julia immediately looked round, then ran round to give Rak a hug. "Bloody hell you, gave me a bloody heart attack yesterday," she lightly slapped his arm. "Be more careful will ya. Happy birthday darlin'," and she planted a big kiss on his cheek.

Rak laughed, "watch out Julia, your husband's watching," and she gave a naughty chuckle.

Nick just shook his head, *'unbelievable'.*

Rak and Nick had just sat down when Slim Jim came over. "All right mate, look I won't keep ya. It looks like it might be a right off," Jim winked at Rak. "Or maybe it can be fixed."

Rak got the message. "Can we discuss it on Tuesday, Jim? Will that be ok?"

Jim quickly realised this was not the time or the place. "Oh, yeah, of course. Eh, what you runnin' round in?"

Rak had not considered this. He would need a car and knew Lisa would not allow him to use hers. "I've not thought about it mate to be honest, have you got something I can borrow?"

Jim smiled a knowing smile. "As it happens, I have. I've got this sporty number, needs test driving, know what I mean? The owner's away so I don't need it back 'til next week. Will that do ya?" Rak was looking unsure. "Don't worry, you'll be insured. I'll just give you some trade plates. Pick it up when you want. Just don't get a speeding ticket." Jim was laughing as he left the pub. Rak and Nick both looked at each other and smiled.

"Happy birthday mate, have you had a good day so far?" Brad was looking straight at Rak.

"Er... yes thanks. Better than yesterday anyway." Rak was feeling guilty, having a drink with the husband of the woman he had been in bed with only an hour before. He couldn't very well say, 'yeah, I made love to your wife twice this morning, good isn't she?'

Rak just wanted to leave and Nick could sense it. "You're not looking too clever mate, maybe you should get a bit of rest after this one. We can have a proper session next Saturday at the fundraiser." Rak felt instant gratitude towards his friend.

"Yeah, mate, if you're not up for it don't make yourself worse" Mark interjected.

Rak nodded his head. "Yeah, I'm sorry. I still feel crap to be honest. The painkillers are slow to kick in. We'll have a proper drink next week." Rak drained his glass and made to leave.

"Catch you in the week mate, we need to put the final plans into action. In fact, I'll walk out with you, I need to check I've locked my car." Nick walked one step behind Rak.

Once safely outside and out of earshot, Nick could not contain himself any longer. "Fucking hell mate, that was awkward."

Rak looked at his friend. "Yeah, tell me about it. I didn't know he was gonna be here. I didn't know where to look."

Nick looked flustered. "What are you gonna do? He's gonna be there next Saturday too, with Charlie. Mate, are you sure about this? Y'know, on your own doorstep and all that?"

Rak looked away. "It's not ideal, I grant you, but I can't stop it now. I'm in too deep Nick."

Nick looked his friend in the eye. "That's what I'm worried about. Have you seen Lisa?"

Rak shook his head. "No, and I don't intend to today. She's not even wished me a happy birthday."

Nick could feel he was becoming exasperated. "Ok, if she rings here I'll say you're staying with us for a bit. Not that she will I suppose, ring here."

Rak shook his friend's hand. "You're a proper mate, y'know that? I owe you big time."

Nick hugged his friend farewell. "Make sure she kisses it better."

Rak had never been happier to send a text.

'Charlie, baby, please come and pick me up. I miss you, hun, and I want to do lots of naughty things to you xxx'

Charlie was there five minutes later.

23

Sunday Evening

Pam's Cottage

Whilst Rak was at *The Bull*, Charlie had quickly gone to the supermarket. She had got a leg of lamb and all the trimmings. She knew Rak loved lamb and wanted to cook him something special.

"Baby, you didn't need to do all this y'know. Thank you."

Charlie smiled at him, "I knew you'd be starving, we haven't exactly eaten much this weekend have we? Anyway, the oven is doing all the work."

Rak looked thoughtful for a moment. "What are you thinking, baby?" Rak looked at her.

"I would love to take you out for the day tomorrow, why don't we go to Stratford? That was where we were meant to be and I know you were looking forward to it." Charlie moved towards him and put her arms around his neck, he put his arms around her waist.

"Yes, I would love that. The weather is supposed to be good and we can sit by the river. We could have fish and chips if you want." A plan was made.

They enjoyed a bottle of red and the lamb, both savouring the peace and tranquillity. Rak had not felt this happy in a very long time. Lisa did not cook for him, favouring take-away food or eating out. He hadn't been cooked for since Amira and he missed it. "This is gorgeous honey, do you enjoy cooking?"

Charlie was actually a very skilled cook but modest with it. "Oh, it's just thrown together but yes, I really enjoy it. Do you cook?"

Rak smiled. "Yeah, when Amira and I got married I promised her I would cook as much as she did. I learnt lots of recipes, not all successful though," he was laughing now. "I once attempted risotto, oh my God, that was awful. It was more like glop. She tried to eat it and encourage me it was fine, that I just needed some practice. I never made it again. But I do make a really good paella. One day I'll make it for you."

Charlie touched his knee, "is that a promise?"

Rak nodded his head and kissed her.

Later that evening they snuggled up on the sofa, holding on to each other tight, but not uncomfortably so. "Would you like to watch a film?" Charlie had spotted 'The Bodyguard' was on in around ten minutes time and Brad never did like watching chick flicks.

"What's on, anything good?"

Charlie looked at him "Well, my favourite film is on, one of my favourites anyway, 'The Bodyguard', do you mind?"

Rak smiled at her and started to laugh, "no, I don't mind, hun, why would I mind?"

Charlie felt slightly awkward now. "Because he never lets me watch it without complaining, that's all."

Rak looked sad suddenly. "When you're with me baby you do what makes you happy. I never want you to ask permission, do you know what I mean?"

Charlie knew she shouldn't have mentioned Brad, she didn't want to compare Rak to him. "Yes, I'm sorry. I know you're different."

Rak kissed her, passionately "Get this film on before I drag you off to bed," he was laughing.

★ ★ ★

"Can you believe they love each other but can't be together?" Charlie was sobbing now.

"I will be your bodyguard, hun, and I'll never leave you on your own without me." Charlie laughed as he tickled her lightly.

"Have you seen it before?"

Rak took a breath. "yes, I took Amira to the cinema to see it when it first came out. She was obsessed with it, and that song. What was it? Number one for around a year?"

Charlie was slightly jealous at that moment of Rak's ex-wife, having all the fun with him before her. "Yeah, something like that. Another drink?"

Rak looked surprised. "Have I said the wrong thing?"

Charlie didn't know what to say. "Err…, no. It's silly really, but I'm slightly jealous of Amira. You had all the firsts with her."

Rak knew he had said the wrong thing. "Not all the firsts, I love you, Charlie. Don't feel threatened by Amira, there's no need." They kissed passionately again.

Their kissing became passionate further. Charlie wanted to show Rak his birthday present. "Wait, I've got something for you." She got up and went into the bedroom to change into her new underwear. Rak was intrigued. Five minutes later Charlie returned in her new La Perla underwear, he looked at her, smouldering. Rak could feel his cock was becoming hard, he wanted her now. "Happy birthday, baby."

They were kissing, Rak was running his hands all over her body, Charlie was letting him enjoy himself. She felt his jeans, she knew he was hard. She wanted him now. Rak slowly removed her knickers, sliding them down her smooth legs and discarding them on the floor of the living room. He put his head between her legs and kissed her, deep and slowly. "Ahh, Rak! Yes, yes. Rak, yes, don't stop." He moved to her clit, slowly and deliberately kissing her and licking her. "Rak, Rak, Rak, yes, yes, please, don't stop!" She was pushing his head further into her, she was going to come, she couldn't stop it. "Rak, ahh! Yesssssss, Rak!" He picked her up, into his arms and carried her to the bedroom.

Once in the bedroom, Charlie unbuttoned Rak's shirt, she wanted to feel his chest. She loved his chest. Next, she loosened his belt and undid his jeans, tugging them off him. His boxers were bulging at the front, she knew he wanted her. They both fell onto the bed, kissing so passionately the world stopped. She pulled off his boxers, his cock was so hard she wanted him there and then. She placed her mouth around his cock and moved her head up and down.

"Honey, oh God, baby, yes. That's so good, so good."

She was moving faster now, using her tongue. He pushed her off him and positioned himself in front of her. He lifted her legs and moved inside of her. Slowly at first, carefully. Then faster, harder. She met every thrust. "Baby, yes, oh god, yes. You feel so fucking good. Yes, yes!" she placed her hands on his bottom and pushed him into her, faster, harder, quicker, stronger. "Rak, Rak, oh my, yes, Rak. I need you, Rak, right now." She knew she was coming again and loved it. This time it was harder, hotter.

He knew he wanted to come, he tried to slow down but he couldn't. "Honey, yes, honey. Ahh! Yes, yes!" He collapsed on top of her. She kissed his head. They both breathed again.

24

9 Church Lane

Tilly and Mark had enjoyed their dinner at *The Bull*, they hadn't planned to eat out but time was getting on and Tilly lost the will to cook. Brad had joined them and it had been a good afternoon. Tilly thought it was odd Rak didn't stay long, she expected he would be glad of a break from Lisa. "Did you think he went home suddenly? I thought he might have had more than one drink."

Mark was not really bothered, his friend had seemed happy and that's all that mattered. "Well, perhaps he wasn't feeling like socialising, bloke crashed his pride and joy yesterday love."

Tilly was not convinced, "hmmm, yeah maybe, seems strange though. Oh well. Have you got an early start in the morning?"

Mark was glad of a subject change. "Yep, another 5:30 start I'm afraid. That's the thing with these big projects, no one lives there so you can start earlier. Finish earlier too, though."

Tilly was concerned Mark was taking on too much. "I've not done your accounts for a while, they must need doing. Let me have the paperwork and I'll have a look tomorrow afternoon when I get home from work."

Mark was petrified now, he knew it was a mess. "If you're sure love, that would be great but don't worry too much."

Tilly looked straight at him. "It's nearly September, Mark, we need to get organised. I'll do it tomorrow." Tilly was not asking.

25

Pam's Cottage

Charlie had woken early, she opened the curtains in the bedroom to reveal the beautiful view to the garden. She still couldn't believe that Nick had allowed her and Rak to stay there as and when they wanted to, it really was most generous of him. Charlie lay in bed, listening to Rak gently breathing, she resisted the urge to touch him, wishing for him to rest instead. She looked over to him and thought to herself how handsome he is, still having the looks of a somewhat younger man but with the experience etched around the edges of his face. Certainly, his physique was of a much younger man, as well as his stamina. Charlie had never experienced passion like she had with Rak, he was happy and willing at any time.

Charlie was really looking forward to visiting Stratford-upon-Avon, she hadn't been for a couple of years, you wouldn't think it was only around an hour away from Upper Loughton. She used to visit regularly as her friend, Anna, lived there. But then Charlie and Anna had not been so close recently, after a falling out over Brad. Anna had intimated that she did not feel Brad was right for Charlie and she should leave him. Charlie had reduced contact with Anna after that, although she knew her friend was right.

Charlie moved quietly to the kitchen to make tea. She crept around, trying to be as quiet as possible when her phoned pinged, she almost dropped the milk, *'oh shit, who's that now?'* she thought to herself.

'Hiya babe, I hope you're ok and had a great day at the trade fair yesterday. I'll be late back tonight, got a meeting in Gloucester. See you later, safe journey home. Love you xxx'

"What's happening baby? Are you all right?" Rak was awake now after he had heard the commotion coming from the kitchen.

"Yes, I'm fine thanks, I won't be a sec," she loved hearing his voice. Charlie finished making the tea and returned to the bedroom. Brad could wait for a reply.

"Good morning gorgeous, did you sleep well?" Rak was smiling at her and looking at her with love in his eyes.

"Yes thanks you gorgeous man, did you?" Charlie handed Rak a cup of tea and a kiss.

"With you next to me, yes of course. Did I hear a phone?" Charlie's face said everything before she could say anything "Oh, ok. Was it him?"

Charlie looked Rak straight in the eye. "Not important baby, only we're important today. I love you." Charlie kissed Rak on the cheek and they both drank their tea, enjoying the view of the garden from their bed.

Rak reached for his mobile, "I'm going to text Slim Jim and see if I can pick that car up he's got for me. Take you out in style."

Charlie playfully smacked him and laughed. "What's wrong with my Mini?"

Rak was laughing. "Well, let's just say, it's not the type of car I'm used to, don't hit me please." Rak was dodging her playful smacks until they rolled together on the bed, into each other's arms. Ten minutes passed before Rak actually texted Slim Jim.

'Hi Jim, any chance I can pick that motor up you were talking about? Don't need to discuss mine until tomorrow if you're busy. Just need a car to run round in. Cheers mate.'

Two minutes later Rak's phoned pinged a message.

'Yes, no worries. I'm at the garage all day. Cheers mate.'

Fantastic. Rak was happy to be able to drive Charlie today, he wanted her to relax and not worry about traffic or parking or anything else. "I just need to text Nick, sorry, I won't be a moment."

Charlie was happy enjoying the view of the garden. "No worries baby, do what you need to," she knew she should really respond to Brad's text but she couldn't face it.

'Hiya mate, hope you're ok. I need a favour, could you please run me up to Slim's, I want to pick that car up he's got for me. Earlier the better if poss, I'm just having a shower now. Cheers mate.'

"Right, I've just told Nick I'm in the shower, do you wanna join me? You can help me wash my hair."

Charlie laughed. "What's left of it," she couldn't help herself. She had been cutting Rak's hair for a few years now and knew he was precious over what he had left.

"You're not married to Lisa! Anyway, think what I save on shampoo." They were both laughing like school kids as Rak smacked Charlie on the bottom and chivvied her towards the bathroom.

Pam had installed a new bathroom shortly

before her departure to Spain. She had wanted a large walk-in shower, for her old age, she had told Nick. Rak switched the shower on and pulled Charlie towards him. He kissed her, slowly at first, then with his tongue. She responded with her tongue, both of them licking and flicking one another's tongues. It was sensual. Rak reached for the shower gel and squeezed some into his hands, he was feeling her body, her neck, her breasts, her stomach. He turned her round so he was behind her, she could feel his erection pushing against the small of her back. His hands wandered further, Charlie was so excited with anticipation as his fingers traced the inside of her thighs, she reached behind to feel his hard cock, it was throbbing in her hand, the warm water rolling off of him. Rak's fingers moved towards her pussy. "Rak, oh Rak, I need you now." He slowly inserted two fingers inside of her and moved them in a circular motion. "Rak! Rak, yes! Yes!" she bent over and supported herself on the shelf inside the shower, he pushed his cock into her, slowly at first, then harder, and harder.

"You feel so fucking good, honey, so good," his hands were feeling her breasts.

"Rak, oh my god, Rak, yes, don't stop! Please don't stop!" she could feel she was going to come any second. "Rak! Rak, yes! Yes! Ohh, Rak!"

He continued thrusting into her, deeper and deeper. She reached behind her and felt his balls, they were tensing, she knew he was about to come.

"Charlie, Charlie baby, ohh God, yes, yes. Oh God yes!" They turned to face each other and kissed passionately, melting into each other, the warmth of the water and their orgasms washing over them.

After they had finished washing each other, they both stepped out of the shower. Rak wrapped Charlie in a towel and kissed her again.

"You had better go and see if Nick's texted you back,"

Rak dried himself off, "Yeah, I'd forgot about him. You are a distraction Charlie Worthing, do you know that?" he smiled as he moved back towards the bedroom to get dressed.

'No problems mate, give me around 30 minutes. Cheers'

Rak needed to hurry up, but he wouldn't have changed the events of their morning for the world. He wished every morning could be like this one.

Charlie was blow-drying her hair when Rak came into the bedroom, she switched off the hairdryer. "Hey, hun, Nick's here so I'm gonna get going. I won't be long, I promise. By the time you're ready I should be back. We're going to have a fantastic day. I love you."

Charlie turned to face him, "I love you too. Be careful on the road, baby." She looked deep into his eyes.

"I will, of course I will."

Then from the kitchen. "Come on Rak, some of us have got a pub to open before lunchtime, you're worse than a pair of kids you two are."

Rak and Charlie both burst out laughing as Rak kissed her. "See you soon," he smiled lovingly. "All right, I'm coming, stop yelling." He shouted to Nick as he made his way back to the kitchen, laughing to himself.

In the car, Nick could tell his friend was superbly happy. "Whatever she's doing for ya, I hope it continues. I've not seen you this happy in years, not since Amira. Do you think you'll leave Lisa?"

Rak looked out of the window "I would love to mate, this weekend's been amazing, I mean absolutely amazing. Charlie's everything, y'know what I mean? When I left your place yesterday, she'd got some lamb in the oven, bloody delicious by the way, then we watched a film, not my usual type of film but apparently boy wonder doesn't let her do much that she wants and I'm not like him. Then we went to bed, mate she's unbelievable. This morning, cup of tea in bed, larking around, laughing. I feel like I'm twenty again. Everything's exciting"

Nick looked at his friend for a brief second "So, are you going to leave Lisa?"

Rak sighed. "That's not the question is it? The question is, would Charlie leave him? I don't know the answer and I'm afraid to ask in case it upsets things between us"

Nick shook his head "Mate, maybe she's thinking the same. How will you know if you don't ask? She seems delirious over you, I know that"

Rak digested his friend's comment. "Yeah, well we'll see. Wonder what Slim's got for me?" Nick knew that meant subject closed.

26

Monday Morning

Catchford Garage aka Slim Jim's

"Morning boys, how are we all doing on this fine morning?" Jim was very chipper for a Monday morning, thought Nick, and glanced at Rak as if to say as much.

"We're good thanks Jim, yourself?" said Nick.

Jim smiled, "top of the world mate, top of the bloody world." Jim was around sixty-five years old, very rotund would be a polite way to describe him, and his attitude was very much what you see is what you get. There were no heirs and graces with Jim. He had owned the garage in Catchford for the previous forty years, he had known Nick's father and looked after his cars before he started looking after Nick and Rak's. Jim had some, shall we say, unorthodox methods, but deep down he was a good man.

"Right, Rak, my old son. Now, come and look at this beauty." Jim walked towards the back of the yard and both Rak and Nick followed, Nick was just as excited as Rak. "You know old Eric Fisher? You do, the old antiques dealer, lives down the road here." Rak was not familiar but knew if he said so, Jim would convince him he did know him.

"Yeah, sort of," was the best he could come up with.

"My dad knew him mate, he used to drink in *The Bull* sometimes. When the old man died, he stopped coming in."

Nick provided some clarity for which Rak was grateful. Jim stopped in front of a black Aston Martin. "Well, this is his, for now. He wants to sell it, asked me if I know anyone who might have an interest. I've serviced it and kept it's MOT up to date since he's had it, it's a good motor. And I was thinking, now you've managed to total your Jag you might fancy a change?"

Rak was smiling to himself as much as anybody else, he knew that Jim would benefit from a generous percentage of any sale he managed to secure. Jim continued, "I can say your Jag's a write off, the insurance will pay out, there's nobody else involved, luckily. What do you reckon? To be honest mate, I could do without the hassle of fixing it."

Rak did like the look of the Aston, he had driven one once, a customer's car when said customer took the term working lunch literally and got drunk at a networking event they had both attended. Rak had driven him and his car home, much to the dismay of his customer's shocked wife. "What's he looking for?"

Jim looked straight at Rak. "He wants market value, to be honest with ya, it does need a bit of attention here and there, nothing major but it'll help you get a better deal."

Rak was thinking, he opened the car door and sat inside, he liked it.

"Put it this way mate, with what you'll get off the insurance plus your normal, predicted motoring expenses for the year, it shouldn't cost you much out of your own pocket."

Rak was thinking that Charlie would love it. "Yeah, ok, let me have it this week. If I get on with it, I'll have it. Any good to ya?"

Jim held his hand out. "Yes mate, you've got a deal. Drop me the paperwork round for the Jag and I'll do the necessary. It was getting old anyway."

Rak shook Jim's hand. "I'll get on to the insurance tomorrow when I'm back in the office. What are we going to do about insuring me to drive this car?" Rak wanted everything above board if he was taking Charlie out.

"I'll ring Eric, explain. If you've got his permission you're covered. Is that ok?"

Rak shook Jim's hand again. "Certainly is, thanks mate. I've got to get going, got an important day."

Jim smiled. "Big business deal, is it?"

Rak laughed. "No mate, pleasure. Can't wait. See you tomorrow afternoon, I'm out at lunch so it might be later."

Jim waved his hand. "Tomorrow or Wednesday mate, whatever suits you better. Enjoy your day, whoever she is." Jim winked and walked off towards his office. Rak followed Nick back to Upper Loughton as far as *The Bull*, then he carried on back to Pam's Cottage.

27

The Bull

Julia was bottling up when Nick returned home. "How did you get on? Is Rak having whatever Jim had got for him?" Julia shouted from the bar as Nick came in from the back.

"Yeah, he's all right love, Jim had this Aston, nice, in black. If Rak gets on with it this week he reckons he'll have it. It belongs to old Eric Fisher, so it would have been well looked after."

Julia looked surprised. "I thought Eric was dead, not seen him in ages."

Nick laughed. "Just because folk stop drinking

145

in here don't mean they're dead. You crack me up you do." Nick took Julia in his arms and kissed her, properly, passionately, like they used to do when they first got together.

"What's got into you?" she asked, shocked, when he put her down.

"Ahh, nothing, just think I take you for granted sometimes, that's all. I do love you, Julia, y'know that, don't ya?" Nick was not looking bad for his age, at fifty-five he still had all his hair, blonde and grey nowadays, he wasn't too fat considering he ran a pub and drank too many pints with the regulars, just to be sociable, and his blue eyes were slightly wrinkled at the edges but he was wearing well.

"Oh, course I know you love me, you wouldn't put up with me otherwise, would ya?" Julia smiled. "I love you too, we need to spend more time together. Why don't I ask Adam and Anthea," Julia's children from her first marriage, "to look after the place for a couple of days next month? We could go away, they could manage."

Nick liked the sound of that idea. "Yeah, not over a weekend though, for a start there's always kids and families around and they'd be better off looking after this place mid-week. I'll get on the laptop and have a look, where do you fancy?"

Julia hadn't really thought about it. "Anywhere, surprise me. I'll ring Charlie tomorrow, book my colour. Want to look respectable, don't I?" Julia had a long bob, coloured in Autumn Cherry. It suited her dark looks, brown eyes and olive skin.

"Yeah, all right, leave it with me. I'm looking forward to it already" and with that, he kissed her again.

They could have taken things further if they were not due a delivery from the brewery, but alas, they were. "Eh? Look at the time, the delivery driver will be knocking on the door in a minute." Julia giggled, feeling almost naughty for kissing her own husband in the bar.

"Can I see you later? If I'm good." Nick winked at her.

"We'll see, be good and you never know," she teased, just as the door knocker went.

28

Monday Morning
3 Church Lane

Lisa was beginning to become concerned for her husband's whereabouts. He had not been home since Saturday evening. He had not even texted her. She checked the wardrobe, he had taken a few shirts with him, wherever he had gone. She was starting to wonder if he had actually left her, Rak had never been away sulking for this long before.

She grabbed her phone, opened the online banking app and checked the balance of the joint account, joint being a joke, as quickly as Rak paid in, she took out. Well, there still money in there, he hadn't left her penniless. While she was holding the phone she considered calling him but was wary that could seem like an apology, which she did not want to make. If anything, he should be the one to apologise to her for all the distress he had caused. She decided to look at his WhatsApp profile, that would tell her the last time he used the app. Yes, she would check he was still alive that way, 'last seen yesterday 18:56', read the message below his name on his profile page. *He was probably chatting with one of his spoilt children*, she thought, Geeta or Amit. Both of whom she despised. Their cards to their father were still on the kitchen table, unopened. The one from Geeta addressed to 'my Daddy'. Really, at twenty-four years old, Lisa felt repulsed by the very sight of it.

Lisa had always been jealous of Rak's children. Jealous of the attention he showered them with; jealous that he would always have a link to Amira; jealous that he had other people to love. Lisa had considered children before she met Rak, in fact she actually thought it might suit her somehow. However, after Amit was born, Rak had opted for a vasectomy. He could not give Lisa children like he had given Amira children. Another reason, in Lisa's head, to hate Geeta and Amit.

Lisa looked out of the window, she could see the delivery truck was outside *The Bull*. She knew Nick would know where Rak was, she considered walking over. Yes, that's what she would do. Lisa got her Gucci shoes out of the cupboard, put them on and she was out the door.

★ ★ ★

"Nick, hello. Where's Rak?" she had taken Nick unawares.

"Oh, hiya Lisa, blimey were you never told not to creep up on people?" Nick was really stalling for time, not sure what to say as he didn't know where his friend was planning on sleeping that evening. Lisa was staring at him, waiting. "How should I know love? I've got a pub to run, I don't keep tabs on him. He's old enough to look after himself. He stayed here over the weekend. Have you tried calling the office or the workshop? Or his mobile?" Nick added as an afterthought.

"No, I assumed you would know where he was. Never mind, if you do see him, tell him I'm going up to London for a couple of days."

Nick really wanted to put his hands round her throat and keep squeezing. "Yeah, I can do that for ya, or you could just text him. Only an idea."

Lisa turned away and walked off. Nick was relieved but made a mental note to text Rak.

As Lisa walked back towards her house, Kate spotted her as she was taking a delivery into the post office. "Oh, hello dear, lovely to see you. How are you keeping? How's Rak after his accident?"

Lisa was now livid inside, having to partake in small talk was not her strong area. "I'm great thank you. I don't know how Rak is, if you can find him, why don't you fucking ask him?"

Kate was truly gobsmacked, Lisa stormed off at lightening pace.

29

Stratford-upon-Avon

The journey to Stratford had been an extremely pleasant one. Charlie could not believe her eyes when Rak arrived back at Pam's Cottage to pick her up. "An Aston! Are you serious? Wow, Rak; amazing baby! I love it." Charlie had never sat in a car so prestigious, it didn't just move along the road, it glided. The leather seats hugged her, it felt special "Do you think you'll keep the car?" Charlie asked when they were just outside of Stratford.

"Do you want me to?" Rak smiled.

"Yes. Yes, I do. It suits you. And I love it."

153

Rak reached over to touch her thigh. "In that case hun, I will keep it. Just for you."

The weather was glorious, the sun was shining and there was not a cloud in the sky. When Rak parked the car, he took out a bag from the boot.

"What have you got in there, Mr?" Charlie was inquisitive.

"Nothing for you to worry about. Now did you promise me fish and chips?" they walked towards the park by the river, holding hands. There was a good chip shop just the other side of the park. Charlie decided they would get their fish and chips and have a picnic on the grass. As they walked into the chip shop the woman serving behind the counter shouted, "five minute wait on chips love, is that ok?"

Rak smiled at her. "No problem, my girlfriend here assures me that your fish and chips are the best in Stratford. So, fish and chips twice please, to take away, when you're ready. Would you mind wrapping them?"

The woman was obviously quite taken with Rak. "Ohh, that is nice to hear. Yes, of course I'll wrap them for you darlin', salt and vinegar?"

Rak smiled his usual charming smile. "Yes, please, that would be fantastic. Thank you." When the chips were ready, Rak paid her before he and Charlie walked towards the park.

Once comfortably seated on the grass, Charlie had thought to bring a picnic blanket she had found back at the cottage, Rak opened the mystery bag. Out came a bottle of champagne wrapped in a cool blanket and two glasses. "Surprise, hun, fish and chips with champagne."

Charlie immediately hugged him and gave him the biggest kiss "You are so thoughtful, I love you, Rak Banerjee!"

Rak popped open the champagne and poured two glasses. "Here's to new beginnings, together," he had been considering his earlier conversation with Nick

"Yes, new beginnings, together. Cheers" they clinked glasses and tucked into their treat of fish and chips.

After they had eaten Charlie lay in Rak's arms, they were looking at the sky and making shapes out of the few white clouds there were. "That looks like a cat, look, look, Rak." Charlie was pointing up to a random cloud.

"Oh yeah, baby, look it's changing again now, now it looks like a boat."

She looked into his eyes, the eyes she could always get lost in and kissed him passionately.

* * *

Anna Dempsey had just finished work for the afternoon, as she walked across the park towards the shops, she could have sworn she saw Charlie Worthing. She was with a man, but it wasn't Brad.

This was an Asian man, very good looking from what Anna could see, older than Charlie. Charlie looked happy, they were laughing together. Anna had to go over, she had to know.

"Charlie, is that really you?"

Charlie knew that voice immediately "Anna, oh my God, Anna. Hello darling, how are you?" Charlie was genuinely happy to see her friend, she was surprised by how happy she felt to see Anna, especially after their last face to face encounter. "I'm very well, thank you. I can't believe it's you. You look so well. It must be two years since we last saw each other."

Anna suddenly recalled why it had been so long but didn't say anything. "Who's your friend?" Anna indicated towards Rak.

"Anna Dempsey, meet Rak Banerjee. Rak and I are together." Rak extended his hand to shake Anna's.

"Pleased to meet you Anna, it's a pleasure. Will you join us? You're more than welcome."

Anna's mind was full of questions, how long had they been together? What happened with Brad? Where had Charlie met this gorgeous man? "If I wouldn't be imposing, that would be terrific, I want to know everything."

Anna got herself comfortable and the three of them sat there chatting "What happened to you and Brad? Are you divorced?" Charlie knew Anna was probably about the only person she could be honest with, Anna had experienced her own fair share of dramas.

"No, no we're not divorced Anna. Rak and I are having an affair and I'm, we're, very happy."

Anna beamed her trademark smile, she had perfect teeth and a perfect smile. "Charlie, I'm so happy for you, I've thought about you a lot since our little 'episode' and I've been meaning to call you but I didn't know what to say. So, I want all the juicy bits, starting with where you found this gorgeous man."

Rak smiled, then laughed, he wasn't sure she was being serious.

They sat and talked for around an hour and a half before Anna made her excuses and left them to the rest of their day out. "Right, I was supposed to be spending money this afternoon shopping. See, Charlie, you've helped me resist." Anna was laughing. "Tell me we'll keep in touch, properly from now on. If you ever need a 'place to be', feel free to say you're with me. For what it's worth, Rak, I approve of you. I haven't seen my friend, one of my oldest friends, this happy in a very long time. Take care of her."

Rak smiled genuinely. "Don't worry Anna, you have my word. She's my world, y'know," and he kissed Charlie lightly on the cheek to prove it.

"We'll keep in touch, I promise. I will keep you informed of any developments. It's been so good to see you Anna. Look after yourself." Charlie embraced her friend, tightly and kissed her cheek. She really was happy to have put things right with Anna.

When Anna had left Rak wanted to know everything. "What did you two fall out about? What happened? She seems lovely, like a true friend." Rak was curious as to what had gone on between them.

"A couple of years ago Brad and I were having problems, rowing all the time, he would call me some terrible things, Rak, things that stick with you, y'know what I mean?" Rak nodded, "I had escaped to stay with Anna for a couple of days, Brad was not very familiar with Anna and I thought he'd leave me alone. He followed me, he turned up at Anna's house, threatening to kick the door in if I didn't speak with him. Anna wanted to call the police but I wouldn't let her. If he lost his job, I would have to pay all the bills, as well as the mortga…"

Rak put his hand up to stop her. "Hang on hun, you pay the mortgage? What the fuck? All of it? What type of man lets his wife pay the fucking mortgage?"

Rak was fuming with anger, he was very old fashioned in this respect and did not like the idea of Brad taking advantage of Charlie, the woman he loved. "He's in *The Bull* every weekend, spending money, buying rounds. He was on the golf course the other week, Nick and I saw him. Why can't he pay the mortgage?" Rak had tears in his eyes, he was so upset for Charlie.

"Because I wanted the house. The only way I

could have it was if I paid for it. Rak, please, don't be angry. Anyway, he was at Anna's house, shouting abuse, threatening me, I went to speak with him and managed to persuade him to leave. That the neighbours would call the police even if Anna didn't. Anna got really angry with me, told me to leave him, start again somewhere he wouldn't find me."

Rak was still in shock. "Then your friend Anna is definitely a friend worth keeping. You fell out with her; why?"

Charlie did not want to cry, not in public. "Because I knew she was right baby, and I couldn't. My salon was there, I'd worked bloody hard to build that business up, Rak. He wasn't taking that from me. I thought if Anna wasn't privy to the problems in my marriage, she would stop telling me to leave him. So, I cut contact with her. We still texted but nothing serious. I didn't want to hear the truth."

Rak was still fuming. "Why didn't you kick that twat out? You were already paying the mortgage."

Charlie was dreading Rak's reaction to the answer she was about to give. "The house is in joint names, I would've had to have bought him out. I couldn't afford to do it Rak."

Rak couldn't believe his own ears, it was a good job they were an hour away from Upper Loughton, because he knew he would of killed Brad if was anywhere near him.

The journey back was strained. Rak did not want

to be angry with Charlie, however, at the same time, he did not have the capacity to engage in normal conversation. His mind was full of thoughts of hatred for Brad. He was imagining the different ways he would like to kill him and ensure he suffered.

Rak could be a very mild-mannered man, very gentle and mellow. However, there was another side to him. Rak was very capable of losing his temper if someone he loved was hurt by somebody else. Rak knew he had a temper and he really endeavoured to control it, most of the time he succeeded. The last time he had properly lost his temper was twenty-five years before, with his father. Rak's mother had been diagnosed with a brain tumour not long after Rak had taken over the business. She managed to recover well after surgery and everyone thought she was on the road to recovery. She was absolutely delighted to be well enough to attend Amira and Rak's wedding. Rak's sister, Meena, had taken care of her. Meena was five years older than Rak and had always tried to shield her little brother from life's awfulness. After a routine check-up four years later, it was found the tumour had returned. Geeta was six months old. Rak was devastated. This time, it was inoperable, terminal. Rak's father was not able to support his wife, instead he was busy gambling. The problem only became apparent to the rest of the family after he gambled away the family home. Rak's mother was not able to die peacefully in her own house, the house she had called home for thirty years. It now belonged to strangers. She died at Meena's house, still with her family, all except her husband. But it was not what she had wanted. After she had died, Rak found his father, drinking himself to oblivion in a rough pub. He beat him half to death. They had never spoken since.

30

Pam's Cottage

After they had arrived back in Upper Loughton, Charlie had asked Rak to take her to Pam's Cottage to collect her car. She knew she had to return home, return to Brad, at some point and she was not sure she wanted to be in Rak's company at the moment either.

When they pulled up at Pam's Cottage Rak checked his phone, a text from Nick.

'Hiya mate, FYI I've seen Lisa. She said she's going up to London for a couple of days. I told her you

were here all weekend. Hope you enjoyed your day. Cheers.'

Rak was relieved, relieved he would not have to contend with Lisa, at least not for a couple of days. He knew she would be staying with her sister, spending his money, but he could not have cared less right now. "Honey, have you fell out with me?"

Charlie knew the answer was no, but she also knew she was not keen on Rak's temper and felt she needed time. "No. No I haven't. But you have to realise Rak, my life isn't like yours, I can't throw money at a problem and it goes away."

Rak looked at her, again with a certain degree of anger in his eyes. "If you want him to fuck off, I'll pay him to fuck off. Is that what this is about?"

Charlie could not help it, she laughed. "Really? Really would you? So, what? I get rid of one control freak for somebody else I'd be indebted to? Don't talk bollocks, Rak."

Rak was demonstrably hurt. "Somebody else, hmm? Is that all I am, somebody else? Just go hun, go on, go away before we both say things we might regret." Rak turned away to look out of the car window, he could feel tears in his eyes and he wanted Charlie to go away, away from him, away from his life. At that moment he believed every time she had said 'I love you,' she had been lying.

Charlie got her car keys out of her handbag, she stayed seated in the Aston, hoping, wishing for Rak to look at her. She knew she should not have referred to him as 'somebody else' this man was her world, her life. When she wasn't with him, she craved him and when she was with him, she never wanted those moments to end. She sat there for what felt like an eternity, too afraid that if she spoke, Rak would tell her they were over. Eventually, Charlie opened the car door, whilst looking over to Rak, expecting a reaction. She was disappointed, he remained looking out of the window, his face turned away from her.

She got into her car and drove away, looking at Rak as she did so, again he turned away from her, choosing now to look down towards the steering wheel. When he was sure she had left, he turned the engine back on and left Pam's Cottage. He needed a drink.

31

5 Main Street

As Charlie drove towards her house, she felt utter dread at the prospect of having to talk with Brad. She would have to be light and easy going, after all, she had just had a fun filled weekend at a trade fair, socialising with other likeminded people, hadn't she?

As she pulled onto the drive of 5 Main Street she could see that Brad's car, the company car he cherished, an Audi Q3, was not there. She was relieved and actually, overjoyed. She prayed he would be home late and she would be in bed.

She let herself in, as she did so she realised she had left some of her belongings at Pam's Cottage. She would not text Rak, she knew he didn't want her. She was sure she had a new toothbrush in the bathroom cabinet and she would wash and dry her hair in the salon tomorrow. As soon as Charlie got into the kitchen, she poured herself a very large glass of red wine, sat at the island and cried her eyes out.

She knew Rak was only concerned for her but he had exasperated her, imagining his money would solve her problems. She knew she was in love with him. What if he had meant it? What if he didn't want to see her again? What would she do without him? This lovely, gorgeous, kind man wanted her, she needed him and yet she was sure it was now over. Her phone pinged with a text, she hoped it was Rak, she needed it to be Rak.

'Hiya babe, hope you're ok, I've not heard from you. Just to let you know, this meeting in Gloucester has run over so I'm getting a hotel tonight, on expenses lol. See you tomorrow. Love you xxx'

Charlie sat, staring at the phone in her hand. She felt like she wanted to throw it across the kitchen. She knew she had to text back this time.

'Hi, yeah no worries. Catch you tomorrow sometime. Enjoy yourself x'

As she had typed the kiss at the end she felt sick, sick that she did not love this man at all, that she was trapped. The thought of this bought on sobs of unhappiness and regret. Charlie could not stop, she sat there sobbing, uncontrollably.

32

Monday Evening
The Bull

Nick was surprised by how busy the bar was for a Monday, especially since he had instructed Julia to take the evening off. He had realised she had been doing the lion's share recently, especially with Nick being pre-occupied with Rak's issues. Julia was never one to complain, however, she would usually allow stress to build up, then blow up. Nick would do anything to avoid a Julia style meltdown.

"Yes love, what can I get ya?"

Kate was at the bar, eager for a chat as well as a drink. "Ohh, a nice V&T would be lovely thanks

Nick, I say, that Lisa Banerjee had a real go at me earlier. I was only enquiring as to how Rak is after his accident."

Nick ordinarily would not have batted an eye lid at someone telling Kate to mind her own business, crikey, he had wished she would often enough, but he also knew how vicious Lisa could be. "I'm sorry to hear that Kate, are you all right?"

Kate nodded. "Yes, I am now but it was an awful shock."

Nick could see Kate was visibly upset. "Yeah, I can imagine, love, look, have that on the house. And I can tell you, Rak is fine. I saw him earlier and he was in good spirits considering."

Kate smiled at Nick, she was now hoping for more details. "Do you know what happened? I mean, it's not like Rak to be driving dangerously."

Nick knew he had to tread carefully now. "I don't think he was driving dangerously, Kate, y'know accidents can happen. Is there anything else I can get ya?"

Kate had got the message. "No, that's lovely. Thank you, Nick, you're a good man." Kate eventually walked back towards her table to read her paper.

The entrance door to the bar opened and Rak walked in, Nick could tell from his face he was not happy. "All right mate, didn't expect to see you tonight. What you having, a pint?"

Rak released a sigh of resignation. "Errr…, yes please mate. Why is life so fucking complicated? Have you got the answer to that behind there?"

Nick could really do without this. "Why? What's up now? Did you not enjoy playing Romeo and Juliet in Stratford?"

Rak tried to smile. "Romeo, don't make me laugh, apparently, I'm just 'somebody else', not her Romeo." Rak was getting resentful now, not a good look on him.

"Oh right, so you've had a tiff, have you? Well, y'know mate, happens to the best of us. You'll get over it."

Rak was surprised by his friend's lack of interest. "Don't you want to know what happened?"

Nick realised he actually did want to know but he also knew by asking Rak, it would just exacerbate his misery. "Yeah, go on then, what's happened? And for fuck's sake mate, cheer up. I can't stand looking at your miserable face all night and Julia's having a night off."

Rak laughed. "Might be better off talking with Julia, she listens to me." Nick looked at him, amusement in his face. "Right, I found out today that Charlie pays the fucking mortgage on that house, always has. Laughing twat won't pay for it because he didn't want it. And another thing an' all, she can't kick him out because it's in joint names, he'll want half."

Nick's amusement had turned to bemusement. "Y'what? What do you mean? She pays for it but can't get rid of him, of course she can. Her bank statements will show she pays for it surely."

Rak shook his head. "Not the case mate, joint names, means he's entitled. Then I offered to pay him off and she went mental, accused me of trying to control her, said I'm just 'somebody else' to control her. I thought she loved me."

Nick could understand why his friend was upset, however he could also appreciate Charlie's point of view. "Right, the way I see it is this, that's their business. I know it's hard but you can't get involved in their marriage, well, not any more than you are. She sees you as an escape, if you start giving her a hard time, she'll wonder why she's bothering, why have two twats when you could just have one? I know you wanna be this knight in shining armour, her hero, but you can't. You've got to let her arrive at her own conclusions mate, you can't influence them. If she started 'advising' you on Lisa, how would you feel?" before Rak could speak, Nick continued "I tell you how you'd feel, you would say that's not for you to worry about honey, that's my problem, not yours. And that's exactly what she's saying."

Rak knew his friend was right, as usual. "Yeah, yeah; ok, I get it. I just hate that little twat laughing at her, it makes me so fucking angry Nick, I wanna kill him."

Nick smiled, "Well, then you'd be in clink and she would meet another bloke, probably a younger, more handsome one. So don't do that, I ain't got time to visit ya anyhow."

Rak laughed now. "What do you mean, more handsome? She'd be hard pushed." They both started laughing, rather loudly.

Kate approached the bar, ready for her second V&T and dose of gossip. "Ohh, Rak, I'm so pleased I've seen you. How are you feeling now?"

Rak could see she was salivating at the possibility of news to share with Dorian. "I'm fine thanks Kate, just a little bump that's all," he knew by tomorrow morning that would be elevated to a full-blown catastrophe.

"Your Lisa had a right go at Kate earlier, didn't she Kate?" Nick was beginning to enjoy this and he also thought it may distract his friend from his real problems.

"Really, what happened Kate?"

Kate's face lit up with delight. "Well, I'm not one to gossip, as you know," Rak nodded his head in acknowledgement, "I was only enquiring as to your health after your little bump and she told me, in no uncertain terms, to 'ask you my effing self.'"

Rak was now trying desperately to suppress the smile he knew was appearing across his face, he could just picture Lisa, being her usual friendly self and it made him laugh. "I am truly sorry, Kate, I don't know what must of gotten into her. It must have been the worry." Now he knew he was stretching the truth. "Let me buy you a drink, as an apology." Rak thought it was worth the price of a vodka and tonic for the entertainment.

After Kate was safely seated back at her table, out of earshot, Nick couldn't help himself. "You see mate, if you don't sort things out with Charlie, there's always Kate, swear she's got the hots for ya."

Rak smiled "Yeah, grab a granny, 'bout sums me up."

Nick was laughing now, "I can see you as a toyboy, yeah that would deffo suit ya. Are you staying for another?"

Rak looked at the clock over the bar, 20:25pm. "Yeah, go on, why not? There's no one waiting for me anymore."

Nick shook his head "Don't you start again, or I'll send you home with Kate."

Rak eventually went home at 11:30pm.

33

Tuesday Morning

3 Church Lane

Rak needed to go into the office. After taking the previous day off he was well aware he would need to catch up on his paperwork and he also liked the team to see him as a visible boss. He knew he would be out from lunchtime so wanted to be in early, however, best laid plans and all.

That morning he had seen Tilly whilst he was walking back from Dorian and Jack's after buying his morning paper. She had been walking the dog, Rollo; Rak had spotted her at quite an inopportune moment. Tilly was busy filling a poop bag as Rak walked past her, he was trying to decide whether to wait until she had finished before saying hello, when she spotted him. "Oh, I know what you're thinking Rak Banerjee, but the shit this dog gives me is nothing compared to the shit Mark gives me." Rak was worried now for his friend, however, before he could speak, Tilly continued. "Do you know what I was doing 'til gone bleedin' midnight?"

Rak really didn't want to think about it. "His fucking books. He had let them build up and up again. Gave me a shitting carrier bag full of receipts and invoices, I had to sort through them all. He's not like you, organised. Then, when I finally get to bloody bed, he tries it on. Can you believe it, since when did sorting through petrol receipts become foreplay?"

Rak was beginning to wish he had bought his paper on the way into the office. "Oh, you know Mark, he is more hands on than I am these days, I've got time for paperwork. Do you want me to have a word with him?" Rak still had a soft spot for Tilly, she had helped him a lot over the years.

"Nah, don't worry about it, he's a twat. How are you now? See you've got a new motor."

Rak knew she was upset but trying to hide it. "Yeah, I'm all right thanks. The car's from Slim, I need to ring him later. Do you fancy a coffee? I was just going home to make some." He wasn't being totally truthful but felt Tilly needed a chat.

"You can bring erm..." Rak gestured towards the Labrador.

Tilly helped him out. "Rollo."

Rak smiled. "Yes, bring Rollo, come on. I've got custard creams too."

They both walked towards Rak's house, Rollo in tow. Rak knew Lisa would have a fit if she knew the dog had been in the house, however he didn't intend to mention it. Once inside, Rak got the coffee machine working and put out a plate of biscuits. "I don't have any doggy treats, Tilly, sorry. He is lovely isn't he, very friendly." Rak was giving Rollo a good fuss, he had wanted a dog himself, but Lisa had forbidden such an idea, claiming it would just make a mess.

"He likes you, must sense how kind you are. Where's Lisa?"

Rak laughed, "in London, spending money. It's her vocation y'know. Do you still take it black, no sugar?"

Tilly was amazed her friend and former boss recalled how she liked her coffee, then again, he never was shy at making the drinks in the office. "Yeah, please, that would be great".

"So, what's happening with Mark? You don't sound very happy." Tilly and Rak had always had a candid friendship, came from years of working closely together. There was a certain level of trust between them.

"Oh, I don't know Rak, I don't seem to see him these days. He's always got some big job on. The days of fixing Mrs. Doodah's pointing are well gone. He's out the door before I'm awake and when he gets home, I'm at work. Well, for three days of the week anyway. He's even working Saturdays now and then he's knackered on Sundays." Rak nodded, he knew she had more to say. "Then there's the kids, they always want ferrying somewhere or another. We don't get any quality time these days. We don't even need the money so much now, but Mark won't turn any job down." Rak felt slightly guilty, if he hadn't introduced Mark to the golf club crowd things might be different, however Mark had indicated he needed the extra cash.

"Have you tried talking to him about it?" Rak took a biscuit and dipped it in his coffee, a habit Lisa despised as the crumbs sat at the bottom of the cup.

"Yeah, but whenever I bring it up, he just says it's better than being skint. I suppose he's got a point. I just wish we could get out more together sometimes, enjoy the money. Do you know what I mean?"

Rak really wished he could find some words of comfort but he really didn't know what to say. "Look Tilly, I don't know what to advise but I will say this, you and Mark have a fantastic marriage, how long is it now, over twenty-five years? I'll never manage that, believe me. Don't give up, eh? Just try talking to him. Us men can be blinkered sometimes; we can't always see what's in front of our face." He held her hand and looked into her eyes. "You can get over this, Tilly, I promise you. He does love you, y'know." They both finished their coffee, and the biscuits, and embraced each other before Tilly made to leave.

"You'll be late Rak, not a good example to your staff." She smiled. "Thank you, sometimes I just feel lost, do you know what I mean?"

Rak smiled back. "Yeah, I sure do. I'm here, any time you need to let off steam or have a laugh." Rak laughed. "You don't fancy your old job back do ya? This one at the minute is not a patch on you." He was being serious and Tilly knew it.

"Maybe, we'll see. Right, come on Rollo, time to let Uncle Rak get to work. Thanks again." They both walked out together.

34

Heirs & Graces

Rak had not left Charlie's mind all night. She had been desperate to call him but was afraid he would still be upset with her. She could not believe she had slept in an empty bed when she could have been with him. She was hoping he would have calmed down by now, however she had resolved to wait to hear from him first.

Charlie's favourite client was in this morning, Jo Hartington. Jo always made Charlie laugh with her tales of dodgy first dates and online dating profile photos from several decades previously. Jo had shoulder length hair, very thick. She always opted for bleach blonde highlights with a caramel contrast and a layered cut. Jo was relaying her latest disappointment on the dating scene when Charlie spotted Tilly French leaving Rak's house with Rollo.

"Hang on Jo, I've just got to check something, won't be a sec." Charlie moved further towards the window, she knew she was staring but couldn't help it. Rak embraced Tilly, then fussed the dog. Tilly left, walking towards her house, Rak made to get into his car, then he looked over towards the salon, Charlie quickly looked away, but she wasn't quick enough, Rak had seen her. She knew he had seen her, she looked back at him again, this time he waved. She felt relief, she waved back. He began to walk over. Her stomach was full of butterflies.

The salon door opened, he walked in. He looked to see if any of the village gossips were in, then stepped in further. "Would you have a moment? I would like to enquire regarding gift vouchers." Rak was smiling, he had a naughty look in his eyes.

"Can you wait just one moment? I'm just finishing this last foil." Charlie smiled.

Rak took a seat on the sofa in the window which faced the main road, he was watching her bottom, she could see him in the mirror.

"Would you like a coffee, Jo? I've got this new latte, it's a dream."

Jo smiled. "Oh yes please darling, would you

have the latest Cosmo, too?" Charlie handed Jo the magazine and went into the back to make the coffee, Rak followed.

As soon as they were in the back room Rak grabbed Charlie, he held her tight, as if his life depended on it. Then he kissed her, passionately, slowly, using his tongue. Charlie knew she was becoming wet, she felt his jeans, he was hard.

"We can't, you know that. Stop it, or you know what will happen," she teased, mumbling between his kisses. Rak stopped kissing her and held her.

"I missed you last night, I'm sorry for interfering, Nick made me see sense. I am sorry baby."

Charlie rested her head against his chest. "I'm sorry too. I said some terrible things to you. I know you were only trying to help me." Charlie kissed him again. "I thought you had finished with me."

Rak laughed. "Well, I did nearly get a chance with Kate so it was a close call to be honest."

They both started laughing, Charlie was aware Jo could possibly hear, however she didn't care. Charlie made the latte and gestured for Rak to move.

"I can't hun, not at the moment," he indicated towards the front of his jeans, "I don't want your client seeing what she could've won." They both laughed again and she kissed him, again.

35

Tuesday Lunchtime

Amira's House

After the morning's delays, Rak had decided the best idea was to head straight over to Amira's place rather than risk getting caught in the office and being late. He knew his ex-wife could not abide lateness, she only previously tolerated it because she loved him, not an affliction she still suffered with. And Rak was hungry now.

He took a slow drive over, Amira lived the other side of Langham, in what was their marital home. Rak always felt awkward whenever he visited Amira, the house no longer felt like home, however, it had been his home for many years. He never knew whether to knock the door and wait or just walk in, he always felt somewhat awkward parking on the drive but didn't want to park down the road. It always seemed he plumped for the wrong choice.

Rak decided he would park on the drive, having not officially bought the Aston yet. He knocked the door and waited patiently. Then he saw Amira approach from the other side. "Why didn't you just come in? For Christ's sake Rak, I'm busy in the kitchen. New car?"

He knew he couldn't do right for doing wrong. "Hello to you too darling, yes, new car, I pranged the Jag last weekend. My own fault, I was driving too fast." If they had one thing still, it was honesty. Amira was looking good he thought, still slim at a size ten, her hair still glossy and long, dark with a red tint. She still dressed well and made the best of herself.

"It's lamb for lunch, is that all right? Do you still like it?"

Rak smiled at her. "You know I love lamb, thank you. You didn't need to go to any trouble, a sandwich would have sufficed." Rak opened the bottle of red he bought with him. "Where are the glasses?"

Amira pointed, "over in that cabinet, help yourself."

Rak looked around the house, into the living room. "Have you decorated?" He was curious.

"Yeah, I was fed up with the same old thing, do you like it?"

Rak smiled to himself. "It's very fifty shades of grey."

Amira laughed. "Hardly, there's no dildos."

Rak laughed "I meant the different shades of grey you have used in the living room. You've got a filthy mind Amira Banerjee." Whilst alone in the living room, Rak was trying to see if there was a man staying there. He knew it was none of his business what Amira got up to, but he still worried about her.

"Are you still single?" he asked as he approached the kitchen again.

"Don't you mean young, free and single? Yes, thank you, I am." She smiled cheekily. "How is the ice maiden?"

Rak laughed. "I don't really know, she's in London." He immediately felt he needed to provide clarity. "Only for a couple of days, staying with her sister. Probably clearing out the bank account" Amira rolled her eyes.

"What's happening with Geeta?" Rak asked after Amira had sat with him at the kitchen table.

"Oh, Rak, it's a mess darling. She was here the other night, crying her eyes out. Sanj is being brutal, he won't look for a job, he won't consider anything. He's always tapping her up for money, and she gives it to him. She's doing really well at establishing her client list but she's not being recognised at that snooty salon, they're still paying her peanuts Rak. I don't think it helps that Amit is doing so well. She said that she's two years older than her brother but feels like a child compared to him." Amit had a career as a solicitor, specialising in criminal law, and he was doing exceptionally well, having been involved in some high profile cases.

"Right, so how did you leave it?"

Amira looked deep into Rak's eyes, "I told her I was going to talk with you about it. She didn't like it, Rak; I think she worries you'll smack him one."

Rak looked away, out to the garden, the garden his children used to play in, so innocently. "I can't pretend I'm not tempted to Amira, he's a waster. But that's what he wants, to cause her to choose between him and her family." Rak was also reminded of Brad, his anger rising again. "But we can't go on like this, Amira; I will not have my daughter made a fool of."

Amira held his hand, to try and calm her ex-husband down. "Have a drink. The lamb's ready."

Rak made a decision. He would ask Charlie if she could offer Geeta a job, that way he could keep an eye on her. And it would allow Charlie more free time to spend with him. A win-win situation. "If I could secure Geeta a job at another salon, where she would have more responsibility and a pay packet to reflect it, do you think she would go for it?" Rak asked Amira in-between mouthfuls of lamb and potatoes.

"Yeah, I don't see why not. Why, what have you got in mind?" Amira knew her ex-husband too well, she knew he was hatching a plan.

"Well, I have a friend, she owns the village salon. It's always busy and she's on her own. If Geeta bought her own clients and could assist Charlie with hers, it could work for both of them."

Amira did have to concur, the plan sounded ideal. "What about Sanj? She thinks she's in love with him. I listen when she's upset but as soon as I suggest she leave him, she closes rank. I just cannot get through to her, Rak."

Rak was aware this was going to be more difficult to rectify. "I don't know, honey, I really don't. Let's just hope if her confidence grows at work, she'll see she's worth more than that twat. I might suggest she stay with me for a while, it would be convenient for her new job and he will not dare show his face near my house".

Rak had enjoyed his lunch, Amira did know how to cook and it had been a treat. He felt they could work together to solve Geeta's problems.

Amira had enjoyed Rak's company, it had been so long since she had seen him, she had forgotten what good company he could be.

They had moved to the conservatory after lunch, to enjoy a coffee and look at the garden. "You're managing the garden well, Amira; it looks great."

Amira laughed. "I wish I could take all the credit,

I have a gardener visit once a month, he keeps on top of it for me." Rak looked further towards the garden. "Have you seen Amit?"

He turned to look at Amira. "Sorry, I didn't catch that, I was miles away."

Amira smiled and shook her head. "I said, have you seen Amit recently?"

Rak turned back to face her. "Yeah, we went for a beer the other week. God, Amira, he's got numerous women on the go. Don't know how he keeps up."

Amira laughed. "Hmmm, and you'd know." Rak looked away again. "Sorry, Rak, that was unnecessary."

Rak looked back at her. "I never had numerous women, honey, I made one mistake." She could see the regret in his eyes.

Amira felt a subject change was needed. "Hey. You'll never guess who I saw in the bank the other week? Your dad."

Rak turned to look at her quickly. "Sorry you had to suffer that."

Amira's face softened. "He's looking old, Rak. He asked about you, I said you're well as far as I know. He asked me to say hello to you from him, he said he wants to see you." Rak could feel his eyes starting to burn with emotion. "Rak, you've got to let this go. If you don't, you'll regret it. I know; I miss my dad every day."

Rak looked Amira straight in the eyes. "Your dad was a good man, I liked your dad. I miss your dad." They had kept in touch even after the divorce. "But my dad is not a good man, I don't miss him and I don't love him. Now leave it. If you see him again, cross the street. Do you understand? And you do not talk to him about me."

Amira was upset for her ex-husband, however Rak had never told her the full story, not in all these years. All she knew was that they had fallen out, he had never divulged the details.

Amira knew he had made himself clear. Rak had never allowed her to take the kids to see his dad, always warning her if she did, she would regret it. She had always wanted to ask him for more details but there never seemed the right time. Again, this was not the right time.

"Hey, before you go, could you do me a favour?"

Rak laughed. "No such thing as a free lunch, eh? What do you need?"

Amira gestured to him to follow her, she began to ascend the stairs. "Can you hang this picture for me please? The decorators took it down but forgot to put it back up. I can't reach" Rak followed his ex-wife upstairs, remembering the times he had previously followed her upstairs, to bed.

Once in the main bedroom Amira showed him where she wanted the picture hanging. "Just there, can you do it?"

Rak moved her out of the way. "Where? Here? Is that right?" Amira nodded and Rak proceeded to hang the picture, ensuring it was straight. "Ok?"

Amira looked. "Yes, perfect. Thank you." She moved towards him. "I miss you Rak, I miss you being here."

She was looking deep into his eyes, then she was kissing him. Rak didn't know what was happening, he began to respond to her kiss, then they were kissing passionately, like they used to. Amira unbuttoned his shirt, she pulled it off of him and threw it on the chair, her hands were feeling through his hair, pushing his mouth closer towards her own. His hands were feeling her bottom, he knew she was getting him hard, he knew he could have her again. Amira began unbuttoning her blouse, her breasts heaving in her black bra, Rak tugged at her blouse, pulling it away from her. They fell onto the bed, the bed they had shared for many years before, they were still kissing, with more and more passion.

Amira's hands wandered to the belt on Rak's jeans, she was beginning to loosen it, she wanted him. She undid the button and the fly, she placed her hand inside his boxers, he was hard, so hard. She felt herself surge with wetness, she wanted him now. He was unbuttoning her trousers and unzipping the zip, his hands were inside her knickers, he could feel how wet she was, wet for him. He was touching her, touching her clit, she thought she was going to come there and then, it had been so long since she had been touched. Rak pulled her trousers off and her knickers, he had his head between her thighs, he was kissing her lips, licking her. "Rak, oh my god, Rak, you still feel so good."

Then he stopped. Just stopped. He sat up, his back turned away from her. He looked at her. "I'm sorry, I can't do this. This should never had happened. This is a mistake. I have to go." He got up from the bed, grabbed his shirt from the chair and proceeded to run down the stairs, doing his jeans up as he went. Amira immediately followed him, in just her bra.

"Rak, what's wrong? Rak, don't do this, don't run away." She was crying now.

Rak did wait, he went to the kitchen to pick up his car keys and knew he couldn't run out on his ex-wife. He knew he had to explain. "Go and get dressed, I'll wait".

After Amira had got some clothes on she returned to the kitchen to find her ex-husband sitting at the table. He had poured them both a glass of wine. She sat down opposite him, she took his hand. "I'm sorry, Rak, that was my fault, I encouraged you."

Rak looked at her, resignation etched on his face. "Honey, it was both our faults. I need to tell you something. I'm seeing somebody else, behind Lisa's back. I think, I know, I love this person and I can't cheat on her, not even with my ex-wife. I am sorry, please know if it wasn't for her, I would not have stopped. I will always love you Amira, you're a very attractive woman, still."

Amira could not take this new information on board. "You're having an affair?"

Rak looked deeper into her eyes. "Yes, I am. With the hairdresser I was telling you about, Charlie. Lisa has not given me any, and I mean any, affection in years. I have needs Amira." They both took a sip of wine, Amira to help her digest this new information, Rak to calm his nerves after admitting to his ex-wife he was having an affair. They both sat there, holding hands, looking at the garden.

Amira spoke first "How long have you been cheating on Lisa?"

Rak was surprised by the question. "What?"

Amira spoke softly. "How long Rak?"

Rak looked at her "A couple of months, she's married too. It's not ideal, I know that, but I can't stop it, Amira."

Amira felt sorry for him, she knew Lisa treated him badly, but she had no idea just how badly. "Do you love her more than you loved Jenna Fallon?"

Rak did not know the answer to this question.

Jenna Fallon was the reason Amira and Rak divorced. Rak had an affair with Jenna when Geeta was aged fifteen and Amit was thirteen. Amira knew he was seeing someone, all the signs were there. Being late home from work, business trips away at weekends, snide phone calls and texts. She really thought it would fizzle out after a while, she was prepared to tolerate it for the sake of the kids. That was until she found out that the mystery woman was her children's French teacher. She could not believe Rak would involve the kids in his secret affair. Jenna started treating the kids differently in school and it was only when Amira took it up with the school and demanded answers, did she find out the truth.

Amira kicked him out, telling him she never wanted to see him again. The biggest problem for Rak was, once he was all Jenna's, she didn't want him either.

36

9 Church Lane

Tilly had not been home long. It was her day off and after her coffee with Rak, she had decided a spot of retail therapy was in order, so had taken herself off to the shopping village just the other side of Langham. She had bought more than she intended to and was placing the purchases in the wardrobe, where Mark wouldn't see them. She heard the front door opening and Mark shouting up. "Honey, I'm home," in a mock American accent.

Tilly looked at the clock, it was only 15:15pm, why was he home so early. "Hiya, what you doing back so early?"

Mark was already making his way upstairs. "What sort of a welcome is that? Come here." He grabbed her and spun her round. "I've missed you Mrs. French, the kids are both out and we've got the house to ourselves."

Tilly smiled naughtily. "What on earth are you suggesting Mr. French? Tiddlywinks?"

Mark took her in his arms and began kissing her, they were kissing like they hadn't in a long time. He was running his hands all over her, Tilly was enjoying herself. He lifted her top over her head, then immediately his lips were back on her mouth. He was unfastening her bra, his hands feeling everywhere. He was fondling her breasts, Tilly could feel she wanted him, it had been so long since they had made love. She began to loosen his belt, then undo his trousers, she placed her hand inside his boxers, he was hard, so hard. Tilly lifted his t-shirt off and was feeling his chest now, then his back. They both fell onto the bed. He was pulling her skirt off, then her knickers. He kissed her neck, then her breasts. "Oh God, Mark, yes"

He stood up to quickly pull off his trousers and his boxers, he was hard for her, his throbbing cock just wanting to be touched. Tilly knelt on her knees and placed her hands over the shaft and bought his cock to her mouth, she was teasing him with her tongue, flicking the head of the shaft, then she took him in her mouth.

"Ahhhh, Tilly, baby yes, yes,"

She was using her hands to fondle his balls, they were tensing up. Mark placed his hand between her legs and began playing with her pussy, he inserted a finger inside her, she was dripping wet. "Ah God, ah God yes, Mark, yes!"

He used his thumb to caress her clit, Tilly knew she was going to come, she couldn't hold out any longer. "Yes, oh fuck, yes!" his cock now in her hands, hard. Tilly wanted him inside her now, she turned around so he was behind her and he pushed his throbbing cock into her wet pussy. It felt so good.

"Oh God Tilly, yes, yes." He was moving faster, deeper inside of her.

"Mark, Mark, yes, please don't stop." His hands were on her breasts now, he was going harder and harder inside of her. Tilly felt she was going to come for a second time. "Oh fuck! Yes!" She was gripping the bedding, the power of her orgasm overtaking her.

He was still banging her, deeper still, harder. "I'm gonna come baby, baby, I'm gonna come." Her pussy was tight around his throbbing cock. "Yes, yes, babe! Oh God, yes!"

It had been six weeks since they had made love together, Tilly had begun to think Mark didn't want her any more. How wrong she had been. As they snuggled up together in bed, Mark looked into his wife's eyes. "I know things have been shit recently,

Tills, I'm sorry. I just don't want us to ever worry about money again, do you know what I mean?"

Tilly kissed her husband. "Yeah, I know why you're working so hard, but really, we need more time together, Mark. I miss you, y'know?" Tilly was still curious about something. "What made you come home early today? Just out of interest."

Mark had a cheeky smile. "I shouldn't really tell you this, I'm sworn to secrecy."

Tilly lightly tapped him in jest "You can't do that, now come on, tell me."

Mark was still smiling "Well, let's just say a guardian angel intervened."

Tilly smiled. "Rak?" Mark nodded, still smiling. "I saw him earlier, he could tell I was pissed off with you, invited me and Rollo for a coffee."

Mark was laughing now. "What? Rollo was allowed into number three?"

Tilly laughed. "Yeah, her ladyship's in London, well anyway, we had a coffee and a chat and Rak basically said we're good together and I should stick with it."

Mark laughed. "Bet you had biscuits too, I know what you pair are like together. Well, anyway, he texted me, said I should treat you to a night out and he'd seen *the Rose & Crown* had got a steak night on tonight. Made me realise I need to treat you a bit better."

Tilly smiled. "A lot better don't ya mean? Y'know,

he offered me my old job back, Rak, I mean. I think he was serious."

Mark looked at his wife. "Would you want it? I mean, you don't need to work at all now Tills."

Tilly thought for a moment. "I know that, Mark, but it gets me out the house. Gives me a purpose. I wouldn't mind working with Rak again, he was always fair and we had a laugh. Don't get me wrong, I like the bus station but there's little to no flexibility. Rak was always fair, as long as the work got done. I wouldn't mind part-time, or maybe work from home a couple of days a week. What do you think?"

Mark thought for split second "What I think is, if you're happy, I'm happy. Now come here, I want to cuddle you some more before I take you out for that steak".

Tilly had made her mind up, she would accept Rak's offer.

37

Tuesday Evening
Amira's House

After his confession to Amira, Rak stayed a while longer with his ex-wife. Amira had made coffee, deciding that if Rak drank too much, he wouldn't be able to drive home. "So, what do you think you'll do?"

Rak was sitting at the kitchen table, they had put some music on, Dionne Warwick, something they both used to enjoy together. Rak turned to face Amira in the kitchen. "What about, honey?"

Amira came towards him and massaged his shoulders. "About Lisa and this Charlie woman, will you leave Lisa?"

Rak rested the back of his head on her chest. "I don't know, hun; I really don't know. I wish I'd got together with Charlie years ago, before Lisa. She's different y'know, we get on but we don't always see things the same way but we embrace each other's different ideas. I love her Amira, I really love her. She's married to a complete prick, imagine Sanj multiplied by a hundred. He even makes her pay the fucking mortgage." Despite Nick's words of advice the previous night, this still angered Rak.

"What? Oh my god, no wonder she's playing away."

Rak gestured for Amira to sit beside him. "That's why I worry for Geeta, I don't want our daughter chained to a waster. I've seen how it can tear people apart."

Amira held his hand "How did you get together with her? Charlie?".

Rak explained everything to Amira, all the details. "Wow, you really have been through hell already for her. Would you have really fallen out with Nick over her?" This was what Amira was having real difficulty understanding, knowing how strong their bond was.

"Yeah, I suppose I would have. She's everything to me. I want her, I really want her. I don't know what to do." Rak could feel tears in his eyes, Amira could sense he needed comfort, she opened her arms and he cried on her shoulder.

They stayed in each other's arms for what felt like an eternity. Amira still loved Rak and hated seeing him so upset, so confused. She wanted to help him but didn't know how.

"I'm sorry, honey, I don't know what came over me. I shouldn't be crying on your shoulder".

Amira felt tears in her own eyes, tears of regret of ever letting her husband go, tears of frustration that neither of them seemed to have their lives sorted out but mostly tears of sadness, sadness that she knew she really had lost him now. "I wish things had been different Rak, I really do. Why couldn't you have shagged somebody else, anybody else but Jenna fucking Fallon?"

Rak looked shocked. "What? You would have forgiven me shagging somebody else?" he wanted to raise his voice but could see how upset Amira was.

"Yes. Yes, I would have. I knew you were knocking somebody else off, I'm not stupid. I thought it was Tilly to be honest with you. Why her though, Rak? Why?"

Rak wanted to laugh at her. "Tilly, really? Shagging the secretary, how very predictable."

Amira looked him straight in the eye. "Oh yeah, I mean you're so original, you had to screw our kids' fucking teacher!" Amira was shouting now, they were both on their feet. "What choice did I have? I had to divorce you. The whole fucking school knew, you couldn't even have an affair properly." Amira was smacking his chest, sobbing her eyes out. They had never had this level of in-depth analysis before.

"I'm sorry; I am sorry, Amira. Everything was getting on top of me, I needed an escape. I met her at parents' evening, the one time you couldn't go. She was flirting with me, she asked what I did. I told her I had an engineering business. She looked me up and called me at the office, asked me out for a drink. I did not intend to sleep with her, please believe me."

Amira could feel her anger increase "Oh! Well then, as long as you didn't intend to fuck her!"

Rak was struggling for the words. "What I meant was, she did all the running, put it on a plate for me."

Amira was further incensed by this. "Like I did earlier y'mean? But you wouldn't fuck me because of this Charlie! Charlie, who you've known all of five minutes! But cheat on your wife of nearly twenty years and the mother of your kids? Yea, no problem! It was on a plate, after all!"

Rak knew he wouldn't get anywhere with Amira in this mood. "Why are you bringing all this up now? Nearly ten years later. Why?" his fist hit the table, he was shouting now, shouting so loud it scared her, she started sobbing.

"Because I always thought you would come back to me, Rak, even when you met Lisa, I knew it wouldn't last. But now you're telling me you love this Charlie, love her so much. I know we will never be together again." The tears streamed down her face.

He opened his arms and took her into them, kissing her head. "I'm sorry. I didn't know you felt that way, I really didn't. I thought you hated me. Why did you never say anything? In all these years?"

Amira just stared into his eyes, both their eyes glistening with emotion. "I would have come back to you Amira, I would have, like a shot."

Amira looked deeper into his face "Because of my stupid pride, that's why. I thought you would ask to come back, but then you never did."

Rak held her tighter. "I was scared to, honey, I thought about it but I thought you'd tell me to fuck off. And you would have been within your rights to. What a mess!"

They stood holding each other, both taking in these revelations. The realisation that they had wasted years; years when they could have been together, if only they hadn't been too proud or too scared to tell each other.

Rak eventually left around 8:30pm. They had made a pact they would be friends from now on, proper friends. Amira took his hand as he was leaving.

"If she ever lets you down, you know where I am. I will always love you, Rak."

He kissed her cheek. "I will always love you too, Amira, always."

38

The Bull

When Rak had driven a little down the road he pulled over and checked his mobile, he had put his notifications on silent whilst he was with Amira. Two new texts, first one from Slim.

> *'Hi mate, just wondering what your thoughts are with regard to the Aston. Let me know, Eric says he'll do a deal if we can sort it out by Friday. Cheers.'*

Shit! Rak remembered he was supposed to have called Slim today, but with everything going on he had completely forgotten.

'Hi mate, sorry for the late reply, difficult day. Yes, I would like the Aston, do you want to talk to Eric or should I? If you do, make sure you get a cut. Cheers.'

Second text, Charlie.

'Hey baby, not heard from you. How's things go with Amira? Have you come up with a plan for Geeta? Xxx text me xxx'

Rak did not know how to respond to this text, 'yes, great time with Amira, we realised we still love each other, oh by the way, I nearly fucked her,' didn't sound so great, or how about, 'nearly screwed her actually, can you give my daughter a job?' *'Oh shit!'* He sat in the car, thinking. Did he want Amira back? He didn't this morning, did he? Rak couldn't figure out what could be wrong with him. Nick only had eyes for Julia, like it's supposed to be, what's wrong with him? Why did he make his life so complicated?

'Hey baby, sorry discussions went on longer than expected. Can you meet me in The Bull, you know, accidentally on purpose? Say half an hour? There's something I need to ask you xxxx'

Rak waited for a reply before driving off, his phone pinged.

'Yes mate, no worries. I'll chat with Eric for you. Drop that insurance paperwork into me tomorrow, let's get this sorted. Cheers mate.'

Not what he was waiting for.

'No worries, will do. See you in the morning. Cheers mate.'

Rak sat there another five minutes. He was trying to work out if he should tell Charlie anything about the afternoon's events, other than to enquire about a job for Geeta. He had agreed with Amira they would not have any relationship other than friendship, did she need to know? Would it be so awful if he had a secret with his ex-wife, really? He had kept enough secrets from her over the years. He knew he should have told Amira the whole truth about his dad, but he couldn't face it. And he knew she would be shocked, shocked at her husband's temper, shocked he could inflict that level of violence. He knew as well he should have told her about the time Tilly tried to kiss him, but it was blamed on too much champagne at a Christmas networking do she had attended with him. And Rak knew that Amira would make him fire Tilly and that was unnecessary. Yes, he had kept many secrets from Amira over the years, he could keep one for her, surely. The phone pinged.

'Hey baby, yes that will be fine. See you in 30 mins, can't wait. Can we escape to Pam's too? Xxx'

Rak read it, he didn't know if he wanted to escape to Pam's yet, so started the engine and drove to *The Bull*.

Rak parked at his house and walked over. Charlie was already there. She had managed to sit at the snug little table in the corner, out of sight of most of the pub. She was enjoying a glass of red and feeling the anticipation of seeing Rak. The entrance door to the bar opened. It was him.

"Evening darlin', what can I get ya? Looking gorgeous as usual." Julia winked.

"Stop it, your husband will hear then we're both for the high jump." Rak was laughing "Looking fabulous yourself, Julia, a large Chivas please, have one yourself as well."

Julia smiled. "Thanks darlin', I will after closing; it's been a right bloody day. I was going to go shopping with Tilly, but it's been mental here, couldn't get away"

Rak looked over towards Nick. "Not letting your wife out again mate? There'll be rumours, y'know."

Nick joined Julia at the bar. "Hello, mate, not stopped all day. Been mad busy, can't complain though, you all right?"

Rak really wanted to tell Nick everything but knew here was not the right place "Yeah, I'm ok thanks. Just left Amira's. Are you free tomorrow to put the final plans in place for the fundraiser? Maybe after work, I've got to show my face in the office at some point this week."

Nick thought quickly. "Yeah, could do. Let's go to *the Rose & Crown* otherwise I'll be on the bar and we won't get anything sorted. Julia, can Adam cover tomorrow evening? We won't be late, we'll come back here to get proper sozzled."

Julia looked over, knowing they would be late. "Yeah, go on then, if he wants to buy that house, he'll be grateful of the cash. I'll text him".

Rak looked around the pub, Nick noticed. "She's over there mate," he whispered, pointing to the snug.

"Oh, Charlie? I didn't see you there. Are you alone? Would you like another drink?"

Charlie flashed her widest smile, Rak felt a pang of guilt. "Oh, hello, Rak, yes that would be lovely, a glass of red please. Would you like to join me?"

He nodded and made his way to the table.

Charlie was so happy to finally have him to herself. "Did you have a good day? How was it with Amira?"

Rak smiled and reached for her hand. "It was ok, I might need your help with something." Charlie smiled naughtily. "No, not that, not yet anyway." He looked into her eyes and knew he loved her, he knew he had done the right thing not sleeping with Amira. "How would you feel about giving Geeta a job? She's fully qualified, got an enviable client list by all accounts and she will work hard."

Charlie was slightly taken aback, this was not the question she had been expecting. "Err… yeah, I could do. Why, what's wrong with where she is now? In my experience stylists only move if there's a problem."

Charlie really wanted more detail. "They're not recognising her skill, shit money and no progression. She could be a manager, hun, it'll give us more time together too."

Charlie thought about this. "Yeah, interesting. Where does she work now?"

Rak didn't really know. "Err, Simon something or other, on the main road just near Langham. Apparently, he's got a chain of salons."

Charlie laughed, she couldn't stop herself.

"What? What's funny?" Rak was bemused.

"I know Simon Freer and what you describe is spot on. He treated me the same until I had a proper tantrum at him, I was around twenty-two and he wouldn't let me manage a salon until I proved I could do it. Lost my temper in the end and got the Lower Chivley salon. He's a hard nut to crack. I made him a fortune." Rak was shocked. "Yes, we're quite good friends now, I'll call him tomorrow. If I'm going to poach Geeta from him, he'll appreciate knowing about it."

Rak breathed a sigh of relief. "Thanks, hun, I can't tell you how much you're helping me. Thank you."

They both sat there, finishing their drinks "You

never answered me baby, about escaping to Pam's?"

Rak looked at her, a naughty smile on his face. "We could do, but what have you told him?"

Charlie knew he was referring to Brad. "That I was going to see a girlfriend, from the old days. Can always say I've had too much to drive home, what do you say?"

Rak did not recall seeing Charlie's car in the carpark. "Where's your Mini? I didn't see it."

Charlie laughed "Up near the church, divine intervention, wouldn't you agree?"

Rak was in the mood for behaving recklessly. "Yeah, ok then. Let's go. I'll leave first, wait outside. Then we can walk up to get your car, I'll take mine too, need it for the morning. Are you ready?"

Charlie squeezed his thigh and smiled.

Rak got up to leave, not taking his eyes off of Charlie. "I'll see you tomorrow mate, I'll call for you after work, say about six-ish? Will that be all right?"

Nick looked over, raising his hand. "Yeah, that's great. See you tomorrow mate, have a good night." Nick was smiling, he knew what Rak was going to do for the rest of the night.

As they both walked up to the church, they were very aware of the possibility of being seen. They both hurried along, walking as quickly as they could. Once Rak knew Charlie was safely in her car, he ran back to get his own and followed her to Pam's Cottage.

39

5 Main Street

To say Brad was disappointed that Charlie had gone out to see an old friend would be an understatement. He had been looking forward to spending the evening with her. He had not seen her properly since the previous Friday night and he wanted them to spend quality time together.

All day he had been planning the perfect evening with his wife. He had decided to opt for a takeaway, rather than going out to eat, he had wanted her all to himself. Brad wanted to have sex with Charlie. He was struggling to recall the last time they had been to bed together, she had not wanted it for so long. He knew their fertility issues were partly to blame, Charlie had stopped wanting sex, just viewing it as a process which would end in disappointment. However, up until around the time he had gone to that conference in June, they had been trying to get their intimate relationship back on track. However, since then, Charlie was less and less interested and now they rarely mentioned it, never mind did it.

Brad was acutely aware he had not been able to satisfy his wife in quite a while, he could not remember the last time he had seen her come. He knew she was only agreeing to sex to please him, and quite selfishly he was happy to take it from her. All day he had been fantasising about her, how good it felt when his cock was in her mouth, how good her pussy felt, how satisfied he felt when he came inside her. Charlie had asked him previously if they could try different things, she wanted him to kiss her in places he wouldn't usually, but he flat out refused. He would make excuses, that he wasn't in the mood or that he didn't think he was very good at it. The truth was, he was only interested in his own satis-faction. He found the idea of giving his wife oral pleasure repulsive.

Brad looked at the clock on the living room wall, it read 22:30pm. Where the hell was she? He considered texting her but decided against it, knowing she could ignore a text, that had been proven all weekend. No, he would call her. He wanted to know what she was doing. He wanted her home. He wanted sex and he wasn't waiting any longer.

40

Pam's Cottage

Rak couldn't open the door quick enough, as soon as they were inside, they were all over each other. In the hallway they were kissing, kissing so passionately. They were bouncing off the walls, going towards the bedroom in circles. Kissing, lips locked, tongues playing in each other's mouths.

Charlie heard her phone, the ringtone of 'Just Dance' by Lady Gaga playing. "Wait, baby, I'd better get that, wait here." Charlie fished her phone out of bag, her bag sitting on the hall floor where it had been dropped. The screen read Brad. Her heart dropped. "Hi, are you ok? I'm at Cassie's, what do you want?" her face relayed what was being said.

"When are you coming home? I want us to spend some time together Char, I want to go to bed with you."

Charlie didn't know what to say, Rak was walking towards her, he took her hand and pulled her gently towards the bedroom. "I'm not coming home tonight, Brad, we got talking and I've had rather a lot to drink. I will see you tomorrow. I've got to go, the pizza has just arrived. Bye." She hung up the phone and dropped it on the bedside table. She could only imagine the temper her husband would be in now.

Charlie pulled Rak towards her, she kissed him, passionately. He kissed her back, his tongue signifying what he wanted to do with her. The bedroom was dark, no lights on, the sensation of touch heightened further. Charlie could wait no longer, she undid his belt, then his jeans, then she pulled off his boxers. His cock was rock hard, throbbing. She sat on the edge of the bed and teased the head of his cock with her tongue, slowly licking in a circular motion.

"Ahh, Charlie, baby, yes." He pushed her blonde hair, her mouth taking all of him, her hands caressed his balls, they were tightening up. "Honey, hun, you'll make me come, ahh, God, oh God!" She was licking him and sucking harder, she used her hand to gently massage the base of his shaft. "Baby, I can't stop, oh God, oh God yes, yes!" His whole body shook.

Rak was literally blown away by the sensations he had just felt. "That was amazing, hun, fucking amazing," he whispered. He took off his shirt, then he took off Charlie's top, then her jeans, pulling off her boots at the same time, then he teased her knickers away from her and parted her legs. His tongue felt so good, he knew exactly what to do. He was licking her lips, his tongue inside her, kissing her. He kissed her clit, slowly at first, softly, gently, then he slid his fingers inside her, he was playing, teasing.

"Rak! Rak, yes! Oh yes. Never stop, never stop, please!" The pleasure was so much she didn't think she could take any more. He licked her clit, faster now, deeper. His fingers still playing with her pussy, quicker. "Rak, yes! Rak, oh God, Rak!" He didn't stop, he wanted her to feel ecstasy. She saw a rainbow of colour in her eyes, she felt her whole body almost levitate. "Oh Goooodddddddddd yeeeesssssssss, yesssssssss!" she was crying with pleasure.

They both lay in the bed, in the dark, holding each other. Charlie was listening to Rak's heartbeat, the rhythmic sound calming her. She was feeling his chest with her fingers, tracing a pattern across his heart. Rak was holding Charlie, feeling her body next to his, warm and smooth. His hand lightly caressing the small of her back.

Rak opened his mouth to speak. "That was amazing, Charlie; fantastic." He held her a little closer still.

"Rak, I love you y'know. I always will."

Rak was very aware this was not the first time this evening he had heard these words, his mind briefly flitted to Amira.

"Do you still have sex with Brad?" He didn't know where this question had come from, he hadn't intended to ask it, it just came out.

Charlie turned to look into his eyes. "What? I mean, well no. No, I don't. But I'm just surprised you asked."

Rak looked at her, his eyes staring into hers. "Sorry, I don't know where that came from. It was just in my head and I said it."

Charlie suspected he wasn't being totally honest. "Are you ok? Has something upset you?" She really was concerned for the man she loved.

"No, nothing has upset me. How can I be upset after what we have just enjoyed. Don't be silly hun, I just want you all to myself." He kissed her, as if to signify the end of the discussion.

41

Banerjee Engineering

Rak had made some excellent progress this morning, the day had started well. He had spoken with the insurance company and got that sorted out, then he had been to see Slim and agreed a deal with Eric to secure the Aston. He was feeling a sense of achievement. Finally, he had arrived at the office, ready for a coffee.

Rak walked into his workshop first, he liked to see what was happening on the shop floor before heading up to the office. He was immediately accosted by Greg, his workshop manager. "Rak, you got a minute?" Greg was good at his job, but personality was certainly lacking.

"Good morning, Greg, yes, what can I do for ya?"

Greg did seem rather flustered. "We had Carl Potter in here yesterday, kicking off that his order was wrong, he wanted four hundred stainless pipes fabricating, he got forty. I looked at the order sheet and it deffo says forty. I asked Alison but she wasn't much help. He was not happy."

Carl Potter was George Potter's son. George had always worked with Rak's father and after some minor disagreements when Rak took over, the Potters' had continued to work with Rak. Carl now ran his father's business and he and Rak had become friendly.

"For fuck's sake, really??" Rak was fuming, this was not the first time Alison, his latest P.A., of just three months had inputted important information incorrectly. "Leave it with me Greg, thanks mate. Looks like I'll be paying overtime soon".

Rak walked into the office, saw Alison Cartwright sat there, filing her nails. "Busy?" She nearly fell off her chair with the shock of her boss's raised voice. "Did Carl Potter come to see me yesterday?"

Alison looked as if her brain was searching for excuses. "Yes, but you said not to disturb you unless it was urgent, don't you remember?"

He could feel his blood pressure skyrocketing. "So, if a client comes in shouting the odds at my workshop manager, you don't think that's urgent?"

Alison was fiddling with her dress now. "Well, no. Not really. I mean the order said forty and he'd got forty. He did say he was going to call you himself, but I told him not to, that you were busy." The vacant look on her face was infuriating Rak.

"Did you fill out the order form Alison?"

She looked away from him. "Yeah, I think so. I don't know, it's my writing though so I suppose I did, yeah."

Rak was trying to remember to breathe. "Did you listen to the order being given to you?"

She looked away further. "Well, sort of, but I was late for my lunch, so when I thought his secretary had said forty, I just put forty. Maybe I should've checked though." This was not the first, or the second time come to think of it, that Alison had made an error; errors which would cost the company and she had received warnings previously.

"Get out! Get out, don't come back and don't expect a reference. A five-year-old could do a better job than you."

Alison started to turn on the tears but it wouldn't work with Rak, although he wasn't totally heartless. "I'll pay you 'til the end of the month, and that's more than I should do. Now go."

Never mind a coffee, he needed a whiskey now. The phone rang. "What?!" Rak had forgot it was the outside line which customers used to call the office.

"Well, I was going to say you've got yourself a new, old, P.A., but if that's what mood you're in…"

Tilly, thank God. "Tilly, hun. Are you serious, when can you start?"

Tilly smiled to herself "Well, I spoke with my manager at the bus station and I'm owed quite a bit of leave so I'm taking that as my notice period, so I'm all yours. How does today sound?"

Rak could have jumped for joy. "Bring the biscuits, we're gonna need 'em".

Rak now had to smooth talk Carl Potter. "Carl, mate. Look, I'm sorry for the mix up. We'll put it right, I promise. Have I ever let you down before?" the phone went quiet for a moment.

"To be honest, Rak, it's a bit more than a mix up. Rumour has it you've not had your mind on the job for a while. Other priorities apparently."

Rak was taken aback by Carl's insinuations. "What exactly are you saying mate? Come on, out with it."

Carl sighed. "Well, it's been noticed that office sees less of you than the pub or the golf course, you're not so hands on anymore and it shows."

Rak knew he'd been less involved in the business recently but didn't know it had been noticed in professional circles. "Yeah, you've got a point mate, can't lie to ya. I've had some family issues recently. But look, I've just spoken with Tilly, you remember, my previous P.A? Yeah, well she's coming back. Carl, she can run this business without me and that's what I need now, some support. Be good if I could count on you for support too mate."

Carl did remember Tilly, in fact he used to have a thing for her. "Tilly's coming back?"

Rak knew he used to have a thing for her. "Yes, starting today. So if you want to pop over and see us, we'll have the kettle on and a plate of biscuits, what d'ya say?"

Carl didn't need to think twice, he knew she was married but he did enjoy a good flirt. "Yeah, ok. But any more cock-ups Rak and that's it. I can get a better deal with Varney's."

Varney's were very much Rak's competition. "Yeah, but not the quality mate, or our stunning personalities." They both ended the call laughing. Rak couldn't pretend he wasn't relieved; he couldn't afford to lose Carl's business.

42

Wednesday Afternoon
Heirs & Graces

Charlie had been very busy for a Wednesday morning, she had done two perms, three colour touch-ups and two cut and blow dries. She actually thought to herself she could use an extra pair of hands. She knew she needed to call Simon, 'oh well, no time like the present.' She had a half hour window before her next client, full head foils. She dialled Simon's mobile number.

"Charlie Redman, how the devil are you, darling? Do you want to come work with me again?"

Charlie laughed, she always found Simon

amusing, and she enjoyed hearing her maiden name. "Hello gorgeous, how's life in the fast lane?"

Simon was very flamboyant, even on the phone. "Oh, you know, it's just one star studded event after the other, darling. Not really, life's busy but I'm enjoying it. Sebastian and I are getting married next year, about time, hey? Would you be a darling and come along?"

Simon and Sebastian had been together over ten years, Charlie was surprised they had decided to marry. "Congratulations, what fab news. Oh, course I'll come, it would be a pleasure." She was thinking by next year she may be able to take Rak as her plus one, a smile enveloped her face.

"Now, as lovely as it is to hear from you, what do you want?" Charlie knew Simon would guess there was a reason for the call.

"Geeta Banerjee, is she any good? And no tales please." Simon could embellish things to suit himself.

"Geeta is a star, reminds me of you actually. Very keen but too involved with the wrong man, like you used to be. Not ready for responsibility yet. Why, do you want her?" Simon was very serious now.

"I know her father, he's asked me to give her a job, Simon. He is a very good friend…"

Simon interrupted. "I bet he is, I've seen pictures of him, Geeta showed me. Shame he's straight, he is straight, isn't he?"

She knew he was fishing. "Well, I think so, he's married, to a woman"

Simon chuckled. "Never stopped you before darling. I definitely would, no questions asked. If you want Geeta, you have my blessing. She'll do well for you. She's got a nightmare fella though, be warned. Although, I imagine daddy knows all about him. Take care Charlie, must dash, I'm late for tea at the Ritz. TTFN."

Charlie smiled to herself. "Take care Simon, and thanks, you've helped me out with this. I'm sure you can imagine. Love to Sebastian."

Simon could imagine, all too well.

43

Wednesday Afternoon
The Bull

Julia was ready for a drink herself, the lunchtime rush had been manic and the thought of Nick going out that evening with Rak, daunted her. "Nick, gorgeous, darling man."

Nick looked over the bar towards his wife. "Yes sugarplum, what do want?"

Julia made her way round to her husband. "Would you and Rak mind staying here tonight? I know Adam is helping out but I need you too. I promise, if it's not too busy, I won't disturb you."

Nick could see his wife was serious. "Yeah. ok

then, I'll text him. At least no one has to drive then either."

Julia kissed him, just a peck at first, then more. "Whoa, there's punters in Julia, later, eh?"

Julia gave him a naughty smile.

The bar door opened and in walked Gary Tyler, the landlord of *The Oak*. Aged around sixty-five and showing it, with a beer belly and scruffy jeans. "Afternoon Nick, how's things going with you?

Nick couldn't deny he was intrigued. "Afternoon Gary, what you having?"

Gary was eyeing up the selection *The Bull* offered. "Err… just a half, no make it a pint of bitter please, Nick, have one yourself too."

Nick was desperate to find out the reason for Gary's visit so took him up on his offer "Cheers mate, I'll have a pint of lager if you don't mind." Gary nodded his head. The two men sat at the bar.

"What can I do for you Gary? Everything all right?"

Gary had an excited look on his face. "Well, the thing is mate, I know you've got this fundraiser on Saturday, I was wondering how you feel about our two pubs working together? The cause is close to my heart too, my brother had MND and I'd like to get involved."

This was not what Nick had expected, him and Gary rarely spoke to each other, never mind worked together, however he could see it meant a lot to him.

"Erm… yeah, ok mate, don't see why not. I usually donate the days takings, which are substantial as we have the beer tent on the green, and then me and Rak match the total amount raised between us. If you wanna double up or something we can. Rak was talking about a classic car display, near Fox Lane, so do you wanna put a beer tent there? I'll help you."

Gary had a smile so wide, even Nick was shocked. "Yeah. Yeah, let's do it. And you'll help me?"

Nick nodded his head. "Yes mate, of course I will. Can I ask you something? Is *The Oak* your first pub?"

Gary and his wife Sheila had been running *The Oak* for around eleven months, taking over the lease just after the fundraiser of the previous year. "Yes mate, and to be honest I don't know what we were thinking. I thought it would be easy, serve drinks, be friendly and that's it, but as you know it's not that simple."

Nick had to agree, even being raised in the pub trade, he still found it challenging. Speaking with Gary, he was reminded of his own father and how his mum had struggled to help him run *The Bull*, having never run a pub previously.

"There's no magic formula mate, I can tell ya that. My old man struggled to run this place and now, touch wood, it's doing all right. Have you tried offers?" Nick knew if Julia heard him, he would be in trouble, assisting the competition, but he felt sorry for Gary.

"We thought about it but didn't know where to start, we don't offer food, not like you. It can be a nightmare."

Nick knew he had to be careful, not wanting to lose business to *The Oak*. "Well, tell you what, let's see how Saturday goes, eh? We might be able to work together on other projects."

Gary was happy with this and Nick thought that maybe his fellow publican did really want to make an effort but didn't know where to start. They both sat, finishing their pints and chatting about the price of beer from the brewery.

44

Banerjee Engineering

Tilly had arrived with what could only be described as a picnic, sandwiches, biscuits, crisps, cheesy bites and sausage rolls. "I thought you might be hungry, you never did stop for lunch." She smiled at Rak, who was quite taken aback by the vast amount of food Tilly was placing on the office table.

"Well, actually I do eat lunch these days thanks Tilly, however, we've got Carl Potter visiting so this little spread will not go to waste." He was laughing, remembering why Tilly was the best he had ever had.

"Oh really, Carl Potter? Not seen him in ages, how is he?" Rak held her shoulder "Actually, he's quite pissed off with me, reckons I'm never here and that's the reason his order was so dramatically wrong, need you Tills, to sweet talk him."

Tilly smiled "Leave him to me, I always did have him in the palm of my hand." She laughed and lightly tapped Rak on the arm.

Carl arrived just after 2:00pm, he made a point of walking through the workshop before making his way to the office. He approached Greg first. "Greg, sorry mate for yesterday. I was out of order giving you grief. You're not paid to listen to problems that should go directly to the gaffer. I hope we're all right?"

Greg was quite shocked by this admission and apology. "No worries, Carl, it's fine. Now we've got Tilly back I'm sure things will improve, for all of us." The two men shook hands and Carl made his way to the office, carrying a very large bouquet of flowers.

"Tilly, my love, my darlin', this place has fell to pieces without you. Rak don't know what he's doing. Welcome back, sweetheart." He handed her the bouquet.

"Bloody hell, Carl, there really was no need. Thanks darlin', they're lovely. Would you like a drink? We've laid some food on for ya too."

Carl smiled, looking deep into Tilly's eyes. "Oh, that would be great, Tilly, has he still got that expensive whiskey?" Carl was winding her up.

"As you're driving it's tea or coffee, I'm afraid, wouldn't want any unnecessary mishaps, would we?" Tilly smiled straight at him.

"No, I heard the man himself had one of them last week. News travels fast round here." Tilly immediately thought Slim, as lovely as he was, did love to gossip.

Once Carl was comfortably seated with a coffee and a plate of food, Rak began his sales pitch. "You know we can deliver Carl, and apart from that, look at the history your old man and mine have. We can't dismiss that surely?" When it suited, Rak would mention his father, if it was to his advantage.

"Yeah, I know mate. I spoke with my dad before coming over here, I was warned not to upset decades of respect and trust. But I can't have any more fuck ups, Rak, you know that." Rak did know, and he knew if he was Carl, he wouldn't tolerate it.

"From now on I can promise you the best deal, no more problems and Tilly will be your go-to person for anything and everything. I know I'm not always available, the problem with grown-up kids, they're worse than toddlers. Any problems or concerns, Tilly is on hand to assist you. How does that sound?" Rak had already discussed this with Tilly, and it had been decided this was the best way to win over Carl.

"You've got a deal mate, but you are in last chance saloon, y'know what I mean?"

Rak extended his hand and the two men shook

on their agreement. "You comin' over on Saturday? It's our annual fundraiser."

Carl was laughing. "Yes, of course mate. Wouldn't dream of missing it".

45

Wednesday Evening
The Bull

Rak had arrived just after 6:30pm, having gotten caught up in the office. "Hiya gorgeous, can I have a glass of Merlot, please? Really fancy a red wine."

Julia was happy to see Rak, she was always happy to see Rak. "Oh, course you can darlin', he won't be long, he's getting ready for your date night." She was smirking.

"What can I say Julia? They're queuing up," Rak laughed.

"Hey, what do think about karaoke in here on Friday night? Get the weekend off to a bang." Julia winked at him.

Rak was not a huge fan of karaoke but knew Julia enjoyed it and it would be a draw to the pub. "Don't see why not, might be a laugh. Don't expect me to sing though," he laughed.

Rak took at a seat at a table near the snug and enjoyed his first drink of the evening, he was ready for it. Carl Potter had been hard work, he was thankful for Tilly. She seemed to have placated him. Rak was aware he had not been fully engaged in the business recently, but he couldn't neglect Charlie. He needed her. Just as she crossed his mind, his phone pinged.

> 'Hey baby, I know you're out tonight, Rose & Crown, but I spoke with Simon and I'm free to approach Geeta. Happy days, eh? Tomorrow would be great, around 3pm, we can sort everything out. Love you xxxxx'

Rak could feel the warmth spreading across his face, and elsewhere.

> 'Hey hun, change of plan. We're in The Bull, pop in if you can. Thanks for helping Geeta, I'll tell her to be there, 3pm tomorrow. I really appreciate it, I'll show you how much later… xxxx'

The memory of the previous night overcame him and he began to feel excited. An overwhelming feeling of happiness and desire overtook him. Just then, Nick appeared, a bottle of red and another glass in hand. "All right mate, how's it going? You look flustered." Nick was looking straight at his friend.

"Oh, I'm great mate, couldn't be better. God, I can't explain how happy I am right now."

Nick smiled and poured himself and his friend some wine. "That's great to hear mate, it really is." Nick was relieved Rak was happy.

They discussed the fundraiser—the logistics. Rak had agreed with Slim that the local classic car club would come along to show their pride and joys, Nick explained how Gary had been to see him and how they had agreed to work together. They both discussed the karaoke and concluded that was wholly Julia's idea, however they were both happy to go along with it. They discussed the catering arrangements, a BBQ being the usual offering. The weather forecast was fantastic, both men were extremely excited.

Rak knew he had to tell his friend what had happened with Amira, however he was reluctant. "You know I went to see Amira yesterday?"

Nick nodded, his mouth full of nuts.

"Well, we nearly, you know."

Nick didn't need to hear this. "What? For fuck's sake mate, how many do you need? I can't cope with one."

Rak knew he had to embellish "It was her, she started kissing me, out of nowhere. Then we were on the bed, thank God I saw sense mate, admittedly, I nearly didn't. I thought about Charlie and stopped. The thing is, we both confessed we still love each other, why didn't she say before, for fuck's sake, I would've left Lisa in the blink of an eye. But I can't hurt Charlie."

Nick was quite shocked by this latest revelation. "You still love Amira? Since when?"

Rak took a gulp of wine. "Since forever, mate; since forever. Ms François was a mistake, a big one. She fooled me and I fell for it, stupid old fool, what do they say? 'no fool like an old fool?' I was a game to her mate and then she lost interest."

Nick felt sympathy for his friend. "So how did you two leave it?"

Rak had some more wine. "We agreed to be friends, properly this time, not just for the kids. I didn't know how much I'd hurt her, I really didn't. She said if I'd been shagging anyone else, she wouldn't have divorced me. It was more about the shame of everyone knowing."

Nick was shocked by this, having had a heart to heart with Amira, without telling Rak, after the big revelation, where she had not indicated any forgiveness for Rak. "Well what's done is done mate. The question is now, is Charlie any better than Ms François? Or do you want Amira back?"

Nick knew Amira would give Rak another chance, no questions asked. "I don't know mate,

I love Charlie and I hope she loves me too. I can't just dump her for Amira, it's not fair and Amira has had years to tell me how she feels, why pick now? Because I'm happy?"

Nick was concerned for his friend, always preferring Amira to any of Rak's other conquests. "I must admit mate, I'm concerned Charlie will hurt ya, she's married too remember. Just be sure before closing a door for good."

Rak had heard his friend. "I know mate, don't worry, I'm not as reckless this time."

The door to the bar opened, in walked in Charlie. And Brad. He had insisted on joining his wife in a trip to the pub, having not spent much time together recently. Rak could not suppress his disdain, even Nick picked up on it. "You see what I mean, you're not going to be free of him, ever. I remember when I met Julia, it really pissed me off that Joe was still around and that was just for the kids. Can you really do this mate?"

Rak was deep in thought. "I don't know mate, but I've gotta try. I don't want Lisa and I don't want to be alone. If me and Amira get back together, she will always have the Jenna thing to hold against me. I need Charlie."

Nick could sense his friend was becoming maudlin. "Well at least you learnt some French from Ms François, always an upside."

Rak smiled and retorted rather too loudly. "She

definitely passed her oral examination," and both men burst into fits of laughter.

Charlie heard this and immediately wanted to know what Rak and Nick were discussing. She wondered if he was filling his friend in on the details of the night before. Charlie felt jealousy, betrayal and a very definite feeling of not wanting to be there. She made a mental note to discuss this later with Rak.

"What you having, babe?" Brad was waiting for an answer.

"What? Oh, a red wine please. I'll find a table" Charlie picked the table immediately adjacent to Rak and Nick, she wanted to hear their conversation, be involved.

Brad appeared with the drinks. "So, I was thinking, why don't we go home early tonight, y'know have some us time?"

Charlie could not think of anything worse. "I'm not sure babe, I'm really tired. The salon has been manic recently and I'm still tired from being at Cassie's last night. It was late when we got to sleep." Charlie hoped this would close the subject.

"But it's been ages, months, Char. You must feel it too." Charlie felt her gaze move towards Rak, she wanted Rak. Even though she was not totally sure of the context of his conversation with Nick, she still wanted him. She wanted to feel his hands on her body, his tongue in intimate places, his cock inside her. She noticed Brad was speaking. "I said, Char, you must feel it too. When was the last time? It must be months ago."

Before she could speak Rak interjected. "Hey, how's it going? We're just discussing the final plans for Saturday, are you coming along?" His eyes were burning into Charlie's, she felt a weakness in the pit of her stomach.

"Yes, wouldn't miss it for the world. I'm closing the salon for the day. Looking forward to it."

Rak smiled at her. "Be great to see you there, enjoy your evening." She was shocked, was that it? Was that all he had to say?

She turned her attention back to Brad when her mobile pinged.

'Meet me outside. 5 mins. Can't take this anymore xxxx'

She smiled over at Rak as an acknowledgement.

Charlie made an excuse to check her appointment book at the salon and left Brad chatting with Nick. She quickly ran over to the salon and switched the lights on. Rak was there two minutes later. "I can't stand seeing him with you hun, I want to kill him."

She knew he was serious "Come here baby, kiss me now." They fell into a moment of passion, kissing, touching, undressing, unbuttoning. "Ahh, Rak, you know we can't. Not here." Rak didn't stop, kissing her more passionately now, kissing her neck "Rak, we can't. Someone will see." She was giggling now. Charlie was wet and she felt he was hard. She pulled him into the back room, undoing his jeans as they went.

As her hand lightly grazed his cock, he gave out a moan. "Ah, honey, yes, yes. I need you now." His hand reached to touch her, in-between her knickers and her smooth, soft skin. He could feel how wet she was, he wanted her now. He slid a finger into her pussy and began to play.

"Rak, Rak, yes. We shouldn't you know."

Rak kissed her neck "Do you want me to stop?"

She looked deep into his brown eyes. "No, don't stop. Fuck me, baby." He pulled her trousers and knickers away, then lifted her onto the tumble dryer. He kissed her mouth as he slid his cock into her hot, wet pussy; slowly to begin, then with more urgency, faster, harder, deeper. Charlie knew she was going to come. "Rak, oh my god, Rak! Yes, oh yes!"

His hands were on the small of her back, pushing her towards his thrusts. Her hands were on his bottom, pushing him further inside her. "Charlie, honey, you feel so fucking good. I wanna come." Rak continued to thrust, hard, deep, he needed her to come, he needed to come.

"Rak, oh my god, yes! I'm coming baby. Oh, yesssssssss! Yesssssss!"

He could wait no longer, they both came together. They both held each other, looking into each other's eyes. They both knew they needed each other.

They both held each other for what felt like hours, in reality it was only a few moments. "Rak, I heard you laughing with Nick about someone passing their oral. What were you talking about?"

Rak looked away, looked past her. "Not you baby, not you. Someone I used to know. I was an idiot when I was with Amira, I shagged our kid's French teacher. We were talking about her, just having a laugh like men do. Nothing for you to worry about" Charlie was shocked.

"You fucked your kid's teacher? Rak, what the fuck were you thinking?"

Rak did not want this conversation now. "Not now, hun; not now, hey? I'll explain everything next time we're at Pam's but not here, please, baby."

Acknowledging he did not want to have this conversation now. "Ok, not now. But I want to know Rak. No secrets remember?"

He responded with a kiss.

They both made their way back to *The Bull*, Charlie first, then Rak. Brad was waiting for her. "Where have you been? It can't take that long to check an appointment."

Charlie thought quickly. "No, sorry. My phone rang, it was Simon Freer, he's getting married. It was good to catch up with him actually. Shall we have another drink?" Charlie was already on her feet and walking towards the bar, walking towards Rak.

"When can you get away again? I need you baby," he whispered.

"I don't know, I'm meeting your daughter tomorrow afternoon, why don't you come along? Rak briefly touched her hand.

"Okay, I'll see you then, but when can we see each other properly, be alone?" His eyes were searching hers.

"After Geeta has left, we can go to Pam's. I want you all to myself baby."

Rak smiled "Definitely, can't wait."

Just then Adam appeared at the bar. "What can I get you?"

Rak smiled. "Same again please, all round".

46

Thursday

Heirs & Graces

Julia could not wait to get her hair done. The colour was looking faded, and it needed a cut. Charlie was looking forward to seeing Julia, it had been so long since they had chatted without Julia having the pressure of the bar

"What we going for then? The same or a change?" asked Charlie.

Julia had been toying with the idea of a change for some time "How about a change? Could you cut it differently, so it's got a few more layers in it? And I wouldn't mind going a couple of shades darker if you can please Charlie."

Charlie took the colour shade chart and the two women decided on a shade to suit Julia. As she was applying the colour, Charlie was thinking about Rak, the night before. About how special he made her feel, how much she wanted to be with him all the time.

"I know, y'know. It's all right, you can talk to me about him."

Charlie was slightly caught off guard. "Oh, I didn't; I mean, I wasn't sure if you did. Sorry, what I mean is, I didn't know if you knew. But of course, it's obvious Nick should tell you. Sorry, Julia."

Julia smiled. "No, it's ok love, it's not the sort of thing you want getting out. And it won't; not from me. Do you love him, Charlie?"

Charlie looked away, out of the window, over towards Rak's house. "Yes; yes, I do, Julia. Very much so. It's not easy—all these secrets. I just hope one day we can stop hiding how we feel and openly be together."

Julia felt sorry for Charlie. "I'm sure you will love. He's got it bad for you, y'know. I've not seen him like this before, certainly not with Lisa. He was prepared to fall out with Nick over you, you mean a lot to him."

Charlie smiled at Julia. "I'm pleased he didn't, and I wouldn't have let him anyway. Can you imagine if those two weren't speaking? I think Rak's life would be over." both women laughed.

After Julia had left, very happy with her new look, Geeta arrived. She wasn't what Charlie had imagined, somehow Charlie imagined a young woman that would look like Rak, Geeta was nothing like Rak, more the image of her mother and this slightly unsettled Charlie. She had not known how beautiful Amira was and the thought of Rak still having contact with her unnerved her.

"Hi, you must be Charlie. My dad said he would be here, but I don't suppose he is—probably stuck at the office. I'm Geeta by the way."

Charlie was finding this awkward, she felt unsure around Geeta, someone who had known Rak her entire life. "Yeah, I'm Charlie, pleased to meet you. Your dad shouldn't be long. Simon speaks very highly of you, he said you'd be an asset to me. Would you like a coffee while we wait for Rak?" Geeta nodded and took a seat on the sofa; she was eyeing up the salon, deciding if it was for her or not.

Just as the kettle boiled Rak rushed in. "I'm sorry ladies, got caught on a call. How are we getting on? Geeta, are you ok?"

Geeta immediately lit up, the sight of her father lifting her spirits. "At last, Dad; thought you had forgotten. I'm good thanks, how are things with you?"

Rak sat beside his daughter "I'm very well, thank you, darling; very well. Now listen, I would really like you to consider what Charlie is offering you.

And also consider moving in with me for a bit, ok?" the latter was news to Charlie, she thought it was a good job she was in the back as her face would've given her away.

"Yeah, Dad, Mum said. Look, I know you two don't like Sanj but you don't know him."

Rak looked straight at his daughter. "No. No, I don't, and I don't want to, either. Amit said what a loser he is too. Are we all wrong?"

Charlie knew she needed to intervene. "Right, Geeta, what would you describe as your strengths in the salon?"

Geeta was grateful for the subject change, Rak was not, and his face told her so

"Well, I love cutting and colouring, I did my Colour Expert course last month and passed. I really enjoyed it too. I would love more responsibility, Charlie; that's something Simon is slow to give me and I feel frustrated by it."

Charlie smiled "I don't know if you're aware, but I used to work with Simon. I had to beg for the opportunity to manage a salon. He is hard work. However, he speaks very highly of your talent. Would you consider working with me? —note: with me, not for me. I believe you have a decent client list and I feel I could offer you more of a managerial role."

Geeta smiled wide, one that reached her eyes. "Yes. Yes, I would. I would be very happy to take the opportunity."

Charlie was hoping this would be her answer "Good, because I've had an idea. Would you like to work here on a self-employed basis? So, what I mean is, we split whatever you take 70/30 in your favour for your own clients and if I ask for help with mine, we split it 50/50. I will expect you to bring your own clients to the salon and put the hours in when needed, although, I will offer flexibility and also work to secure future business, what do you say?"

Geeta looked at Rak. "It sounds very favourable Geeta; I would say yes if I were you. Charlie is a very good friend to me and you won't find anybody fairer."

Rak winked at Charlie, she wanted to kiss him there and then. She had to control herself and he knew it.

"Yes, I would be very interested, thank you. I would need to check with Simon when I can finish working...."

Charlie put her hand up to stop Geeta. "No need, I've texted Simon and he agreed that if you would like to work here, you can collect your kit and he will give you your client list, you can start here next week. How does that sound?"

Geeta was almost jumping for joy. "Yeah, that's wicked! Thanks Charlie. I owe you one."

Charlie laughed. "You don't owe me anything, just work hard," and she rolled her eyes.

They decided they would all have a drink in *The Bull* to celebrate, Charlie shut up shop early.

47

Thursday Evening
The Bull

What had begun as a celebratory drink in aid of Charlie and Geeta's new arrangement had now grown into a quite a party. Tilly and Mark had popped in—Tilly had not seen Geeta for almost ten years and was thrilled to catch up with this young woman, aged nearly 25, who she remembered as being a teenage girl.

Then Amit had texted his dad:

'Hey old man, I've just been to see a client in Catchford, you got time for a beer?'

Rak had laughed to himself, recalling when he was his son's age and referred to his own father as the old man.

'Less of the old man!! Yeah, actually, your sister is here too. We're in The Bull, your Uncle Nick's pub. Pop over xx'

Charlie could not quite comprehend she was meeting both of Rak's children now, at the same time. She knew it was silly, but she really hoped they liked her.

When Amit walked into the pub she knew immediately who he was. He was a younger version of Rak, tall, broad shouldered, thick, dark, hair, as his father's would have been once, and he was very good looking.

"Dad, how you going? Been a while since I've been in here."

Rak hugged Amit. "I'm good, Son. Yeah, everything's great. Your sister just got a new job, that's excellent isn't it? What's everyone having? On me, I'm so proud of my kids today."

Rak's face was beaming with pride and Charlie felt very emotional towards him. "I'll give you a hand, hang on." She got to her feet and they approached the bar together.

"Thank you, hun, I know she'll work hard, I'll make sure of it," and he winked at her.

"I know she will too. I would do anything for

you, Rak, you know that." She was desperate to touch him. "Can you get away tonight? I want to see you."

Rak looked over at the table, with both his children sitting there, teasing each other like five-year-old kids, he had missed this for so long. "I'm not sure, see how the evening pans out, eh? I've not seen both of them in the same room for ages, I would really like to see my kids, Charlie." He saw her face change. "You will be part of their lives too someday, if everything works out. Get to know them, I know you'll get to know Geeta but give Amit a chance too." Rak was staring deeply into her eyes.

"Come on Dad; what you doing? Brewing it yourself?" Amit shouted over, laughing.

"Ok Son. Hang on would ya? I'm on my way."

Julia approached the bar and Rak ordered the drinks, including a couple for Julia and Nick. "Bloody hell, Rak, don't they grow up fast? Don't seem five minutes ago they were at school and now look, Amit, suited up smart and Geeta, starting a new adventure."

Rak smiled. "Makes me feel old, Julia, to be honest. Where do the years go, eh? At least I'm not a grandad yet." They both laughed, "Not that I know of anyway, y'know what I mean?"

They returned to the table where Tilly was asking Amit about his work. "So do you meet actual criminals then?"

Amit looked at her, "Yeah, I do. Some of them have just had bad luck, but others, for fuck's sake, you wouldn't wanna get on the wrong side of 'em"

Rak looked over, "Amit! Language."

Tilly laughed. "Rak, get a grip. Used to hear worse from you at his age. He's, what are you now Amit? Twenty something?"

Amit laughed. "Yeah, twenty-two. Don't worry, the old man can't take the pace."

Rak had to laugh.

Tilly was right, he had always used bad language himself; just something about hearing his kids swear made him realise they're not kids anymore. Rak had the realisation that he had missed the most important years of his children growing up. That Amira had had to deal with the tantrums and the tempers but that she had also had the good times over the years, the years he would never get. "I'm really enjoying us all being together. We should do this more regular." He looked at both Geeta and Amit, love in his eyes and hope.

"Yeah, that would be fab, Dad. Maybe if Amit could meet us in here once or twice a month or something. I'm loving us being together again." Geeta had a bright smile on her face and Rak secretly hoped this would help her see Sanj for what he was.

"Sounds good to me sis, especially if the old man's buying, eh?" both Geeta and Amit started laughing like kids at their father's expense.

"Yeah, ok. So, I have to buy time with my kids, fair enough." Rak was laughing now, happy to see they were enjoying themselves.

Charlie was enjoying herself, and she was enjoying seeing Rak happy, more. She had not seen this side of him before and she liked it.

Mark noticed Charlie watching Rak. "Magic innit? Seeing him with his kids. I can't believe how they've grown. They're adults themselves now."

Tilly had heard her husband. "Yeah, it's great. Still, ours will be fully grown soon, perhaps we'll get some peace then, eh, Mark?"

Mark nodded and smiled a cheeky smile at his wife.

The party carried on until nearly 22:00. Rak invited both Geeta and Amit to stay with him, so they didn't have to drive and could stay in the pub longer, with him. Lisa was still in London, so it made sense. They had both agreed and it was settled. Charlie knew she would not get Rak to herself tonight, but she also understood if she gave him time now, he would be thankful later.

When they left *The Bull*, Rak gave Amit his house keys. "Go and let yourselves in, I'm going to walk Charlie home. I won't be long. Try not to wreck the place, please?"

Amit took his dad's house keys. "Can we order pizza? I'm starving."

Rak smiled. "Yeah, whatever. Just don't make

a mess, mate. Can you order me something too, please? I'm hungry."

Amit looked at his father. "Yeah, no worries. See you in a bit."

As they walked towards Charlie's house Rak took her hand. "Stop a minute hun, I want to say something."

Charlie looked at him, wanting him.

"Thank you for the making the effort tonight. I know you wanted to go to Pam's but I've not seen them together in ages. I promise you, over the weekend I will make it up to you. Can you get away after the fundraiser on Saturday? We could make a night of it."

Charlie really wanted to say 'yes', but was mindful of Brad "I don't know. It depends on Brad and what mood he's in, baby. I don't know where I can say I am. Just lately he's been pressuring me, y'know what I mean? Maybe we could escape for an hour or two though?" Charlie smiled, trying to reassure Rak.

"What do you mean, putting pressure on you? For sex?"

She knew he would go mad, "A bit, yes, but nothing I can't handle. I promise. Saturday sounds great, we'll make it happen." She looked around quickly, no one around, she kissed him. On the mouth, slowly and deliberately.

"Stop, hun, someone will see. Are you busy tomorrow? Meet me at lunch."

Charlie quickly scanned her appointment book in her head. "No. I can do half one—meet you at Pam's? Now go; go and eat your pizza."

Rak kissed her quickly. "Yes, half one works for me, see you there. I love you hun."

Charlie embraced him, she could smell his after-shave, it turned her on. "I love you too. See you tomorrow." And with that they walked to their own houses.

48

Friday Morning
The Bull

Julia was awake early. She was so excited about the karaoke that evening, she wanted to begin the preparations now. She also had a plan to help Charlie and Rak have some fun, without raising suspicion.

Nick awoke to find he was alone, not something he was familiar with as Julia usually needed her morning cup of tea in bed before getting up. He went downstairs to look for her, he didn't need to look too hard. The tones of Julia singing Adele came from the bar.

"What are you doing up this early? Are you all right?"

Julia continued her version of 'Rolling in the Deep', and grabbed her husband, trying to encourage him to dance with her.

"Get off, it's too early." He said playfully. "You'll be knackered by tonight then you won't enjoy it."

Julia laughed. "Guess what? I've got a plan."

Nick looked over, thinking he would prefer to eat his breakfast before being convinced to partake in a 'Julia plan'. He continued to just look at her.

"Well, I thought we could have a duet round right, where the lucky couple of singers are drawn from a hat, by you. The thing is, the only names in the hat will be Charlie and Rak, what do you reckon?" Julia was animated with excitement.

"Do you think that's wise? Really?" Nick was not convinced.

"Yeah, of course. If you don't know they're together, which nobody does, who would find it odd? And it'll give them a chance to fool around together."

Nick knew better that to argue, Julia's mind was made up. "Yeah, ok. Whatever you wanna do, but if it goes wrong, don't come crying to me."

Julia smiled cheekily. "Oh yeah, I don't want you telling Rak either, promise?"

Nick was walking towards the kitchen now, he just waved his hand to her, in recognition he could not win this one.

270

After having a cup of tea and a round of toast together and watching the news headlines, Julia went to sit on Nick's knee. "Are you looking forward to tonight?"

Nick kissed her "Yes. Yes I am but don't push things too far Julia, y'know what I mean."

Julia kissed him full on the mouth. "I'll be good, promise. Now, we've got time to be bad, upstairs" she took his hand and led him back to bed.

49

Heirs & Graces

Charlie was fully booked that morning; having transferred her Saturday regulars to today so she could close for the fundraiser—she was really looking forward to it.

Kate was the client in the chair, having booked for a cut and blow dry. "So, Charlie, are you keeping busy?" she enquired.

"Oh, yeah, it's very busy at the moment Kate— in actual fact, I've got a new stylist starting next week." Charlie knew Kate would appreciate this bit of news

"Oh, really. Hmmm, that is interesting and where are they from?"

Charlie saw her client's interest pique "Well actually, it's Rak's daughter, Geeta. She has worked for my former old boss, and he assures me she is very competent, talented even." Charlie was half hoping to lose Kate to Geeta.

"Oh, I see. Rak's daughter you say? He must be very proud of her in that case."

Charlie was loving this too much. "Yes, he is. She's a very well-presented young woman, I'm sure she'll do very well."

Kate's mind was now working overtime, trying to decide which bits of information she needed to extract from Charlie.

"How old is Geeta? Is she very young?"
Charlie played simple for moment, to see Kate's anguish at the possibility of learning nothing further. "Err, oh, now you're asking Kate. Well, Amit, Rak's son, is twenty-two and Geeta's a couple of years older so, twenty-four." She was daring Kate to ask more.

"Ohh, right. She must be up on all the trends then. They must have been young when Rak left his first wife."

'*Bingo!*' Charlie thought to herself. "I don't know, it's quite personal, isn't it?" and with that, she switched on the hairdryer.

The phone was ringing. "Excuse me Kate, I just need to get that." Charlie ran over to the reception desk, "Good morning, Heirs and Graces, how may I help you? Oh, no. That's awful, no, don't worry Mrs Weston, I'll move it to next week. I hope you're feeling better soon. Take care, bye now." Charlie immediately picked up her mobile.

'Hey baby, good news. I'm free all afternoon, client cancelled. See you later, can't wait much longer xxxxxxxx'

Charlie walked back to Kate with a spring in her step, knowing they would not have to rush their lunch date. The smile on her face showed her excitement.

"Not a cancellation love? Really some people have no sense of loyalty. You should charge a fee y'know."

If only Kate knew; if only. Charlie quietly giggled to herself.

50

Friday Morning

Banerjee Engineering

"Right Tilly, I'm going to out for a while this afternoon, will you be all right?"

Tilly looked at him as if he had just asked if he could run off with Mark. "Oh, let me think, can I manage here on my own? Hmmm, tricky that. Of course I can. Anyway, I'm not alone am I? I've got Rollo to keep me company."

Rak had agreed that Tilly could bring Rollo into the office as he got lonesome without her at home. The truth was that Rak enjoyed the dog being in the office, he was good company. "Honestly Rollo, your mummy is very rude." He was fussing him now "Do you know that? Do you? Eh? Good boy." Rak was fussing Rollo further when his mobile pinged with a text

'Hey baby, good news. I'm free all afternoon, client cancelled. See you later, can't wait much longer xxxxxxxx.'

Rak could not stop the huge smile spreading across his face, even Tilly noticed "Good news? You look pleased."

Rak nodded his head. "Very good news, Tills, but it does mean I may be out longer. I tell y'what, close at 3:30 today. I know we're busy but it's Friday. I'll let Greg know as well. Are you going to the karaoke tonight?"

Tilly was laughing. "Only to watch, you'll not get me singing."

Rak laughed too. "Yeah, we'll see after a couple of drinks, eh? I've seen you and Julia before, remember?"

Rak then replied to Charlie's text.

'Fantastic news hun. Don't have lunch, let me look after you. I'm really looking forward to seeing you, having you all to myself. Love you xxxxxxx'

Rak only stayed another hour and then headed over to the supermarket, he needed to get some supplies.

51

Pam's Cottage

Rak arrived at Pam's around 12:30. He wanted to prepare their lunch before Charlie arrived. He had gone slightly over the top in the supermarket, buying tiger prawns, expensive champagne and an extravagant dessert as well as the ingredients for the main course.

Rak was just preparing the tiger prawns when his mobile rang, he quickly washed his hands and took the call. It was Lisa. "Hello, how are you? Are you having a good time in London?" He was aware he sounded maybe too happy for Lisa's liking.

"I'm fine thank you. I just thought I'd let you know, I've been invited to stay down here for a couple of weeks. Belinda's on her own and asked me to stay. How are you now? Did you get your car sorted?"

Rak rolled his eyes, the concern for his car was obviously uppermost in her mind "Yeah, I'm good thanks, the kids were here last night, Geeta's got a job with Charlie. Great news, isn't it? I've got a new car, from Slim, no need to worry. Enjoy yourself, love to Belinda." Rak was keen to end the call, he wanted to get on with his preparations

"Thanks, I'm pleased you're sorted out. What's happening with us, Rak?"

He really did not need this. "Not now hey? Wait 'til your back and we'll talk properly. I'm at work y'know? Not the right time. Now go on, enjoy yourself." He heard Lisa sigh in defeat.

"Ok, if that's what you want, don't say I didn't try," and with that she hung up.

Rak had put the vinyl record player on, Pam used to love playing her records, describing it as an escape. He found an album by The Kinks, and put it on. He was enjoying himself, lovingly preparing a meal for the woman he loved and dancing around the kitchen. He hadn't realised Charlie had let herself in and was watching him from the kitchen door.

"Wow, you're some mover," she laughed.

"For fuck's sake, Charlie; you made me jump. Come here and kiss me, help me get over the shock." He grabbed her and pulled her close to him, mouths locked together, both dancing now to 'Lola'.

She was very impressed by the spectacular lunch Rak had made for them, they started with the prawns, peeling them with their fingers, feeding each other. Then for the main course they enjoyed paella. "I promised you I'd make this for you one day, do you remember?" He took her hand and slowly caressed it.

"Yeah, I do remember. It's gorgeous, Rak; where did you learn to make this?"

Rak took a sip of wine. "Amira and I took the kids away to Spain, years and years ago. One of these cheap all-inclusive hotels. The food was horrendous, so we ate out most of the holiday. Anyway, we hired a car one day and went up into the hills, found this restaurant, traditional, y'know?" Charlie nodded as Rak took another sip of wine. "Well, we had this paella dish, we both loved it. So much so, we went back there every day for the rest of the holiday, I extended the car hire and we explored everywhere. Then on the final day, we explained we were heading home and how much we had enjoyed the food, especially the paella. The lovely old lady offered to show me how she made it. I'm telling you hun, she knew her stuff. I don't speak much Spanish and she didn't speak much English, but I jotted down everything she was doing."

Charlie looked amazed. "Really? That sounds fabulous baby."

"Yeah. Well, I tried it when we got home, and it tasted nearly as good as hers had. I kept making it, even the kids loved it in the end. It became my, what do they say? signature dish." Rak was smiling, and Charlie felt so proud of him, she also felt immensely happy.

They finished the paella and the bread. Rak was happy Charlie had enjoyed it. He wanted to make her feel special. "I do have a dessert, but would you like to save that for later?" they were both holding hands, gazing into each other's eyes.

"Yes, later. I'm so content at the moment. Would you like to go to bed?"

Rak kissed her. "Yeah, of course I would, hun. Wait here, I've got a surprise for you."

Charlie was shocked. "Another surprise, what, really?"

He got up and gestured for her to stay seated at the table. "Close your eyes."

Rak went into the bedroom to put the finishing touches to his surprise treat for Charlie. "You can come in now honey."

She couldn't believe the sight that greeted her; flowers everywhere, champagne on ice with two glasses and Norah Jones playing softly in the background on the CD player.

"Is it all right?"

Charlie was amazed. "No, it's not all right," she was smiling. Rak was confused. "It's fabulous, Rak; truly fabulous. Thank you, baby."

They fell into each other's arms, kissing so passionately, they couldn't stop. Rak was feeling her body, her breasts, her bottom, her waist. He was holding her closer to him, needing her to be part of him. She had her hands in his hair, enjoying the sensation of running her fingers through it. Their tongues were playing games, licking and flicking each other's.

Charlie unbuttoned his shirt and slipped it off him, her hands feeling his chest, moving down towards his stomach.

Rak unzipped her skirt, letting it fall to the floor. His hands were lifting off her top, over her head. He started to remove her tights, then sat her on the bed while he took them off, casting them aside.

Charlie undid his belt, slowly, knowing he was desperate for her to touch him. She then unbuttoned his jeans and slowly pulled them away from him—his boxers were straining from the throbbing of his cock.

Rak undid her bra, touching her breasts, lightly fondling them, kissing them. Charlie placed her hand inside his boxers, feeling the silky smoothness of his hard cock. "Ohh, Charlie. Yes, yes!"

Her eyes met his as she pulled his boxers off, his

cock hard and begging to be touched.

Rak slowly took her knickers off, sliding them away from her with his fingers. The anticipation of him touching her was overwhelming. Rak lay on the bed with her, both of them naked, kissing, touching, rolling in between the sheets. Rak looked her in the eyes, his eyes full of love and excitement. "What do you want me to do to you, honey?"

She guided his hand between her thighs, towards her wet pussy, and moved it slowly along her lips. "Ahhh, Rak! Rak, yes. Oh God, yes!" He slipped a finger inside her, slowly fingering her, exciting her.

Charlie felt his cock in her hands, she was softly, lightly teasing him. She felt his balls, then caressed the length of his shaft.

"Sexy, baby; that's good, so good. Oh God!" Rak whispered in her ear

Charlie could feel she was close. Rak touched her clit; massaging her slowly. Her pussy felt hot, so hot. "Rak, Rak, oh yeah, baby. Don't stop. Please!"

Rak knew she was coming, he felt it. "Can I slowly fuck you honey? Slowly and naughtily?" They were laying facing each other, on their sides, he slowly lifted her thigh and pulled her towards him. She guided his throbbing cock inside her, and they both began to move slowly, together. They were staring into each other's eyes, both getting lost in each other. He felt so good inside her she felt she would come undone again.

"Oh God baby, kiss me, kiss me now." Charlie wanted to feel his mouth on hers

They kissed passionately as they continued to slowly thrust together, so slowly it was magical. Rak moved deeper inside of her, deeper, but just as seductively slowly. "Honey, you feel so good. I love you Charlie, I love you so much."

Charlie held his bottom, pushing him further inside her. "I love you too, Rak. I'm coming baby! Oh God, yes!"

Rak continued slowly thrusting inside her until the pleasure was too much. "I'm coming honey, oh fuck, yes! Oh God, yes!" There were tears in his eyes.

They lay in bed all afternoon in each other's arms, enjoying the view of the garden whilst drinking champagne. They were both in heaven, nothing or no one else mattered at that moment in time. If there had been a war happening outside, they would not have known about it. They were so engaged in each other.

"Did you enjoy that honey?"

Charlie kissed his chest. "Yes, you know I did. Only you can make me feel like that Rak—only you."

Rak kissed her. "You're not too bad yourself, y'know?" he laughed.

They lay together, Charlie's head resting on Rak's chest, listening to his heart beating. As far as she was concerned, this was the best sound in the world.

"Thank you for being kind yesterday, not putting

too much pressure on me. I really enjoyed seeing my kids."

She looked up, into his eyes. "It must be difficult, not seeing them all the time. Hopefully, now Geeta is in the village, that will change"

"I hope so, Charlie. I know it was me that caused all the upset. Do you know, she wouldn't talk to me for over a year after her mother and I split up? It was so hard. I am so happy now to have them both in my life again."

Charlie could hear his voice was tinged with sadness. "Why did you split up from Amira? What happened baby? Tell me everything."

Up until now Rak had been vague around the reasons Amira had divorced him, he had mentioned there was a teacher involved but he hadn't given any details. He was deciding right now just how much he should disclose.

Rak poured some more champagne for both of them. "It was a long time ago baby, but I'll tell you. I met the kid's French teacher at a parent's evening, I'd gone alone as Amira wasn't well. Her name was Jenna Fallon. She made a play for me, Charlie, asking me about my business, making jokes, flirting, y'know." He paused for a sip of champagne but also to try and judge Charlie's reaction. "Anyway, we got on, parents' evenings are a tad repetitive, and it was good to have a laugh, but I thought no more about it. Then around a week later she rang the office, I was alone, Tilly had gone home, so I answered it. She asked if I wanted to take her out for a drink, I was flattered—y'know what I mean?"

Charlie nodded and caressed his chest.

"We went out for a drink—it was just a drink. I didn't consider anything else, I promise you. Amira and I had been arguing a bit, the kids were becoming teenagers, giving the attitude, especially Geeta. Amira thought I hid at work to avoid it; my defence was that I had to work to pay the bills. I suppose in all honesty, it was a bit of both. I was happy to let Amira play bad cop. We met for a drink, we got on really well, made each other laugh. At the end of the evening, she asked if she could see me again, I'd enjoyed myself so said, 'yeah, why not?' The next time she invited me to her place, I know, I should've said no but I didn't. I took a takeaway and we had a few drinks, it felt like an escape, just a friendly bit of fun. But then she kissed me, properly. Said I was exactly what she needed. She turned me on, Charlie, but I told her no, that I'm married. I left and went home."

Charlie looked in Rak's eyes, "so, what happened then? What happened next?"

Rak took another sip from his glass. "A couple of weeks later Amira and I had this blazing row, about other things. I was so pissed off with her I just stormed out the house. I should've gone to Nick's, had a few beers, but I went to Jenna's place. We shared a bottle of wine, she made me laugh, forget about my problems, about Amira, about the kids. We kissed but this time I didn't stop, we went to bed. She wanted me so much, more than Amira had done lately. I was weak and she knew it. She took the lead; she made it happen."

Charlie wanted to know more, she wanted to know everything. "So, did you have an affair with her?"

Rak looked ashamed. "Yes, we did. Believe me hun, I felt guilty afterwards, I went home and saw my wife and kids and felt so guilty. But then Jenna wouldn't leave me alone, she was addictive. It was mad. It was just sex, not like us, I promise you. Jenna hinted she wanted more, but I couldn't give it. Amira found out when she started treating Geeta and Amit differently at school—talking to them in a familiar way—like she was their friend more than teacher. She crossed boundaries. Amira went to the head teacher and complained that the kids felt awkward around her, she was intimidating them. They looked into it and Jenna was suspended pending an enquiry. She begged me to help her, to save her career. She promised it wouldn't happen again. I told Amira to drop it, said the kids were probably just playing up because they didn't like French. Amira didn't fall for it, she demanded answers. I had to confess. She kicked me out, told me that I'd shamed our kids."

Charlie could hear Rak's voice faltering. "It's ok baby, it's ok. You don't need to tell me anymore."

Rak kissed her "No, I must tell you everything. I went to Jenna, explained that to save her career, I had to tell Amira the truth. I said that she'd kicked me out and if I could stay with her. She let me in, fucked me one last time, then told me it wasn't gonna work. She actually said go back to your wife. Can you fucking believe that? Said it was only supposed to be a bit of fun, she didn't want a relationship, just a shag now and again. I was broken, Charlie. I believed this woman wanted me, but she just used me. I stayed with Nick for a while, but he had only just got with Julia and her two kids weren't that old, I didn't want to be in the way. So, I got a flat, lived alone. Saw Amit at weekends, Geeta wouldn't see me. I went on a few dates, nothing special. Then I met Lisa four years after Amira divorced me. She was a laugh; I needed a laugh. We got married a year later, then she soon stopped being a laugh. There, you know everything baby. Permission to hate me."

Charlie could feel Rak's pain, the pain of missing out on all of them years, of not being there every day to watch your kids grow up. She just needed to hold him, she held him so close, she didn't want to let go. "I don't hate you baby. I appreciate your honesty. What happened to Jenna?"

Rak sighed, "I don't know, the enquiry was halted as Amira didn't want the kids being made a laughingstock. Jenna moved to another school. I don't know any more than that. I do know she ruined my life." Charlie kissed his chest. "Do you see why last night was so important? Time with both my kids, it doesn't happen very often. I worry as well, hun; Amit seems to have numerous girlfriends, I hope that's not the example I set him."

Charlie did laugh now "Rak, baby, he's twenty-two and a good looking young man, he will have lots of girlfriends, don't worry about that."

Rak held her tighter, "and what about Geeta with this tosser she's seeing, did I make her think that's how men behave?"

Charlie shifted round to look him straight in the eyes. "I used to be the same, believe me, or ask Simon. I'll persuade her that Sanj isn't the best choice, leave it with me. And stop beating yourself up. Now, what's for dessert?"

Rak smiled. "Chocolate".

52

Friday Evening

The Bull

The atmosphere in *The Bull* was electric, Julia had prepared a buffet and the karaoke machine was set up and ready to go. There was quite a crowd already and it was only 7:30pm.

Charlie was sitting with Brad at a table with Tilly and Mark; Rak had told her he'd be there around 8:00pm. They hadn't left Pam's Cottage until 6:30pm, not wanting to tear themselves away from their bed.

Tilly was at the bar chatting with Julia. "Wow, what a great turn out. You must be happy it's this busy."

Julia was cheerful, "yeah, I am Tills. I'm glad I asked Adam and Anthea to help out too, get them some practice for next week."

Tilly was intrigued. "Oh, yeah? What's happening next week then?"

Julia couldn't contain herself. "Nick's taking me to Brussels for two nights, Tuesday to Thursday. It's been so long since we've been away. The kids can manage here, it's not too busy mid-week, usually."

Tilly knew her friend needed a break. "Fantastic news, Julia, I'm sure you'll enjoy it. I'll keep an eye on the kids for you too. Be a good excuse to get out for a drink, not that Mark needs an excuse, eh?" Tilly rolled her eyes and smiled.

"What's everyone having? It's my round." Brad announced to the table; he was keen to impress Charlie tonight and thought flashing the cash would work.

"I'll have a pint please mate and I'm sure Tills will have a rosé—do ya want a hand?" Mark got to his feet to walk to the bar with Brad.

"All right Nick, can I get two pints, one large red and one large rosé please, and whatever you and Julia are having."

Nick obliged. "No problem, mate; how ya doing? Keeping busy?"

"Ahh, y'know, up and down. People always need shoes, don't they? I'm looking forward to tomorrow, you must be pleased—sunshine is forecast."

Nick was looking forward to the fundraiser, traditionally himself and Rak got very drunk and had a silly time. "Yeah, I am mate. I'm planning on having a session with my best mate. Speak of the devil; Rak, how you going?"

Rak had just walked through the bar entrance, he immediately looked for Charlie, needing her. "Nick, my old friend; I'm good thanks, very good. Quite a turnout, eh? Who you got signed up to sing?"

Before Nick could speak Brad interjected "What you having, Rak? It's my round."

Rak knew he had to behave, for Charlie's sake, but it was bloody difficult being civil.

Nick rescued him. "No, don't worry Brad, I owe him a couple from the other night, I'll get Rak one. That'll be £17.50 please, mate."

Nick had not taken one for himself or Julia, he didn't want to be hypocritical.

"Thanks mate, nice save. I will not have that no-good twat buying me drinks while Charlie's slaving away to pay the fucking mortgage."

Nick poured his friend a pint. "All right, mate; don't ruin tonight—I mean it, Rak. It means a lot to Julia. Did you have a good afternoon?"

Rak knew he'd been told. "Yeah, sorry, mate. I just can't stomach him. What do ya mean? Did I have a good afternoon?"

Nick smiled. "I called by your office, needed some advice about Brussels, I'm taking Julia next week, but Tilly said you were out and that she could close up early. I take it you were otherwise engaged?"

Rak smiled, recalling the afternoon he and Charlie had not long ago been enjoying. "Yeah, erm... I was busy. You could say I was busy. You'll enjoy Brussels mate, make sure you visit the Grand Place, it is something."

"Thanks mate, it's on the list. Now, you enjoy tonight, don't worry about laughing boy. Think of it as you're out with her, not him." They both exchanged a knowing look.

Julia was so excited. She started the singing first, opening with 'Like A Virgin' by Madonna. Julia hadn't got the finest singing voice, but she made up for it with enthusiasm. As the drinks continued to flow, more willing participants were discovered, including Charlie. She enjoyed singing but wasn't very confident. However, after three large glasses of red wine, her confidence grew.

"Have you got any Diana Ross? I can do that." She asked as Julia went around the table.

"I'm sure you can sing anything honey, you have a voice like melted gold." Rak said, knowing he was pushing his luck, but he didn't care.

"I've got 'Chain Reaction', do ya wanna do that?"

Julia knew this would be a hit. "Yeah, go on then, I know that one too."

Next Julia turned to Rak, "so, come on then, what you having?"

Rak smiled, "I told you, I'm not singing; I'm terrible at it, Julia."

Julia was having none of it. "No, that's not gonna work, Rak. You've got to take your turn; now, what you 'aving?" Julia was laughing her head off now, digging his ribs.

"Have you got anything old? I know! Have you got 'You Really Got Me' by The Kinks?"

Julia sighed "Bloody hell, trust you—something old... Yeah, I'll put you down for that."

Tilly signed up for Kylie Minogue's 'Spinning Around'.

"You ain't got the hot pants too, have ya?" asked Mark, laughing his head off.

"No, but I could wear them if I wanted to, couldn't I, Rak?" Tilly was looking for support.

"If you want to, then yeah, don't see why not." Rak was mindful, he did not want to upset Tilly, especially now they were working together.

"See, Rak's a man of the world and he said I'd look good."

Mark was almost choking now. "He did not say you would look good. He said wear them if you wanna. This is what she's like Rak, hears what she wants to; y'know what I mean mate?" the whole table erupted into laughter, even Tilly.

Brad was looking to get some buffet food. "Do you want anything Char? You must be starving, busy day at the salon."

One thing Charlie was not, was hungry. Rak had cooked a perfect lunch for her

"Y'know what? I'm all right actually. You go past it after a while, don't you?"

Brad looked, quizzically at her. "So you don't want anything? Is that what you're saying?"

Charlie looked at him, trying to smile. "Yes, that's what I'm saying, I'm not hungry. Thank you." Charlie was left alone with Rak. Tilly had gone to the buffet with Mark and Brad.

"Is he always like that? Questioning you hun?"

Charlie touched his thigh. "Please don't, Rak; I loved our naughty afternoon, please don't spoil it." She smiled wickedly, it actually turned him on.

"Stop it, or shall have to take you over this table. With Kate and Dorian watching, imagine the shock waves." He was laughing, so was Charlie as she imagined it.

Brad returned from the buffet with two plates. "You'll be pissed if you don't eat anything. I got you this."

Charlie saw Rak clench his fists; she didn't want him to lose it. "Thanks, leave it there—we'll see, might fancy it later."

Brad looked at her, as if Rak wasn't there. "You've not fancied it in fucking months."

Rak could not contain himself. "Mate, I think you're the one that's pissed, you don't talk to a lady like that; apologise, now!" Rak was staring straight at Brad.

"You what? You're telling me how I can talk to my wife? Where's yours again? 'cos she ain't with you."

Charlie was wishing for Mark to return to the table with Tilly.

"I won't tell you again, fucking apologise!"

"Rak, leave it please, he's not worth it. Like you say, he's had too much to drink. Please." She glared at Brad, "if you're going to continue showing me up, you can go home, or you can start to enjoy yourself and stop ruining everyone else's night. Do you understand?" Brad looked away, "I said, do you understand?"

He nodded his head and carried on with his sausage roll. Charlie glanced at Rak, she needed him, she wished they could be open and be together.

Rak felt her look at him, he looked back, his eyes asking her if she was ok. She smiled to him.

"Right, everyone, next up is our lovely, gorgeous, local businessman, Mr Rak Banerjee as Ray Davies." Julia had got the microphone, "don't let me husband hear that though," she tittered away.

Nick was laughing, "can she borrow your dog, Tilly? She needs a guide dog."

Rak made his way up towards Julia, "I've told you before, not in front of your husband."

Charlie was watching this, wishing Rak was her husband, so easy going, getting along with everyone.

The opening bars to the song started "I have told her I can't sing" Rak laughed. He was looking straight at Charlie as he sang. She was sure other people would notice.

Rak was laughing whilst he was singing it, pleading eyes at Nick to help him out, Nick just shook his head in disbelief of his friend's awful singing voice.

When he eventually finished, he did get a round of applause, much to his surprise. "I thought that was a short track, it's not when you're up there. I need a drink, anyone else?" Everyone except Brad accepted Rak's offer of a drink, saying he would rather buy his own.

"I'll help you, and I want to see what gins they've got." Charlie got to her feet.

As they were waiting to be served, being kept waiting on purpose by Nick to give them chance to talk. Rak asked Charlie, "are you ok hun? You shouldn't let him talk to you like that y'know."

Charlie wanted to touch him so badly. "Yes, I'm fine. You shouldn't have intervened, Rak; he might suspect something."

Rak looked at her "Believe me honey, if I heard any man speak to a woman like that, I'd intervene. He's a twat. What gin do you want?"

Charlie looked before responding, "may I have a pink gin with elderflower tonic? Lots of ice please."

Nick had heard this and was on to it.

"Make it a double mate, she deserves it" Rak wanted to kiss her so badly.

Next Julia introduced Tilly. "Please welcome to the stage my very dear friend and all-round glamour puss, Tilly."

The song started and she was really enjoying herself. She was not keeping up with the words on the screen and quite a large percentage of the lyrics were missed out altogether; however, it did prove very entertaining.

Julia then introduced Charlie, "please welcome our resident stylist to the stars, well she does mine." Julia gave a twirl and played with her hair. "The very lovely, Charlie!"

Charlie was feeling very tipsy now and was looking forward to a sing-song, especially her favourite 'Chain Reaction' by Diana Ross. She was really getting some applause and was enjoying herself. She was looking at Rak, and was beginning to dance now too; she carried on to the end, feeling like she was putting a show on just for Rak.

When she returned to the table everyone was cheering—everyone except Brad. He was sulking after their words earlier, but Charlie was not going to let him ruin her night out.

Next up was Julia and Tilly, Julia had persuaded Tilly she would be fantastic singing Girls Aloud's 'Sound of the Underground'. It was certainly an experience. "Sounds of the underground, the beat of the drum goes upside down," Tilly was making up her own lyrics and Julia was laughing so much she could hardly sing a word.

Other stars of the evening included Kate—surprisingly—singing Bob Dylan's, 'Rolling Stone', Adam had a decent stab at 'Mr Brightside' and Nick and Julia sang, 'Don't Go Breaking My Heart'.

Julia was on the microphone once more. "Right, you lucky people, everyone that has graced us with a song has had their name put in my magic hat. My glamorous assistant," she was referring to Nick, who just smiled and flicked his hand in a camp manner, "will select two names from the hat, the two extremely lucky people will sing a duet together to finish this evening's excellent entertainment. Nick, please pick out a name and read it out" Nick made a point of really searching the hat "The first name out of the hat is… Rak."

Rak looked up sharply, "Really? No. Pick again. Can't inflict my singing on people twice in one night."

Julia was laughing "No, the names picked are the names doing it, there's the rules. Nick, who's Rak singing with please?" Nick again made a play of searching the hat "It is… Charlie! So that's Charlie and Rak." Charlie looked over to Rak, laughing so much she didn't think she'd be able to sing. "Good, you can sing honey and I'll just sway in the background, that's what they do these days innit?"

He laughed and looked into her eyes.

Brad was not amused, and it showed. "I'm sure you'll enjoy yourselves," was all he could muster.

"Right, you've got a choice of songs, either, 'It Takes Two' or 'Islands in the Stream', what do you want?"

Both Charlie and Rak looked at each other "Ask the audience Julia, see what they would prefer." Rak said laughing.

"All right you lot, cheer now for 'It Takes Two'." There was quite a loud cheer. "Cheer now for 'Islands in the Stream'." There was an eruption. "There's your answer; enjoy yourselves".

Rak was very aware Brad was watching, he knew they shouldn't get too close.

"It's your bit first; are you ok doing this?" Charlie was smiling.

"Not really; I'm rubbish. Hold my hand and I might be all right, if not, you'll have to carry on." The music started and Rak began the first lines of the song.

Charlie was ready to sing her part and as they progressed towards the chorus, Rak pulled her close, putting his arm around her waist. Their faces were only centimetres apart as they sang the chorus.

Nick was feeling worried for his friend, he was also watching Brad and could see this performance was not being well received. Julia had also noticed Brad's disdain and began to wonder if this idea could have been better thought out. Both Julia and Nick just wanted the song to end.

At the table Tilly was really enjoying it. "Aren't they good? Charlie's really carrying Rak, though; don't you think?"

Mark smiled at his wife. "Yeah, they're doing a great job, not an easy song to sing. Brad? Just saying, they're doing a great job, aren't they?" Mark was genuinely enjoying the performance.

"They look like a pair of idiots, slobbering all over each other."

Tilly immediately shot Mark a look. "Look, come on mate, that's the song innit?" Mark was really supporting his two friends up on the stage "They're doing a good job, if you'd had a go then your name would have been in the hat, and it might be you up there with her. But you refused to sing, give 'em a break."

Brad looked at Mark, very aware that he was not showing himself in his best light "Yeah, sorry mate, you're right. They're doing a great job."

Tilly raised her eyebrows at Mark, as if to say, 'careful'.

At the end of the song the whole pub erupted into applause, Rak gestured towards to Charlie, microphone still in hand. "The true star, the real voice. Thank you honey" then he kissed her cheek.

She was shocked but smiled. "Come on, you can buy me a drink now"

"With pleasure hun; with pleasure".

53

Friday Night

3 Church Lane

Rak had left the pub with everyone else, arranging to meet Nick at 8:30 the next morning to put the final preparations in place and help him set up the beer tents with Gary.

As he made his way home, he began to think what a fantastic night he had enjoyed with Charlie. He thought about all the laughs they had shared and how much he had enjoyed holding her, in public. He thought about their afternoon, how he had shared intimate details of his life with her, things not many other people knew about him. How he could feel vulnerable in front of her without her judging him or telling him to get a grip.

Rak turned the front door key and let himself in. He went straight upstairs, he wanted to feel comfortable. He went into the bedroom and undressed, recalling how it felt when Charlie undressed him, and he put his old t-shirt and pyjama bottoms on.

He went back downstairs, poured himself a large Chivas and sat on the sofa in the living room. His head was full of Charlie, how he wanted her with him, right now and forever. How he loathed the idea of her being with Brad; the way Brad spoke to her and how he treated her. He knew he felt malice towards Brad, he actually wished him dead.

Rak knew thinking like this would do him no good, he switched on the television. He knew there was golf being shown from America, he would sit and watch that until he felt he wanted to go to bed, alone.

54

Friday Night

5 Main Street

Charlie and Brad had left the pub with Tilly and Mark and Rak. As they wished their friends a good night, Charlie knew Brad was in a mood. She was dreading going home with him.

As they got through the front door, Charlie kicked off her boots. She was tired and needed to go to bed, then she heard Brad from the kitchen. "You want another drink?"

She really didn't, as she had drunk quite enough for one day, however she also knew if she refused, it would just exacerbate Brad's bad mood further.

"Yeah, but just a small one".

Charlie walked towards the kitchen, Brad was seated at the kitchen table, two glasses of wine in front of him. Charlie could sense an atmosphere, she immediately went towards the CD player, she was not going to sit in silence. She grabbed the CD which was nearest the front of the pile, she wasn't in the mood for searching. It happened to be 'Greatest Hits of Whitney Houston' —it would do.

They sat opposite each other, hardly a word spoken. Charlie decided she'd had enough. "Did you plan to ruin tonight? Or do you just hate seeing me enjoying myself? Hmm, which is it? All night you've behaved like a fucking twat," all the anger she had contained throughout the night escaped in that moment.

Brad just looked at her, hatred in his eyes and a sneer of arrogance on his face. "You really need me to tell you? You've got no idea? Do you think I'm fucking stupid?" his fist clenched tightly around the stem of his wine glass.

Charlie looked at him, not daring to speak.

He stood up and came around to face her, standing right in front of her. Then he began shouting, "well, do you? You fucking bitch! You don't think I see what's going on? You flirt with every fucking man in the pub, but you won't fuck your husband!"

Charlie was scared, he was right in front of her face, she wanted to calm him down. "What? What do you mean, every man in the pub? I only spoke to Mark and Ra..."

"Oh, yeah! I saw you with Rak. Enjoy it did ya? Having his filthy fucking hands all over ya!"

Charlie was petrified now, she could see the whites of his eyes. As he shouted at her, his spittle hit her face. Then he dragged her off the chair and bent her over the table, he ripped off her tights and her knickers, she could hear him undoing his belt, she was scared, so scared. He pushed her over the table, she could feel him behind her. He forced her legs apart, she did not want this. "Brad! Stop! Stop now! Please." She was crying. "I said stop!" then she was screaming. She reached behind her, somehow, she found the strength to push against him. She could feel his cock, hard. She grabbed it and squeezed as hard as she could. Brad released his grip on her, moving his hand to hers, to try to get her to stop squeezing. She quickly got to her feet; she didn't know where the strength had come from. She ran into the hall, threw on her boots, and ran out the door.

Charlie was scared, she couldn't catch her breath. She was scared he would come after her. She had to go somewhere he wouldn't find her. She started running, running towards the salon, then realised she didn't have the keys. She saw a light coming from Rak's house. She ran as fast as she could and banged on the door so loud she could of woke the dead.

55

3 Church Lane

Rak was nearly falling asleep in front of the television. He had finished his whiskey and was considering going to bed. He had got a big day tomorrow and he wanted to enjoy it.

Just as he picked up the television remote to switch it off, there was loud banging on the front door. It startled him, he almost dropped his empty glass.

He went towards the door, thinking 'who the fuck is that?' What he saw scared the life out him.

"Charlie, baby, what's wrong?" Rak was shocked.

"Can I come in?" Charlie asked, white as a sheet and trembling.

"Yeah, of course, come on." He gestured her inside. Rak went straight in the kitchen a poured two large whiskeys, he gestured towards the sofa for Charlie to sit down.

"What's happened honey? What's happened to you?"

Charlie was shaking, she was shaking that much she couldn't speak. She took a large sip of the whiskey Rak had just handed to her. He sat next to her and held her

"Honey, please, what's happened? Has he hurt you?"

She looked into Rak's kind face, she could see concern in his eyes. "He… he tried… he tried…" she burst into tears. She was scared; scared of Brad and scared to tell Rak. She knew he would kill him.

"Ok baby, come on. Tell me, I promise I won't get angry. Please, what has he done?" Rak knew his promise was a lie but he needed her to tell him.

"He tried… oh God, Rak." She was sobbing, wailing, tears rolling down her face

"Charlie; please, honey; come on. Please." she took a deep breath and another large sip of whiskey.

"Rak, he tried to force me."

Rak's blood ran cold. He couldn't comprehend what she had just said. "What? What did you just say?"

Charlie looked into his eyes; she could see love; she could see pain, and she could see anger. "He tried to force me. He held me over the kitchen table, he ripped off my tights and knickers." She wailed again, recalling the fear she had felt.

Rak was shocked, he was dumbstruck. "Did he… did he force himself inside of you?"

Charlie was really trying to regain her composure. "No, I managed to stop him. I hurt him. Then I ran away, out of the house. I'm sorry… I'm sorry I came to you. I'm so sorry." She was crying again; Rak held her even closer

"Why are you sorry honey? I love you, don't be sorry. You're safe now, I promise." As angry as Rak was there and then, he knew Charlie needed him more. Rak wanted to kill him with his bare hands, but he knew she needed him to stay with her—to comfort her. "Do you want me to call the police?"

She had not even considered this, but she knew the answer. "No. No please, no. Don't Rak; please, baby."

He held her even closer "Ok hun; ok. Do you want a bath? I'll run you a bath"

She kissed him, tenderly "Yes, please. Please." They went upstairs to the bathroom, Rak held onto her while the bath was running, both of them staring at the water.

After her bath, Charlie and Rak went to bed. They held each other all night, he was scared she would have nightmares, and she was scared he would do something that could put him behind bars.

56

Saturday Morning

3 Church Lane

Charlie awoke to the sound of the radio playing downstairs. She could just make out the sound of 'Babylon' by David Gray—it was only 6:30am. She climbed out of Rak's massive bed and looked for a dressing gown or something to put on. She found one of Rak's shirts and slipped it on.

As she made her way into the kitchen, she saw Rak sitting at the kitchen table, looking out to the garden. He seemed to be lost in thought, she didn't know whether to disturb him or not. He was wearing his pyjama bottoms from the night before, nothing else. There was a cup of coffee on the table next to him, still steaming hot, she knew he hadn't been awake long. "Hello, baby; are you ok?"

Rak turned to look at her, a startled look upon his face. "Morning, honey; yeah just thinking, y'know? How are you feeling? Tea or coffee?"

She walked over towards him and sat on his lap. "I'm alright, I think. Still can't quite believe what happened last night, I don't know what to do Rak. I don't even have my door key, I've got nothing to wear, and I don't want to go back there." She could feel tears burning her eyes again; she clung to him; she needed him.

"Don't worry about what to wear hun, Lisa has enough clothes to open a chain of shops, take something out of the wardrobe, you're the same size." Rak knew the real problem had nothing to do with what Charlie might wear. He kissed her, slowly and softly "Would you like a coffee?"

Charlie smiled, one of trust, that this man could look after her. "Yes please; that would be great. Why don't we take them back to bed?"

As they stood up together she held him, she wanted to feel his bare chest against her face, to listen to his heartbeat.

"Yeah, that sounds good. I'm supposed to be meeting Nick in a couple of hours, do you want me to stay here instead?"

Charlie moved her head towards his face, to look

into his eyes "No; no I don't, I want you to see your friend and enjoy your day. If you don't then he's won. I might even join you later." She kissed him, as if to signify there would be no arguments.

As they both sat up together in Rak's bed; the bed he shared with Lisa; drinking their coffee, Charlie turned towards him. "What do you think I should do baby?"

Rak looked away slightly, he felt uncomfortable "It doesn't matter what I think honey, only you know the answer to that. What do you want to do?"

Charlie couldn't deny she was slightly shocked by Rak's response. "Oh, ok. I just wondered what you thought, that's all. Well, I need to get my house keys, I've not paid the mortgage all these years so he can live there, and I can't even get in. I suppose I should kick him out, but I don't know." She could see Rak was not happy, his face had a way of portraying his feelings.

"I'll get the keys for you, leave it with me."

Charlie had never seen him like this before "Rak; baby, hold me. Kiss me, kiss everything away." She moved towards him and he opened his arms to her. Her lips met his and they kissed passionately, Charlie wanted him, needed him right now.

Rak could feel he was becoming hard, he knew he wanted her but something in his head was stopping him. "I'm not sure baby, I don't want to hurt you, y'know what I mean? Maybe it's too soon."

Charlie felt rejected—hurt. "Don't you want me anymore? Am I damaged goods, Rak?"

Rak held her, tight, and looked into her eyes. "No, hun; don't be silly, please. I just don't want to hurt you. I don't want you to think about what he tried to do to you, and I just think it might be a bit soon. Believe me honey, I want you, I want you so much." He took her hand and placed it between the top of his legs, she could feel how much he wanted her. She slipped her hand inside his pyjamas, she could feel his cock was hard, she slowly and carefully ran her hand down the length of his cock.

Rak felt himself becoming harder, he really, really wanted her. "Charlie; Charlie, baby, oh God. Are you sure? Are you?"

She moved her body further down the bed and pulled his cock away from his pyjamas, her mouth was still hot from the coffee, hot and wet. She carefully placed her lips around him.

"Oh God, honey. Oh, yeah; yeah, ahh, yes."

She teased the head of his cock with her tongue before moving her head further down to take all of him in her mouth. Rak was in ecstasy, he pushed her head slowly, her tongue teasing him all the time.

"Honey, if you want me to fuck you, you'll have to stop. I'm so close."

She slowly moved her mouth up the hard shaft, teasing with her tongue one more time.

"Oh God, sexy; you're so fucking good. Come here, I want you to enjoy yourself."

Rak carefully pulled her towards him, so his face was just centimetres away from her wet pussy. "Sit on my face sexy, come on, you'll enjoy it."

Charlie was giggling, having never tried this position before, she did as Rak said and straddled his face. Then his face changed from smiling at her to sudden upset.

"What? Am I doing it wrong? Show me then." She laughed.

"No, it's not that. He's bruised you baby, in between your legs. I don't want to hurt you."

Charlie knew she was sore from where Brad had forced her legs apart, she hadn't realised he had bruised her. "Kiss it better for me then baby; I need you to kiss it better." She sat closer to Rak's face, his tongue teased her lips, licking her. He used his hands to part her lips, slowly, carefully, until he was licking her clit. Charlie moved herself where she wanted to feel his tongue, she unbuttoned the shirt she was wearing to reveal her breasts. She played with her breasts as Rak slowly licked her clit. "Oh, Rak, yes, yes! Oh God. Don't stop; don't stop, please!" She was crying for him not to stop, she could feel she was going to come, hard, strong. He slipped a finger inside her as he continued playing with her with his tongue, with more intensity than ever. "Rak! Rak, I'm coming, yes! Yes! Yes! Oh fuck, yes!"

With his other hand he spanked her bottom, lightly, carefully. He felt a sudden surge of wetness, he knew she had enjoyed herself.

"I want to feel you inside me, Rak, please."

He carefully placed her on the bed next to him and climbed on top of her, she guided him inside her pussy. She was wet and hot; he was hard, so hard for her. He started to move slowly, very slowly. He was desperate to fuck her hard and deep, he knew she wanted him to, but he didn't want to hurt her. "Is that ok honey? Are you alright?"

Charlie lifted her legs higher. "Harder baby, harder. I want you to fuck me."

That was all Rak needed to hear, he immediately thrust harder, needing her so much. "Oh honey, yes. You feel so fucking good."

Charlie pushed his bottom, pushing him further inside her, deeper. She met every thrust, his massive cock filling her with ecstasy. "Oh, Rak! Rak, you're so good. Never stop; never."

His smile filled his face. "I'll have to stop soon, sexy; I can't last all day." He was laughing, "I'm an old man, you know that!" He met her lips and kissed her, his tongue playing with hers. Rak felt her pussy clench around his cock, he knew she was coming. Still kissing, still playing with each other's tongues, he felt himself come, the pleasure was immense.

They lay together in bed, holding each other. The view from the bedroom window was that of trees, the house backed onto woodland. Charlie was looking out of the window, Rak's arms around her. "What time do you have to meet Nick baby?"

Rak looked at the bedroom clock, it read 07:45. "In around forty-five minutes, I should really have a shower and a shave and get ready. What are you going to do today? You're welcome to stay here as long as you want or you can come to the fundraiser with me."

Charlie wanted to go out, to go out with Rak but she was afraid of seeing Brad. "I'm not sure. I'd like to meet you later; maybe around half eleven, but what about…"

Rak could see she was struggling. "Meet me, I'll look after you hun. I promise." He kissed her, once more before heading to the shower.

57

Saturday Morning
The Green

It was 8:35. Nick knew Rak would be late and he was right. He and Julia were setting up the beer tent on The Green, then Nick had promised Gary he would help him set up at Fox Lane.

"What time's Rak meant to meet ya?" Julia was looking over towards Rak's house as she shouted to Nick.

"Five minutes ago, love, don't worry, he'll be here".

The sun was already shining bright in the sky—not a cloud in sight. Nick was excited, this was one of his favourite days of the year. "Julia love, do me a favour, you wouldn't go and make me and Rak a couple of breakfast baps would ya? I'm starving."

Julia smiled "Yeah, go on then, do you want egg as well?" Nick smiled and nodded his head, winking at his wife.

Five minutes later Rak arrived. "Sorry mate, lost track of time. You alright?"

Nick could sense something wasn't right. "Yeah, I'm alright. Julia's just gone to make us some breakfast. Are you alright? You don't seem it." Nick had known Rak a long time, he could read his friend like a book.

"I'm not supposed to say anything, this ain't my secret to tell, y'know what I mean?" Nick nodded. "That bastard tried to rape Charlie last night when they got home."

The colour drained from Nick's face. "What the fuck? Is she alright? I mean, did he, you know…?"

Rak hugged his friend. "No, thankfully not. She got away somehow, I don't know where she found the strength, mate, to be honest. I was just going to bed after watching the golf and then there was this hammering on the front door. Opened it, and there she was. She was petrified, shaking, everything. She stayed with me. She hasn't even got her house keys, mate."

Nick immediately switched his thinking away from Charlie for a second. "You've not done anything have ya? Rak, have you done anything to him?" Nick knew Rak had a temper.

"No, not yet. But he's got it coming and don't you try and stop me." Rak said defiantly.

Nick knew better than to try and reason with him, he also knew that if Rak hadn't done anything yet, he may have calmed down. If he'd done anything last night, Brad would be on life support by now. "Just don't get banged up, mate, ok?" Nick was not really asking. "Don't worry, I won't say anything either, I don't suppose Charlie wants everyone knowing."

"Morning gorgeous, looking fab as usual." Julia was smiling at Rak as she delivered the breakfast baps to the two friends.

"Good morning, Julia. Looking sexier than ever. Mornings must suit you."

Nick was laughing, trying to hide his dismay at the revelation his friend had just sprang on him. "You two get worse, you know that? I am standing right here, y'know."

Julia kissed Nick on the cheek. "Don't worry, I won't run off with him. Anyway, he's too busy." Julia smiled and raised her eyebrows at Rak. "What were you two talking about? Looked intense when I was walking over. The golf club putting their prices up again?" Julia knew something serious had been discussed and she wanted to know.

Rak looked at Nick, he knew he hated keeping

secrets from her. "Look don't say anything, Julia, please. But Brad tried to attack Charlie last night. She's alright, she's over at my place. I just know he doesn't like keeping things from you, so I've told you."

Julia immediately hugged Rak. "You sure she's ok? This is all my fault, if I hadn't engineered that duet round. For fuck's sake, Rak, I'm so sorry."

Rak was a little surprised "What do you mean, engineered?" he looked hard at Julia.

"I thought you two might like to sing a duet together, for a laugh. So, I only put your names in the hat, it was my idea. I am sorry if that's what pushed Brad to hurt Charlie."

Rak hugged her. "No, it's not your fault, I promise. The man's a fucking coward—hurting women. It's all his fault. I enjoyed the duet round, so did Charlie, so thank you." He kissed her on the cheek. Both men then tucked into their baps; Nick was very aware he would need to keep an eye on Rak, his temper could erupt at any time.

After setting up on The Green, Nick had to help Gary. "Look mate, I've got to give Gary a hand now, what are you doing?"

Rak looked at his watch—9:40. "I'll come and help you, then perhaps we can have a sample, eh? Start the day off as we mean to go on."

Nick was well practised in the art of daytime drinking, especially on fundraiser day, but even he thought it was a little early. "Yeah, we'll see. Come on."

They both arrived at Fox Lane and were surprised to find Gary already there and seemingly without a hangover from the night before. "Morning you two, you both ok?"

Both men nodded their heads and shook Gary's hand. "Yeah, we're good thanks mate. Couldn't get a better day for it, could we?".

As they were setting up the beer tent, Slim and his mates from the classic car club arrived with some gorgeous cars to show off. "Alright boys, how's it going? All good?"

Rak walked over to his old friend "Yeah, everything's great thanks, Jim; what about you?"

Slim was looking towards the newsagents. "Do they sell ciggies? Left mine on the kitchen table at home."

Rak thought he'd seen cigarettes in the shop, but not being a smoker, he wasn't sure "They might do, shall we take a walk over?"

Slim nodded and the two men wandered over to the shop.

58

Saturday Morning

Upper Loughton News

Dorian was looking forward to the day's events. She had agreed to meet Kate around lunchtime, and they were planning to walk around the various stalls and then have something from Julia and Nick's BBQ for lunch. Jack had agreed to mind the shop, on the condition he could close after lunch to look around himself at the classic cars.

The shop was very busy, people wanting their morning papers, kids in buying sweets with their pocket money and a couple of elderly customers, who didn't wish to experience the faff of the super-market, much preferring to buy their milk and bread from Dorian.

Slim and Rak walked in and were surprised at just how busy the shop was.

"Morning you two, what can I get you?" Dorian knew Slim from days gone by, she recalled he used to service David's cars, that was a lifetime ago.

"Morning love, have you got any ciggies? Gone and left mine at home."

Dorian looked at the shelf behind her. "Only these I'm afraid, not much of a selection. Less and less people smoke now you see."

Slim had a smile spread across his face. "Aww, yeah; you've got my brand, you're a star!! Twenty Bensons please love. I know what y'mean though, we really are a dying breed, know what I mean?" Slim was laughing.

Dorian knew exactly what he meant. "I agree, it's since they banned it inside—especially the pubs. I still have the odd one myself now but not like I used to." Suddenly there was a commotion coming from the back of the shop. Both Dorian and Slim went to investigate.

"How fucking dare you show your fucking face. Make you feel like a man did it?" Rak punched Brad, straight in the face. "I'm gonna fucking kill ya; get up!"

Brad was staggering around; he really wasn't expecting a smack in the face with his morning paper. "Been crying to you, has she? What a fucking surprise. I saw you last night, your fucking dirty hands all over her."

Rak hit him again, this time in the stomach. "You don't even pay for your own fucking house, what type of man are ya? You fucking waste of space!"

Brad got to his feet, regaining his composure; he hit Rak straight in the mouth, knocking him back. Rak checked his lip with the back of his hand, he was bleeding. "How come you know so much about my fucking sham marriage? Are you and her cosy? Is that it?" Brad hit Rak again, harder, right in the ribs.

All Rak could see was Charlie last night, scared, shaking, feeling humiliated. He could not control himself. He tackled Brad to the floor, pinning him down and repeatedly punched him, over and over. He would have killed him if Slim had not pulled him off of him.

"Rak, for fucks sake mate, you'll kill him."

Rak was like a man possessed. "Let go of me, I wanna kill him. He fucking deserves it!"

Slim was struggling to hold Rak—Rak being a good fifteen years younger and a lot fitter. "Come on mate, nothing's worth this."

Rak was so angry he couldn't contain himself. "He tried to rape his wife last night, I'd say that's justification, wouldn't you?"

Dorian looked horrified, not in a gossipy way, just pure horror across her face. "Rak, leave it. Now!" she glared at Brad, "get out and don't ever set foot in this shop again. Get out!"

Slim let go of Rak when he was sure Brad had left the shop. "Mate, are you alright? You're bleeding."

Rak was still livid. "Yeah, I'll live and thanks to you, so will he."

Dorian asked Slim and the other customers to leave, announcing, "show's over." She asked if Rak wanted a drink, a proper drink. "I've got a whiskey, I think you might need it for the shock"

Rak nodded, still holding his chest. "Please. I think he's broken a rib."

Dorian fetched Rak a whiskey, put closed on the door and cleaned his lip. "Was that true? Did he try to rape Charlie?" she asked, quietly.

"Yes, Dorian. It's true. Very sad, but true. I'm sorry about the mess and I'm sorry it happened in here."

Dorian dismissed Rak's last comment. "No, don't worry about it. The bastard deserved it, Rak; I wish you'd gone further."

Rak took Dorian's hand, he sensed there was more than she was telling him. "Are you alright? Do you want to talk?".

Dorian poured herself a drink too and sat opposite Rak. "You know me and Nick's father, David, had an affair. I know you know so don't pretend otherwise."

Rak nodded his head. "I was going to run off with David, I loved him so much Rak. I was very unhappy with Jack; he always drank too much, made my life a misery. He never wanted to move down here from Yorkshire, I made him not long after we met, you see. He was working down here, on a short contract, he never intended to stay. I didn't want to live up there, with no friends or family." Dorian took a sip of whiskey, her eyes were miles away, miles away in the past.

"Jack found out about David, it was hardly a secret, the whole village knew. The thing was, Rak, it wasn't like now; things were different. Jack couldn't let me leave him; he wouldn't, you see. Not that he actually loved me, more his pride would be damaged."

Rak looked into her eyes, this woman he hardly knew, who he just bought his paper from every morning, and he could see pain and regret. "What happened? If you want to tell me, that is."

Dorian took his hand. "It's difficult as your best friends with David's son, but I'll tell you. David and I had been carrying on for years, Jack knew, he wasn't bothered. Not until I was going to leave him. He came home early, found me packing a bag. He…" she paused, trying to decide if she wanted to disclose the next part of the story "He went mad, hit me, he used to hit me a lot back then but this time he knocked me to the floor. Then he raped me, Rak. I couldn't, hmmm, I hadn't got the strength." Rak felt tears burning his own eyes, he held her. "I didn't leave him, I told David we needed to wait. David wasn't happy, he wanted to start a new life with me. No disrespect to Pam but they were not well matched, I knew David treated her unfairly but he wasn't like that with me. A few weeks later, I found out I was pregnant. I told David first, I thought the baby was his. He knew what Jack had done to me, he didn't try to defend me. Men controlled women more then. He would never have defended me, not like you just have for Charlie." They both took a sip of their drink. "David said the baby could be Jack's, he wanted nothing to do with it. He said that Nick was nearly grown up, why would he want to start having babies again with me. He said to stay with Jack, it's probably Jack's anyway." Dorian was beginning to cry.

Rak put his arms out to her "You don't have to tell me any more Dorian, you really don't".

They both sat, drinking their whiskeys and thinking for a moment. "You see Rak, I still don't know who Sally's father is, don't think I ever will. I let Jack believe she was his and he did calm down when she was born. If anything, Sally saved our relationship. But sometimes, when I look at her, I see David. She could be David's. But it was all a long time ago." Dorian sighed in resignation that she would never know what life she may have had. "Can

I ask you something Rak?" He nodded. "Are you seeing Charlie?"

Rak was not expecting that, should he tell one of the village's greatest gossips his biggest secret? Ordinarily, his answer would be no, definitely not, but after what she had just shared with him, he had to be honest. "Yes. Yes, I am. I love her Dorian and I think she feels the same. I'd do anything for her, even kill for her."

Dorian squeezed his hand "Don't do that, what would she do without you? Enjoy it, and don't worry, I won't say a word. I promise. You're a good man, Rak, better than most."

Rak looked her in the eye. "Thank you. And thank you for trusting me as well. I promise I won't say anything, not even to Nick. Although, he does know about you and David, as I'm sure you're aware, but what's the point in dragging it all up again."

They both sat, quietly for a few moments, when suddenly there was a knock on the door of the shop. "I'd better see who that is, you sit for another minute or two." Dorian went towards the door, checking her face in the mirror on the way. "It's Nick, should I let him in?"

Rak knew he would have to face him, "yeah, go on then."

Nick ran in, straight passed Dorian towards Rak. "Mate, for fuck's sake! I lose you for two minutes. Are you ok?"

Rak smiled. "Slim tell you then? Yeah, I'm fine. Sore ribs, maybe a broken one. Nothing to worry about. Come on. Let's go and enjoy our day."

The two men walked towards the door, Nick leading the way. As Rak passed Dorian, he flashed a smile of sincerity and mutual trust that neither would share the other's secret.

59

Saturday Morning

5 Main Street

Brad returned home. He was livid. Livid with Charlie for running to Rak, he was now convinced they were seeing each other. He was also worried about the amount of people who may have heard Rak shouting about how he had hurt Charlie. He had always tried to portray an image of the good, supportive husband. Now people may think him a monster.

Brad knew he had to leave the village, he just wanted to rewind to last night, to not have spoiled the night at the pub, to not be the man his wife despised and to not have attacked her. He went upstairs and packed a bag, he wasn't even looking at the clothes he was packing, just randomly throwing items into the suitcase. He had no idea where he would go, he just needed to get away from there.

He was just about to walk out of the front door when he realised Charlie had not got her keys, her phone, or the keys to the salon. He knew if he stood any chance of her forgiving him, he should take them to her.

He collected Charlie's things and started to walk over to Church Lane.

60

3 Church Lane

Charlie had enjoyed her shower. Rak had a fabulous power shower and she emerged feeling invigorated. She was drying her hair at Lisa's dressing table, using Lisa's hair dryer. It felt strange; it felt as if she was intruding; invading Lisa's life. After she had put on some make-up and finished drying her hair, she looked through the wardrobe.

Charlie could not believe the amount of clothes Lisa owned—designer clothes and expensive clothes. She knew that Lisa enjoyed spending money; Christ! Rak had complained enough times about the amount Lisa spent, but this was extreme. Some items still had the tags on, unworn. The prices actually frightened Charlie; she couldn't believe it. It was as if Lisa just spent money for fun, or maybe as a way of escaping her problems. Whatever it was, it was like an addiction. Charlie didn't dare wear anything too expensive, she found a pair of Armani jeans and a Calvin Klein t-shirt, that would more than suffice. She decided she would borrow a pair of socks from Rak.

Charlie decided to make herself another coffee before going out to meet Rak. She was apprehensive about leaving the house, she did not wish to see Brad. The silence in the kitchen was unnerving, she switched the radio on. They were playing 'Call Me' by Blondie, a favourite of Charlie's; she began singing along and dancing around the kitchen. She had actually relaxed.

Just as Charlie poured the water into the coffee cup, she heard the door. It startled her, she was sure Rak had his key. She stood still in the kitchen, quickly trying to turn the volume of the radio down. There was a second knock. She felt her heartbeat increase. Then there was a voice through the letterbox. "Char, I know you're in there. Just open up, I've got your keys and phone. Please Char, open the door"

Charlie froze, her mind racing, shit! *'What does he want?'* she began to panic *'how does he even know I'm here?'* Then the voice again, through the letterbox.

"Charlie, come on babe. We need to talk, please. I've got your stuff, your phones been pinging, I think you've got messages. Open the door"

★ ★ ★

Rak and Nick were heading back towards *The Bull*, Nick needed to put the finishing touches to the outside bar and see if Julia needed any help in the kitchen, preparing the BBQ food. "Hey mate, you've got blood on your shirt, do you wanna go home and change?"

Rak looked at his shirt "Oh, for fuck's sake; I've just bought this. Yeah, I'll pop over, I need to check Charlie's ok too. See you in a minute."

Then Nick quickly thought. "Hang on, I'll come with ya. Julia can wait a minute."

As the two friends turned towards Rak's house, Nick saw his friend's face change, then Rak broke into a run. Nick looked towards his friend's house, then he quickly ran after him.

"What is it with you? Do you want some more?" Rak was shouting.

Nick knew he was beyond angry. "Just calm down mate, please. You're not doing her any favours."

The look on Brad's face was of extreme fear, he knew Rak could and would hurt him. "I was just bringing her stuff; so she's here then? My wife."

Charlie heard the commotion, she heard Rak. She wondered what had happened, she opened the door. "Yes, she is here…" then she saw the blood on Rak's shirt. "What have you done to him? What the fuck have you done to him?!"

Brad started speaking, "nothing; he attacked me in the shop."

Charlie could see Brad had been involved in a fight, he had cuts and bruises on his face.

"Don't you care if I'm alright?" Brad asked, incredulously.

Rak was getting ready to throw another punch, Nick was trying to stop him, but he wasn't able to.

Just as Rak raised his fists. "Rak! Baby, no. He's not worth it. Leave it please, for me."

Brad could not comprehend what he had just heard. "Rak, baby? Baby! What the fuck?" he bellowed.

Charlie was scared, her face showed it. "Just give me my keys and my phone and fuck off. I don't want to do this now." She was grateful for Nick being there, she knew Rak would have killed Brad and there would be no way she could stop him.

Nick saw the fear in Charlie's eyes, he needed to do something before Rak did. "You heard the lady, Brad; give her stuff to her and go away. While you still can."

Brad threw Charlie's keys and phone at her, she only just caught the phone. "I'm going away for a bit. I'm sorry about last night."

Charlie did not want to discuss anything with

him, she just stared at him until he eventually turned and walked away, down the drive.

All three of them went inside, Charlie immediately holding Rak.

"Not too tight hun," he winced.

"Why? What's wrong? What's he done to you?"

Rak shot a look at Nick. "They had a to do in the paper shop, I left him on his own for two minutes. He's got sore ribs, but more so, sore pride. I've got to say, Charlie, since my friend's been with you, he just seems to keep getting hurt."

Rak had not expected this. "Nick, please. Come on, mate; you know what he did to her. Why you having a go at Charlie?"

Nick took a deep breath and looked away "Because you seem to be getting hurt mate, all the time. Car crash last week, fighting this week. This ain't like you, I'm worried."

Charlie let go of Rak and walked towards Nick "I'm sorry, Nick; you're right."

Rak opened his mouth to speak but Charlie gestured for him to shut up. "I am very much in love with your friend, this gorgeous, selfless man. I won't apologise for that. But you're right, he can't continue getting hurt, I'm scared he will do something that will either kill him or put him in prison."

Rak had just about had enough. "Can I speak in my own fucking house? Nick, I know you're concerned and thank you for that, but I know, if anything like this happened to Julia, you wouldn't just sit there and take it. And my car accident was just that, an accident. I will not have you two falling out, I'm old enough to look after myself."

Both Charlie and Nick looked at Rak, then at each other.

"Alright, but don't do anything else. Now go and change your shirt, this beer won't drink itself." Nick said.

While Rak was upstairs changing, Charlie knew she had to say something. "I do worry about him, Nick. I promise, from now on, things will be better."

Nick saw the love in Charlie's eyes. "Yeah, I know you do, but he's my best mate and I love him. I shouldn't really tell you this, but he wants you two to be together, properly. Do you know what I mean?"

Charlie looked out towards the garden. "It's not that easy, I want that too but it's not that easy."

"What's not that easy? What you two talking about?" Rak asked.

Nick looked over to see Rak just coming into the kitchen. "You mate; you. It's not easy keeping you under control. Now come on, let's go. I need a drink".

61

Saturday Lunchtime
The Green

The atmosphere between Nick and Charlie had improved, thankfully, and now they were all enjoying a drink together with Julia, Tilly and Mark.

"What you done now? You been in the wars again?" Tilly asked.

Rak smiled. "Yeah, something like that, Tilly; maybe I should get a canine companion like Rollo." Rak reached down, carefully, to fuss Rollo, who was devouring a sausage.

Rak saw Dorian and Kate approaching the pop-up bar, himself and Dorian exchanging a knowing look.

"I'll get whatever Dorian and Kate are having Adam, would you put it on my tab please?"

Dorian smiled. "There's really no need, Rak."

"Yes, there is. I shouldn't have caused a disruption in the shop, please accept my apologies by accepting a drink."

Kate was waiting with bated breath for tales of scandal.

"Rak accidentally knocked over a display of greeting cards this morning, I told him not to worry. Thank you for the drinks, we'll have two halves of cider please."

Kate was most disappointed there was not more to it than knocked over greeting cards but took the drink without hesitation.

The day was going well, all things considered. Rak had taken some painkillers and now decided his ribs were just sore, not broken. Charlie seemed to be enjoying herself, relaxed knowing that Brad had disappeared, at least for now and the whole atmosphere of the day was one of fun and laughter.

Slim was wandering over towards the group of friends. Rak knew he needed to speak with him, so he got up to meet him halfway.

"Rak, you alright now? Is that right what you said? Did he try to force himself on her?" Rak gestured Slim towards the edge of The Green where it was quiet.

"Yeah, I've been better but I'm alright thanks

344

mate. Look, it's true, but Charlie doesn't want it broadcasting, ok? The story is I walked into a display of cards, knocked it clean over, alright?"

Slim took a cigarette out of the pack in his hand and lit it, inhaling deeply. "Pissin' hell, mate; it's unreal innit? Who does that to a woman? Don't worry, I won't say anything. Come on, you can buy me a drink."

The group were all enjoying the day, the drinks were flowing as was the conversation. The whole event was busy, attracting people from the neighbouring villages. Families were enjoying the attractions, including a bouncy castle, face painting, two live bands, which Nick had secured for free once he had explained what the event was in aid of and, of course, the BBQ.

"When's Geeta starting with you Charlie? Bet you'll be glad of an extra pair of hands."

Charlie was happy to be talking about normal things and forgetting about the previous night. "On Tuesday, Tilly; I'm looking forward to it to be honest. Someone else to chat with when it's not so busy too. She'll be a great addition."

Rak smiled, he was desperate to hold her hand. "Don't let her sit around too much hun, make sure she gets the kettle on and puts the brush round."

Charlie laughed "She's not a junior Rak, she's a fully qualified stylist. We'll share the boring bits. I'm really looking forward to her starting."

Tilly looked pensive, as if she wanted to ask Charlie something.

"Are you ok, Tilly?"

Tilly looked at Charlie.

"Would you mind if Geeta did my hair next week? I've not had a proper catch up with her in ages."

Charlie was relieved, thinking that was the least of her problems. "Of course not, we're working together. Just hope I don't get left with all the oldies." She laughed and looked towards Rak.

"Hey, what you trying to say? I only trust you with my hair."

Charlie laughed louder "That's what I meant, the oldies."

Rak gave her a playful tap, on the bottom. It didn't go unnoticed.

Later, Tilly and Mark were walking around the classic cars, on their own. "Mark, can I ask you something?"

Mark was busy drooling over a Lotus Elan. "If you want to darlin', yeah. Can I have one of these?"

Tilly looked at the car, she had to agree, it was superb. "I suppose, if you want one." She knew he was only kidding, "no, listen; do you think there's something going on between Charlie and Rak?"

Mark stopped strolling and looked at his wife. "You what? I don't know, do I? You work with him every day, what do you think?"

Tilly was trying to think back, to what Rak's mood had been like recently. She had to admit he had been happier. She put it down to Lisa being away but now she wasn't so sure. "He did tap her arse earlier, I saw him. That's a classic Rak move, he used to tap Amira's arse too. He's a bottom man you see."

Mark was looking at her, quizzically now. "What's a bottom man when they're at home?"

Tilly was laughing now, aware that the owners of the Lotus had heard. "Well, y'know," she was trying to whisper, not successfully, "you like boobs, some men like legs, Rak likes arses."

Mark was shaking his head and laughing "Right, I see. Well, yes then probably. If he tapped her arse, he probably is tapping her off. They did do well with that duet last night; perhaps they are together. None of our business though, is it?"

Tilly could be easily infuriated by Mark at times, and this was one of those times. "Is that all you're going to say? None of our business?"

Mark looked at her a little dumbfounded. "What do you want me to say? It isn't, is it? If they're happy then fair enough, just hope Brad don't work it out, eh?"

Tilly looked away, deep in thought. "Yeah, that's another thing that doesn't add up, Rak doesn't walk into things, especially them massive greeting card stands Dorian's got; I wonder if he had a scrap with

Brad? I've not seen him all day and Charlie's not mentioned him."

Mark was getting tired of this conversation now. "I don't know, why don't you go and see Julia? Let me have a look round these motors, look there's Nick and Rak, leave me here."

Tilly looked over where Mark had indicated. "And Charlie; look; look, Mark, with Rak."

Mark had heard enough, although he did secretly agree with Tilly. "Here's twenty quid, go buy yourself and Julia a couple of drinks. I'll catch you later. And take Rollo with you before he decides to piss up one of these cars."

Both Tilly and Mark were laughing, looking down at Rollo.

62

Saturday Afternoon
The Green

Julia had asked Adam to look after the BBQ and Anthea to look after the bar, she needed a break, and when Tilly arrived, they decided to have a couple of drinks and a cheeseburger each, Rollo had another sausage.

"Hey Julia, what a great day it's been so far? Really enjoying it." Julia took a swig of her cider, nodding her head.

"Yeah, the weather's made it good too, hopefully they've raised a bit. The raffle's been busy—some great prizes—we donated a meal at *The Bull* for two,

The Rose & Crown did the same, which surprised me. Slim donated a free service for any car, 'to be used within three months.'" Both women laughed, just picturing Slim thinking up that particular caveat. "Dorian donated a weeks' worth of free newspaper deliveries, the golf club gave us two free rounds of golf for two people and Charlie donated a gift voucher with a value of fifty quid, so not bad, eh?"

Tilly was surprised by the last one. "Fifty quid, you say? That's a lot; does she normally do that?" Tilly then took another bite out of her cheeseburger.

"No, it's normally a tenner but this year she's been more generous." Julia knew Tilly was asking with other questions in mind. "Why, what you getting at, Tills?"

Tilly moved nearer to her friend. "Do you think her and Rak have got something going on? I've seen how he looks at her, have you seen it?"

Julia had been dreading this question, already knowing exactly what was going on "Look, I'm not supposed to say anything, I only found out myself last weekend," Julia looked at her friend, the friend she used to share a house with when they were both in their very early twenties. "He's been seeing her a couple of months, reckons they're in love. The thing is, he's not been hiding it very well recently." Julia was looking at her friend, trying to judge her reaction

"Well exactly, I saw him tap her arse earlier, that's

what made me suspicious. They are well matched though, don't you think?"

"Better than Lisa." Both women chimed in at the same time, and fell about laughing.

Julia did not want to mention, even to Tilly, the events of the previous night. She decided it was not her place. Charlie seemed relaxed; she had looked happy with Rak. Julia respected that it wasn't her place to discuss Charlie's most personal business.

The two women sat chatting further. "Are you getting excited now? Y'know, about Brussels?"

Julia smiled naughtily. "Yeah; y'know what? I am. Nick needs a break, and so do I to be honest. We've not had any quality time recently; we really need it, Tills."

Tilly waited, knowing Julia wanted to say more.

"Just lately, our sex life has been, shall we say, lacking. We do try but after closing time we're both knackered. To be honest, Nick hasn't been in the mood, says he is but then when we get to bed, he goes off the idea. I don't know what to try, I just feel rejected. Do you think he's got another woman?"

Tilly had to laugh. "No I do not. He's not Rak, just like Mark's not. The difference is, Julia, Rak can organise himself. He can remember where he was supposed to have been. Both Nick and Mark are shit at thinking on their feet or remembering what they've told us. He's probably just knackered; the break will do you both good."

Julia knew her friend was right, she had just needed to hear it.

63

Saturday Afternoon

Fox Lane

Charlie and Rak were enjoying wandering around the classic cars. There really was a thrill to appreciating other people's pride and joys.

"Have you ever owned a classic?" Charlie asked.

"Yeah, when I was first training in engineering, I had this little MG. I loved it. Used to tinker with it all the time. That was years ago though, hun, not got the time so much now."

Charlie looked at him, she could see he was reminiscing. "Y'know, you could get yourself something, it'd be a bit of fun."

Rak smiled, looking into her eyes "Oh, I know I could, but I don't want to. Got better things to do in my spare time" he grabbed her and pulled her behind the newsagents. Rak was sure nobody could see, he kissed her. Charlie felt a warm surge of pleasure, she knew this was very naughty.

They were getting carried away further when Rak heard a familiar voice, he immediately stopped, placing his finger on Charlie's lips, signalling her to be quiet. The voice was getting closer, they could both clearly hear.

"I'm at this fundraiser thing, shouldn't be too long. I did promise Rak I'd show my face, although I can't bloody find him now. Yeah, ok, Dad, I'll come over later this afternoon, we can have dinner together if you like. Yeah, see you later." It was Carl Potter.

Charlie wanted to laugh so much as Rak was making funny faces whilst they listened to Carl's phone call, she was desperate to giggle but knew she'd be heard. He kissed her on the lips, a quick peck, leaving her wanting much more, and walked back towards the car display. "Carl, how you doing? Thanks for coming mate."

Carl quickly turned around. "Been looking every-where for you. I'm good thanks mate, nice day for it."

Rak gestured towards the pop-up bar being run by Sheila and Gary "Do you fancy a beer? Nick shouldn't be too far away."

Carl nodded in agreement, walking now towards the bar. "Is Tilly here?"

Rak had to smile to himself, he knew Carl didn't stand a chance with Tilly, but you couldn't fault his perseverance. "Yeah, she'll be somewhere mate, you really do like Tilly, don't you?"

Carl looked at the selection of drinks on offer. "What you having?"

Rak looked. "A pint please, mate; lager."

Carl ordered the drinks and stood with Rak, soaking up the atmosphere. "Yeah, you know I've always liked her, she's a very attractive woman"

Rak knew his friend was serious. "She's married mate, you know that. And believe me, that's not a mess you want to get into." Rak was considering his own problems, "can't you meet someone who's available? Successful business owner like you shouldn't have a problem."

Carl had tried online dating but without success. "Mate, come on, I'm not exactly fit, am I? Fifty-two years old, divorcee, two kids, fat and bald." Carl was laughing but Rak could see his point.

"Yeah, but the women our age have got their own baggage, believe me mate, they could do worse than you. Where are you looking?"

Just then Charlie approached Rak. "Oh, hello. Would you like a drink? Carl, please meet our local businesswoman and salon owner, Charlie Worthing. Charlie, this is my old friend, Carl Potter. I've known him nearly as long as I've known Nick."

Charlie extended her hand to Carl. "Pleased to meet you, Carl; bet you've got some stories about him, eh?" Charlie smiled at Rak "I'll have a G&T please if you're offering."

Carl was animated now. "Oh, Charlie, the stories I could tell you would make your hair curl without the need for perming solution. He used to be real hard work, mellowed with age though."

Rak was laughing "Don't believe a word of it, Charlie, can you imagine me ever being anything but convivial?"

Charlie laughed "I couldn't possibly comment. So, Carl, who are you with? Is there a Mrs. Potter?"

Carl laughed "No, unfortunately not; well, not any more anyway."

Rak interjected. "Carl's trying to meet someone new, any ideas?"

Charlie really didn't have a clue. "Have you tried actually going out? I know it's meant to be online these days but some of the stories I hear in the salon would make you howl. Two words, 'profile pictures.'" The group all laughed.

"I've not, no; got no single wingmen you see."

Charlie looked towards Rak. "Take him with you, see who you can meet. Just for support obviously".

Just then Rollo appeared, shortly followed by Tilly and Julia. "Hello Carl, how you doing? Good day for it. Rollo, come here."

Carl's face lit up at the sight of Tilly. "Hello beautiful, how are you today? Is this your dog?" Rollo was sniffing Carl, looking for further treats.

"Yeah, this is Rollo. He comes into the office with me now, you'll see him next time you pop in. I'm ok thanks; enjoying today. Do you know Julia?"

Julia had not missed how excited Carl was to see Tilly and answered for him. "I've seen you in *The Bull* sometimes with Rak, I'm Nick's wife, Julia Carr, pleased to meet you."

Carl did recall meeting Julia previously. "Yeah, I remember now. Would you two ladies like a drink?"

Both Tilly and Julia nodded in agreement. "Yes please, two halves of cider, please; Carl, if you don't mind".

Charlie sensed Carl really liked Tilly, she could see it in his face. What she couldn't decipher was how Tilly felt about him. Rak saw Charlie watching them both, he smiled over to her. She knew he was happy, she wished they were like the other couples here, openly affectionate towards each other. Nick's words were running around in her head, 'he wants you two to be together, properly,' that was exactly what she wanted too but why hadn't Rak told her himself? Why was he keeping his feelings from her? She knew Rak was very mindful of not causing any trouble for her but if only he would say how he really felt. She thought to herself that she could not read his mind, he needed to tell her.

The afternoon was passing by so quickly, it was already 3pm. The band had been a real hit; they were still playing, their penultimate track, before the second band of the day took over for the afternoon/evening session. The opening bars of 'When a Man Loves a Woman' started up, Rak felt overcome with romance. "Would you like to dance with me?"

Charlie was slightly taken aback. "What? Now? In front of everyone? I think you've probably had a couple too many." She laughed.

"No, come on, please," he took both her hands and gently pulled her towards him, encircling her waist with his arms.

Nick and Mark were making their way over towards the group, Nick thought his eyes were deceiving him. As he walked over to Julia, he shook his head. "Can they make it any more obvious? Last week he wanted it all kept hush-hush."

Julia sighed. "Yeah well, Tilly worked it out. I couldn't say she was imagining things. I had to tell her. I suppose he could just say he got caught up in the emotion of the day. How are you feeling? Alright?"

Nick had just asked for two pints, one for Mark and one for himself. "Yeah, I'm ok thanks love. It always feels like we're remembering Pete rather than being maudlin, do you know what I mean?" then Nick realised what his wife had just said to him, "what do you mean, Tilly worked it out?"

Julia tapped his arm. "She saw Rak touch Charlie's arse, asked me if they were getting it on. I couldn't lie to her. If they want it kept quiet, they had better be more careful Nick".

Just as Charlie and Rak had finished their dance, Geeta and Amit arrived.

"What time do you pair call this? Out last night we're you?" Rak said to the pair.

Geeta rolled her eyes, Amit spoke. "Yeah, I was. But she just couldn't be bothered to get ready. In the end I had to go and get her. That's why we're late."

Rak looked concerned. "Are you ok honey? What's going on?"

Geeta was trying not to look at her father. "Nothing, I'm fine. Are you going to buy me a drink?"

Rak didn't want to cause a scene so left his questioning there, although he was sure something had occurred between Geeta and Sanj; he made a mental note to revisit this conversation at another time. "Yeah sure, what would you like? You too Amit, what you having?"

The second band was even better than the first, performing various covers as diverse as The Beatles to Adele, and then Van Morrison to Al Green. They really added to the atmosphere.

Amit was speaking with Rak; he wanted some advice. "Dad, I need another car, what do you reckon I should get?"

Rak was used to advising Amit, he found his son easy; he found his daughter more of a challenge. "What do you want? Sporty or safe and boring?"

Amit was excited. "I want sporty, Dad; something to impress the ladies, y'know what I mean?"

Rak had to smile, his son wasn't that different to himself. "If you want, we can look together next week. And don't forget Slim, he sells the occasional motor. How many 'ladies' are you entertaining at the moment anyway?"

Amit took a gulp of his pint. "That would be telling old man, didn't you say a gentleman never tells? Put it this way, I'm busy most nights of the week." Amit grinned back at his dad.

Rak shook his head. "Then why didn't you bring someone with you this afternoon? You could've, y'know."

Amit looked away, into the distance. "There is this one girl I really like, but the thing is, Dad, she's with someone. I think I want more from her than just the two nights a week I'm getting but I don't think she'll leave him."

Rak knew that feeling all too well. "Well, you need to knock the others on the head then son, show her that you only want her. But don't waste your life waiting, if she doesn't want to know, move on."

Rak knew he was being hypocritical, but he didn't want his son to get hurt.

64

Saturday Evening

The Green

The afternoon soon gave way to the evening; the day had been a success. Sheila and Gary had really enjoyed running the pop-up bar at Fox Lane with Gary commenting how much he had felt involved in the community spirit. Nick had chatted with Gary further and a plan was made to involve Gary in further village projects.

Geeta was on her phone when Rak glanced over; he could see from his daughter's face she was not happy. He looked towards Charlie, gesturing for her to look over at Geeta. "Something's not right hun, she's been off all afternoon. If I ask her, she don't say anything. What do you think?"

Charlie could see he was getting agitated "You need to leave it baby, she won't tell you anything if you interfere. Speaking of which, I do wish you hadn't hit Brad, two wrongs don't make a right, y'know."

Rak was looking deeply into her eyes. "Are you seriously defending him? Charlie, do you not remember what he tried to do to you?"

Charlie knew he was wounded by her last comment. "Yes, of course I remember, how could I not? But you shouldn't have hit him, and you've got yourself hurt again. That upsets me. Leave Geeta to me, I'll have a talk with her next week. She might tell me more as we're not so close. It's sometimes easier speaking with someone who isn't involved."

Rak did appreciate her help, but he was also angered inside by her defence of Brad. He felt at that moment he would always be playing second fiddle to her husband.

There was now a hog roast on the BBQ—it smelled delicious. Tilly could see Rollo was very keen on a sample. She was just walking over to get a hog roast bap when Carl approached her. "Hey Tilly, what you having? Do you want a bap?"

Tilly looked up to see Carl staring back at her, waiting for an answer. "Oh? Yeah, go on then. That would be great, thanks. Are you enjoying the day so far?"

Carl gave a warm, full smile. "Yeah, I am thanks. Even better seeing you here. Tilly, would you like to go out, for a drink sometime, just as friends?"

Tilly had not been expecting this. "Oh, Carl; you know I'm married. Men and women don't go out for drinks just as friends, do they? It's a lovely thought but I'll have to say no. I'm sure you'll meet someone soon enough—it will happen for you."

Carl's face portrayed disappointment, he knew he had been pushing his luck asking, but he hadn't expected her to be so reluctant. "Ok; sorry, Tilly. I shouldn't have asked, my mistake. Let's get a bap, eh?"

If Tilly was to be honest, she did find Carl attractive and if she were single herself, she would have snapped his hand off.

As the evening progressed, Nick and Rak started on the whiskey. Nick knew he would suffer the next morning, but he was enjoying himself too much right now. They were sitting with Charlie, Tilly, Mark, Julia and Carl, who had also called George inviting him to join them; however, he declined, stating he was watching the cricket and didn't want to move.

Nick looked over towards Julia. "You know Julia, it's been great of Anthea and Adam to help out today, we should give them a bit of cash for their time."

Julia nodded, "yes, I offered them some but they said they'd enjoyed themselves so much they weren't bothered. Just that they are expecting a decent wedge for looking after the place next week." She rolled her eyes.

Nick laughed. "Don't worry, they'll be looked after".

Rak had gone quiet since his reprimand from Charlie, he was mulling things over in his mind. Did she really want Brad to get away with nearly raping her? Did she really love him, or Brad? He knew he was getting tired of this, of not having their relationship out in the open, of hiding behind closed doors, of her almost seeking defence for Brad's actions of the previous night. Why couldn't she realise that he would have killed him, for her, to protect her? He began to wonder if Nick was right; wasn't this going to end well? What did she actually want from him? Just sex? Or something more? He knew he enjoyed sex with her. Christ, he had never experienced passion like it, but he was too old for just sex, he wanted more.

Amit and Geeta had just approached the table. Geeta saw her father was lost in thought. "Are you ok, Dad? You were miles away."

This was the first time she had spoken properly to him all afternoon; Rak was slightly taken by surprise. "Oh? Hello, honey; yeah, I'm ok. Are you enjoying yourself? Is everything alright? Come and sit with your old man." Rak gestured towards an empty table just slightly away from the crowd, Geeta obliged. This was the first time he had sat with his daughter, just the two of them, in months. Rak was not going to upset the equilibrium.

"What's new?" he was looking at her, patiently waiting for her to speak.

"I'm not happy, Dad—with Sanj. I wish he was more like you, y'know? Some get up and go. He didn't even say well done on my new job. I've wanted to talk to you for a while, but I was worried you'd go mental."

Rak knew he had to control himself, his entire relationship with his daughter hinged on what he said next, he was careful. "What do you want, honey?"

Geeta took a sip of her white wine. "I want to feel important to him, Dad; do you know what I mean? I don't feel like he's that bothered about me sometimes. But then other times, he's great. Then I feel bad for thinking bad thoughts."

Rak could see she was visibly upset. "Look, we all do things like that—think bad things sometimes— if he's not right for you, though, you must end it, Geeta. Please don't waste your life on someone who doesn't love you." Rak was also thinking of Charlie now, how Brad had wasted her life, from what he could see.

"Can I stay with you tonight, Dad, please?" Rak smiled warmly, comforting his daughter. "Yeah, course you can. You never need to ask. I know I've not been 'father of the decade' but I do love you, Geeta; both you and Amit, and I'm always here for you, do you understand?"

Geeta took her father's hand and held it. "Yes, Dad; I understand. I know things were difficult for you and mum, but you two were excellent when you were together. That's what I want."

Rak squeezed her hand a little tighter. "Your mother and I still love each other very much, and we both love you. I'm sorry I fucked up, but never doubt how much you and Amit mean to me."

Geeta look confused. "If you and mum still love each other, why don't you get back together?"

Rak laughed, "you're still so innocent and naive honey; because life isn't like that, that's why. Come on, let's get some food".

Rak was waiting for the BBQ when Charlie appeared by his side. "Are you ok? Is everything alright with Geeta?" she was genuinely concerned.

"Yeah, everything's fine, thanks. Geeta's staying with me tonight so we can't stay with each other, ok?" he was very short with her, and she noticed.

"Why are you being like this, Rak? Cold towards me?" she felt an immense feeling of sadness

"I'm not being cold towards you, I'm just telling you that Geeta needs me, so I need to be there for her. She's my priority at the moment." Rak's face was like thunder.

"What's happened baby? Why are you being like

this?"

Rak looked through her. "Not here, too many people around. Meet me later, in the church yard."

Charlie was shocked by his attitude; she couldn't figure out what had changed.

65

The Bull

As the evening became night, the party moved into the warmth of *The Bull*. Nick had arranged for a juke box to be installed in the pub, initially just for the one night but he was considering acquiring one if it was successful. The track of the moment was 'Change' by Lisa Stansfield, chosen by Charlie. She had hoped the message would translate to Rak.

Tilly and Mark were looking after a table with Charlie and Geeta, Amit had already left, having an important date to keep. Rak was at the bar, talking to Nick whilst he got some drinks in, oblivious to the track playing through the pub.

"Are you alright mate? You seem a bit distracted."

Rak looked his friend in the eyes. "I'm fine thanks, fine and dandy," the sarcasm was not lost on Nick.

"What's up? Come on." Nick was pouring a pint whilst also looking at his friend, years of practice not wasted.

"Apparently, I shouldn't have smacked him, the rapist that is. I went too far; can you fucking believe it mate? I just wanted to protect her, be there. I don't know what she wants anymore, I really don't. I've got a funny feeling it ain't me." Rak's eyes portrayed sadness, sadness that Charlie couldn't see his way of thinking.

Nick really didn't know what to say, he hated seeing his best friend so upset, so desolate. "Only you know mate, I can't tell ya. But don't be too hasty, eh? I know you love her, don't be a twat because your temper's getting the better of ya."

Rak knew Nick was right, but he couldn't deny how hurt he was feeling right now.

Back at the table, Rak tried to be jovial, enjoying tales of Rollo and how the dog had enjoyed the day.

"I swear he can smell a BBQ from two miles away, he's ate better than me today. Everyone that's met him has fed him something." Tilly was laughing at how popular Rollo had been, she was also trying to put Carl's offer out of her mind.

Mark had also enjoyed the day, but for different reasons. "It was inspired, getting Slim to bring the classic car club along—really made the day mate. Great idea."

Rak was pleased, it was the first year the classic car club had got involved, and he didn't think it would be the last. "Yeah, it went well didn't it? I think Slim enjoyed himself too, he seemed happy enough."

Charlie was waiting for Rak to finish his drink; she needed to talk with him. She needed to know what he was thinking. She was trying to think back, through their day together, what could have upset him? She saw him drain his glass, she looked at him, eyes saying 'now'.

Rak made an excuse to leave, Charlie was close behind him.

66

Saturday Night

St Michael's Church Yard

The night was still. The cemetery was deadly quiet. After all the hustle and bustle of the day, the contrast was palpable. The entrance to the church was lit by a dim light, Rak stood there, waiting.

He saw Charlie approach, she was looking for him, stumbling slightly. "I'm over here," Rak called to her.

She immediately looked towards him, walking over to him. "What's wrong baby? Why are you being like this, cold to me?" her voice was fragile, and he knew it.

"This isn't working Charlie. I can't do this anymore." His words cut through her like a knife, she stopped where she stood.

"What do you mean? What have I done wrong?" Charlie could feel tears burning her eyes.

"You have a go at me for defending you. I don't know, perhaps you'd prefer it if I wasn't bothered. After all, he's your husband, what happens between you is your business"

Charlie knew he was serious; she knew she was losing him "Don't do this; don't do this please baby. I love you; you know that. Why would you say we're finished?"

Rak came closer towards her, the light showing just half of their faces. "I can't be second best to a man like that. And what's more, I won't be. If you feel you have to tell me not to defend you against someone like him then, well I'm sorry Charlie, you deserve to be with him. I need to focus on my kids, they need me"

Charlie scoffed at this, unable to understand what he was saying "Do you really think I want to be with him? Do you? Rak, I love you"

Rak was not giving in. "My kids need me. I've let them down enough. This was a mistake, I think you know that."

Charlie felt the heat of her tears in her eyes,

streaming down her face. "No, Rak; it's not. It's not a mistake. I'm sorry I had a go at you, please, don't do this. Your kids are grown up now, you need to put yourself first. I need you."

Rak could not believe she was trying to put herself above his children. "Fuck you, Charlie! You had your chance; you chose wrong! Fuck you!" he walked away, leaving her wailing in pain.

67

The Bull

Julia could not face getting up to clear the bar, having left the clearing up last night until the morning. The party had gone on quite late, past midnight, with Tilly and Mark being the last to leave around 1:00am. Nobody knew what had happened to Rak and Charlie, they just disappeared; Julia thought maybe they needed to be alone. Geeta had left around 11:30pm.

"Morning darlin', have we really got to tidy up downstairs, or has a fairy been in the night and done it?" Julia asked as Nick had just brought her a cup of tea.

"No, sorry love, no fairies I'm afraid. Here you are." He handed over the hot cup of tea.

"How's your head? You feeling rough?" Julia asked before taking a sip of her tea.

"No, actually, love; I'm feeling alright. I've got a proposition for you as it goes."

Julia looked at him, a naughty glint in her eye. "Oh, yeah? What's that then, hmm?"

Nick smiled cheekily before proceeding to explain further. "Not what you're thinking. No. I was gonna say, if I clear up downstairs, is there any chance I can escape later for a round of golf with Rak? Don't know what happened to him last night."

Julia thought for a millisecond. "Ok, you got a deal. I might feel more like doing something later, and the Sunday lunch bookings aren't as busy, I made sure of that. You gonna text him then?"

Nick gave her a kiss on the cheek and then grabbed his phone:

'Alright mate, I've got a pass later, around lunchtime. Do you fancy a round? We could have a catch up. Let me know.'

Nick was really hoping Rak would say yes, he wanted to talk to him about something that had been bothering him, and he wanted to discuss it in private.

Julia cuddled up to Nick, holding him a little tighter than usual. "Are you looking forward to our break? Only a couple of days to go, eh? I can't wait"

Nick knew they both needed this, they hadn't been away from the pub for nearly a year now. He recalled his parents hardly ever took breaks away, he didn't want to be like his dad. "Yeah, I can't wait. And I don't want you worrying about the place; the kids will be fine, and Tilly said she'd pop by too, didn't she?"

Julia was grateful for her friend. "Yeah, she's a diamond ain't she? Talking of which, isn't Belgium famous for diamonds?" Julia was laughing.

"Yeah, I think so. Rak mentioned something about it, not that he's ever bought one from there. If the kids do alright with the pub maybe we can go away for longer next time, what do you think?"

Julia knew this was probably a fantasy, the pub was a massive commitment, but the idea sounded fabulous. "Yeah, we'll see. Right, if you wanna go golf, you'd better make a start downstairs. Rak not texted back yet?"

Nick checked his phone. "No, not yet. Probably busy." Nick smiled cheekily.

Julia thought what a lucky cow Charlie must be.

68

Sunday Morning
Charlie

The sun was shining through the bedroom curtains; it was promising to be another beautiful day. Charlie awoke with a start, a bad dream jolting her out of her slumber. She was amazed she had managed to sleep at all, she was so upset about Rak.

She could not understand what had happened the night before, why he had said the things he had said. What had happened? Why did he want to end things? He said he loved her, and she knew she loved him. She was going over and over their conversations through the day in her head, what tipped him over the edge?

Charlie got out of bed, slipped on her dressing gown and went downstairs. She needed a coffee, her head still swimming in alcohol. Charlie put the kettle on and checked her phone for messages, she was sure Rak would've woken up regretting their argument. There was nothing from Rak.

'Hello babe, look I'm sorry about Friday night. I'm sorry I went too far. Can we meet? I need to see you. I do love you xx'

If Charlie was feeling hungover before she read the message from Brad, she was feeling particularly nauseous now. The message had been sent just after midnight, *'he was probably pissed',* she thought to herself. Charlie didn't want to meet Brad, that she definitely did know. She decided to ignore it, for now anyway.

As she sat at the island, cradling her coffee cup and looking out to the garden, she knew she needed to contact Rak—she needed him. This could not be the end. She picked her phone up, selecting the text button initially. She then changed her mind, she would call him, she needed to hear his voice, to hear the emotion in his voice. She needed him to tell her everything would be ok. She dialled the number and waited.

"Hello, Rak's phone, it's Geeta, is that Charlie?"

Charlie was taken aback, she was not expecting to hear Geeta's voice, why was she answering her father's phone. "Hi Geeta, yes, it's... it's me, Charlie. Is, erm, is... is your dad there, please?" Charlie felt awkward now, maybe she should have texted after all, this might upset him more.

"Oh, hi Charlie, yeah, I'll just get him. He's in the garage, looking at some old engineering books; yeah, I know, boring, huh?" she heard Geeta walk through the house, into the garage, then she heard. "Dad, it's Charlie for you; here you are."

She must of handed him the phone, she could hear him breathing, then the door shutting.

"What do you want?"

Charlie felt tears immediately burn her eyes. "I thought, I hoped we could talk. I don't know what... oh, Rak; don't do this!"

He could hear her sobs, his heart was breaking, he was close to breaking. "Charlie, look, I said everything last night. You know why; you can't expect to tell me how much he's hurt you and then ask me to do nothing about it. And you cannot make me choose between you and my kids; I won't have it. It was fun while it lasted, baby, but please, accept it's over. I'm hanging up now, ok? Bye."

The line went dead, he had actually hung up. He didn't want to hear her. He had made up his mind. Charlie felt empty, empty inside. Her stomach on the floor. Her face drowning in her tears.

69

Sunday Morning
Rak

The time on the clock read 4:56am. Rak was wide awake, thoughts of Charlie running through his head. He lay in bed, naked, the duvet wrapped around him. He wished she was next to him, he wanted to hold her in his arms. Feel the silky smoothness of her skin next to his, to smell her hair, to kiss her.

He did not want to end things with Charlie, that was the last thing he wanted to do. But he also felt they would never be more than a secret, a couple who had to be satisfied with snatched afternoons or the occasional night spent together. Rak didn't know if that was enough for him, he wanted more. He was too scared to put pressure on her to give it to him.

He lay in bed, his mind racing through the last couple of months, the happiest couple of months he'd had in a very long time. His thoughts turned to that Saturday night, on 'The Green'. He had said it wouldn't work between them, that she had too much to lose. He realised now that he had been right. He had never anticipated falling this hard, this deeply for her, he had really believed that she could just be a fling, a bit of fun, he never envisaged falling in love with her.

Rak was getting himself in a state, the more he lay in bed thinking of her, the more upset he was becoming. He didn't want to lose her, but he knew it was the kindest thing to do. That they would only go on to hurt each other, really hurt each other, and he did not want that.

He knew if he ended it now, she would still have the possibility of making her marriage work, she would see that all that was missing was the spark. She could work to reignite it, couldn't she? Yes, of course she could. Charlie could be happy and he would go back to being who he was before.

Rak decided to go downstairs, make a coffee. He sat at the kitchen table, looking out to the garden. He was watching a sparrow, pulling up a worm and eating it. He thought for a moment how fragile life is, how everything needs to be managed. He began thinking about his own fragility, what should he do about his marriage? Could it be saved? He knew Lisa would never be capable of bringing him as much happiness as Charlie. Should he just accept it? After all, he was no longer a young man.

He wondered if Nick would be awake yet, then he decided obviously not, it would be far too early. He turned on the TV in the kitchen, the news headlines were just starting for 6am news. He had hoped this would take his mind off of his own problems, however stories of war-torn countries, homeless children, people fleeing their homes in fear of persecution, they just added to his anguish.

Rak knew he had been unfair to Charlie, she wasn't really asking him to choose between her and his children, she just wanted more of him—still in secret though. He felt immense guilt for the way his relationship with his children had developed. He knew it was his own fault, he resolved he could not let another woman come between them again.

Just as the news finished, he picked up his phone. He needed to send a text.

'Hello darling, I do hope you're ok. Just to let you know, Geeta stayed here last night. She might finally be seeing sense, let's hope. Told me she's not been happy with him for a while. I'm not pressuring her, she'll make her own decision, it had better be the right one. I hope you're well, let me know if you're free for a drink in the week.'

He hit the send button before he had chance to change his mind. Rak felt immediate trepidation, should he have suggested meeting Amira for a drink? Oh fuck; what was he thinking?

Around ten minutes later his phone pinged

'Hi Rak, yes I'm well thank you. Good news about Geeta, let's keep everything crossed. I'm busy this week but I am free this evening, Rose & Crown? *7pm? x'*

Rak knew the only person he could talk to right now was Amira. After their last meeting he felt he could trust her, he knew they still had something

'Yeah, sounds good. Would you like to have dinner? On me xxx'

He walked over towards the fancy coffee machine Lisa had bought; he needed another coffee. The phone pinged.

'Yes, that would be good thanks. You know I hate cooking for one. See you later, I'm looking forward to it xxx'

As he sat and drank his coffee, looking out over the garden, he had convinced himself that they were only meeting as friends, to discuss their children. Although Geeta's words were running through his head, 'why don't you get back together?'

A couple of hours later, after a refreshing shower

and a chance to collect his thoughts, Rak decided to go and play in his garage—something he hadn't done for a long time. He had different bits and pieces he used to tinker with, not something he had done recently. Lisa complained about the mess and the noise.

He was just taking apart a component he was experimenting with when Geeta came in. "Dad, it's Charlie for you, here you are."

His heart missed a beat, he felt his stomach hit the floor, he held out his hand and took the phone from Geeta. He waited for her to leave before speaking, he was aware his breathing felt heavy. "What do you want?" he was trying to focus on anything except the phone call.

"I thought, I hoped we could talk. I don't know what… oh, Rak; don't do this!"

He could feel tears, hot tears in his eyes, his heart ached, he just wanted to hold her, right then. "Charlie, look, I said everything last night. You know why; you can't expect to tell me how much he's hurt you and then ask me to do nothing about it. And you cannot make me choose between you and my kids; I won't have it. It was fun while it lasted, baby, but please, accept it's over. I'm hanging up now, ok? Bye."

Rak knew he did not mean it; he knew he loved her, and he wanted to be with her more than anything. But he also knew he could not come second to another man, especially a man like Brad. As he was putting his phone on the work bench, he noticed a text.

'Alright mate, I've got a pass later, around lunchtime. Do you fancy a round? We could have a catch up. Let me know.'

Rak looked at the message for a couple of minutes, did he want to see Nick? He knew he would have to tell him everything but then he thought about his friend.

'Hello mate, yeah go on then. If you've managed to get a free pass, be a shame not to. 2pm suit you? Cheers.'

A couple of minutes later the phone pinged.

'Great, yeah. See you at 2. Cheers'

70

Sunday Lunchtime

5 Main Street

Charlie decided she needed some perspective on what was happening in her life. After her telephone call with Rak, she had texted Anna. She needed to hear someone else's thoughts on what was happening. She decided to invite her over for lunch.

"So why, exactly, has he got the arse with you?" Anna was filling her plate from the mezze of cooked meats, cheeses, olives, salad and crusty bread Charlie had prepared. Surprisingly, for a petite woman, only a size eight, Anna ate quite a lot, and Charlie had already considered this.

"He says that I need to let him look after me. That I shouldn't have bollocked him for smacking Brad." Charlie had already filled Anna in regarding the events of the previous Friday night."

"Well, I have to say Charlie, he's right. Why on Earth did you tell him off? For fuck's sake, Brad's had it coming long enough."

Charlie wasn't expecting her friend to defend Brad, but she was taken aback by her defence of Rak. "I know that, but he keeps getting hurt. For me. Oh, Anna, I wish I was married to him instead."

They had a couple more glasses of wine, continuing to enjoy the platter of food "There's something else as well, he thought I was trying to make him choose between me and his kids."

Anna looked at her friend, surprised. "Why, what do you mean?"

Charlie took a bite of her bread and cheese. "I might have said that I need him more than they do because they're grown up. The thing is, his daughter really needs him at the moment, which I'm aware of. When he divorced his first wife, the kids didn't bother with him much, especially Geeta."

Anna put her hand up, a gesture that she needed to interrupt. "Why did you say that? You can't be jealous of his kids Charlie, they're a permanent fixture. You need to sort this out." She was giving her friend a knowing look, looking through her thick, black fringe at her. "What are you going to do about

Brad? You can't seriously take him back now?" Anna had a look of certainty in her eyes, sure her friend would see sense now

"I don't know what to do Anna. We are still married and well, let's be honest, he owns half this house on paper. I don't know if I can afford to divorce him. I think he knows about Rak. He could have me for adultery"

Anna was shocked by her friend's revelation. "Does he have proof? Photos? Phone calls? Because if not, he's not got a leg to stand on. You know, you should've called the police on Friday night, got it properly recorded what he tried to do to you."

Charlie knew her friend was right. "No proof but he heard me call Rak, baby, that's it. But he thinks there's something going on. And let's face it, he's right. Well, he was." Charlie started crying, again. "It's over; he said it's over, 'a bit of fun while it lasted', that's what he said. Anna, I love him. It can't be over, it can't be."

Anna held her friend tightly, not sure what to say.

"His friend, Nick, he said he wanted more, to be together properly. But he's never told me that. And now he doesn't want anything." Charlie cried even harder; Anna held her even tighter.

Anna decided she would stay with Charlie, she would call work tomorrow morning, say she would be late in, emergency dental appointment would do.

She didn't dare leave her friend in this state. Anna hoped she would see Rak herself, things needed to be said. "Look, I'm staying here tonight, no arguments. Now, I need my hair colouring and this evening, we'll go for a drink in that pub over there. It will be alright Charlie, I promise."

Charlie composed herself, got her salon keys and a bottle of wine and they both walked over to *Heirs & Graces*. Sunday special for friends.

As the pair walked over towards the salon, Charlie glanced over at Rak's house. She saw him, on the drive. He was putting his golf clubs into the boot of his car. He looked sad, withdrawn. She was desperate to go over, hold him. Say everything would be ok, that they could work everything out. Then he looked up, he was looking straight at her. He saw her and immediately put his head down, looking away from her. Charlie felt her heart break into a thousand more pieces. She continued to watch; he got into the car, reversed off his drive and drove past, not looking at her once.

Charlie continued to the salon, opened the door, both women went inside, then she cried her heart out all over again.

71

Sunday Afternoon

Upper Loughton Golf Club

Nick had arrived at the club first, eager to escape before Julia had a change of mind. The pub had been extremely busy all lunchtime, busier than expected, and he didn't want to forsake his game of golf. "All right, Ted? We've not booked a tee-time, but any chance me and Rak can have a round?"

Ted Walsh was in his sixties, he had been the course manager for nearly twenty years and had quite a soft spot for both Nick and Rak since they always bought him a bottle of something expensive at Christmas. "Don't see why not. How did yesterday go? I was gonna pop down, but it was manic here. Did you raise much?"

Nick smiled. "Not added it all up yet, Ted, but yeah, I would say around five hundred quid, so not bad. Me and Rak'll match it as well, so about a grand. Thanks for the raffle prize, Dorian and Kate won it."

Ted chuckled, "are you having a laugh? I'll have to close the bloody course if them two are going round for the day."

Nick laughed. "Don't worry mate, Rak won the meal for two at my place, he'll swap 'em."

Ted looked relieved. "Thank Christ for that, where is he anyway? Not like him to be late."

Nick looked at his watch. "I was early, Ted, to be honest. We arranged to meet at two. He'll be here in a minute."

Just then the Aston pulled into the car park. Nick made his way towards Rak's car, to greet his friend. "All right mate? How you feeling? Rough?"

Rak got out, shaking his head. "No mate, feel all right, not got a hangover, anyway. You?"

Nick smiled, "No mate, woke up feeling ok. Good day for a spot of golf, eh? What you done with Charlie, left her in bed?"

Rak's face changed to reflect the mood he was in. "No. No, erm... look, it's over. I've ended it," he looked through Nick, looking away into the distance, "it wasn't working. I told her last night we're finished. She's not taking it too well, rang this morning, upset. I told her to accept it, that it was fun while it lasted." Nick knew Rak too well.

"Maybe you should tell yourself that mate, because from where I'm standing you ain't too happy either. Could it be that it's just a row? We all have 'em. You knew what you were getting into mate, you can't say you didn't. You told me you were happy; that you've never been happier." Nick was genuinely confused.

"I was happy but I don't think I was making her happy. She wanted me to put her above the kids. And she had the nerve to bollock me for smacking that loser she's married to. I don't need it, I have enough shit from Lisa, don't need two of 'em. Come on, let's go and play golf."

Nick knew his friend was bluffing, he knew he was more upset than he would ever show. Nick knew he had to do something.

As they made their way around the course, Nick was very aware he had asked his friend to meet with him for personal reasons—he wanted to ask him something. Although now his nerves were getting the better of him. "Eh mate, can I ask you something? It's personal though."

Rak looked back at Nick, he'd just hit a hole in one on the ninth hole. "Yeah, course you can, but I'm not talking about Charlie, you got it?"

Nick knew he was serious. "No, it's not about Charlie."

Rak nodded.

"You see, the thing is, you're nearly my age, ain't ya?"

"Yeah, I suppose, four years younger though." Rak laughed but seeing Nick hadn't, he stopped.

"I don't know how to ask you this."

Rak wanted to move onto the next hole. "Come on mate, what is it? I'm meeting Amira at seven for Christ's sake."

Nick could not hide his surprise, however, he didn't want to get side-tracked by asking for further details. "As you've gotten older, have you found you can't last as long? Y'know, in bed?" Nick was embarrassed and Rak could tell.

"Well, what do you mean? Before the point of no return? Yeah, not as long as I used to, but I still enjoy myself. Why, what's going on?"

Nick began walking towards the next hole. "I can't last now mate, about ten minutes and that's it, and then only once. I think Julia's getting frustrated, she wants more."

Rak could see his friend had been struggling with this for a while. "Well, I can't go for hours mate; fucking hell, we're not twenty anymore. Do you enjoy yourself?"

Nick looked at his friend, slightly more embarrassed now. "Yeah, I do but she ain't…, you know…, get what I mean?"

Rak understood perfectly. "Have you discussed it with her?"

Nick shook his head. "No, I've just made excuses not to get close to her, y'know, too tired, too pissed. I'm embarrassed mate to be honest. Last time we did y'know, she said, 'is that it?'"

Rak was slightly lost for words, never having been in this position himself. He always made sure the woman he was with was satisfied. "Why don't you mix it up a bit? When I noticed I was getting, shall we say, less longevity, I made it a priority that the lady was satisfied first. Never had any complaints." Rak took his shot, missing the hole by millimetres.

"I have tried mate, but she's always keen to get on with the main event, that used to work for both of us you see. I feel under so much pressure, it makes it worse."

Rak had got an idea, an idea that reminded him of Charlie, something they had done only the week before. He felt an ache, a longing, as he recalled the sensations. "Have you tried just playing around?"

Nick looked confused. "No, I love Julia. Anyway, that won't change my problem, will it?"

Rak realised what he had said and smiled. "No mate, I mean together, with Julia. Don't go all the way, just play. Y'know, mouths, hands, tongues? Do you need a diagram?"

Nick took his shot, straight in the hole; Rak had

to smile. "Don't do that basically mate."

Even Nick laughed. "Very funny, trust me to get it straight in the hole now. No, we don't do that so much, she never says what she wants. I think she's gonna buy a vibrator, I saw her internet history. Mate, I don't want her to prefer some battery-operated toy to me."

Rak was surprised but not shocked. "Amira had one once, we had fun with it together. She got it because her mate had got one, raving about it. But Amira said she didn't want to use it on her own. So, one night, the kids were at her parent's house, we tried it together. Fucking hell, it was magic. We didn't use it all the time, but it was a toy. Might be good for you, make it more fun again. Why don't you surprise her and get one, take it to Brussels?"

Nick thought for moment. "Do you think? Do couples use 'em?"

Rak nodded. "Yeah. Takes the pressure off, mate, I can tell ya. And you can find out what she likes in a playful way. Get a couple, they work on different areas, know what I mean?" Rak's eyes lit up, the memory of Amira making him smile.

"All right, yeah, I will. Just one thing though, what do I get?"

Rak laughed, "I'll look on the internet with you, but I draw the line at going shopping together."

Nick laughed, the image of them both in Ann Summers amused him.

As they were playing the last couple of holes, Nick knew he had to ask Rak. "Why are you meeting Amira anyway?"

Rak looked at him, trying to decide himself why he was meeting his ex-wife. "I don't really know mate. I texted her to say that Geeta stayed with me last night, we're both totally against this twat she's seeing as you know, and I ended up asking her out for dinner. We both put kisses at the end of our texts. I don't know what I'm doing."

Nick could see Rak was struggling, struggling to understand his emotions. "Do you want to sort things out with Charlie? And don't piss me around because I know when you're lying."

Rak looked away and sighed. "Yeah, of course I do. I love her, mate, but I can't see past how she defended him, after what he did."

Nick shook his head. "Well, look, don't shag Amira, eh? You might regret it. Give Charlie another chance, she loves you and you know she does. I told you it wouldn't be easy, didn't I?" Nick was looking right at him now.

"Yes; yes, you did. I wouldn't listen. Anyway, I thought you'd be happy I was meeting Amira; you always did get on well with her, better than Lisa or Charlie."

Nick laughed. "Yeah, that's true, I'll give you that. I always did like Amira. She was good for ya. But you, my friend, love Charlie and as much as you say otherwise, it ain't over yet."

Rak knew Nick was right, but he didn't know what to do next.

72

The Rose & Crown

Amira had not been sure how to dress. She wasn't sure why she was meeting Rak. Was it to discuss the kids? To enjoy a meal as friends? Or for something more? She couldn't even decide what she hoped the reason might be, although she did experience a warm sensation when she thought about him. *The Rose & Crown* always evoked good memories for Amira. After all, it was the place she got engaged to Rak; the place where her life had really began. She knew they still both frequented the pub, neither choosing to avoid it after the split. Amira had dated a couple of men after

Rak, but she had never suggested here as a meeting point. It would always be her and Rak's place.

Amira was early, she wanted to get settled before Rak arrived. She sipped a glass of Merlot and sat at the exact table she had been seated at when she got engaged. She was thinking how over the years things had altered. The feeling of excitement she had on that night some twenty-nine years or so ago had diminished over the years, now she felt more as if she had to be grateful for what had gone before, feeling there were more good times behind her than in front of her.

The door opened and in walked Rak; he saw her immediately and waved before strolling over to her. "Hey, you look good; shall I get a bottle?"

Amira smiled, she welcomed the compliment. "Thanks, not looking too shabby yourself. Yes, get a bottle, save us having to keep getting up at our age," she laughed, and his eyes smiled. "Get a couple of menus as well, I'm starving."

They both settled, enjoying a glass and perusing the menus. "The food has changed over the years, what the hell is a Poke Bowl?"

Amira laughed "Probably not what you think it is. Sorry, couldn't resist." They both shared a naughty laugh. "Where's the ice maiden? Surprised you could meet tonight."

Rak was still smiling. "Still in London, at her sisters. She could've left me, I've no idea. The wardrobe is still full of clothes but that means nothing. How have you been?"

Amira laughed, looking into his eyes—the eyes she used to get lost in. "Not bad thanks, keeping busy. Rak, why did you ask me out?" she knew she should have waited before asking; to see how the evening progressed, but she wanted to know.

"Oh hun, I wanted to see you. I don't know why, I don't know what I want anymore." The eye contact between them was intense.

"How's the hairdresser?"

Rak took a breath, "We…, we had a falling out last night. I ended it."

Amira could not hide her shock. "What? Last week you said you loved her, what happened?"

Rak now had to decide how much to divulge. "Her husband attacked her, Amira, tried to force her on Friday night," Amira's mouth hung open, gobsmacked, "I smacked him about a bit—he deserved worse believe me. Then she bollocked me for it. Me? Can you believe that?"

Amira knew her ex-husband's temper was awful. She could imagine what he would have done. "So, what happened? Are you over?"

Rak didn't know the answer. "Shall we order some food? Service ends soon. Then we can talk properly. What you having?"

Amira was familiar with this particular distraction technique. "Ok, I see. Tell me what you want to darling; don't tell me anything you don't want to; we're not married any more. Chicken; the chicken casserole with dumplings. You?"

Rak took her hand. "I will try to explain, I promise, but I don't understand myself. I quite fancy the pie. I'll go and order".

As he walked to the bar, Amira thought on how much she still loved him and wanted him. Rak took a couple of moments to collect his thoughts, did he want Amira back? Perhaps he was better off without Charlie?

He returned to the table, and a full glass—Amira had topped them both up. "Food ordered. I'm really looking forward to it, not had pie in ages."

Amira decided in that instant that he would only tell her what he wanted to, so she would enjoy his company and not quiz him. "How was the fundraiser? Amit said he enjoyed it, he popped in earlier."

Rak appreciated the subject change, he knew she wouldn't question him too much. "It was good, hun, Slim bought his classic car mates along, the weather was super and the beer flowed. There were a couple of live bands too, you should've come along."

Amira had to smile. "I don't think that would've gone down too well, do you? Pleased you enjoyed it; did you raise much?"

Rak chose to ignore the former comment. "Yeah, about a grand when Nick and I make our contribution, so a good day all round. Well, until the end." Rak looked away. "How was Amit today? He said last night there's this girl he's seeing; apparently, he's serious about her."

Amira chose to stick with treading carefully. "Yeah, he was in a good mood. You two going car shopping next week, or something. He's really looking forward to it, Rak."

He sensed the warning in her voice, not to let him down.

"I know, so am I, hun. Geeta was still at mine when I came out to meet you, she said she needed some clothes from home, I offered to pick some up for her and she agreed, so I'm going there afterwards."

Amira raised an eyebrow. "Don't have a scrap with Sanj, she won't trust you again if you do. I mean it, Rak."

He knew she meant it and he agreed, now was a critical time, Geeta was finally confiding in him, why would he jeopardise that?

As the evening progressed, they both agreed the meal was excellent, savouring every mouthful. "This is fantastic, honey; tastes home-made too. How's your chicken?"

Amira was mid-mouthful. "Fab, thanks, better than mine actually."

"I don't believe that. Yours was always fantastic." Rak replied, taking a sip of wine. "I don't know if

Charlie's worth the hassle, I really don't. I do love her, but I think she's still in love with her husband; how can I compete with that?"

Amira was rather surprised the conversation had moved from the food to more personal matters. However, she was pleased he'd raised the subject. "Have you asked her? I know what you're like, you always make your mind up before asking the question."

Rak was a little taken aback, but then recalled how long she had known him. "Yes, I know what I can be like. No, I've not asked her. But why would she defend him after what he did if she didn't still love him? Hmm? Answer me that. You're a woman." Rak was beginning to get ever so slightly irritated

"I don't know darling, I'm not her. If any man tried that with me, it would be the last thing they ever did. Do you love her?" Amira had placed her knife and fork down; she was really looking into Rak's eyes.

"Yes. Yes, very much. I had hoped we could become more but that doesn't seem likely. I thought, after she had met Geeta and Amit, she would realise how I felt, but she doesn't seem to acknowledge how important it is to me that the kids got on with her. Perhaps she was never serious in the first place."

Amira placed her hand over Rak's. "Have you told her? Perhaps she's feeling the same, unsure of what your intentions are. The kids have no idea you two are together, you know that don't you? They don't recognise her as being important in your life, Geeta thinks she is just her new boss and Amit, well Amit didn't say anything."

Rak was surprised now. "You asked them about her? Really?" he laughed.

"Yeah, caught red handed. I was curious, ok? Anyway, have you told her, how you feel?"

Rak was still laughing. "No, I haven't, ok? I'm scared; scared she'll run a mile. I told Nick but…"

Amira interrupted, "You told Nick? For fuck's sake Rak, you're not shagging Nick. You need to tell her. If you love her and you think she loves you, then don't lose it!" Amira was serious and he knew it.

"But what if she chooses him? What then? It's called self-preservation, honey."

They both took quite a large sip of wine.

"Sort it out Rak, I want you to be happy."

"I want you to be too. Why haven't you met anyone new?"

Amira looked past him, her mind trying to decide what he needed to hear. "Because I don't want to, ok?" she wanted to say because she was waiting for him, but then he already knew that.

They enjoyed the remainder of the wine then made their way to the car park together. "Will you be alright getting Geeta's stuff? Do you want me to come with you? I'm going home that way after all."

Rak thought it might not be the worst idea he had heard all day. "Yeah, that would be good, thanks hun."

73

Sunday Night

The Bull

Charlie really hadn't wanted to go to *The Bull* but Anna had insisted. "It'll get you out, now go and change into something suitable. Quickly. And put some make-up on too. Bring back Charlie Redman." Anna was clapping her hands and smiling but she was also serious, her friend would have happily sat and cried the evening away, and Anna wasn't going to let that happen.

They arrived at *The Bull* at 9pm; the pub was half busy, not manic. Nick was on the bar and Julia had gone for a lie down after contending with the lunchtime crowd. When he saw Charlie walk in, he was rather surprised. He also felt relieved Rak wasn't there. He noticed the first thing she did was scour the bar area for Rak.

"Hello, you two lovely ladies, what can I get for you? I don't think I've had the pleasure before." Nick was looking towards Anna.

"Anna please meet Nick. Nick owns the pub— has done for years. Nick, Anna is my best friend. We all need best friends, don't we? Two G&T's please, doubles."

Nick had got the sense that Charlie was not in the mood for being sociable, especially with him. "Pleased to meet you, Anna. Take a seat, I'll bring 'em over." Nick was rather upset, he did feel he was being unfairly blamed for Rak's decisions, they weren't a double act.

The two friends took a seat at the table which faced the bar entrance, if he did show his face she wanted to know and be in a position to compose herself. "Oh, hang on, I need the loo now. This is because you rushed me." Charlie made her way towards the ladies. Anna was secretly pleased when Nick appeared with the drinks.

"I think we might need a quick chat, best friend to best friend, get my meaning?"

Nick did agree but was also hesitant, he didn't want any blame to come back to him. "Yeah, ok, but quickly. I don't wanna be in the middle of this and

I'm sure you don't either."

Anna gestured for him to sit down. "Ok, in a nutshell, she loves your best friend, Rak, does he love her?"

Nick had to admit, he liked the direct approach. "Yeah. Yeah, he does. But the pair of 'em are a nightmare. Neither says anything to the other in case they get it wrong. They could be the next Burton and bloody Taylor. What do you suggest?"

Anna rolled her eyes, "I've no idea darling, but this can't go on. I saw them in Stratford, and they were so happy together. They are good together."

Nick was smiling, Anna looked at him, quizzically. "Stratford? Yeah, another fine example. After they saw you, they had a row, Rak had an episode because he found out Charlie pays the mortgage on her place. He went mental. They fell out. You see, that's how fickle it is."

Anna nodded. "But from what I can gather, your Rak only has her best interests at heart. She's stubborn, Nick."

Nick laughed. "Yeah, but so is he. That's the problem, when they're good, they're bloody fantastic, but when they have an argy-bargy, there's no talking to either of 'em. Leave it with me, I'll have a chat with him, no promises mind."

Anna smiled. "I'll do the same. Although, I do feel they need to come to the same conclusion by themselves. Brad doesn't help matters as I'm sure you're more than aware. I hate that excuse of a man. I quite like your Rak, I just don't think she's used to being looked after."

Nick nodded. "And he ain't used to being told off. He's like a child sometimes but I've said enough now. Enjoy your evening, good to meet ya."

Anna smiled and took his hand. "Likewise. If you're ever in Stratford and fancy a drink, let me know."

Nick laughed. "Sorry love, I am happily married. I like the easy life." They both erupted into laughter together.

Charlie came out of the ladies to hear Anna and Nick laughing. She wondered what on Earth was happening now. She made her way back to the table just as Nick was turning round to return behind the bar. She got comfortable then took a large sip of her G&T. "What were you two laughing about? Looked cosy."

Anna was smiling to herself inside. "I wanted his number, but he's married. Never mind, the best ones so frequently are. How are you feeling?"

Charlie didn't know whether to believe this or not. "You fancy Nick?" she whispered.

"Yeah, why? What's wrong with him?"

Charlie looked over towards the bar, she had never really appraised Nick's looks before. "Hmm, he's alright I suppose. I prefer dark men, you know that. Never have fancied fair hair. He's a bit old for you, he's older than Rak, y'know."

Anna laughed. "Well, that's quite funny as Rak seems to behave like a child. Why would he ignore you? He needs to act his age. What's his wife like?" Anna was gesturing towards Nick again now.

"Julia? She's lovely. Don't get any ideas Anna; it doesn't end well, believe me."

Anna looked her friend straight in the face. "It's not ending well for you, darling, because you won't let it. Let him look out for you. Women need to be wanted and men want to be needed. He wants to be needed, and he wants you."

Charlie felt as if she had just been reprimanded by a teacher at school like when she was ten years old. She also knew her friend was right. She knew Rak loved being needed and she knew he wanted her—he wanted her so much.

The two friends remained in the pub until nearly closing time, both feeling rather tipsy as they made their way back over to Charlie's house. Nick had offered to walk them both back over the road, but they insisted they would be safe.

Rak was just driving into the village as they walked out of the pub, he initially saw the Audi TT on Charlie's driveway. He was curious as to who it belonged to having not spotted it earlier. As he drove up 'The Jitty', he spotted Charlie and Anna leaving *The Bull*. He did consider stopping, to see if she was ok, but then quickly thought now was not the right time. He wanted to get a quick drink in with Nick before he closed up. Rak parked on his drive and wandered over to the pub.

Charlie had seen him, she had hoped he would stop, ask if she was ok. She was upset he didn't. *'This is hopeless,'* she thought.

"Evening landlord, how goes it?"

Nick had his back to the door. "We're closed, piss off." He knew it was Rak, Nick was laughing, "lock the door behind ya, mate. Do you want a Chivas?"

Rak locked the door and took a seat at the bar. "Yeah, a large one. Has Charlie just been in with her mate?"

Nick poured Rak and himself a drink, his was not as large. "Yeah, why? You see 'em?"

Rak took a sip. "Yeah, just now. Walking back over to her place. Was she all right?"

Nick looked up. "Did you stop and ask her?"

Rak took another sip. "No, I thought you'd be all locked up if I was any later. Was she? All right?"

Nick took a sip of his whiskey before replying, "no, not really herself to be honest mate. How was Amira?"

Rak was still trying to find out about Charlie. "What do you mean, not herself. Has that twat been bothering her again?"

Nick shook his head. "Unless that twat is you, then no, I don't think so. She still loves you, mate, for some bizarre reason."

Rak sighed. "I know that. I feel the same. I'm sure we'll figure something out. But I'm not rushing into anything. Not this time."

Nick knew better than to push it. "How was Amira? Is she keeping well?"

Rak lightened his attitude. "Yeah, she's good thanks, mate. We had a good chat; she still knows how I think." Rak looked thoughtful. "We had to meet the layabout who is Sanj tonight. Geeta wanted some fresh clothes, asked me to pick some up for her. Y'know what? I actually thought he was ok. So did Amira. I just think he's young and strug-gling to find where he fits into the world. He let us in, made us a drink. Made us welcome. Talked about Geeta, asked how she was, if she'd be back soon. He said he's looking for a job, but nothing stands out to him. I might offer him something with me, what do you think? After all, our paths were mapped out for us, weren't they? He said he doesn't have much to do with his dad, doesn't fancy taking over the business."

Nick thought for a moment. "Be a good way to keep an eye on him too. Yeah, why not?" Nick took his phone out of his pocket. "Looked at these earlier, y'know what we were talking about this afternoon?"

Rak took his friend's phone out of his hand. "Oh? Hmmm… very interesting. Did you order anything?"

Nick smiled. "Yeah, these two," he was showing Rak two sex toys, one advertising amazing clitoral stimulation and a rampant rabbit. "I can collect them tomorrow. Do you think she'll like the idea? And I found this gel too, meant to delay the inevitable, so I got one of them too."

Rak was quite amazed by how proactive his friend had been in the few hours they had been apart. "Fucking hell, mate, you don't mess around do ya? Yeah, I think Julia will be very happy with that. Surprise her though, wait 'til you get there." Rak smiled.

"I thought I heard voices, hello gorgeous, you're late tonight." Nick quickly put his phone away, it was Julia. "What you talking about? Diamonds?" Julia chuckled.

Rak got up and went behind the bar to embrace Julia. "Hello, sexy lady, where you been all my life?"

Julia was laughing. "Get off, will ya? You couldn't handle me if you had the chance."

Nick was laughing. "Hey, you two, guess what? I got propositioned tonight. By an attractive young woman. What do you reckon about that, eh?"

Julia looked at her husband, mock dismay on her face. "I think I need one of them," she pointed to the whiskies both friends were enjoying.

Nick obliged. "Yeah, Charlie's mate, Anna. Asked if I fancied going out for a drink with her."

Rak smiled. "What did you say?"

Nick shook his head. "Nah, I'm happily married. Don't need any hassle. She was disappointed to be honest."

Julia squeezed him tight. "Yes, you are happily married. Remember that. So, was she good looking? And young?"

Nick looked at Rak, perfectly aware he had met Anna. "Anna's all right, Julia, but she's not a patch on you. And she's a bit posh for this reprobate, not saying you're rough or anything."

Nick shook his head at his friend's attempt at a save. Julia playfully smacked his arm. "If I didn't like you, Rak Banerjee, I'd bar you for that. So, shall I be worried?"

Nick grabbed her. "No, darlin', you've got no reason to be worried. I've seen him struggling to keep up, I can't be arsed with that."

All three of them laughed.

74

Banerjee Engineering

Rak had arrived in the office early, even before Tilly and Rollo. He wanted to look at the possibility of recruiting a business development manager—in particular, Sanj. Earlier at home over breakfast he had asked Geeta her thoughts on the matter. He had resolved that to have a decent relationship with his daughter, he needed to stop making decisions for her. He had consulted with Geeta and she agreed it could work well. He had her blessing.

After looking at the figures and moving around the responsibilities of the office, he could see there was an opportunity waiting to be filled. He was also keen after finding out the previous night that Sanj's father ran a similar business. Rak knew he needed to increase his customer base and he thought Sanj might be the answer. He dialled the mobile number Geeta had given him.

"If you're selling anything, piss off. I'm busy."

Rak mused at how novel this approach to answering the phone was. "No, I'm not selling anything. It's Rak, Rak Banerjee. I'd like to have a chat with you. Can you come over to my office this morning, say around 11:00?" he heard Sanj immediately sharpen himself up.

"Sorry Mr. Banerjee, I didn't know the number, thought it was cold callers. Is Geeta all right?"

Rak had to smile to himself. "Yeah, she's fine thanks. And it's Rak, ok? I'm not ninety; not yet. I would like to discuss an opportunity that's arisen within my business. I understand you studied business management at uni, am I right?"

Sanj was obviously trying to sound awake now. "Yeah, I did, that's right. But I haven't found the right thing. The old man keeps ramming the business down my throat but it's not what I want. I want to do it for myself, not just step into the old man's shoes."

Rak had to smile, again. "Yeah, that's what I did," he knew he would have embarrassed the younger man now.

"Oh, I'm sorry. I didn't mean that how it sounded."

Rak was laughing, "Yes you did. And you're right. I admire your honesty; it's too easy sometimes to pick up where the old man left off. Come and see me, we'll have a coffee." He could hear Sanj breathe again.

"Ok, sounds great. See you at 11:00. Will you text me the address?"

Rak smiled, he was beginning to warm to Sanj. "Yeah, no worries, see you then".

Rak was happy, he already felt a sense of achievement. He picked up his phone,

'Hi Amira, hope you're alright. I had an idea last night; I'm going to offer Sanj a job. Geeta approves too. I enjoyed last night, enjoyed seeing you. Don't leave it too long 'til the next time xxx'

Tilly had arrived, Rak heard Rollo first, he had a way all his own of clambering into the office. "Will you calm down? Now!"

Rak couldn't resist. "If you really want me to, I was only making us a coffee."

Tilly was giggling to herself. "Not you, this bloody dog. Honestly, Rak, he's hyper this morning. What you doing here so early?"

Rollo came bounding up to Rak, ready for his daily fuss and cuddle. "Good boy; hello, boy. Good, sit, sit then." Rak fed him a treat.

"That's why he loves it here so much, don't get easy treats all weekend. You spoil him, you do. He's got you right where he wants ya."

Rak smiled, "They're not called man's best friend for nothing y'know. Good boy, Rollo; good boy. Come on, settle down now." The dog sat at Rak's feet under his desk, he would stay there as long as Rak did. Rak's phone pinged.

'That's great news, good idea. Yes, I enjoyed last night too. I enjoy seeing you, Rak. Thanks for dinner, my treat next time xxx'

Rak was mindful he could be giving Amira the wrong impression, but she wasn't stupid. She knew where his heart was at. If the truth be told, he was happy having her on his side. He still wasn't ruling out a reconciliation of some sort. What do they call it? Keeping one's options open?

Rak was fussing Rollo and drinking his coffee. "Tills, I've got Geeta's boyfriend, Sanj, coming to see me around eleven. I want your opinion on him so join me for the meeting would you? Nothing formal, just in here. I'm going to offer him a job."

Tilly was surprised. "Thought you thought he was a tosser? What's changed?"

Rak smiled, "I met him."

The time on the office clock read 11:10, no sign of Sanj. Rak was beginning to think his initial thoughts were correct, that Sanj was a waste of space, then his phone rang. "Hello, Rak Banerjee."

A flustered voice was on the other end. "Rak, I'm lost. I'm going round in circles, I'm near a pub called *The Bull*. The satnav keeps taking me in and out of this village."

Rak laughed. "Ok mate, park up and go into the pub, tell Nick, the landlord, who you are and he'll give you a diagram of how to find us. Is that ok?"

Sanj sounded relieved. "Thanks, hopefully I won't be long."

Rak smiled. "You're literally five minutes away, Nick'll tell ya. See you soon, kettle's on. Take your time." Rak was thinking more and more about how wrong he had been about this young man.

Around ten minutes later Sanj arrived. "I'm so sorry for being late, it's so easy to find when you know where you're going to."

Rak shook Sanj's hand. "No worries, you passed the first test." Sanj looked worried. "I'm only kidding, come on, sit down. Tea or coffee?"

Sanj was grateful to take a seat. "Coffee, please; black, no sugar"

Tilly smiled. "Just how I have mine and I get on all right with him." she laughed as she went to make the drinks.

Rollo was sniffing Sanj, checking him out. "Are you all right with dogs?" Rak hadn't thought.

"Yeah, love dogs. He's a handsome chap, isn't he? Good boy."

Rollo was just happy to have made a new friend.

"Right, I won't mess around. I need someone to take this business further, y'know networking, all that stuff. To be honest, I can't be arsed and I'm getting too old to be nice to people just for their business. I had hoped to pass it onto the kids, but they're not interested and I can't blame them. If you're going to make a go of things with Geeta, well you're nearly family. Are you interested?"

Sanj was a bit shell shocked, he wasn't expecting that speech. "Wow, you don't mess around do ya? Are you only offering me this job because of Geeta or because of my talents, what I can bring?"

It was Rak's turn to be shocked, this kid really was a breath of fresh air. "To be honest, both. I want, I need, my daughter to be happy. However, if you work for me, you would be treated like any other member of staff, even if you and her were to finish. If, however, you two make a go of things, well let's just say, there could be more for you. Do you understand?" Rak was looking him straight in the eye now.

"Yeah, I understand. Before we go any further, Rak, I want you to know, I do love your daughter and I also need her to be happy. I know I've been a twat recently, but I need to show her I can be better. This would be a great start. So yes, I would like to look at your offer."

Rak took a sip of his coffee, wishing it was something stronger. "I appreciate your honesty Sanj, how does 30k a year sound, to start with, and what you driving at the moment?" Rak got out of his chair to look out of the window. "And a company car, you can't meet customers in that boy racer wagon?"

Sanj was taken aback. "Thanks for your honesty too, mate." He was laughing, "yeah, sounds great; when can I start?"

Rak extended his hand. "How about now?"

Both men shook hands.

75

Monday Lunchtime
The Bull

"Right Sanj, welcome to your first working lunch. Don't get used to it every day though." Rak had decided a celebratory lunch was called for. He had invited Geeta along as well as Tilly, after all she would be working with Sanj. "Nick, I believe you met my new business development manager earlier, but this is Sanj Mistry. Please meet my best mate, Nick Carr."

Both men extended their hands to each other. "Pleased to meet ya, Sanj, if you can't find him in the office try here or the golf course, know what I mean?" Nick was laughing.

"Thanks mate, likewise. Nice place you've got here."

Rak smiled, he had made the right choice. "What's everyone having? You too, Nick."

Tilly went to find a table.

They ordered a selection of sandwiches, baguettes, chips and salad. "So Sanj, whereabouts are you from, originally?" Tilly was interested in people,

"I grew up the other side of Langham, but my family are originally from Kent. We moved when I was around five years old. My grandparents still live down there though."

Tilly liked Sanj and she had let Rak know in the car on the way over.

"Thanks, Dad; you're a star. I'm sure Sanj will work hard for you." Geeta was beaming, happy to see her father welcome her boyfriend into the fold, she was also mindful Rak would be watching his every move.

"No worries honey, it works for both of us. Now, you two need to find a place in the village. I heard there's a house going up to let next month, would you be interested?" Rak wanted to keep her close.

"That's a lovely thought, Dad, but I doubt we could afford it."

Rak squeezed her knee. "Leave that to me, would you be interested? You both work here now." Rak wanted to help his daughter, he felt he owed her.

"We'll see, Dad; let's see what happens in the next month."

Rak knew not to push it, but he couldn't deny he was excited.

The entrance door to the bar opened, it was Charlie. Rak's heart skipped a beat. He looked for an escape. "I just need the gents, carry on, I won't be long." He was up like a shot and straight into the gents. Charlie had seen this sharp exit, she just felt desolate now, unable to figure him out. She could see there was a cosy family lunch going on, she wouldn't stay.

"What can I get you Charlie? Glass of wine?"

There were tears in her eyes, she couldn't stop her voice from shaking. "Err; no, Nick. Sorry, I erm, this was a mistake."

She was just about to run out of the pub when Geeta spotted her. "Charlie, how you doing? Are you still ok with me starting tomorrow?"

Charlie didn't want to become embroiled in this conversation. "Yeah, nine would be great. Can't stop, see you then," and with that she ran towards the door.

Rak returned five minutes later to a concerned look from Nick.

76

Tuesday Morning

Heirs & Graces

Charlie arrived at the salon early, she wanted to give the place a spruce up before Geeta arrived. Geeta had texted her the previous evening to say she already had two clients booked in for her first day, Charlie was relieved, she didn't want to be finding her things to do.

The radio was playing 'I Will Always Love You' by Whitney Houston, Charlie immediately thought of Rak, recalling them watching 'The Bodyguard', happy with each other, together. She felt hot tears in her eyes, she knew she wouldn't be able to stop crying if she started. She picked up her phone, she needed to hear his voice. Just as she turned it on, it started ringing, Charlie was startled, she read the display. Brad.

"Hello," she knew she had to answer.

"Char, babe, I'm sorry. Please, listen to me."

Charlie stared out of the window, she was looking over towards Rak's house, wishing she was speaking with him, she let out a sigh.

"Char, I want to come home babe. Please. I want to make us work again. Please. I am so sorry."

Charlie felt the tears overtake her, but not for Brad. "Do what you like. I'm past caring," with that, she hung up.

Brad was left not knowing what his wife wanted but he had a good idea it wasn't him.

Charlie went into the back; she needed a coffee and to pull herself together. She couldn't let Geeta see her like this. It wouldn't be fair. The clock read 8:45; she had fifteen minutes to put her face back on and get happy. Firstly, the radio station was changed, no more sad love songs, not today. Then the make-up bag was out, full refresh, hair styled, clothes smoothed down, coffee drank. Charlie was ready.

The door opened at 8:55. "Hi Charlie, I'm not late am I? Dad was lecturing me on how to behave and 'make the most of this generous opportunity', you know what he's like."

Charlie felt a warm feeling, knowing that Rak must have been thinking of her. "Yes, I know what he's like. No, you're not late, anyway, I'm not your boss as such, remember? We're working together."

Geeta beamed the widest smile. "Thank you so much. Hey, you'll never guess what, Simon texted this morning, wishing me luck, isn't that lovely?"

Charlie laughed "Did he say, 'you can always come back if Charlie is a nightmare darling?' or similar?"

Geeta was laughing now, "Yeah; yeah, he did. How did you know?"

Charlie was shaking her head. "He said the same to me when I left him, 'always here for you darling', shame he never actually is. Would you like a coffee?"

Geeta nodded and walked towards the back room. "I'll make them, how do you take yours?"

Charlie was impressed "White please, not too much milk though, and no sugar, please. How's your dad? Is he alright?" Charlie knew she shouldn't be gleaning information from Geeta but reasoned it would be odd if she didn't ask.

"Yeah, he's ok thanks. He's given Sanj a job with him in the business. I hope they get on. To be honest, Dad's been in a funny mood all weekend, a bit moody really. Probably because Uncle Nick is going away, you know how inseparable they are. I asked him if he wanted to pop in later, but he said he'd got a really busy day. I don't think he's heard from Lisa, although for my money, that should please him. I shouldn't really say anything Charlie, but I don't like her. She uses my dad. I wish he'd meet someone else or get back with Mum. He said they both still love each other, I don't understand them."

Charlie could not believe what Geeta had just said, they both still love each other? Since when? Had Rak wanted to fall out with her so he could go back to Amira? He always promised her Amira wasn't a threat to her. Had he been lying? "Oh, right. Do you think they'll get back together then?" she had to know more.

"I don't know, Dad said no, but then they had dinner together on Sunday. I think he enjoyed himself, he decided to offer Sanj a job. Amit and I were talking about it, Amit doesn't think they will. I wish they would. They were good together."

Charlie hoped her face wasn't portraying how she felt: used, discarded, alone. Most of all angry. Angry with him for lying to her, angry with herself for believing him.

77

Tuesday Morning
Rak

Rak wanted to have breakfast with Geeta, it was important to wish her well on her first day at the salon. Geeta told him that she would be returning home to Sanj tonight, she felt she had punished him enough and she wanted to spend time with him. Rak wished he could spend time with Charlie, he was craving her. He knew it would take just one phone call or even a text and they could be together. But what if she didn't want him anymore, what then?

Rak was scared of rejection. It was the one thing that made him insecure. He knew he had a problem, but he didn't know what to do about it. Nick had told him to just call Charlie, then he would know one way or the other. That was the problem, whilst he was in limbo there was always a possibility but if the definite answer was no, that would kill him. Anyway, if Charlie wanted him back, she would call him, wouldn't she? She had made her choice very obvious.

Rak left home and wandered over to *The Bull*. He wanted to wish Julia and Nick a good break away, they both needed it. "Morning you lovely people, are you ready?"

Nick was just loading the cases into his car and Julia was looking in her handbag for the millionth time to see if the passports were still there.

"Great mate, looking forward to it. Can you tell her, we've got the passports—doing my head in."

Rak did love seeing Nick exasperated, it was a rare sight and it made him laugh when it did happen. "Calm down mate, romantic break away remember? Just being cautious aren't you, darling? Nothing wrong with that." Both Julia and Rak laughed.

"Oh, you know what he's like, Rak; he doesn't check anything. I'm just making sure we've got everything. How are you? Any news?"

Rak knew to what Julia was referring. "No, not yet. I don't think we..., I think it's run it's course to be honest. Knew she was too good to be true. Back on the shelf, eh? Well, apart from Lisa, and I don't know if she's even coming back. Not to worry, I want you two to enjoy yourselves, I'll keep an eye on the pub for you."

Nick shook his friend's hand. "Cheers mate, appreciate it. Y'know, you need to call her mate. You might be surprised."

Rak shook his head. "No. No, I don't think so. Do you need the keys to Pam's back?"

Nick laughed.

"What? What's funny?"

"Nothing, mate; nothing. No, hang on to 'em. You might need 'em" Nick winked at his friend before embracing him.

Julia gave Rak a tight squeeze and a quite a big kiss. "Easy, honey; you'll get Kate talking."

Julia looked him the eyes. "Call her, you listening? Promise me."

Rak was not promising anything and had learnt a long while ago not to make promises he wouldn't keep.

"We'll see. Get a diamond out of him, honey, a big one."

They got into the Porsche and drove away out of the village.

Rak knew time was getting on, he checked his watch. It was an Omega watch he had bought a very long time ago. He still loved wearing it. It read 10:34am. He needed to get into the office, Sanj would be waiting for him.

He walked back to his house, grabbed his phone, wallet and car keys. Straight into the Aston, radio on. He wanted to be in a good mood, he knew Sanj would no doubt report back to Geeta, who would report back to Amit, who would then tell Amira. This had been the chain of communication when the kids were little, Geeta always with her dad and Amit always telling Amira what was going on. Nothing had really changed, he was happy his children were friends as well as siblings—it was important.

Rak was enjoying driving his car, he decided he had got time for a little play and drove up to the main road. After last time he was more cautious, not taking the bends quite a fast, but still quite swiftly. He was recalling how worried Charlie had been that day, how concerned she was for him. Did she still love him?

The radio was playing a favourite of Rak's, 'I Heard It Through The Grapevine', by Marvin Gaye. He couldn't help himself, he found he was singing along. Rak was very aware that this was exactly how he was feeling. His fingers were tapping the steering wheel to the beat. He knew he had to do something, he had to see Charlie.

★ ★ ★

Zoe Jones was running late for her hair appointment. She was rather put out that her stylist, Geeta, had moved to Upper Loughton, although she had enjoyed bragging about the location of her new hair salon to anyone who would listen. She was on her mobile, using the handsfree function—her hands were actually flailing around, not even on the wheel. "Yeah, I know that dun I? How much will that be then? I've got the money, don't matter 'bout the money. Hang on, I don't know where I fucking am!" She was talking to her architect; Zoe was extending her house near to Langham and to say costs had run over would be an understatement. Zoe had illusions of being rich when in actual fact she owed so much on her credit cards and bank loans she was now seen as a risk.

Zoe had little to no regard for other road users, being preoccupied with her own thoughts and importance. Just then she spotted the tiny signpost directing her to Upper Loughton. Immediately, without indicating, she turned right. Straight into the path of an oncoming black Aston Martin. Rak slammed his brakes on, missing her by millimetres, if he hadn't been concentrating, he would have driven straight into the side of her car. He hit the horn so hard he thought he might break it.

Zoe was still on her call, not slightly phased by the near miss she had just created. "What's his fucking problem? You wanna try looking mate!" she shouted to Rak, having the roof of her convertible down. As Rak was about to reply with something unsavoury Zoe sped off. "They're a nightmare, these sports car drivers. Now, when can you have the plans with me for?" she was totally oblivious.

Rak was fuming mad now, he followed her, right into the village. She parked up outside *Heirs & Graces*. Rak jumped out of the Aston. "You do know I had the right of way. You were turning right. You should've waited."

Zoe looked at him like he was speaking a foreign language "What? What's your problem? You should get your eyes tested mate."

Rak knew he wasn't going to get anywhere.

"Fuck off; you should read the fucking highway code. You shouldn't be on the fucking road!"

Charlie and Geeta heard the commotion outside the salon, they both looked out of the window at the same time, naturally curious as hairdressers are. "Oh God, your dad's rowing with some woman in the street. He looks really angry." Charlie couldn't believe what she was witnessing.

"Oh no, that's my 11:15, Zoe Jones—she's a nightmare. Charlie, go and stop it. He'll listen to you!" Charlie really did not want to get involved, already telling Rak off for losing his temper recently, she was cautious of upsetting him further.

"No, leave them. He'll calm down in a minute. He won't bring it in here." That, she was certain of. That would mean having to see her and she knew he wouldn't do that.

"Shall I go outside? He looks so mad" Geeta was concerned for her client as much as her father.

"No, leave it. Come on, we shouldn't stare. He'll see us." Charlie was getting worried now, worried he would see her and become even more indignant. She wanted to move away from the window but somehow, she could not tear herself away, this was better than the television programmes of late. They could hear through the glass

"Yeah, you fuck off too. You dopey bitch. Fuck you!" Rak was getting back into the Aston. Zoe was walking straight into the salon. Both Charlie and Geeta were suppressing the urge to laugh, having both been on the receiving end of one of Rak's tantrums before.

Both were aware he liked to have the last word.

Rak was so angry now he had considered going home and having a whiskey, however it was not yet midday and he knew that was a slippery slope.

He decided to go into the office, he needed to calm down and he knew who would help him. Rollo.

Rak took a very careful drive, covering the short distance it was to his office. He decided against walking through the workshop, he wasn't in the mood for Greg and his complaining about anything and everything. He went up the back stairs, straight into the office.

"Afternoon." Tilly was being sarcastic and Rak knew it. "You all right? You're a bit late. Sanj has been here since nine."

Rak fussed Rollo who had ambled over to him. "Good boy; hello, Rollo. Good boy. Sit. Sit; that's it. There you go; good boy." Treat distributed, Rak then proceeded to recall the events of his morning. "She just comes outta nowhere, turns right, right in front of me then says I need to get my eyes tested. Can you fucking believe it? On her fucking phone she was."

Tilly knew it was best to let him vent, get it out of his system. "Would you like a coffee?" Rak looked at her, "and a biscuit too then?"

He smiled, "now you're talking, yes please." Rollo sat at his feet, enjoying a fuss. "So, Sanj, what have you been doing? Sorry I'm so late."

Sanj realised he could now speak, not being very familiar with Rak's temper he was slightly taken aback and made a mental note to never upset him. "I've been contacting some of your old contacts, Tilly gave me an old file. We've got a meeting with Walkers next Monday, they're fed up with their current supplier, want to see what we can do. And I rang my old man, he gave me some useful contacts too, ones who he can't supply to anymore since he downsized slightly. So, yeah, good morning; better than yours anyway." Sanj had got a smile across his face.

Rak had to smile too, he'd done well. "Fantastic. Well done. What you doing for lunch? Do you fancy the pub? I've got to go in; I promised Nick." Rak winked at Sanj

"Oh, yeah; why not? Be rude not to, don't ya think?"

78

Tuesday Afternoon
Heirs & Graces

Zoe was still there, having the works done to her hair. A full-head colour followed by highlights through the top sections, followed by a conditioning treatment and then finally a cut and blow dry. Charlie thought to herself how valuable Geeta could be if all her clients spent this much money, although she was hoping they weren't all as brash as Zoe.

"Honestly, right, it was like five grand, and I just said yeah, get on with it then. What's five grand, I've spent thirty already. I ain't even picked the kitchen yet," Zoe rolled her eyes in exasperation.

Geeta found the idea of Zoe picking a kitchen highly hilarious, being a keen cook herself, like her mother. "So, what type of kitchen are you after then? Have you got any ideas?" Geeta was trying not to laugh.

"Nah, I've seen one for like fifteen grand, so I think I'll have that, I don't know what to do in it though; know what I mean?"

Geeta glanced over at Charlie, who was trying and failing not to laugh. The two women hadn't mentioned Zoe's earlier altercation, deciding it was best left, however they both kept having flashbacks of Rak's temper fit and began giggling spontaneously every now and again. Charlie had to admit, she was enjoying Geeta being there.

Tuesday was usually a quiet day, a few of the regular pensioners would be in for their shampoo and sets and blow dries, but ordinarily it was a boring day. Zoe had certainly changed that.

Zoe eventually left at 4:00pm. Both the women were exhausted with laughing, Charlie didn't think she could laugh any more. Geeta made them both a coffee.

"You know, Simon calls her 'loadsa money', he said something about some comedy character."

Charlie laughed and took out her phone, she typed in, 'Harry Enfield, Loadsa Money.' A video began to play of this loud mouth cockney character flashing around a load of money. Charlie continued to Google, showing Geeta a link to 'Loadsa Money' (Doin' Up The House). Geeta could immediately see how Simon would have related this character to Zoe.

"Oh my God, Charlie, he's spot on isn't he? Fab, I do love Simon's sense of humour." Both women were falling about laughing. Charlie selected the text button

'Hi Simon, hope you're well. Loving Geeta being here, breath of fresh air. Just met loadsa money, OMG what a character xxxx'

Charlie knew Simon would appreciate that nugget of information, he always was a gossip. Two minutes later.

'Hello darlings, so happy things are working out— Geeta don't forget us darling. Charlie, so pleased you're meeting the clientele pmsl xxxx'

Just then all the lights went off, the radio went silent. Charlie realised the electrics were out. This was all she needed. "Geeta, try the kettle, it might be a single fuse."

Geeta put the kettle on, but nothing happened. "Nothing, the hairdryers won't work either."

This was all Charlie needed. "Ah, shit. It'll be ages for an electrician."

Geeta took out her phone "I'll get Dad, he'll know what to do" she had dialled before Charlie could stop her.

CAROLINE HOOD

79

Tuesday Afternoon
Brussels

The hotel Nick had chosen was perfect. Located in the city centre, within easy reach of restaurants, bars and of course, shops, Julia could not have wished for more. Once inside their room the indulgence continued; the room boasted a super-king size bed, a roll-top bath positioned at the bottom of the bed, fantastic views of the city and a chilled bottle of champagne was awaiting their arrival.

"God, Nick! This is fabulous. I can't believe you booked somewhere this fantastic." Julia had just dropped her case on entering the room, blown away was she by the splendour.

"Yeah, not bad, is it?" Nick was smiling, confident he had made the right choice, "you deserve it darlin', you've been working so hard recently in the pub. I do appreciate you; you know that, don't ya?" Nick opened the champagne and poured two glasses, he then proceeded to undress and get into the massive bed. "Are you joining me or what?"

Julia was slightly overwhelmed, usually when they went away they would drop the bags and immediately go out to explore "Are you offering?" she giggled, before taking all of her clothes off.

They were both enjoying the view from the window whilst sipping champagne, wrapped in each other's arms. "I bought you a couple of presents, would you like to see them?"

Julia was excited by this, imagining jewellery might be the gifts Nick had chosen. "Yeah, go on then, what is it?"

Nick left the bed, quickly making his way towards his case, he retrieved two individually wrapped gifts and got back into the bed. "I hope you approve Mrs. Carr." He had a lightness to his voice but he was a little apprehensive at the same time. He handed her the first gift. "Open it carefully, take your time."

Julia was so excited she wanted to rip off the pink paper he had wrapped it in but she attempted to restrain herself. She removed the paper carefully to reveal a silicone, pebble shaped object. "Nick, what is it? Does it open or something?"

Nick had already read through the instructions so was well prepared, he took it from her and turned it on. The pebble began to buzz, vibrate, in his hand. Even Nick was slightly surprised how strong the vibrations were, Julia was shocked. "Let me show you." He placed his hand and the vibrator between her legs, Julia was amazed. He placed the pebble on her clit.

"Ohhhh, God. Yes, yes, oh my God, Nick."

He could see she was enjoying herself; her pussy was becoming wet.

"Nick; yes, Nick. Oh yes."

Nick felt himself starting to get hard, he knew he wanted her, but he wanted her to come first. He pressed a button which increased the sensations on her clit, more intensity now.

"Nick, I'm gonna come baby, I'm coming! Oh God. Yes, yes. Aahhhh, yesssssssss!"

He then took the pebble away and placed his mouth on her clit, kissing her, licking her.

"Nick, I can't take any more. Oh my God. Yes, yes, yes!" She came, hard; harder than she had in a long time. Her pussy was hot and wet. Nick wanted to fuck her, he needed to fuck her. His cock was throbbing, he wanted her so much, he lifted her legs and guided himself inside her, immediately he was thrusting deeply, hard and deep.

"Fuck! Oh God, Julia, I love you." He was banging her harder, quicker, he knew he couldn't last much longer.

"Nick! You feel so good, Nick. Yes yes yes." She grabbed his bottom, pushing him further inside her. Julia hadn't enjoyed herself this much in a long time. Nick knew he had to slow down—he didn't want it to end. He slowed down until he felt he could bang her hard again. Julia was guiding his hands towards her breasts, she wanted him to touch her.

"Nick, yes, oh yes!" she was coming again. He felt it, he needed her to enjoy herself. As she came, so did he; they both melted into each other. The other present remained unopened, both of them more than satisfied.

80

Tuesday Afternoon

Heirs & Graces

Geeta was waiting for Rak to pick up.

"Hello honey, are you ok? How's your first day going?"

Geeta could hear he was genuinely interested but she just needed him to help her and Charlie. "Yeah, I'm fine, Dad. Look, the electrics have gone off, we've both tried everything we can think of. Are you free? Can you help please?"

This put Rak in a position he didn't want to be in, he couldn't deny Geeta help, that just wasn't in his nature, but if he did agree he knew he would see

Charlie. He had to think quickly "Have you checked the fuse box?"

Geeta pulled a face and sighed, her annoyance obvious "No, Dad, we haven't. We don't know what to do. Please, if you're not busy, can you pop over?" Charlie was listening, knowing why he was being obstinate. She wanted to tell Geeta to just leave it but then she heard. "Good; thanks, Dad. See you soon. Bye." Geeta hung up, "he said he'll be ten minutes; do you need me to stay?" Charlie could tell Geeta couldn't see the point of staying if there weren't any clients for the rest of the day. "It's just I'm going home tonight, to Sanj, and I really would like to cook something special. Y'know, celebrate his new job. But I need to go shopping."

Charlie could see she wanted to make a special evening of it with Sanj, she couldn't refuse. "Ok, I don't see why not. Are you going to hang on for your dad though?"

Geeta shook her head. "No, because if I do, he'll keep me talking and none of us will get home. Will you tell him I'll see him tomorrow please?"

Charlie felt torn, torn between helping Geeta and not upsetting Rak. "Ok, I'll tell him. Enjoy your evening. See you tomorrow. Thanks for today."

Geeta hugged her "Thanks so much Charlie, you're the best. See you tomorrow".

She sat alone in the salon, butterflies in her stomach. She was excited and apprehensive about seeing him. She heard the door open. "Geeta? It's your old man."

Charlie was a little wounded by this. "She's gone home, there's just me here. Sorry about this, if you want, I can call a sparky."

He came into the salon, looking gorgeous, he smelled delicious. He looked into her eyes. "No, I'm here now. Are you all right?"

She stared back into his eyes, the eyes she dreamed of floating away in. "Yeah, I'm fine. You?"

Rak knew he only had this one chance to get it right. "No, not really. I'm not all right, hun. I miss you, I still love you."

Charlie felt her heart skip a beat, then she recalled what Geeta had said earlier in the day. "Like you still love Amira?"

Rak looked shocked, she saw him trying to comprehend what she had said. "What? What are you on about?"

Charlie looked straight at him. "Geeta told me, apparently both you and Amira still love each other. Had a cosy dinner for two on Sunday as well. Anything else you've forgot to mention, Rak? I asked you about her, and you promised me that there was no need for me to worry. What is it, is she in reserve?" she could see she had gone too far, he looked hurt.

"No, it's not like that. We've got two kids together—we need to get on. We need to talk to each other. I was talking to her about you actually, y'know what she said? Hmm? She said to sort things out with you. We're not getting back with each other Charlie. I still love you, it's you I want."

Charlie realised he had told her twice now that he still loved her, she knew she felt the same. "I love you too, Rak. I've missed you so much. I've missed holding you, I missed you being next to me."

He held open his arms and she walked into them, "I love you hun. I want us to try again. But I don't want us to be a big secret, not anymore. I want everyone to see us together, to know we're together."

Charlie didn't know what to say, she was confused. She moved her lips to meet his and they kissed passionately, so passionately she never wanted it to end.

They pulled away from each other after a few blissful moments. "Right, do you want me to look at these electrics before it gets dark?"

She looked into his eyes, she felt lost in them. "I suppose you'd better. Rak, I want us to work, I really do."

He looked at her, a worried look, "But… Come on, where's the but?"

Charlie knew she needed to be honest with him, she had to be honest with him. "I can't let Brad find out Rak, it's not that I care about him or anything like that. It's because I can't afford for him to find out—financially, I mean. And I won't have you interfering. I love you so much, it's you I want to be with, just you. I wish we could disappear somewhere and never come back but that's not reality, is it?"

Rak held her, tight to him. "I don't want to always be your little secret, but I do understand. I'll give you the time you need but one day Charlie I want everyone to know we're together. Is that fair enough?" he knew he needed to compromise if he was going to keep her.

"Yes, yes that's fair. Give me time to get things in order. I promise, I love you and I'm in love with you."

Rak kissed her forehead, "Let me sort these electrics out. It's probably the fuse. Are you alone tonight?"

Charlie smiled, she had gotten him back. "Yes, I am. Why, what we're you thinking?"

He smiled naughtily, "I want you to stay with me." He was holding her hand, rubbing his skin against hers, she was already turned on.

"Yes, yes that would be most enjoyable".

Rak looked at the fuse box, the master fuse had blown. "I've got something at the factory which I need to do the job, can it wait 'til the morning? What's times your first client?"

Charlie quickly checked the appointment book, "9:30, but the hot water needs to come on at eight."

Rak smiled "Ok, I'll get up early. Come on, let's go baby," he lightly smacked her bottom, he knew what he wanted and so did she.

81

Tuesday Night

3 Church Lane

Once they had arrived at Rak's, they couldn't keep their hands off each other. They were hardly through the front door before they began kissing passionately—tongues playing in each other's mouths, hands feeling everywhere. They fell into the living room and collapsed onto the sofa, Rak on top of Charlie, kissing her with such intense passion. Charlie had her hands in his hair, feeling him pushing against her.

After a few moments they both smiled, then giggled together. "As much as I would love to make to love to you right here and now hun, would you like some dinner? I'm starving."

Charlie smiled, she was looking deeply in his eyes and all she could see was love. "Dinner? Hmm, ok then, dinner."

He saw she was mocking him slightly. "Sorry honey, but I am hungry, for both food and you. But food first, I need to keep my energy up to satisfy you."

Charlie smiled naughtily. "Yeah, you do. I have serious needs that need attending to Mr. Banerjee, I've been neglected you see." She pulled him towards her and kissed him, long, meaningful kissing, symbolising how much she wanted him. After a moment, she pulled away. "Right, what's for dinner?" as he got off her to stand up, she could see very clearly he was still interested in her.

He spotted her looking towards the front of his jeans "That's for dessert. Dinner is a recipe my mum taught me, chicken curry, Mama Banerjee style. Come on, I'll show you".

In the kitchen Charlie thought to herself how impressed she was by the way Rak knew his way around a kitchen. He was a confident cook and she found it very sexy. "Shall I pour some wine? Where are your glasses?"

Rak pointed towards the cabinet on the wall, "Just in there, there's a bottle of red in that cupboard over there too, open that one."

Charlie found two wine glasses in the wall cabinet then opened the cupboard. "There's only a really expensive one in here, looks like a vintage. Are you sure you want to open this?" She was holding up a bottle of vintage Bordeaux 1985, Rak turned to face her.

"I was saving it for something special honey. You being here is special; yeah, open it."

She walked over to him and held him close, she wanted to feel him next to her body. "Thank you."

Rak looked at her, staring into her. "For what?"

Charlie could feel a well of emotion rising inside her. "For everything, for letting us be us again. I love you."

Rak held her even closer "I love you too, hun. Now, come on, let me show you this recipe."

"My mum taught it to me before I left home, it's very special to me. It always reminds me of her and brings me comfort whenever I make it. I've only ever made it in front of Amira, and now you."

Charlie realised he was becoming emotional and also he was trusting her with a very personal part of his life. "What happened to your mum Rak? I mean, if you want to tell me."

Rak was chopping onions but she could see there were tears in his eyes for other reasons.

"Ohh, God, yeah. I knew you would ask me about this," he took a sip from his glass, he was really trying to compose himself. "When I was around twenty-two she was diagnosed with a brain tumour."

Charlie was shocked he had never mentioned this before. "Oh God, Rak; why did you never say?"

Rak carried on chopping the garlic. "It's never come up in conversation, has it? Anyway, she had surgery, got over it. My sister, Meena, nursed her back to health. She was doing well, she even managed to come to our wedding—mine and Amira's. We all thought she was going to be fine. Then around three and half years later at a routine check-up," he took a deep breath but carried on chopping, not daring himself to look at Charlie, "they found it had returned. Different this time though, inoperable. Geeta was only six months old. My mum never saw Amit. I wanted her to have these grandchildren to spoil, and she would have had them earlier, except Amira had a miscarriage, a few months after we got married. It shook both of us. It took a while for her to become pregnant again; we didn't even know if we would."

Charlie felt a pain stab her right through her own heart, she knew that feeling all too well.

"Then Geeta was on the way, at last I thought things were turning round, Mum was better, Amira was pregnant. Then, like I say, Geeta was only six months old when they found this new tumour. My mum passed away three months later. I never really have got over it, Charlie. I used to tell her things, private things, funny things, y'know everyday sort of stuff. Then she wasn't there anymore."

Charlie had to hold him, she needed to hold him, but she could see he didn't want that. "What about your dad? How did he cope?"

Rak was trying to decide how much he wanted to divulge, he took another sip of wine, turned around, looked straight at Charlie, sitting at the kitchen table. "I'm not discussing that, not today."

Charlie couldn't hide her shock. "Ok, sorry. I didn't mean to, y'know? I didn't mean to cross the line."

Rak knew he had been a little too harsh. "No baby, I'm sorry. I shouldn't have answered you like that. It's just, it's not something I like to talk about. All I will say is, we haven't spoken in a very long time, and I doubt we ever will again. He never saw my kids growing up and if I have anything to do with it, he never will. That is not a privilege he deserves."

Charlie took a sip of wine, she couldn't deny she wanted to know everything but she knew not to push things. "All right, no pressure to tell me. I appreciate you telling me about your mum, couldn't have been easy."

Rak had already turned away to continue chopping. "I hope you're hungry, this makes quite a lot. Put some music on if you want, help yourself," and with that she knew that chapter was closed.

Charlie was looking through Rak's record collection, she couldn't believe the variety he had amassed over what must have been decades. "I can't decide what to listen to, you've a huge collection. Have you always been interested in music?" Charlie suddenly had the realisation they had spent the majority of their time together in bed so far, she had not really ever asked about Rak's taste in music or television, it had never come up. She knew he didn't like modern pop music but that was about all she knew. The record collection in front of her was an eclectic mix of bands from the 60s, 70s and maybe slightly later mingled in with classic soul and Motown as well as some classical albums; Charlie had never seen a collection like it.

"Put what you like on, something soulful maybe? Then we can still talk, how about Diana? You like her, put that on. It's there somewhere, sorry they're not in alphabetical order or any order at all come to that. There just never seems time to sort them out."

Charlie looked through the albums until she stumbled across 'The Greatest Hits of Diana Ross', that would do nicely.

As the first track began to play, 'Touch Me In The Morning', she took a seat back at the kitchen table, happy to sit and watch Rak who was now starting to cook the onions at the hob.

"Tell me about your family, you got sisters? Any brothers I should be worried about?"

Charlie laughed. "Really, you'd be worried, would you? That is funny. No, you've nothing to worry about, I've got one sister, Danni. She's two years older than me, she's a lecturer at Bath uni. She's the clever one, she must be, she never wasted her time on marriage."

Rak laughed as he looked over towards her, "Then you must be the beautiful one, honey." his eyes were soft with emotion, she laughed but also thought what a smooth talker he could be.

"That will get you everywhere. My mum and dad used to live in Chivley, that's where I grew up, then they moved to Portugal. They still live there now. I miss them being just up the road, but the move was right for them. Dad had a heart attack, be around ten years ago now, just before I got married, should have been a sign." She laughed but quickly noticed Rak wasn't.

"Charlie, you shouldn't laugh at that. Is he alright now?"

Charlie smiled, "Yeah, thankfully. The climate is better for him, he exercises everyday—swimming in the sea, as well as their pool, walking, playing golf, which I'm sure you'll approve of, and he eats much better. He used to work as a sales rep, early starts, driving miles and grabbing whatever he could for lunch. It caught up with him in the end. My mum had wanted to move abroad for a while and saw this as a sign, so off they went. I'd only been married a year and they were off to live in the sun."

Rak noticed a distant look in her eyes. "What is it hun? What's upset you?"

Charlie looked out towards the garden, the flowers in full bloom and the grass very green for late August. "Oh, it's nothing. I just could've done with them being here more, that's all. Things weren't easy, Rak"

Rak turned the gas down and came over to sit at the table, all the ingredients now cooking away nicely. "What do you mean? With Brad?"

Charlie had not told him about their fertility issues, she hadn't felt it necessary before now. "Have you ever wondered why we haven't got kids?"

Rak thought carefully, thinking he may know where this was leading. "I just thought you were more career focussed, y'know? With the salon. Why?"

Charlie felt tears in her eyes and she didn't want to be upset tonight, she had waited too long to be with Rak. "I don't really want to talk about it, baby, but let's just say, it never happened."

Rak suddenly felt awful, awful for mentioning how himself and Amira had struggled to conceive, but mostly he felt awful for accusing Charlie of not realising how important his own kids were to him. "I'm sorry hun, I really am. I'm sorry I mentioned the miscarriage earlier too, if I'd had known"

Charlie took his hands in hers and kissed them. "Don't be, you can't change the facts of the past.

What's done is done. But please, I do need you to know, I will never ask you to choose between me and your kids, I know just how important they are to you."

Rak already knew this and felt guilty for ever thinking she was asking him to do just that, he looked away, feeling slightly ashamed that he had ever accused her. "I thought you were asking me to choose, I got scared, honey; scared I'd choose you I suppose, and lose them all over again. I find you intoxicating, do you understand? I need you and it scares me sometimes. Do you know what I mean?"

Charlie knew exactly what he meant, she felt exactly the same. The difference being, she never felt the need to pull away. "I feel like that too sometimes, like I'm drowning in you. But I don't pull away like you do, and when you do, Rak, you can hurt me with words, or no words, to be more accurate. I don't like the silent treatment, Rak, it hurts me more than anything. If you need space, just say. Don't just hide away, please."

He didn't say anything, just looked towards the floor, his face tensing slightly, he then took her in his arms and held her. He knew he had been wrong.

82

The Bull

The Bull was busy for a Tuesday, even though Julia had made the decision not to offer food whilst her and Nick were away. Tilly and Mark had popped in around 6:30, Mark promising Tilly a takeaway for dinner from the local Indian in Catchford. Tilly did love an excuse not to have to cook, especially on a weeknight.

"I really fancy a lamb bhuna, with some Bombay potatoes, mushroom rice and them chapatis you like. What you having?" Mark had been imagining and picturing his evening meal all day.

"Well, I really fancy a lamb naga; y'know, the spicy one but it can get too spicy for me—unless we share each other's curries, what do you reckon?"

Mark had wanted his bhuna all to himself but could see Tilly had been thinking about this. "Yeah, go on then. But don't think you're eating all mine if yours is too hot, you listening?" both laughed, knowing this exact scenario had played out many times over the years, with Tilly picking something and Mark ending up with most of hers and not much of his. It wasn't happening tonight.

"What else you having? Rice, sides?" Tilly loved it when Mark got excited about a takeaway, especially mid-week, a special treat.

"I'm having the spinach and potato thing, pilau rice, chapatis and why don't we get the cauliflower thing too? Convince ourselves we're eating all the right things." Tilly laughed, knowing that was far from the truth.

"Yeah, have what you like. Do you fancy another glass of wine? I wouldn't mind another pint, we can get the takeaway delivered."

Tilly smiled, "why not, make it a large. Rak texted, said I can start later tomorrow if I want as I've been working so hard recently. Go and get the drinks and I'll tell you some gossip."

Mark shook his head, not really one to enjoy talking about other people. "If you must, hang on, I need the gent's first."

Mark re-joined his wife around five minutes later, drinks in hand.

"Oh, thanks love. Right y'know I told you Rak's took Sanj on at the factory?" Mark nodded his head, mid swig of his pint. "Well, he told Sanj he was just popping out earlier, said he wouldn't be long, just going to help Geeta and Charlie with something. Well, that was around half four and he never came back. I reckon he spent the rest of the day with Charlie. And he's been in a bit of mood this week, then he seemed happier that he was going to see Charlie. I reckon they had a tiff then they've made it up."

Mark looked straight at Tilly. "Is that it? Good God, woman; you already told me at the weekend he's knocking her off. Obviously, that's where he was; not rocket science, is it?"

Tilly did feel annoyance sometimes at Mark's inability to gossip about people, she was sure he saw more when he was out and about than he ever let on. "That's just typical of you, never interested in people's lives."

Mark couldn't help but laugh. "Interested in people's lives? That's a novel way of looking at it. Does he seem happier with her?"

Tilly knew he was trying to indulge her now so decided to play along rather than diminish his interest. "Yeah, I would say so. Put it this way, his face said it all this afternoon. I do hope they can work things out, shame about Lisa and Brad really. I'm going to have my hair done Thursday afternoon, I don't think Geeta knows about her dad and her boss."

Mark looked serious now, "Then don't let on Tills, I mean it. These things have a nasty habit of getting out. If you really respect Rak, you'll keep this to yourself."

Tilly knew he was right. "Don't be daft, of course I wouldn't say anything. It's not my place". She meant it as well; her loyalties would always be to Rak.

83

Tuesday Night
Brad

It was around 8:30pm. Brad arrived home to try
to talk with Charlie. He had made the decision he
wanted to sort things out with his wife, to try and
recapture the feelings they had when they first met.
He had been staying with his colleague, Andy, but
now he felt he needed to see Charlie. Brad was also
aware he could lose everything if he didn't salvage
his marriage.

He let himself into the house, noticing all
the lights were turned off. He dropped his bag in
the hallway and walked into the living room. The

television was off, there was silence, no music from the kitchen. He wandered into the kitchen, looking out of the bi-fold doors to the garden; still, he could not see Charlie. He had spotted her Mini outside the salon as had drove into the village; he knew she wouldn't have gone far. He wondered if she was in *The Bull*, after all, why would she be home alone? Brad decided to quickly freshen up and walk over to the pub, he would surprise her.

He ascended the stairs and made his way towards their bedroom. He opened the door, went into the room and dropped his bag. He knew he needed a shower before seeing Charlie. As he was undressing himself, he thought that maybe he should text her, let her know he was home. But then again, what if she didn't want to see him? What then? She might ignore him, or worst still, say she didn't want to see him at all. He resolved to shower first then just go over to *The Bull*—stick with his original plan.

After his shower, Brad dressed in his favourite shirt and a smart pair of jeans. He splashed on some aftershave, he felt good. He felt ready to save his marriage.

As he left the house, he was feeling excited as well as apprehensive. He hadn't forgot the reason they had fell out; he knew he had done wrong. He also wondered what the relationship was between his wife and Rak Banerjee. He got a very real sense they were more than friends. He really wanted to believe their relationship was one of friendship, after all, both parties were married, they wouldn't pursue anything further, would they?

Brad left the house and began walking over to *The Bull*, he saw Dorian and Kate making their way over there too, then they spotted him. He saw Dorian's face change. He recalled what Rak had said in the shop at the weekend. He felt ashamed of himself. He raised his hand to wave, he didn't want them to think him a monster. "Evening ladies, nice evening for it."

Kate smiled, also waving. "Good evening, Brad, I've not seen you in a while. How are you keeping?"

Dorian just stared at him, a cold stare which cut straight through him. "I'm well thank you. Hoping to catch up with Charlie, actually. I imagine she's in the pub, she's not at home you see."

Kate never missing an opportunity was quick to respond. "Oh, I saw her close the salon early. Just before five, actually," Dorian slightly jabbed Kate, a signal to keep quiet, "but I don't know where she was going. She could be in the pub I suppose." Kate was curious as to her friend's unexpected, and quite frankly unexplained, rudeness towards Brad.

"Oh, thanks, Kate; better go and see then. Would you two like a drink?"

Dorian quickly interjected before Kate had the opportunity. "No, we can buy our own. Come along Kate, I can't leave Jack all night."

Kate was most perplexed by Dorian's attitude. Brad, however, knew the reasoning behind her coolness towards him. Quite frankly, he couldn't blame her.

84

3 Church Lane

Charlie and Rak were sitting at the kitchen table, savouring every mouthful of the curry Rak had made. "This is absolutely delicious, baby; I've never tasted anything like it. Thank you."

Rak smiled, which reached all the way to his eyes. "Thank you, honey, thank you for being patient."

She wasn't sure if he meant by waiting for the food or being patient with him, she decided not to ask. "You're welcome; I've enjoyed this evening. I really have missed you, y'know? Rak, when's Lisa due home? Do you know?"

This surprised Rak, his wife not being at the forefront of his mind. "A week or so apparently, why, what's wrong?" he rested his fork on the side of his plate.

"Nothing, it's just, well, I feel slightly uncomfortable being here. Y'know what I mean? Maybe we should just go to Pam's from now on."

Rak took her hand into his own. "Whatever makes you happy, hun, but stay with me tonight, I need you. I really need you."

Charlie beamed a wide smile. "I really need you too baby. I can't wait to go to bed with you".

They had very nearly finished dinner. Rak moved the plates away from the table, he pulled Charlie's chair away from the table and gestured for her to let him hold her. As she stood up, he undid her jeans, pulling them and her knickers away from her and sat her the on edge of the kitchen table. He slowly and gently parted her thighs, kissing her mouth as he did so. He kissed her slowly, deeply, using his tongue. His finger glided inside her; he could feel she was so wet for him.

"Rak! Oh yes, Rak! You feel good."

He slowly took his mouth away from her neck, and gently pushed her back towards the table, his body moving down towards her pussy. He lightly kissed her lips, licking them with his tongue before softly parting them to caress her clit with his tongue.

"Rak! Rak! Yes, yes, Rak!"

Rak could feel himself becoming harder; he needed her; he wanted to be inside of her.

Charlie pushed his head, holding his tongue on her clit, she was going to come. "Rak! Oh God, Rak, I love you. Rak! Rak!" he used his tongue, with more intensity now. "I'm coming, Rak! Oh God, yes, yes, yesssssss!"

He picked her up under her bottom, Charlie wrapped her legs around him. He carried her up the stairs, up to his bedroom.

He pushed the door to the bedroom open and carefully placed Charlie on the bed, he undid his belt and took his jeans off; his cock was straining against his boxers. Charlie sat up to remove his underwear, but he gently pushed her back onto the bed.

"Just lay there, sexy; relax," he took off his shirt, his chest was heaving. He sat her up slightly to remove her top, then her bra. Her breasts were full, her nipples hard. He gently caressed her breasts before licking her nipples. He placed his hands underneath her bottom and lifted her towards the edge of the bed, he took off his boxers, his cock was hard, throbbing, the veins pumping blood towards the head of his cock. He carefully parted her legs, touching her lips softly, she was wet; a slick of wetness just for him. He gently thrust into her, deeply, so deep inside. "Fuck! You feel so good; so good, you sexy minx." He began thrusting harder, quicker, deeper.

"Rak! Oh yes, Rak! That's so good. So good. Don't stop, please!" Charlie was crying. Tears of pleasure; pleasure she had only ever experienced with Rak. She felt every single thrust; every time he banged into her, she felt herself become weaker. She was looking deep into his eyes; she saw love but mostly desire—hot desire.

He used his fingers to play with her clit, as he banged into her pussy, harder and harder. "Play with your tits honey, play with yourself. I want to watch while I fuck you."

Charlie used her hands to gently push her breasts together, she teased her nipples, showing Rak. He massaged her clit with more intensity while banging her harder, he knew he was going to come, he wanted it so much. "Play with your clit, honey, I want to see you play with yourself. I want to watch you come."

Charlie used her fingertips to touch her clit, she was so wet; she was going to come. Rak felt weak, he could feel he was losing control, he didn't want to slow down, he wanted to fuck her. He wanted her to cry out his name.

"Rak! Rak! I'm coming; oh yes, Rak!" he thrust into her deeper, he was going to come any second, the pleasure surging through his cock was immense.

"Charlie, oh God, Charlie, baby! Yes. Yes. Yes. Ahhhhh, yes!" It was one of the best he had ever had.

They both lay there together, in each other's

arms. A feeling of warmth and pleasure between them. Rak wished in that instant that Charlie could be with him every night, that they were together, every night. "Would you like a glass of wine? I need one after that."

Charlie looked up at his face, into his eyes. Eyes filled with love and wanting. "Yeah, that's a good idea."

Rak kissed her forehead. "You stay here, I'll be right back," he climbed out of the sheets, his bottom looking as sexy as ever as he walked towards the stairs.

Charlie knew she wanted him, she wanted him for the rest of her life.

Rak got back into bed, handing a glass to Charlie. "To us hun."

She smiled and kissed his cheek. "To us baby. I don't want us to fall out again."

"Neither do I; neither do I."

He kissed her, full on the mouth, before they both sipped from their glasses. Rak was enjoying holding her close as they sat together, enveloped in the sheets, Charlie's head was resting on his chest, listening to his heartbeat, the beat she had missed so much.

"How did Geeta get on today anyway? Was she alright?"

Charlie smiled, happy to talk about Geeta. "She was great, we had a fantastic day. I'm sure she'll work out fine. Anyway, that reminds me Mr. Banerjee, why were you shouting at her client in the street? We saw you."

Rak started to laugh, he had forgotten his earlier altercation. "Oh that. You two saw that?" Rak laughed, that moment in time seeming so unimportant now.

"Yes, we saw you. We both found it quite funny actually, both of us being more than familiar with your temper."

Rak tickled her slightly. "Oh, did you? Right, ok. Well, actually she nearly drove into me, well my car to be more precise, up on the main road. I was fuming, she just pulled out in front of me then said I needed an eye test. Who is she anyway? Vulgar woman."

Charlie was laughing now. "She's a client of your daughter's, quite a character, actually. More mouth than anything else. Apparently, Simon refers to her as 'Loadsa Money', y'know? Like Harry Enfield's character?"

Rak laughed, "Yes, I can quite imagine. Why on Earth is Geeta looking after clients like that?"

Charlie touched his thigh. "Because she pays, very well actually. And she made us both laugh, just the tonic I needed. I for one hope she's a regular feature."

Rak laughed. "You do, do you? Well, keep her away from me. Is Geeta busy tomorrow?"

Charlie wasn't too sure "I'm not sure to be honest, why?"

Rak looked at her, smiling, "because I wanted to take her out for lunch. I'm seeing Amit on Thursday, going shopping for a new motor with him. Didn't want Geeta feeling left out."

Charlie was enjoying hearing Rak talk about his children, it gave her a fuzzy feeling. "The best thing to do would be to ask her in the morning. Y'know, you're doing well with both of them Rak. I know she appreciates you giving Sanj a job. How is he working out?"

Rak took a sip of his wine. "He's doing well, hun; keen to work and enthusiastic. Tilly likes him too, which means I can leave them together to be with you. I offered him the job because I want to spend more time with you, and to help Geeta out, obviously."

Charlie felt a smile spread across her face and a warmth spread through her groin, she wanted him so much. "I want you too baby, every day. Geeta and Sanj could be just what we need, if you get my meaning?"

Rak understood perfectly. "Oh yeah, honey; I know exactly what you mean. Now come here and kiss me."

They both embraced in a passionate kiss, tightly holding each other close.

85

Tuesday Night
The Bull

Adam was amazed how busy the pub had been, not imagining a Tuesday would be as manic. He knew his mum and Nick would be pleased when they returned home. The clock above the bar read 10:45pm. Adam was ready to close up, he was knackered. "Eh, Anthea, what time does Nick usually close up in the week? Do you know?"

Anthea, Adam's older sister by five years, was also ready to call it a night. "I reckon we can call it a night at eleven, don't think Mum would mind. I didn't realise how hard it is, working behind here.

No wonder she's always knackered."

Adam laughed. "This is the first time you've done it for years, try nearly every weekend like I do. No wonder they needed a break".

Brad was sitting alone, staring into his glass. He had not found Charlie; in fact he had no idea where she was. He had tried calling her, but the phone had gone straight to voicemail; she must have turned it off. He had been sitting with Tilly and Mark, but they had left a couple of hours ago to have a takeaway, they had invited Brad to join them but he declined, not wanting to impose. He was now feeling slightly worse for wear, choosing to switch from pints to shots; he was already on his third. There was only a couple of other customers in the bar, not regulars as such, although Brad did recall seeing them previously.

"All right folks, that's it for tonight. Can we ask you drink up and go to your lovely homes?" This was a line Adam had heard Nick use many times—it usually worked. After all, who doesn't want to say their home is lovely? Adam was just moving the night's takings into the back.

"Ahhh, come on babe, it's not even eleven yet. What you closing up for?" Brad was on his feet, approaching the bar, the other customers were making their way outside

"We're closing, love, go home. Looks like you need to." Anthea was looking at Brad, knowing she wasn't going to serve him any more drinks.

"Look, just one more then I'll go. I promise." Anthea wanted to close up, she was tired.

"Look, I've said we're closed. Go home, will ya? We're here again tomorrow, see ya then."

Brad could feel the alcohol taking over, he walked closer to Anthea who was walking towards the door of the bar to open it for Brad. "I want another drink, you bitch. Now serve me." He grabbed Anthea's arm. "Or do you want to give me something else?" he had his hand up her skirt; he grabbed her in between her legs. "Do you want me to fuck you, you little tart?"

Anthea screamed, as loud as she could. "Get the fuck off me, now!" she kicked him in between his legs, he let go of her just as Adam came running into the bar, to see why his sister was shouting.

"Anthea! What's wrong?"

Adam could see Brad was holding himself, wincing in pain. "He tried to assault me sexually. He tried to finger me. He said he was going to fuck me!" Anthea was crying, unable to believe the words coming out of her mouth.

Adam couldn't believe the words he was hearing, his sister was saying this man tried to assault her. "Call the police, now."

Adam kicked Brad whilst he was on the floor, still rolling round, holding his balls, whining in pain.

Ten minutes later the sound of police sirens

screeched into the quiet village. Two police cars sped into the village, halting outside *The Bull*.

86

Tuesday Night

The Bull

Rak had just dozed off to sleep, Charlie in his arms after they had made love for a second time that evening. Rak was a deep sleeper; once he was gone nothing could wake him. Charlie was just getting settled, trying to ignore the constant snoring from Rak, the one foible she did find annoying if she was to be honest.

Suddenly, she heard the sound of sirens blaring. It sounded close; in the village. "Rak; Rak, wake up. I can hear sirens. Go and see."

Rak awoke, grunting about being woken up.

"What? What do you want, baby? I was asleep."

Charlie put the lamp on. "Rak, I heard sirens, just outside. Go and see."

Rak climbed out of bed. "For fuck's sake, hun; I've got work tomorrow. Wait here, I'll look from the front bedroom." He made his way to the bedroom at the front of the house. "It's outside *The Bull*, two police cars. Baby, I'd better go and see. You stay here, promise me. I love you."

Charlie watched him throw on his jeans and a sweater. "Be careful baby, I love you too."

Rak was worried, he knew the kids were looking after the pub. He also felt guilty, he had promised Nick he would keep an eye on the place, but instead he had been busy shagging. Rak ran over to the pub, only to be met by a policeman outside the pub. "Good evening, sir; can I help you?"

Rak looked confused. "Err, yeah; this is my mate's pub but he's away. The kids are looking after the place, what's happened?"

The police officer, similar age to Rak and well-built was deciding how much he could divulge. "There's been a report of an assault. I'm not at liberty to say anything further."

Rak couldn't believe what he was hearing. "What? What kind of assault? What do you mean? Is anyone hurt?" Rak was struggling to process the information when he spotted Adam "Adam, mate what's happened? What's this about an assault?"

Adam looked relieved to see Rak "Rak, I'm pleased to see you, Brad's assaulted Anthea, sexually assaulted Anthea" the younger man was visibly shaking.

Just then two more police officers emerged from the pub, escorting Brad to a waiting police car. "You bastard! What you done now? Twice in less than a week!"

The police officer was trying to restrain Rak. "Calm down, sir; or I'll have no choice but to arrest you too. Understand?"

Rak nodded, he knew he had to stay calm. He began thinking if he had just been in the pub, if he had just gotten Charlie to report what had happened the previous Friday night. Suddenly, his mind flitted to Charlie, he prayed she wasn't watching from the bedroom window, he briefly looked but couldn't see anything.

Rak was allowed into the pub, immediately Anthea ran over to hug him. "Thank God, Uncle Rak, I was so scared! He had his hand between my legs, I thought, I thought, he was going to, I thought he was."

Rak held her close. "Don't be scared now, honey; come on, tell the police lady what happened."

The female police officer was sitting at a table, taking notes. Rak went to speak with the male police officer.

"What will happen to him now?"

The police officer ushered Rak to the other side of the bar. "Most probably nothing. There's no witnesses, the lady has said he touched her but we're going to struggle for evidence. All he needs is a hot shot lawyer, and he'll walk out of there. If she even presses charges, which she probably won't. See it every week, mate."

Rak knew the police officer was speaking with him off the record, he also knew he was speaking the truth. The ramifications of his son's career suddenly became very real to Rak, that Amit played a part in assisting criminals to evade the law.

The police officers were speaking with Anthea, explaining she would need to be examined by a specialist doctor. Anthea was thinking all this over, did she really need this drama, would they have enough evidence, after all, he hadn't actually raped her, had he? She just wanted her mum.

Adam had called Nick and explained. They were getting the first plane back as soon as they could.

After a lot of thinking, Anthea decided not to press charges.

87

Thursday Morning

Amit's House

The sun was shining and the air was warm. *'It was the perfect day to go shopping for a car with his son'*, Rak thought to himself as he pulled up outside Amit's home. Amit's house was nestled away in woodland, just off Catchford Road. If you didn't know it existed, you would never find it.

Rak was quite amazed when Amit bought the house only six months earlier. He had been concerned for his son on two levels; firstly, he felt the location may be a little too remote. After all, Amit was still only twenty-two—hardly ready for the quiet life, his father felt. Secondly, he was concerned regarding the cost of the property. Yes, it was well priced considering its size and location. Rak could almost imagine living there himself. However, he was worried that Amit was taking on too much debt to pay for it. That was until his son divulged how much he actually earned, and his projected earnings for the next few years if his career path remained on target. To say Rak was shocked would be an understatement.

Rak approached the front door, solid oak no less, and rang the doorbell. He thought it wise to ring the bell as he wasn't sure if Amit would be entertaining a lady, more than aware of his son's popularity with women.

As Rak stood and waited for the door to be answered, his mind flitted back to Tuesday night. He was thinking about Anthea and how she must have felt. He had spoken with Nick before setting off to Amit's. He had said she was all right, just shook up really. Brad hadn't been seen around the village; didn't dare show his face was Rak's guess. Charlie didn't know where he was, although she imagined he would be staying with a work colleague—until the dust settled anyway. Julia and Nick had been livid that he got away with hurting Anthea; livid their well-earned and anticipated break had been disrupted and even more livid that the police couldn't do anything. Adam felt guilty for leaving his sister on her own in the bar at closing time, he should have stayed with her and cashed up when all the customers had left. Rak felt he should shoulder some blame also, he had promised to keep an eye on the place, then got distracted by Charlie and failed in his duty to his best friend.

Rak was shook back into the present as the front door opened. It was Daisy, Amit's cleaning lady. "Oh hello, Rak; he said you'd be calling in. He's just popped to the post office, said he won't be long. Come in, love."

Rak did as instructed, removing his shoes in the hallway. "How are you keeping Daisy? Well, I hope."

She was already making her way back to the extensive kitchen that ran the width of the house at the back. "Yeah, I'm good ta; you?"

Rak began walking towards the kitchen, "yeah, not so bad thanks." He then saw the door to the study was slightly ajar. Daisy must have been cleaning in there. Rak knew strictly speaking Amit's study was off limits, but his curiosity got the better of him. He wanted to know just exactly what his son was involved with.

He slowly and quietly pushed the door open. The room was dark, not being positioned on the sunniest side of the house. The wooden floor creaked slightly as Rak wandered further into the study, as he tried to tip toe away from the door, he was engrossed further into the study and its contents.

His eyes were immediately drawn to a tall, glass display cabinet. It was housing awards Amit had worked hard to achieve, especially this soon into his career. There were numerous photos, Amit's graduation photo took up central position, Rak immediately felt a sense of pride for his son. He realised he needed to show Amit how proud he felt more often. There were photos of Amit with Geeta; on nights out; at a family wedding; some of when they were both younger. Rak thought Amira must have given them to Amit. He saw photos of himself with his son—taken at car shows they had attended together. There was one which Rak recalled being taken, they had gone to Monza to watch the Formula One. Amit looked so happy to be with his dad, only aged around fourteen. This was the first time he had gone away with just his dad, as the family was fractured by then. There were photos of Amira with her son, some taken recently it seemed. Then there were others which were years old. Photos depicting the family as a whole; Amira with her arms around Rak; Amit and Geeta clinging to their parent's legs and smiling. Rak realised how happy he looked in those old photos, with his wife and family. He felt a sense of sadness wash over him. Sadness that he'd lost it all. There was one more photo. Rak didn't recognise the lady in the picture with his son although she looked a similar age to Amit. It was taken in Paris, the Eiffel Tower stood in the background. They both had the look of love in their eyes. Rak wondered if this was the girlfriend Amit had mentioned at the fundraiser, the one who was already taken.

As his eyes moved away from the cabinet, he saw Amit's desk. An old oak desk, very sturdy. Above the desk two pictures were hanging, both quite amusing. Rak moved nearer for a closer look. Both pictures were by the same artist, Mr. Controversial. Rak was not familiar with this artist, however he liked what he saw. The first picture being of a blonde beauty. 'Very Marilyn', Rak mused to himself. She was almost falling into a sea of rose pink, her arms resting behind her head, a suggestive look in her eyes. The caption read, 'I don't make mistakes, I date them'. He felt himself smiling, knowing that feeling all too well. The second picture was not dissimilar, this artist definitely has a style he thought. It was again of a blonde woman, standing sideways on, however this time she was naked except for a blue shirt she was holding against her breasts; her bottom was visible. Her head turned towards the admirer of the picture, her eyes portraying a, 'could not care less', attitude. The caption this time reading, 'Always late but worth the wait'. Rak imagined a woman like that would certainly be worth the wait.

There was a bookshelf on the adjacent side of the desk, titles included biographies and autobiographies of Amit's sporting heroes as well as a collection of law books—well-thumbed and obviously well used. Rak spotted an old joke book, Amit had asked for it one birthday; he must have been around ten. Rak couldn't believe he had kept it all these years. There was also a mug on the end of the bookshelf with the caption, 'World's Best Brother'. As Rak saw it, he was grateful that his children got along so well, even as adults.

He could not help but glance down to the papers residing on Amit's desk, alongside the Montblanc pen he had gifted to him upon his graduation. He wanted to know more about his son's work; what it actually entailed; what he really saw on a daily basis. Rak was aware that if Amit were to know he had looked at his paperwork, paperwork of a sensitive nature, they would fall out. But he couldn't stop it. The urge to know. He moved round to behind the desk, leaning on the soft leather chair as he picked up a file from the desk. As he opened it, he felt tension; his heart was beating faster; he felt his palms become moist; his mouth was dry. His fingers slowly opened the file, immediately he felt sick. He swallowed the bile which had risen in his mouth, he could taste it. The image he was confronted with was the very reason Amit never would have allowed him or anyone else he was close to into his study.

The image was horrific, blood everywhere. This man on the floor had his throat slashed; blood had obviously surged from his neck. There were other pictures of further injuries, bruises, cuts, the post-mortem. Rak knew he should leave it as he had found it and walk away, but he felt this grotesque need for more. More information, more detail. He picked through the papers, skim reading. He ascertained this was a murder, the defence being a moment of madness due to a crime of passion. A thought enveloped his brain quite voluntarily, he would kill for Charlie. He would kill Brad for Charlie. This thought scared him, he quickly started to put the papers back in the file, he couldn't recall the order they had been in, he began to panic, his hands wouldn't behave, he was shaking. From the kitchen, Rak heard the radio being turned up, he faintly recognised the song, 'Born of Frustration' Daisy was singing along. Rak was still panicking, he could not remember how he had found the papers, the order of the photos. He was starting to become hot, stressed. he had to get this right. Amit would know. If he got this wrong, his relationship with his son would be fucked. All the photos became a blur, all blood, all a mess. The bile rising inside him again, he could taste it again, his own sick in his mouth. A noise from the kitchen 'Wooooowooooowooowooo'

Then something else caught his attention, something he couldn't ignore. Something that could end all of his problems, permanently. His mind was awash with thoughts, different decisions hitting his brain every second, different questions. How? When? Who? Could he really? Was it possible? Could he cease to exist? The idea was in Rak's head now, but could he really make it happen?

There was a voice from the hall. "Yeah mate, it's in the second file. You'll find all the information you're looking for in the second one. Gotta go, my old man's here. Read the second one mate. Cheers. See you Saturday for a beer." It was Amit, "Dad, where are ya? Come on, I'm here now."

Website:	www.carolinethenaughtyauthor.com
Instagram:	www.instagram.com/carolinethenaughtyauthor/
LinkedIn:	www.linkedin.com/in/caroline-hood-0376a5213
Facebook:	www.facebook.com/profile.php?id=100090030676011

Printed in Great Britain
by Amazon